Louisa May Alcott

Louisa May Alcott was born in 1832 in Germantown, Pennsylvania, and grew up in the Boston-Concord area of Massachusetts. She received most of her early education from her father, Bronson Alcott, a renowned educator and writer, as well as from the writers Ralph Waldo Emerson and Henry David Thoreau, who were family friends.

Bronson Alcott left teaching to study philosophy when Louisa was very young, and she began earning money to help her mother support the Alcott family by working as a teacher, as a household servant and seamstress, and by writing lurid stories (under a fictitious name) as well as poems for newspapers and magazines. In 1868 she became editor of the children's magazine *Merry's Museum* and published the first version of *Little Women*, a novel about four young sisters growing up in a small New England town during the Civil War. The immediate success of *Little Women* established Louisa May Alcott as a celebrated writer and was one of the first American novels to become a classic in children's literature. It remains one of the best-loved books for girls.

By the time *An Old-Fashioned Girl* was published in 1870, Alcott's income from *Little Women* and her several other novels had enabled her to pay off her father's debts and provide a comfortable home for her family. She spent the rest of her life traveling in Europe and writing until her death in Massachusetts in 1888.

An Old-Fashioned Girl

Louisa May Alcott

With an Afterword by Isabelle Holland

Published by
Dell Publishing Co., Inc.
1 Dag Hammarskjold Plaza
New York, New York 10017

Afterword copyright © 1987 by Isabelle Holland

Yearling ® TM 913705, Dell Publishing Co., Inc.

ISBN: 0-440-46609-1

RL: 7.9

Footnotes were supplied by the Editors.

Printed in the United States of America

April 1987

10 9 8 7 6 5 4 3 2

W

Preface

As A preface is the only place where an author can with propriety explain a purpose or apologize for shortcomings, I venture to avail myself of the privilege to make a statement for the benefit of my readers.

As the first part of *An Old-Fashioned Girl* was written in 1869, the demand for a sequel, in beseeching little letters that made refusal impossible, rendered it necessary to carry my heroine boldly forward some six or seven years into the future. The domestic nature of the story makes this audacious proceeding possible, while the lively fancies of my young readers will supply all deficiencies and overlook all discrepancies.

This explanation will, I trust, relieve those well-regulated minds who cannot conceive of such literary lawlessness from the bewilderment which they suffered when the same experiment was tried in a former book.

The "Old-Fashioned Girl" is not intended as a perfect model, but as a possible improvement upon the Girl of the Period, who seems sorrowfully ignorant or ashamed of the good old fashions which make woman truly beautiful and honored and, through her, render home what it should be—a happy place where parents and children, brothers and sisters, learn to love and know and help one another.

If the history of Polly's girlish experiences suggests a hint or insinuates a lesson, I shall feel that, in spite of many obstacles, I have not entirely neglected my duty toward the little men and women for whom it is an honor and a pleasure to write, since in them I have always found my kindest patrons, gentlest critics, warmest friends.   L.M.A.

Contents

An
Old-Fashioned
Girl

Chapter 1

Polly Arrives

"*I*t's time to go to the station, Tom."

"Come on, then."

"Oh, I'm not going, it's too wet. Shouldn't have a crimp left if I went out such a day as this, and I want to look nice when Polly comes."

"You don't expect me to go and bring home a strange girl alone, do you?" And Tom looked as much alarmed as if his sister had proposed to him to escort the wild woman of Australia.

"Of course I do. It's your place to go and get her, and if you wasn't a bear, you'd like it."

"Well, I call that mean! I supposed I'd got to go, but you said you'd go too. Catch me bothering about your friends another time! No, *sir!*" And Tom rose from the sofa with an air of indignant resolution, the impressive effect of which was somewhat damaged by a tousled head and the hunched appearance of his garments generally.

"Now, don't be cross, and I'll get Mama to let you have that horrid Ned Miller, that you are so fond of, come and make you a visit after Polly's gone," said Fanny, hoping to soothe his ruffled feelings.

"How long is she going to stay?" demanded Tom, making his toilet by a promiscuous shake.

"A month or two, maybe. She's ever so nice, and I shall keep her as long as she's happy."

"She won't stay long, then, if I can help it," muttered Tom, who regarded girls as a very unnecessary portion of creation. Boys of fourteen are apt to think so, and perhaps it is a wise arrangement, for, being fond of turning somersaults, they have an opportunity of indulging in a good one, metaphorically speaking, when, three or four years later, they become the abject slaves of "those bothering girls."

"Look here! How am I going to know the creature? I never saw her, and she never saw me. You'll have to come, too, Fan," he added, pausing on his way to the door, arrested by the awful idea that he might have to address several strange girls before he got the right one.

"You'll find her easy enough. She'll probably be standing round looking for us. I daresay she'll know *you*, though I'm not there, because I've described you to her."

"Guess she won't, then." And Tom gave a hasty smooth to his curly pate and a glance at the mirror, feeling sure that his sister hadn't done him justice. Sisters never do, as "we fellows" know too well.

"Do go along, or you'll be too late, and then what *will* Polly think of me?" cried Fanny, with the impatient poke which is peculiarly aggravating to masculine dignity.

"She'll think you cared more about your frizzles than your friends, and she'll be about right too."

Feeling that he had said rather a neat and cutting thing, Tom sauntered leisurely away, perfectly conscious that it *was* late, but bent on not being hurried while in sight, though he ran himself off his legs to make up for it afterward.

"If I was the President, I'd make a law to shut up all boys till they were grown, for they certainly are the most provoking toads in the world," said Fanny as she watched the slouchy figure of her brother strolling down the street. She might have changed her mind, however, if she had followed him, for as soon as he turned the corner his whole aspect altered: His hands came out of his pockets, he stopped whistling, buttoned his jacket, gave his cap a pull, and went off at a great pace.

The train was just in when he reached the station, panting like a racehorse and as red as a lobster with the wind and the run.

"Suppose she'll wear a topknot and a thingumbob, like everyone else, and however shall I know her? Too bad of Fan to make me come alone!" thought Tom as he stood watching the crowd stream through the depot and feeling rather daunted at the array of young ladies who passed. As none of them seemed looking for anyone, he did not accost them, but eyed each new batch with the air of a martyr. "That's her," he said to himself as he presently caught sight of a girl in gorgeous array, standing with her hands folded and a very small hat perched on the top of a very large "chig-non," as Tom pronounced it. "I suppose I've got to speak to her, so here goes." And, nerving himself to the task, Tom slowly approached the damsel, who looked as if the wind had blown her clothes into rags, such a flapping of sashes, scallops, ruffles, curls, and feathers was there.

"I say, if you please, is your name Polly Milton?" meekly asked Tom, pausing before the breezy stranger.

"No, it isn't," answered the young lady, with a cool stare that utterly quenched him.

"Where in thunder is she?" growled Tom, walking off in high dudgeon. The quick tap of feet behind him made him turn in time to see a fresh-faced little girl running down the long station and looking as if she rather liked it. As she smiled and waved her bag at him, he stopped and waited for her, saying to himself, "Hullo! I wonder if that's Polly?"

Up came the little girl, with her hand out and a half-shy, half-merry look in her blue eyes as she said, inquiringly, "This is Tom, isn't it?"

"Yes. How did you know?" And Tom got over the ordeal of handshaking without thinking of it, he was so surprised.

"Oh, Fan told me you'd got curly hair, and a funny nose, and kept whistling, and wore a gray cap pulled over your eyes, so I knew you directly." And Polly nodded at him in the most friendly manner, having politely refrained from calling the hair "red," the nose "a pug," and the cap "old" —all of which facts Fanny had carefully impressed upon her memory.

"Where are your trunks?" asked Tom as he was reminded of his duty by her handing him the bag, which he had not offered to take.

"Father told me not to wait for anyone, else I'd lose my chance of a hack, so I gave my check to a man, and there he is with my trunk." And Polly walked off after her one modest piece of baggage, followed by Tom, who felt a trifle depressed by his own remissness in polite attentions.

"She isn't a bit of a young lady, thank goodness! Fan didn't tell me she was pretty. Don't look like city girls, nor act like 'em, neither," he thought, trudging in the rear and eyeing with favor the brown curls bobbing along in front.

As the carriage drove off, Polly gave a little bounce on the springy seat and laughed like a delighted child. "I do like to ride in these nice hacks, and see all the fine things, and have a good time, don't you?" she said, composing herself the next minute as if it suddenly occurred to her that she was going a-visiting.

"Not much," said Tom, not minding what he said, for the fact that he was shut up with the strange girl suddenly oppressed his soul.

"How's Fan? Why didn't she come too?" asked Polly, trying to look demure while her eyes danced in spite of her.

"Afraid of spoiling her crinkles." And Tom smiled for this base betrayal of confidence made him feel his own man again.

"You and I don't mind dampness. I'm much obliged to you for coming to take care of me."

It was kind of Polly to say that, and Tom felt it, for his red crop was a tender point, and to be associated with Polly's pretty brown curls seemed to lessen its coppery glow. Then he hadn't done anything for her but carry the bag a few steps, yet she thanked him. He felt grateful, and in a burst of confidence offered a handful of peanuts, for his pockets were always supplied with this agreeable delicacy, and he might be traced anywhere by the trail of shells he left behind him.

As soon as he had done it he remembered that Fanny considered them vulgar and felt that he had disgraced his family. So he stuck his head out of the window and kept it there so long that Polly asked if anything was the matter. "Pooh! Who cares for a countrified little thing like her," said Tom manfully to himself, and then the spirit of mischief entered in and took possession of him.

"He's pretty drunk, but I guess he can hold his horses," replied this evil-minded boy with an air of calm resignation.

"Is the man tipsy? Oh, dear! Let's get out! Are the horses bad? It's very steep here. Do you think it's safe?" cried poor

Polly, making a cocked hat of her little beaver by thrusting it out of the half-open window on her side.

"There's plenty of folks to pick us up if anything happens, but perhaps it would be safer if *I* got out and sat with the man." And Tom quite beamed with the brilliancy of this sudden mode of relief.

"Oh, do, if you ain't afraid! Mother would be so anxious if anything *should* happen to me, so far away!" cried Polly, much distressed.

"Don't you be worried. I'll manage the old chap, and the horses too." And opening the door, Tom vanished aloft, leaving poor victimized Polly to quake inside while he placidly reveled in freedom and peanuts outside with the staid old driver.

Fanny came flying down to meet her "darling Polly" as Tom presented her with the graceful remark "I've got her!" and the air of a dauntless hunter producing the trophies of his skill. Polly was instantly whisked upstairs, and having danced a double shuffle on the doormat, Tom retired to the dining room to restore exhausted nature with half a dozen cookies.

"Ain't you tired to death? Don't you want to lie down?" said Fanny, sitting on the side of the bed in Polly's room and chattering hard while she examined everything her friend had on.

"Not a bit. I had a nice time coming, and no trouble, except the tipsy coachman, but Tom got out and kept him in order, so I wasn't much frightened," answered innocent Polly, taking off her rough-and-ready coat and the plain hat without a bit of a feather.

"Fiddlestick! He wasn't tipsy, and Tom only did it to get out of the way. He can't bear girls," said Fanny with a superior air.

"Can't he? Why, I thought he was very pleasant and kind!" And Polly opened her eyes with a surprised expression.

"He's an awful boy, my dear, and if you have anything to do with him, he'll torment you to death. Boys are *all* horrid, but he's the horridest one I ever saw."

Fanny went to a fashionable school where the young ladies were so busy with their French, German, and Italian that there was no time for good English. Feeling her confidence much shaken in the youth, Polly privately resolved to let him alone and changed the conversation by saying, as she looked admiringly about the large, handsome room, "How splendid it is! I never slept in a bed with curtains before, or had such a fine toilet table as this."

"I'm glad you like it, but don't, for mercy sake, say such things before the other girls!" replied Fanny, wishing Polly would wear earrings as everyone else did.

"Why not?" asked the country mouse of the city mouse, wondering what harm there was in liking other people's pretty things and saying so.

"Oh, they laugh at everything the least bit odd, and that isn't pleasant." Fanny didn't say "countrified," but she meant it, and Polly felt uncomfortable. So she shook out her little black silk apron with a thoughtful face and resolved not to allude to her own home if she could help it.

"I'm so poorly Mama says I needn't go to school regularly while you are here—only two or three times a week, just to keep up my music and French. You can go, too, if you like. Papa said so. Do, it's such fun!" cried Fanny, quite surprising her friend by this unexpected fondness for school.

"I should be afraid, if all the girls dress as finely as you do and know as much," said Polly, beginning to feel shy at the thought.

"La, child! You needn't mind that. I'll take care of you and fix you up so you won't look odd."

"Am I odd?" asked Polly, struck by the word and hoping it didn't mean anything very bad.

"You are a dear, and ever so much prettier than you were last summer, only you've been brought up differently from us, so your ways ain't like ours, you see," began Fanny, finding it rather hard to explain.

"How different?" asked Polly again, for she liked to understand things.

"Well, you dress like a little girl, for one thing."

"I *am* a little girl, so why shouldn't I?" And Polly looked at her simple blue merino frock, stout boots, and short hair with a puzzled air.

"You are fourteen, and *we* consider ourselves young ladies at that age," continued Fanny, surveying with complacency the pile of hair on the top of her head, with a fringe of fuzz round her forehead and a wavy lock streaming down her back; likewise, her scarlet and black suit, with its big sash, little *pannier*, bright buttons, points, rosettes—and heaven knows what. There was a locket on her neck, earrings tinkling in her ears, watch and chain at her belt, and several rings on a pair of hands that would have been improved by soap and water.

Polly's eye went from one little figure to the other, and she thought that Fanny looked the oddest of the two, for Polly lived in a quiet country town and knew very little of city fashions. She was rather impressed by the elegance about her, never having seen Fanny's home before, as they got acquainted while Fanny paid a visit to a friend who lived near Polly. But she didn't let the contrast between herself and Fan trouble her, for in a minute she laughed and said, contentedly, "My mother likes me to dress simply, and I don't mind. I shouldn't know what to do rigged up as you are. Don't you ever forget to lift your sash and fix those puffy things when you sit down?"

Before Fanny could answer, a scream from below made both listen. "It's only Maud, she fusses all day long," began Fanny, and the words were hardly out of her mouth when the door was thrown open and a little girl of six or seven came roaring in. She stopped at sight of Polly, stared a minute, then took up her roar just where she left it and cast herself into Fanny's lap, exclaiming wrathfully, "Tom's laughing at me! Make him stop!"

"What did you do to set him going? Don't scream so, you'll frighten Polly!" and Fan gave the cherub a shake, which produced an explanation.

"I only said we had cold cweam at the party last night, and he laughed!"

"Ice cream, child!" and Fanny followed Tom's reprehensible example.

"I don't care, it *was* cold, and I warmed mine at the wegister, and then it was nice, only Willy Bliss spilt it on my new Gabwielle!" and Maud wailed again over her accumulated woes.

"Do go to Katy! You're as cross as a little bear today!" said Fanny, pushing her away.

"Katy don't amoose me, and I must be amoosed 'cause I'm fwactious. Mama said I was!" sobbed Maud, evidently laboring under the delusion that fractiousness was some interesting malady.

"Come down and have dinner, that will amuse you," and Fanny got up, pluming herself as a bird does before its flight.

Polly hoped the "dreadful boy" would not be present, but he was, and stared at her all dinnertime in a most trying manner. Mr. Shaw, a busy-looking gentleman, said, "How

do you do, my dear? Hope you'll enjoy yourself," and then
appeared to forget her entirely. Mrs. Shaw, a pale, nervous
woman, greeted her little guest kindly and took care that she
wanted for nothing. Madam Shaw, a quiet old lady, with an
imposing cap, exclaimed on seeing Polly, "Bless me my
heart! The image of her mother—a sweet woman—how is
she, dear?" and kept peering at the newcomer over her
glasses till, between Madam and Tom, poor Polly lost her
appetite.

Fanny chatted like a magpie, and Maud fidgeted till Tom
proposed to put her under the big dish cover, which produced such an explosion that the young lady was borne
screaming away by the much-enduring Katy. It was altogether an uncomfortable dinner, and Polly was very glad
when it was over. They all went about their own affairs, and
after doing the honors of the house, Fan was called to the
dressmaker, leaving Polly to amuse herself in the great drawing room.

Polly was glad to be alone for a few minutes and, having
examined all the pretty things about her, began to walk up
and down over the soft, flowery carpet humming to herself
as the daylight faded and only the ruddy glow of the fire
filled the room. Presently Madam came slowly in and sat
down in her armchair, saying, "That's a fine old tune. Sing it
to me, my dear. I haven't heard it this many a day."

Polly didn't like to sing before strangers, for she had had
no teaching but such as her busy mother could give her, but
she had been taught the utmost respect for old people, and
having no reason for refusing, she directly went to the piano
and did as she was bid.

"That's the sort of music it's a pleasure to hear. Sing some
more, dear," said Madam in her gentle way when she had
done.

Pleased with this phrase, Polly sang away in a fresh little voice that went straight to the listener's heart and nestled there. The sweet old tunes that one is never tired of were all Polly's store, and her favorites were Scotch airs such as "Yellow-haired Laddie," "Jock o' Hazledean," "Down Amang the Heather," and "Birks of Aberfeldie." The more she sang, the better she did it, and when she wound up with "A Health to King Charlie," the room quite rang with the stirring music made by the big piano and the little maid.

"By George, that's a jolly tune! Sing it again, please," cried Tom's voice, and there was Tom's red head bobbing up over the high back of the chair where he had hidden himself.

It gave Polly quite a turn, for she thought no one was hearing her but the old lady dozing by the fire. "I can't sing anymore, I'm tired," she said, and walked away to Madam in the other room. The red head vanished like a meteor, for Polly's tone had been decidedly cool.

The old lady put out her hand and, drawing Polly to her knee, looked into her face with such kind eyes that Polly forgot the impressive cap and smiled at her confidingly, for she saw that her simple music had pleased her listener and she felt glad to know it.

"You mustn't mind my staring, dear," said Madam, softly pinching her rosy cheek. "I haven't seen a little girl for so long, it does my old eyes good to look at you."

Polly thought that a very odd speech and couldn't help saying, "Aren't Fan and Maud little girls too?"

"Oh, dear, no! Not what *I* call little girls. Fan has been a young lady this two years, and Maud is a spoiled baby. Your mother's a very sensible woman, my child."

"What a very queer old lady!" thought Polly, but she said "Yes'm" respectfully and looked at the fire.

"You don't understand what I mean, do you?" asked Madam, still holding her by the chin.

"No'm, not quite."

"Well, dear, I'll tell you. In my day, children of fourteen and fifteen didn't dress in the height of the fashion, go to parties, as nearly like those of grown people as it's possible to make them, lead idle, giddy, unhealthy lives, and get *blasé* at twenty. We were little folks till eighteen or so, worked and studied, dressed and played like children, honored our parents, and our days were much longer in the land than now, it seems to me."

The old lady appeared to forget Polly at the end of her speech, for she sat patting the plump little hand that lay in her own and looking up at a faded picture of an old gentleman with a ruffled shirt and a queue.

"Was he your father, Madam?"

"Yes, dear, my honored father. I did up his frills to the day of his death, and the first money I ever earned was five dollars, which he offered as a prize to whichever of his six girls would lay the handsomest darn in his silk stockings."

"How proud you must have been!" cried Polly, leaning on the old lady's knee with an interested face.

"Yes, and we all learned to make bread, and cook, and wore little chintz gowns, and were as gay and hearty as kittens. All lived to be grandmothers and fathers, and I'm the last—seventy, next birthday, my dear, and not worn out yet, though daughter Shaw is an invalid at forty."

"That's the way I was brought up, and that's why Fan calls me old-fashioned, I suppose. Tell more about your papa, please. I like it," said Polly.

"Say 'father.' We never called him 'papa,' and if one of my brothers had addressed him as 'governor,' as boys do now, I really think he'd have him cut off with a shilling."

Madam raised her voice in saying this and nodded significantly, but a mild snore from the other room seemed to assure her that it was a waste of shot to fire in that direction.

Before she could continue, in came Fanny with the joyful news that Clara Bird had invited them both to go to the theater with her that very evening and would call for them at seven o'clock. Polly was so excited by this sudden plunge into the dissipations of city life that she flew about like a distracted butterfly and hardly knew what happened till she found herself seated before the great green curtain in the brilliant theater. Old Mr. Bird sat on one side, Fanny on the other, and both let her alone, for which she was very grateful, as her whole attention was so absorbed in the scene around her that she couldn't talk.

Polly had never been much to the theater, and the few plays she had seen were the good old fairy tales dramatized to suit young beholders—lively, bright, and full of the harmless nonsense which brings the laugh without the blush. That night she saw one of the new spectacles which have lately become the rage and run for hundreds of nights, dazzling, exciting, and demoralizing the spectator by every allurement French ingenuity can invent and American prodigality execute. Never mind what its name was, it was very gorgeous, very vulgar, and very fashionable, so, of course, it was much admired, and everyone went to see it. At first Polly thought she had got into fairyland, and saw only the sparkling creatures who danced and sang in a world of light and beauty, but presently she began to listen to the songs and conversation, and then the illusion vanished, for the lovely phantoms sang Negro melodies, talked slang, and were a disgrace to the good old-fashioned elves whom she knew and loved so well.

Our little girl was too innocent to understand half the

jokes, and often wondered what people were laughing at, but as the first enchantment subsided Polly began to feel uncomfortable, to be sure her mother wouldn't like to have her there, and to wish she hadn't come. Somehow things seemed to get worse and worse as the play went on, for our small spectator was being rapidly enlightened by the gossip going on all about her, as well as by her own quick eyes and girlish instincts. When four and twenty girls dressed as jockeys came prancing onto the stage, cracking their whips, stamping the heels of their top boots, and winking at the audience, Polly did not think it at all funny but looked disgusted, and was glad when they were gone, but when another set appeared in a costume consisting of gauze wings and a bit of gold fringe around the waist, poor unfashionable Polly didn't know what to do, for she felt both frightened and indignant, and sat with her eyes on her playbill, and her cheeks getting hotter and hotter every minute.

"What are you blushing so for?" asked Fanny as the painted sylphs vanished.

"I'm so ashamed of those girls," whispered Polly, taking a long breath of relief.

"You little goose—it's just the way it was done in Paris, and the dancing is splendid. It seems queer at first, but you'll get used to it, as I did."

"I'll never come again," said Polly, decidedly, for her innocent nature rebelled against the spectacle, which, as yet, gave her more pain than pleasure. She did not know how easy it was to "get used to it," as Fanny did, and it was well for her that the temptation was not often offered. She could not explain the feeling, but she was glad when the play was done and they were safe at home, where kind Grandma was waiting to see them comfortably into bed.

"Did you have a good time, dear?" she asked, looking at Polly's feverish cheeks and excited eyes.

"I don't wish to be rude, but I didn't," answered Polly. "Some of it was splendid, but a good deal of it made me want to go under the seat. People seemed to like it, but *I* don't think it was proper."

As Polly freed her mind, and emphasized her opinion with a decided rap of the boot she had just taken off, Fanny laughed and said, while she pirouetted about the room like Mademoiselle Therese, "Polly was shocked, Grandma. Her eyes were as big as saucers, her face as red as my sash, and once I thought she was going to cry. Some of it *was* rather queer, but of course it was proper or all our set wouldn't go. I heard Mrs. Smythe Perkins say, 'It was charming, so like dear Paris,' and she has lived abroad, so of course she knows what is what."

"I don't care if she has. I know it *wasn't* proper for little girls to see or I shouldn't have been so ashamed!" cried sturdy Polly, perplexed, but not convinced, even by Mrs. Smythe Perkins.

"I think you are right, my dear, but you have lived in the country, and haven't yet learned that modesty has gone out of fashion." And with a good-night kiss, Grandma left Polly to dream dreadfully of dancing in jockey costume on a great stage while Tom played a big drum in the orchestra and the audience all wore the faces of her father and mother, looking sorrowfully at her, with eyes like saucers and faces as red as Fanny's sash.

Chapter 2

New Fashions

"I'm going to school this morning, so come up and get ready," said Fanny a day or two after as she left the late breakfast table.

"You look very nice. What have you got to do?" asked Polly, following her into the hall.

"Prink half an hour and put on her wad," answered the irreverent Tom, whose preparations for school consisted in flinging his cap onto his head and strapping up several big books that looked as if they were sometimes used as weapons of defense.

"What is a wad?" asked Polly while Fanny marched up without deigning any reply.

"Somebody's hair on the top of her head in the place where it ought not to be," and Tom went whistling away with an air of sublime indifference as to the state of his own "curly pow."

"Why must you be so fine to go to school?" asked Polly, watching Fan arrange the little frizzles on her forehead and settle the various streamers and festoons belonging to her dress.

"All the girls do, and it's proper, for you never know who you may meet. I'm going to walk, after my lessons, so I wish you'd wear your best hat and sack," answered Fanny, trying to stick her own hat on at an angle which defied all the laws of gravitation.

"I will, if you don't think this is nice enough. I like the other best, because it has a feather, but this is warmer, so I wear it every day." And Polly ran into her own room to prink also, fearing that her friend might be ashamed of her plain costume. "Won't your hands be cold in kid gloves?" she said as they went down the snowy street, with a north wind blowing in their faces.

"Yes, horrid cold, but my muff is so big I won't carry it. Mama won't have it cut up, and my ermine one must be kept for best," and Fanny smoothed her Bismark kids with an injured air.

"I suppose my gray squirrel is ever so much too big, but it's nice and cozy, and you may warm your hands in it if you want to," said Polly, surveying her new woolen gloves with a dissatisfied look, though she had thought them quite elegant before.

"Perhaps I will, by and by. Now, Polly, don't you be shy. I'll only introduce two or three of the girls, and you needn't mind old Monsieur a bit or read if you don't want to. We shall be in the anteroom, so you'll only see about a dozen, and they will be so busy they won't mind you much."

"I guess I won't read, but sit and look on. I like to watch people, everything is so new and queer here."

But Polly did feel and look very shy when she was ushered into a room full of young ladies, as they seemed to her, all very much dressed, all talking together, and all turning to examine the newcomer with a cool stare which seemed to be as much the fashion as eyeglasses. They nodded affably when Fanny introduced her, said something civil, and made room for her at the table round which they sat waiting for Monsieur. Several of the more frolicsome were imitating the Grecian Bend,* some were putting their heads together over little notes, nearly all were eating confectionery, and the entire twelve chattered like magpies. Being politely supplied with caramels, Polly sat looking and listening, feeling very young and countrified among these elegant young ladies.

"Girls, do you know that Carrie has gone abroad? There has been so much talk, her father couldn't bear it and took the whole family off. Isn't that gay?" said one lively damsel who had just come in.

"I should think they'd better go. My mama says if I'd been going to that school, she'd have taken me straightaway," answered another girl with an important air.

"Carrie ran away with an Italian music teacher, and it got into the papers and made a great stir," explained the first speaker to Polly, who looked mystified.

"How dreadful!" cried Polly.

"I think it was fun. She was only sixteen, and he was perfectly splendid, and she has plenty of money, and everyone talked about it, and when she went anywhere, people looked, you know, and she liked it, but her papa is an old poke, so he's sent them all away. It's too bad, for she was the jolliest thing I ever knew."

Polly had nothing to say to lively Miss Belle, but Fanny observed, "I like to read about such things, but it's so incon-

---

* An affected way of walking, with the upper part of the body bent forward from the hips.

venient to have it happen right here because it makes it
harder for us. I wish you could have heard my papa go on.
He threatened to send a maid to school with me every day,
as they do in New York, to be sure I come all right. Did you
ever?"

"That's because it came out that Carrie used to forge ex-
cuses in her mama's name and go promenading with her
Oreste when they thought her safe at school. Oh, wasn't she
a sly minx?" cried Belle as if she rather admired the trick.

"I think a little fun is all right, and there's no need of
making a talk if, now and then, someone does run off like
Carrie. Boys do as they like, and I don't see why girls need to
be kept so dreadfully close. I'd like to see anybody watching
and guarding me!" added another dashing young lady.

"It would take a policeman to do that, Trix, or a little man
in a tall hat," said Fanny slyly, which caused a general laugh
and made Beatrice toss her head coquettishly.

"Oh, have you read *The Phantom Bride?* It's perfectly thrilling! There's a regular rush for it at the library, but some
prefer *Breaking a Butterfly.* Which do you like best?" asked a
pale girl of Polly in one of the momentary lulls which occurred.

"I haven't read either."

"You must, then. I adore Guy Livingston's books, and
Yates's. Ouida's* are my delight, only they are so long, I get
worn out before I'm through."

"I haven't read anything but one of the Muhlbach novels

---

* Ouida is the pseudonym of Marie Louise de la Ramée (1839–1908), who
was known at this time (1870) as the author of long novels about high
society. She later turned to animal stories and children's books, and is
remembered today mainly for *A Dog of Flanders* (1872).

since I came. I like those because there is history in them,"
said Polly, glad to have a word to say for herself.

"Those are well enough for improving reading, but I like
real exciting novels, don't you?"

Polly was spared the mortification of owning that she had
never read any by the appearance of Monsieur, a gray-
headed old Frenchman who went through his task with the
resigned air of one who was used to being the victim of
giggling schoolgirls. The young ladies gabbled over the lesson, wrote an exercise, and read a little French history. But it
did not seem to make much impression upon them, though
Monsieur was very ready to explain, and Polly quite blushed
for her friend when, on being asked what famous Frenchman fought in our Revolution, she answered Lamartine instead of Lafayette.

The hour was soon over, and when Fan had taken a music
lesson in another room, while Polly looked on, it was time
for recess. The younger girls walked up and down the court,
arm in arm, eating bread and butter; others stayed in the
schoolroom to read and gossip, but Belle, Trix, and Fanny
went to lunch at a fashionable ice-cream saloon nearby and
Polly meekly followed, not daring to hint at the gingerbread
Grandma had put in her pocket for luncheon. So the honest
brown cookies crumbled away in obscurity while Polly tried
to satisfy her hearty appetite on one ice and three maca-
roons.

The girls seemed in great spirits, particularly after they
were joined by a short gentleman with such a young face that
Polly would have called him a boy if he had not worn a tall
beaver. Escorted by this impressive youth, Fanny left her
unfortunate friends to return to school and went to walk, as
she called a slow promenade down the most crowded streets.
Polly discreetly fell behind and amused herself looking into

shop windows till Fanny, mindful of her manners, even at such an interesting time, took her into a picture gallery and bade her enjoy the works of art while they rested. Obedient Polly went through the room several times, apparently examining the pictures with the interest of a connoisseur and trying not to hear the mild prattle of the pair on the round seat. But she couldn't help wondering what Fan found so absorbing in an account of a recent German, and why she need promise so solemnly not to forget the concert that afternoon.

When Fanny rose at last Polly's tired face reproached her, and taking a hasty leave of the small gentleman, she turned homeward, saying confidentially, as she put one hand in Polly's muff, "Now, my dear, you mustn't say a word about Frank Moore or Papa will take my head off. I don't care a bit for him, and he likes Trix, only they have quarreled, and he wants to make her mad by flirting a little with me. I scolded him well, and he promised to make up with her. We all go to the afternoon concerts and have a gay time, and Belle and Trix are to be there today, so just keep quiet and everything will be all right."

"I'm afraid it won't," began Polly, who, not being used to secrets, found it very hard to keep even a small one.

"Don't worry, child. It's none of our business, so we can go and enjoy the music, and if other people flirt, it won't be our fault," said Fanny impatiently.

"Of course not, but then, if your father don't like you to do so, ought you to go?"

"I tell Mama, and she don't care. Papa is fussy, and Grandma makes a stir about every blessed thing I do. You will hold your tongue, won't you?"

"Yes, I truly will, I never tell tales." And Polly kept her

word, feeling sure Fan didn't mean to deceive her father, since she told her mother everything.

"Who are you going with?" asked Mrs. Shaw when Fanny mentioned that it was concert day just before three o'clock.

"Only Polly. She likes music, and it was so stormy I couldn't go last week, you know," answered Fan, adding, as they left the house again, "If anyone meets us on the way, I can't help it, can I?"

"You can tell them not to, can't you?"

"That's rude. Dear me! Here's Belle's brother Gus—he always goes. *Is* my hair all right, and my hat?"

Before Polly could answer, Mr. Gus joined them as a matter of course, and Polly soon found herself trotting on behind, feeling that things were not "all right," though she didn't know how to mend them. Being fond of music, she ignorantly supposed that everyone else went for that alone and was much disturbed by the whispering that went on among the young people round her. Belle and Trix were there in full dress, and, in the pauses between different pieces, Messrs. Frank and Gus, with several other "splendid fellows," regaled the young ladies with college gossip and bits of news full of interest, to judge from the close attention paid to their eloquent remarks. Polly regarded these noble beings with awe, and they recognized her existence with the condescension of their sex, but they evidently considered her only "a quiet little thing," and finding her not up to society talk, blandly ignored the pretty child and devoted themselves to the young ladies. Fortunately for Polly, she forgot all about them in her enjoyment of the fine music, which she felt rather than understood, and sat listening with such a happy face that several true music lovers watched her smilingly, for her heart gave a blithe welcome to the melody which put the little instrument in tune. It was dusk when they went out, and Polly was much relieved to find the carriage waiting for them because playing third fiddle was not to her taste, and she had had enough of it for one day.

"I'm glad those men are gone. They did worry me so talking when I wanted to hear," said Polly as they rolled away.

"Which did you like best?" asked Fanny with a languid air of superiority.

"The plain one, who didn't say much. He picked up my muff when it tumbled down and took care of me in the crowd. The others didn't mind anything about me."

"They thought you were a little girl, I suppose."

"My mother says a real gentleman is as polite to a little girl as to a woman, so I like Mr. Sydney best because he was kind to me."

"What a sharp child you are, Polly. I shouldn't have thought you'd mind things like that," said Fanny, beginning to understand that there may be a good deal of womanliness even in a little girl.

"I'm used to good manners, though I do live in the country," replied Polly rather warmly, for she didn't like to be patronized even by her friends.

"Grandma says your mother is a perfect lady, and you are just like her, so don't get in a passion with those poor fellows and I'll see that they behave better next time. Tom has no manners at all, and you don't complain of him," added Fan with a laugh.

"I don't care if he hasn't. He's a boy, and acts like one, and I can get on with him a great deal better than I can with those men."

Fanny was just going to take Polly to task for saying "those men" in such a disrespectful tone when both were startled by a smothered "Cock-a-doodle-doo!" from under the opposite seat.

"It's Tom!" cried Fanny, and with the words out tumbled that incorrigible boy, red in the face and breathless with suppressed laughter. Seating himself, he surveyed the girls as if well satisfied with the success of his prank and waiting to be congratulated upon it. "Did you hear what we were saying?" demanded Fanny uneasily.

"Oh, didn't I, every word!" And Tom exulted over them visibly.

"Did you ever see such a provoking toad, Polly? Now I suppose you'll go and tell Papa a great story."

"P'r'aps I shall, and p'r'aps I shan't. How Polly did hop when I crowed! I heard her squeal and saw her cuddle up her feet."

"And you heard us praise your manners, didn't you?" asked Polly slyly.

"Yes, and you liked 'em, so I won't tell on *you,*" said Tom with a reassuring nod.

"There's nothing to tell."

"Ain't there, though? What do you suppose the governor will say to you girls going on so with those dandies? I saw you."

"What has the governor of Massachusetts to do with us?" asked Polly, trying to look as if she meant what she said.

"Pooh! You know who I mean, so you needn't try to catch me up, as Grandma does."

"Tom, I'll make a bargain with you," cried Fanny eagerly. "It wasn't my fault that Gus and Frank were there, and I couldn't help their speaking to me. I do as well as I can, and Papa needn't be angry, for I behave ever so much better than some of the girls. Don't I, Polly?"

"Bargain?" observed Tom with an eye to business.

"If you won't go and make a fuss, telling what you'd no right to hear—it was so mean to hide and listen; I should think you'd be ashamed of it!—I'll help you tease for your velocipede and won't say a word against it when Mama and Granny beg Papa not to let you have it."

"Will you?" And Tom paused to consider the offer in all its bearings.

"Yes, and Polly will help, won't you?"

"I'd rather not have anything to do with it, but I'll be quiet and not do any harm."

"Why won't you?" asked Tom curiously.

"Because it seems like deceiving."

"Well, Papa needn't be so fussy," said Fan petulantly.

"After hearing about that Carrie, and the rest, I don't wonder he *is* fussy. Why don't you tell right out, and not do it anymore if he don't want you to?" said Polly persuasively.

"Do you go and tell your father and mother everything right out?"

"Yes, I do, and it saves ever so much trouble."

"Ain't you afraid of them?"

"Of course I'm not. It's hard to tell sometimes, but it's *so* comfortable when it's over."

"Let's!" was Tom's brief advice.

"Mercy me! What a fuss about nothing!" said Fanny, ready to cry with vexation.

" 'T isn't nothing. You know you are forbidden to go gallivanting round with those chaps, and that's the reason you're in a pucker now. I *won't* make any bargain, and I *will* tell," returned Tom, seized with a sudden fit of moral firmness.

"Will you if I promise never, never to do so anymore?" asked Fanny meekly, for when Thomas took matters into his own hands, his sister usually submitted in spite of herself.

"I'll think about it, and if you behave, maybe I won't do it at all. I can watch you better than Papa can, so if you try it again, it's all up with you, miss," said Tom, finding it impossible to resist the pleasure of tyrannizing a little when he got the chance.

"She won't. Don't plague her anymore, and she will be good to you when you get into scrapes," answered Polly, with her arm around Fan.

"I never do, and if I did, I shouldn't ask a girl to help me out."

"Why not? *I'd* ask you in a minute if I was in trouble," said Polly in her confiding way.

"Would you? Well, I'd put you through, as sure as my name's Tom Shaw. Now, then, don't slip, Polly," and Mr. Thomas helped them out with unusual politeness, for that friendly little speech gratified him. He felt that one person appreciated him, and it had a good effect upon manners and temper made rough and belligerent by constant snubbing and opposition.

After tea that evening Fanny proposed that Polly should show her how to make molasses candy, as it was cook's holiday and the coast would be clear. Hoping to propitiate her tormentor, Fan invited Tom to join in the revel, and Polly begged that Maud might sit up and see the fun, so all four descended to the big kitchen, armed with aprons, hammers, spoons, and pans, and Polly assumed command of the forces. Tom was set to cracking nuts, and Maud to picking out the meats, for the candy was to be "tip-top." Fan waited on Polly cook, who hovered over the kettle of boiling molasses till her face was the color of a peony. "Now, put in the nuts," she said at last, and Tom emptied his plate into the foamy syrup while the others watched with deep interest the mysterious concoction of this well-beloved sweetmeat. "I pour it into the buttered pan, you see, and it cools, and *then* we can eat it," explained Polly, suiting the action to the word.

"Why, it's all full of shells!" exclaimed Maud, peering into the pan.

"Oh, thunder! I must have put 'em in by mistake and ate up the meats without thinking," said Tom, trying to conceal his naughty satisfaction as the girls hung over the pan with faces full of disappointment and despair.

"You did it on purpose, you horrid boy! I'll never let you have anything to do with my fun again!" cried Fan in a passion, trying to catch and shake him while he dodged and chuckled in high glee.

Maud began to wail over her lost delight, and Polly gravely poked at the mess, which was quite spoilt. But her attention was speedily diverted by the squabble going on in the corner, for Fanny, forgetful of her young ladyism and her sixteen years, had boxed Tom's ears, and Tom, resenting the insult, had forcibly seated her in the coal hod, where he held her with one hand while he returned the compliment with the other. Both were very angry and kept twitting one another with every aggravation they could invent as they scolded and scuffled, presenting a most unlovely spectacle.

Polly was not a model girl by any means, and had her little pets and tempers like the rest of us, but she didn't fight, scream, and squabble with her brothers and sisters in this disgraceful way and was much surprised to see her elegant friend in such a passion. "Oh, don't! Please, don't! You'll hurt her, Tom! Let him go, Fanny! It's no matter about the candy, we can make some more!" cried Polly, trying to part them and looking so distressed that they stopped ashamed, and in a minute sorry that she should see such a display of temper.

"I ain't going to be hustled round, so you'd better let me alone, Fan," said Tom, drawing off with a threatening wag of the head, adding, in a different tone, "I only put the shells in for fun, Polly. You cook another kettleful, and I'll pick you some meats all fair. Will you?"

"It's pretty hot work, and it's a pity to waste things, but I'll try again if you want me to," said Polly with a patient sigh, for her arms were tired and her face uncomfortably hot.

"We don't want you—get away!" said Maud, shaking a sticky spoon at him.

"Keep quiet, crybaby. I'm going to stay and help. Mayn't I, Polly?"

"Bears like sweet things, so you want some candy, I guess. Where is the molasses? We've used up all there was in the jug," said Polly good-naturedly, beginning again.

"Down cellar. I'll get it." And taking the lamp and jug, Tom departed, bent on doing his duty now like a saint.

The moment his light vanished Fanny bolted the door, saying spitefully, "Now, we are safe from any more tricks. Let him thump and call, it only serves him right, and when the candy is done, we'll let the rascal out."

"How can we make it without molasses?" asked Polly, thinking that would settle the matter.

"There's plenty in the storeroom. No, you shan't let him up till I'm ready. He's got to learn that I'm not to be shaken by a little chit like him. Make your candy and let him alone, or I'll go and tell Papa, and then Tom will get a lecture."

Polly thought it wasn't fair, but Maud clamored for her candy, and finding she could do nothing to appease Fan, Polly devoted her mind to her cookery till the nuts were safely in and a nice panful set in the yard to cool. A few bangs at the locked door, a few threats of vengeance from the prisoner, such as setting the house on fire, drinking up the wine, and smashing the jelly pots, and then all was so quiet that the girls forgot him in the exciting crisis of their work.

"He can't possibly get out anywhere, and as soon as we've cut up the candy, we'll unbolt the door and run. Come and get a nice dish to put it in," said Fan when Polly proposed to go halves with Tom, lest he should come bursting in somehow and seize the whole.

When they came down with the dish in which to set forth their treat, and opened the back door to find it, imagine their dismay on discovering that it was gone—pan, candy, and all—utterly and mysteriously gone!

A general lament arose when a careful rummage left no hopes, for the fates had evidently decreed that candy was not to prosper on this unpropitious night.

"The hot pan has melted and sunk in the snow, perhaps," said Fanny, digging into the drift where it was left.

"Those old cats have got it, I guess," suggested Maud, too much overwhelmed by this second blow to howl as usual.

"The gate isn't locked, and some beggar has stolen it. I hope it will do him good," added Polly, returning from her exploring expedition.

"If Tom *could* get out, I should think he'd carried it off, but not being a rat, he can't go through the bits of windows, so it wasn't him," said Fanny disconsolately, for she began to think this double loss a punishment for letting angry passions rise.

"Let's open the door and tell him about it," proposed Polly.

"He'll crow over us. No, we'll open it and go to bed, and he can come out when he likes. Provoking boy! If he hadn't plagued us so, we should have had a nice time."

Unbolting the cellar door, the girls announced to the invisible captive that they were through, and then departed much depressed. Halfway up the second flight, they all stopped as suddenly as if they had seen a ghost, for looking over the banisters was Tom's face, crocky but triumphant, and in either hand a junk of candy, which he waved above them as he vanished with the tantalizing remark, "Don't you wish you had some?"

"How in the world did he get out?" cried Fanny, steadying herself after a start that nearly sent all three tumbling downstairs.

"Coal hole!" answered a spectral voice from the gloom above.

"Good gracious! He must have poked up the cover, climbed into the street, stole the candy, and sneaked in at the shed window while we were looking for it."

"Cats got it, didn't they?" jeered the voice in a tone that made Polly sit down and laugh till she couldn't laugh any longer.

"Just give Maud a bit, she's so disappointed. Fan and I are sick of it, and so will you be if you eat it all," called Polly when she got her breath.

"Go to bed, Maudie, and look under your pillow when you get there," was the oracular reply that came down to them as Tom's door closed after a jubilant solo on the tin pan.

The girls went to bed tired out, and Maud slumbered placidly, hugging the sticky bundle, found where molasses candy is not often discovered. Polly was very tired and soon fell asleep, but Fanny, who slept with her, lay awake longer than usual, thinking about her troubles, for her head ached, and the dissatisfaction that follows anger would not let her rest with the tranquility that made the rosy face in the little round nightcap such a pleasant sight to see as it lay beside her. The gas was turned down, but Fanny saw a figure in a

gray wrapper creep by her door and presently return, pausing to look in. "Who is it?" she cried, so loud that Polly
woke.

"Only me, dear," answered Grandma's mild voice. "Poor
Tom has got a dreadful toothache, and I came down to find
some creosote for him. He told me not to tell you, but I can't
find the bottle and don't want to disturb Mama."

"It's in my closet. Old Tom will pay for his trick this
time," said Fanny in a satisfied tone.

"I thought he'd get enough of our candy," laughed Polly,
and then they fell asleep, leaving Tom to the delights of
toothache and the tender mercies of kind old Grandma.

Chapter 3

Polly's Troubles

*P*olly soon found that she was in a new world, a world where the manners and customs were so different from the simple ways at home that she felt like a stranger in a strange land, and often wished that she had not come. In the first place, she had nothing to do but lounge and gossip, read novels, parade the streets, and dress; and before a week was gone she was as heartily sick of all this as a healthy person would be who attempted to live on confectionery. Fanny liked it because she was used to it, and had never known anything better, but Polly had, and often felt like a little wood bird shut up in a gilded cage. Nevertheless, she was much impressed by the luxuries all about her, enjoyed them, wished she owned them, and wondered why the Shaws were not a happier family. She was not wise enough to know where the trouble lay; she did not attempt to say which of the two lives was the right one; she only knew which she liked best and supposed it was merely another of her "old-fashioned" ways.

Fanny's friends did not interest her much. She was rather

afraid of them, they seemed so much older and wiser than herself, even those younger in years. They talked about things of which she knew nothing, and when Fanny tried to explain, she didn't find them interesting. Indeed, some of them rather shocked and puzzled her, so the girls let her alone, being civil when they met, but evidently feeling that she was too "odd" to belong to their set. Then she turned to Maud for companionship, for her own little sister was excellent company, and Polly loved her dearly. But Miss Maud was much absorbed in her own affairs, for she belonged to a "set" also, and these mites of five and six had their "musicals," their parties, receptions, and promenades as well as their elders, and the chief idea of their little lives seemed to be to ape the fashionable follies they should have been too innocent to understand. Maud had her tiny card case and paid calls, "like Mama and Fan," her box of dainty gloves, her jewel drawer, her crimping pins, as fine and fanciful a wardrobe as a Paris doll, and a French maid to dress her. Polly couldn't get on with her at first, for Maud didn't seem like a child and often corrected Polly in her conversations and manners, though little mademoiselle's own were anything but perfect. Now and then, when Maud felt poorly, or had a "fwactious" turn, for she had "nerves" as well as Mama, she would go to Polly to be "amoosed," for her gentle ways and kind forbearance soothed the little fine lady better than anything else. Polly enjoyed these times, and told stories, played games, or went out walking, just as Maud liked, slowly and surely winning the child's heart and relieving the whole house of the young tyrant who ruled it.

Tom soon got over staring at Polly, and at first did not take much notice of her, for, in his opinion, "girls didn't amount to much, anyway," and, considering the style of girl he knew most about, Polly quite agreed with him. He occa-

sionally refreshed himself by teasing her, to see how she'd
stand it, and caused Polly much anguish of spirit, for she
never knew where he would take her next. He bounced out
at her from behind doors, booed at her in dark entries,
clutched her feet as she went up stairs, startled her by shrill
whistles right in her ear or sudden tweaks of the hair as he
passed her in the street. And as sure as there was company
to dinner, he fixed his round eyes on her and never took
them off till she was reduced to a piteous state of confusion
and distress. She used to beg him not to plague her, but he
said he did it for her good, she was too shy, and needed
toughening like the other girls. In vain she protested that
she didn't want to be like the other girls in that respect. He
only laughed in her face, stuck his red hair straight up all
over his head, and glared at her till she fled in dismay.

Yet Polly rather liked Tom, for she soon saw that he was
neglected, hustled out of the way, and left to get on pretty
much by himself. She often wondered why his mother didn't
pet him as she did the girls; why his father ordered him
about as if he was a born rebel and took so little interest in
his only son. Fanny considered him a bear and was ashamed
of him, but never tried to polish him up a bit, and Maud
and he lived together like a cat and dog who did not belong
to a "happy family." Grandma was the only one who stood
by poor old Tom, and Polly more than once discovered him
doing something kind for Madam, and seeming very much
ashamed when it was found out. He wasn't respectful at all;
he called her "the old lady" and told her he "wouldn't be
fussed over," but when anything was the matter, he always
went to "the old lady" and was very grateful for the "fuss-
ing." Polly liked him for this, and often wanted to speak of
it, but she had a feeling that it wouldn't do, for in praising

their affection she was reproaching others with neglect, so she held her tongue and thought about it all the more.

Grandma was rather neglected, too, and perhaps that is the reason why Tom and she were such good friends. She was even more old-fashioned than Polly, but people didn't seem to mind it so much in her, as her day was supposed to be over and nothing was expected of her but to keep out of everybody's way and to be handsomely dressed when she appeared "before people." Grandma led a quiet, solitary life up in her own rooms, full of old furniture, pictures, books, and relics of a past for which no one cared but herself. Her son went up every evening for a little call, was very kind to her, and saw that she wanted nothing money could buy, but he was a busy man, so intent on getting rich that he had no time to enjoy what he already possessed. Madam never complained, interfered, or suggested, but there was a sad sort of quietude about her, a wistful look in her faded eyes, as if she wanted something which money could not buy, and when children were near she hovered about them, evidently longing to cuddle and caress them as only grandmothers can. Polly felt this, and, as she missed the home-petting, gladly showed that she liked to see the quiet old face brighten as she entered the solitary room, where few children came, except the phantoms of little sons and daughters who, to the motherly heart that loved them, never faded or grew up. Polly wished the children would be kinder to Grandma, but it was not for her to tell them so, although it troubled her a good deal, and she could only try to make up for it by being as dutiful and affectionate as if their grandma was her own.

Another thing that disturbed Polly was the want of exercise. To dress up and parade certain streets for an hour every day, to stand talking in doorways, or drive out in a fine carriage was not the sort of exercise she liked, and Fan would take no other. Indeed, she was so shocked when Polly, one day, proposed a run down the mall that her friend never dared suggest such a thing again. At home, Polly ran and rode, coasted and skated, jumped rope and raked hay, worked in her garden and rowed her boat, so no wonder she longed for something more lively than a daily promenade with a flock of giddy girls, who tilted along in high-heeled boots and costumes which made Polly ashamed to be seen with some of them. So she used to slip out alone sometimes, when Fanny was absorbed in novels, company, or millinery, and get fine brisk walks round the park, on the unfashionable side, where the babies took their airings, or she went inside, to watch the boys coasting and to wish she could coast, too, as she did at home. She never went far, and always came back rosy and gay.

One afternoon, just before dinner, she felt so tired of doing nothing that she slipped out for a run. It had been a dull day, but the sun was visible now, setting brightly below the clouds. It was cold but still, and Polly trotted down the smooth, snow-covered mall, humming to herself and trying not to feel homesick. The coasters were at it with all their might, and she watched them till her longing to join the fun grew irresistible. On the hill some little girls were playing with their sleds—real little girls, in warm hoods and coats, rubber boots and mittens—and Polly felt drawn toward them in spite of her fear of Fan.

"I want to go down, but I darsn't, it's so steep," said one of these "common children," as Maud called them.

"If you'll lend me your sled, and sit in my lap, I'll take you down all nice," answered Polly in a confidential tone.

The little girls took a look at her, seemed satisfied, and accepted her offer. Polly looked carefully round to see that no fashionable eye beheld the awful deed, and finding all safe, settled her freight and spun away downhill, feeling all over the delightsome excitement of swift motion which makes coasting such a favorite pastime with the more sensible portion of the child world. One after another, she took the little girls down the hill and dragged them up again, while they regarded her in the light of a gray-coated angel, descended for their express benefit. Polly was just finishing off with one delicious "go" all by herself when she heard a familiar whistle behind her, and before she could get off, up came Tom, looking as much astonished as if he had found her mounted on an elephant.

"Hullo, Polly! What'll Fan say to you?" was his polished salutation.

"Don't know, and don't care. Coasting is no harm, I like it, and I'm going to do it, now I've got a chance, so clear the lul-la!" And away went independent Polly, with her hair blowing in the wind and an expression of genuine enjoyment, which a very red nose didn't damage in the least.

"Good for you, Polly!" And casting himself upon his sled, with the most reckless disregard for his ribs, off whizzed Tom after her and came alongside just as she reined up "General Grant" on the broad path below. "Oh, won't you get it when we go home?" cried the young gentleman, even before he changed his graceful attitude.

"I shan't if you don't go and tell, but of course you will," added Polly, sitting still while an anxious expression began to steal over her happy face.

"I just won't, then," returned Tom, with the natural perversity of his tribe.

"If they ask me, I shall tell, of course. If they don't ask, I think there's no harm in keeping still. I shouldn't have done it if I hadn't known my mother was willing, but I don't wish to trouble your mother by telling of it. Do you think it was very dreadful of me?" asked Polly, looking at him.

"I think it was downright jolly, and I won't tell if you don't want me to. Now, come up and have another," said Tom heartily.

"Just one more; the little girls want to go, and this is their sled."

"Let 'em take it, 't isn't good for much, and you come on mine. Mazeppa's a stunner, you see if he isn't."

So Polly tucked herself up in front, Tom hung on behind in some mysterious manner, and Mazeppa proved that he fully merited his master's sincere if inelegant praise. They got on capitally now, for Tom was in his proper sphere and showed his best side, being civil and gay in the bluff boy fashion that was natural to him, while Polly forgot to be shy, and liked this sort of "toughening" much better than the other. They laughed and talked, and kept taking "just one more" till the sunshine was all gone and the clocks struck dinnertime.

"We shall be late, let's run," said Polly as they came into the path after the last coast.

"You just sit still, and I'll get you home in a jiffy." And before she could unpack herself, Tom trotted off with her at a fine pace.

"Here's a pair of cheeks! I wish you'd get a color like this, Fanny," said Mr. Shaw as Polly came into the dining room after smoothing her hair.

"Your nose is as red as that cranberry sauce," answered Fan, coming out of the big chair where she had been curled up for an hour or two, deep in *Lady Audley's Secret*.

"So it is," said Polly, shutting one eye to look at the offending feature. "Never mind, I've had a good time, anyway," she added, giving a little prance in her chair.

"I don't see much fun in these cold runs you are so fond of taking," said Fanny with a yawn and a shiver.

"Perhaps you would if you tried it," and Polly laughed as she glanced at Tom.

"Did you go alone, dear?" asked Grandma, patting the rosy cheek beside her.

"Yes'm, but I met Tom, and we came home together." Polly's eyes twinkled when she said that, and Tom choked in his soup.

"Thomas, leave the table!" commanded Mr. Shaw as his incorrigible son gurgled and gasped behind his napkin.

"Please, don't send him away, sir. I made him laugh," said Polly penitently.

"What's the joke?" asked Fanny, waking up at last.

"I shouldn't think you'd make him laugh when he's always making you cwy," observed Maud, who had just come in.

"What have you been doing now, sir?" demanded Mr. Shaw as Tom emerged, red and solemn, from his brief obscurity.

"Nothing but coast," he said gruffly, for Papa was always lecturing him and letting the girls do just as they liked.

"So's Polly, I saw her. Me and Blanche were coming home just now, and we saw her and Tom widing down the hill on his sled, and then he dwagged her ever so far!" cried Maud with her mouth full.

"You didn't?" And Fanny dropped her fork with a scandalized face.

"Yes, I did, and liked it ever so much," answered Polly, looking anxious but resolute.

"*Did* anyone see you?" cried Fanny.

"Only some little girls and Tom."

"It was horridly improper, and Tom ought to have told

you so if you didn't know any better. I should be mortified
to death if any of my friends saw you," added Fan, much
disturbed.

"Now, don't you scold. It's no harm, and Polly shall coast
if she wants to, mayn't she, Grandma?" cried Tom, gallantly
coming to the rescue and securing a powerful ally.

"My mother lets me, and if I don't go among the boys, I
can't see what harm there is in it," said Polly before Madam
could speak.

"People do many things in the country that are not
proper here," began Mrs. Shaw in her reproving tone.

"Let the child do it if she likes, and take Maud with her. I
should be glad to have one hearty girl in my house," interrupted Mr. Shaw, and that was the end of it.

"Thank you, sir," said Polly gratefully, and nodded at
Tom, who telegraphed back, "All right!" and fell upon his
dinner with the appetite of a young wolf.

"Oh, you slyboots! You're getting up a flirtation with
Tom, are you?" whispered Fanny to her friend, as if much
amused.

"What!" And Polly looked so surprised and indignant
that Fanny was ashamed of herself, and changed the subject
by telling her mother she needed some new gloves.

Polly was very quiet after that, and the minute dinner was
over she left the room to go and have a quiet "think" about
the whole matter. Before she got halfway upstairs she saw
Tom coming after, and immediately sat down to guard her
feet. He laughed and said, as he perched himself on the post
of the banisters, "I won't grab you, honor bright. I just
wanted to say if you'll come out tomorrow sometime, we'll
have a good coast."

"No," said Polly, "I can't come."

"Why not? Are you mad? I didn't tell." And Tom looked amazed at the change which had come over her.

"No, you kept your word and stood by me like a good boy. I'm not mad, either, but I don't mean to coast anymore. Your mother don't like it."

"That isn't the reason, I know. You nodded to me after she'd freed her mind and you meant to go then. Come, now, what is it?"

"I shan't tell you, but I'm not going," was Polly's determined answer.

"Well, I did think you had more sense than most girls, but you haven't, and I wouldn't give a sixpence for you."

"That's polite," said Polly, getting ruffled.

"Well, I hate cowards."

"I ain't a coward."

"Yes, you are. You're afraid of what folks will say, ain't you, now?"

Polly knew she was and held her peace, though she longed to speak, but how could she?

"Ah, I knew you'd back out." And Tom walked away with an air of scorn that cut Polly to the heart.

"It's too bad! Just as he was growing kind to me, and I was going to have a good time, it's all spoilt by Fan's nonsense. Mrs. Shaw don't like it, nor Grandma either, I daresay. There'll be a fuss if I go, and Fan will plague me, so I'll give it up and let Tom think I'm afraid. Oh, dear! I never did see such ridiculous people."

Polly shut her door hard, and felt ready to cry with vexation that her pleasure should be spoilt by such a silly idea, for, of all the silly freaks of this fast age, that of little people playing at love is about the silliest. Polly had been taught that it was a very serious and sacred thing, and, according to her notions, it was far more improper to flirt with one boy than to coast with a dozen. She had been much amazed, only the day before, to hear Maud say to her mother, "Mama, must I have a beau? The girls all do, and say I ought to have Fweddy Lovell, but I don't like him as well as Hawry Fiske."

"Oh, yes, I'd have a little sweetheart, dear, it's so cunning," answered Mrs. Shaw. And Maud announced soon after that she was engaged to "Fdeddy, 'cause Hawry slapped her" when she proposed the match.

Polly laughed with the rest at the time, but when she thought of it afterward, and wondered what her own mother would have said if little Kitty had put such a question, she didn't find it cunning or funny, but ridiculous and unnatural. She felt so now about herself, and when her first petulance was over, resolved to give up coasting and everything else rather than have any nonsense with Tom, who, thanks to his neglected education, was as ignorant as herself of the charms of this new amusement for schoolchildren. So Polly tried to console herself by jumping rope in the backyard and playing tag with Maud in the drying room, where she likewise gave lessons in "nas-gim-nics," as Maud called it, which did that little person good. Fanny came up sometimes to teach them a new dancing step, and more than once was betrayed into a game of romps, for which she was none the worse. But Tom turned a cold shoulder to Polly and made it evident, by his cavalier manner, that he really didn't think her "worth a sixpence."

Another thing that troubled Polly was her clothes, for, though no one said anything, she knew they were very plain, and now and then she wished that her blue and mouse-colored merinos were rather more trimmed, her sashes had bigger bows, and her little ruffles more lace on them. She sighed for a locket and, for the first time in her life, thought seriously of turning up her pretty curls and putting on a "wad." She kept these discontents to herself, however, after she had written to ask her mother if she might have her best dress altered like Fanny's and received this reply:

"No, dear, the dress is proper and becoming as it is, and the old fashion of simplicity the best for all of us. I don't want my Polly to be loved for her clothes, but for herself, so wear the plain frocks Mother took such pleasure in making for you and let the *panniers* go. The least of us have some influence in this big world, and perhaps my little girl can do some good by showing others that a contented heart and a happy face are better ornaments than any Paris can give her. You want a locket, deary, so I send one that my mother gave me years ago. You will find Father's face on one side, mine on the other, and when things trouble you, just look at your talisman, and I think the sunshine will come back again."

Of course it did, for the best of all magic was shut up in the quaint little case that Polly wore inside her frock and kissed so tenderly each night and morning. The thought that, insignificant as she was, she yet might do some good made her very careful of her acts and words, and so anxious to keep heart contented and face happy that she forgot her clothes and made others do the same. She did not know it, but that good old fashion of simplicity made the plain gowns pretty, and the grace of unconsciousness beautified their little wearer with the charm that makes girlhood sweetest to those who truly love and reverence it. One temptation Polly had already yielded to before the letter came, and repented heartily of afterward.

"Polly, I wish you'd let me call you Marie," said Fanny one day as they were shopping together.

"You may call me Mary, if you like, but I won't have any *ie* put on to my name. I'm Polly at home, and I'm fond of being called so, but Marie is Frenchified and silly."

"I spell my own name with an *ie,* and so do all the girls."

"And what a jumble of Netties, Nellies, Hatties, and Sallies there is. How 'Pollie' would look spelt so!"

"Well, never mind, that wasn't what I began to say. There's one thing you must have, and that is bronze boots," said Fan impressively.

"Why must I, when I've got enough without?"

"Because it's the fashion to have them, and you can't be finished off properly without. I'm going to get a pair, and so must you."

"Don't they cost a great deal?"

"Eight or nine dollars, I believe. I have mine charged, but it don't matter if you haven't got the money. I can lend you some."

"I've got ten dollars to do what I like with, but I meant to get some presents for the children." And Polly took out her purse in an undecided way.

"You can make presents easy enough. Grandma knows all sorts of nice contrivances. They'll do just as well, and then you can get your boots."

"Well, I'll look at them," said Polly, following Fanny into the store, feeling rather rich and important to be shopping in this elegant manner.

"Aren't they lovely? Your foot is perfectly divine in that boot, Polly. Get them for my party; you'll dance like a fairy," whispered Fan.

Polly surveyed the dainty, shining boot with the scalloped top, the jaunty heel, and the delicate toe, thought her foot did look very well in it, and after a little pause said she would have them. It was all very delightful till she got home and was alone; then, on looking into her purse, she saw one dollar and the list of things she meant to get for Mother and the children. How mean the dollar looked all alone! And how long the list grew when there was nothing to buy the articles.

"I can't make skates for Ned, nor a desk for Will, and those are what they have set their hearts upon. Father's book and mother's collar are impossible now, and I'm a selfish thing to go and spend all my money for myself. How could I do it?" And Polly eyed the new boots reproachfully as they stood in the first position, as if ready for the party. "They *are* lovely, but I don't believe they will feel good, for I shall be thinking about my lost presents all the time," sighed Polly, pushing the enticing boots out of sight. "I'll go and ask Grandma what I can do, for if I've got to make something for everyone, I must begin right away or I shan't get done." And off she bustled, glad to forget her remorse in hard work.

Grandma proved equal to the emergency and planned something for everyone, supplying materials, taste, and skill in the most delightful manner. Polly felt much comforted, but while she began to knit a pretty pair of white bed socks, to be tied with rose-colored ribbons, for her mother, she thought some very sober thoughts upon the subject of temptation, and if anyone had asked her just then what made her sigh, as if something lay heavy on her conscience, she would have answered, "Bronze boots."

Chapter 4

Little Things

"*I*t's so wainy, I can't go out, and evwybody is so cwoss they won't play with me," said Maud when Polly found her fretting on the stairs and paused to ask the cause of her wails.

"I'll play with you, only don't scream and wake your mother. What shall we play?"

"I don't know, I'm tired of evwything, 'cause my toys are all bwoken, and my dolls are all sick but Clawa," moaned Maud, giving a jerk to the Paris doll which she held upside down by one leg in the most unmaternal manner.

"I'm going to dress a dolly for my little sister. Wouldn't you like to see me do it?" asked Polly persuasively, hoping to beguile the cross child and finish her own work at the same time.

"No, I shouldn't, 'cause she'll look nicer than my Clawa. Her clothes won't come off, and Tom spoilt 'em playing ball with her in the yard."

"Wouldn't you like to rip these clothes off, and have me

show you how to make some new ones, so you can dress and undress Clara as much as you like?"

"Yes, I love to cut." And Maud's face brightened, for destructiveness is one of the earliest traits of childhood, and ripping was Maud's delight.

Establishing themselves in the deserted dining room, the children fell to work, and when Fanny discovered them Maud was laughing with all her heart at poor Clara, who, denuded of her finery, was cutting up all sorts of capers in the hands of her merry little mistress.

"I should think you'd be ashamed to play with dolls, Polly. I haven't touched one this ever so long," said Fanny, looking down with a superior air.

"I ain't ashamed, for it keeps Maud happy, and will please my sister Kitty, and I think sewing is better than prinking or reading silly novels, so, now." And Polly stitched away with a resolute air, for she and Fanny had had a little tiff because Polly wouldn't let her friend do up her hair "like other folks" and bore her ears.

"Don't be cross, dear, but come and do something nice, it's so dull today," said Fanny, anxious to be friends again, for it was doubly dull without Polly.

"Can't, I'm busy."

"You always *are* busy. I never saw such a girl. What in the world do you find to do all the time?" asked Fanny, watching with interest the set of the little red merino frock Polly was putting onto her doll.

"Lots of things, but I like to be lazy sometimes as much as you do, just lie on the sofa, and read fairy stories, or think about nothing. Would you have a white muslin apron or a black silk?" added Polly, surveying her work with satisfaction.

"Muslin, with pockets and tiny blue bows. I'll show you

how." And forgetting her late contempt for dolls, down sat Fanny, soon getting as much absorbed as either of the others.

The dull day brightened wonderfully after that, and the time flew pleasantly as tongues and needles went together. Grandma peeped in and smiled at the busy group, saying, "Sew away, my dears, dollies are safe companions, and needlework an accomplishment that's sadly neglected nowadays. Small stitches, Maud; neat buttonholes, Fan; cut carefully, Polly, and don't waste your cloth. Take pains, and the best needlewoman shall have a pretty bit of white satin for a doll's bonnet."

Fanny exerted herself and won the prize, for Polly helped Maud and neglected her own work, but she didn't care much, for Mr. Shaw said, looking at the three bright faces at the tea table, "I guess Polly has been making sunshine for you today."

"No, indeed, sir, I haven't done anything, only dress Maud's doll."

And Polly didn't think she *had* done much, but it was one of the little things which are always waiting to be done in this world of ours, where rainy days come so often, where spirits get out of tune, and duty won't go hand in hand with pleasure. Little things of this sort are especially good work for little people; a kind little thought, an unselfish little act, a cheery little word, are so sweet and comfortable that no one can fail to feel their beauty and love the giver, no matter how small they are. Mothers do a deal of this sort of thing, unseen, unthanked, but felt and remembered long afterward and never lost, for this is the simple magic that binds hearts together and keeps homes happy. Polly had learned this secret. She loved to do the "little things" that others did not see, or were too busy to stop for, and while doing them, without a thought of thanks, she made sunshine for herself as well as others. There was so much love in her own home that she quickly felt the want of it in Fanny's, and puzzled herself to find out why these people were not kind and patient to one another. She did not try to settle the question, but did her best to love and serve and bear with each, and the goodwill, the gentle heart, the helpful ways and simple manners of our Polly made her dear to everyone, for these virtues, even in a little child, are lovely and attractive.

Mr. Shaw was very kind to her, for he liked her modest, respectful manners, and Polly was so grateful for his many favors that she soon forgot her fear and showed her affection in all sorts of confiding little ways, which pleased him extremely. She used to walk across the park with him when he went to his office in the morning, talking busily all the way, and saying "Good-bye" with a nod and a smile when they parted at the great gate. At first Mr. Shaw did not care much about it, but soon he missed her if she didn't come, and found that something fresh and pleasant seemed to brighten all his day if a small, gray-coated figure, with an intelligent face, a merry voice, and a little hand slipped confidingly into his, went with him through the wintry park. Coming home late, he liked to see a curly brown head watching at the window, to find his slippers ready, his paper in its place, and a pair of willing feet eager to wait upon him. "I wish my Fanny was more like her," he often said to himself as he watched the girls while they thought him deep in politics or the state of the money market. Poor Mr. Shaw had been so busy getting rich that he had not found time to teach his children to love him. He was more at leisure now, and as his boy and girls grew up, he missed something. Polly was unconsciously showing him what it was, and making child-love so sweet that he felt he could not do without it anymore, yet didn't quite know how to win the confidence of the children, who had always found him busy, indifferent, and absentminded.

As the girls were going to bed one night, Polly kissed Grandma, as usual, and Fanny laughed at her, saying, "What a baby you are! We are too old for such things now."

"I don't think people *ever* are too old to kiss their fathers and mothers" was the quick answer.

"Right, my little Polly." And Mr. Shaw stretched out his hand to her with such a kindly look that Fanny stared, surprised, and then said, shyly, "I thought you didn't care about it, Father."

"I do, my dear." And Mr. Shaw put out the other hand to Fanny, who gave him a daughterly kiss, quite forgetting everything but the tender feeling that sprang up in her heart at the renewal of the childish custom which we never need outgrow.

Mrs. Shaw was a nervous, fussy invalid who wanted something every five minutes, so Polly found plenty of small things to do for her, and did them so cheerfully that the poor lady loved to have the quiet, helpful child near, to wait upon her, read to her, run errands, or hand the seven different shawls which were continually being put on or off.

Grandma, too, was glad to find willing hands and feet to serve her, and Polly passed many happy hours in the quaint rooms, learning all sorts of pretty arts and listening to pleasant chat, never dreaming how much sunshine she brought to the solitary old lady.

Tom was Polly's rock ahead for a long time because he was always breaking out in a new place, and one never knew where to find him. He tormented yet amused her, was kind one day and a bear the next. At times she fancied he was never going to be bad again, and the next thing she knew he was deep in mischief and hooted at the idea of repentance and reformation. Polly gave him up as a hard case, but was so in the habit of helping anyone who seemed in trouble that she was good to him simply because she couldn't help it.

"What's the matter? Is your lesson too hard for you?" she asked one evening as a groan made her look across the table to where Tom sat scowling over a pile of dilapidated books with his hands in his hair, as if his head was in danger of flying asunder with the tremendous effort he was making.

"Hard! Guess it is. What in thunder do I care about the old Carthaginians? Regulus wasn't bad, but I'm sick of him!" And Tom dealt *Harkness's Latin Reader* a thump, which expressed his feelings better than words.

"I like Latin, and used to get on well when I studied it with Jimmy. Perhaps I can help you a little bit," said Polly as Tom wiped his hot face and refreshed himself with a peanut.

"You? Pooh! Girls' Latin don't amount to much anyway" was the grateful reply.

But Polly was used to him now and, nothing daunted, took a look at the grimy page in the middle of which Tom had stuck. She read it so well that the young gentleman stopped munching to regard her with respectful astonishment, and when she stopped he said suspiciously, "You are a sly one, Polly, to study up so you can show off before me. But it won't do, ma'am. Turn over a dozen pages and try again."

Polly obeyed, and did even better than before, saying, as she looked up, with a laugh, "I've been through the whole book, so you won't catch me that way, Tom."

"I say, how came you to know such a lot?" asked Tom, much impressed.

"I studied with Jimmy, and kept up with him, for Father let us be together in all our lessons. It was so nice, and we learned so fast!"

"Tell about Jimmy. He's your brother, isn't he?"

"Yes, but he's dead, you know. I'll tell about him some other time. You ought to study now, and perhaps I can help you," said Polly, with a little quiver of the lips.

"Shouldn't wonder if you could." And Tom spread the book between them with a grave and businesslike air, for he felt that Polly had got the better of him, and it behooved him to do his best for the honor of his sex. He went at the lesson with a will, and soon floundered out of his difficulties, for Polly gave him a lift here and there, and they went on swimmingly till they came to some rules to be learned. Polly had forgotten them, so they both committed them to memory. Tom, with hands in his pockets, rocked to and fro, muttering rapidly, while Polly twisted the little curl on her forehead and stared at the wall, gabbling with all her might.

"Done!" cried Tom presently.

"Done!" echoed Polly, and then they heard each other recite till both were perfect.

"That's pretty good fun," said Tom joyfully, tossing poor Harkness away and feeling that the pleasant excitement of companionship could lend a charm even to Latin grammar.

"Now, ma'am, we'll take a turn at al*gibb*era. I like that as much as I hate Latin."

Polly accepted the invitation and soon owned that Tom could beat her here. This fact restored his equanimity, but he didn't crow over her, far from it, for he helped her with a paternal patience that made her eyes twinkle with suppressed fun as he soberly explained and illustrated, unconsciously imitating Dominie Deane, till Polly found it difficult to keep from laughing in his face.

"You may have another go at it any time you like," generously remarked Tom as he shied the algebra after the Latin reader.

"I'll come every evening, then. I'd like to, for I haven't studied a bit since I came. You shall try and make me like algebra, and I'll try and make you like Latin. Will you?"

"Oh, I'd like it well enough if there was anyone to explain it to me. Old Deane puts us through double-quick and don't give a fellow time to ask questions when we read."

"Ask your father. He knows."

"Don't believe he does. Shouldn't dare to bother him if he did."

"Why not?"

"He'd pull my ears, and call me a 'stupid,' or tell me not to worry him."

"I don't think he would. He's very kind to me, and I ask lots of questions."

"He likes you better than he does me."

"Now, Tom! It's wrong of you to say so. Of course he loves you ever so much more than he does me," cried Polly reprovingly.

"Why don't he show it, then?" muttered Tom, with a half-wistful, half-defiant glance toward the library door, which stood ajar.

"You act so, how can he?" asked Polly after a pause in which she put Tom's question to herself and could find no better reply than the one she gave him.

"Why don't he give me my velocipede? He said if I did well at school for a month, I should have it, and I've been pegging away like fury for most six weeks, and he don't do a thing about it. The girls get their duds because they tease. I won't do that, anyway, but you don't catch me studying myself to death and no pay for it."

"It is too bad, but you ought to do it because it's right, and never mind being paid," began Polly, trying to be moral, but secretly sympathizing heartily with poor Tom.

"Don't you preach, Polly. If the governor took any notice of me, and cared how I got on, I wouldn't mind the presents so much, but he don't care a hang, and never even asked if I did well last declamation day, when I'd gone and learned 'The Battle of Lake Regillus' because he said he liked it."

"Oh, Tom! Did you say that? It's splendid! Jim and I used to say Horatius together, and it was *such* fun. Do speak your piece to me, I do so like 'Macaulay's Lays.' "

"It's dreadful long," began Tom, but his face brightened, for Polly's interest soothed his injured feelings, and he was glad to prove his elocutionary powers. He began without much spirit, but soon the martial ring of the lines fired him, and before he knew it he was on his legs thundering away in grand style, while Polly listened with kindling face and absorbed attention. Tom did declaim well, for he quite forgot himself and delivered the stirring ballad with an energy that made Polly flush and tingle with admiration and delight, and quite electrified a second listener, who had heard all that went on and watched the little scene from behind his newspaper.

As Tom paused, breathless, and Polly clapped her hands enthusiastically, the sound was loudly echoed from behind him. Both whirled round, and there was Mr. Shaw, standing in the doorway, applauding with all his might.

Tom looked much abashed and said not a word, but Polly ran to Mr. Shaw and danced before him, saying, eagerly, "Wasn't it splendid? Didn't he do it well? Mayn't he have his velocipede now?"

"Capital, Tom, you'll be an orator yet. Learn another piece like that and I'll come and hear you speak it. Are you ready for your velocipede, hey?"

Polly was right, and Tom owned that "the governor" *was* kind, did like him, and hadn't entirely forgotten his promise.

The boy turned red with pleasure and picked at the buttons on his jacket while listening to this unexpected praise, but when he spoke he looked straight up into his father's face while his own shone with pleasure as he answered, all in one breath, "Thankee, sir. I'll do it, sir. Guess I am, sir!"

"Very good, then look out for your new horse tomorrow, sir." And Mr. Shaw stroked the fuzzy red head with a kind hand, feeling a fatherly pleasure in the conviction that there *was* something in his boy after all.

Tom got his velocipede next day, named it Black Auster, in memory of the horse in "The Battle of Lake Regillus," and came to grief as soon as he began to ride his new steed.

"Come out and see me go it," whispered Tom to Polly after three days' practice in the street, for he had already learned to ride in the rink.

Polly and Maud willingly went, and watched his struggles with deep interest till he got an upset, which nearly put an end to his velocipeding forever.

"Hi, there! Auster's coming!" shouted Tom as he came rattling down the long, steep street outside the park.

They stepped aside, and he whizzed by, arms and legs going like mad, with the general appearance of a runaway engine. It would have been a triumphant descent if a big dog had not bounced suddenly through one of the openings and sent the whole concern helter-skelter into the gutter. Polly laughed as she ran to view the ruin, for Tom lay flat on his back, with the velocipede atop of him, while the big dog barked wildly and his master scolded him for his awkwardness. But when she saw Tom's face, Polly was frightened, for the color had all gone out of it, his eyes looked strange and dizzy, and drops of blood began to trickle from a great cut on his forehead. The man saw it, too, and had him up in a minute, but he couldn't stand, and stared about him in a

dazed sort of way as he sat on the curbstone while Polly held
her handkerchief to his forehead and pathetically begged to
know if he was killed.

"Don't scare mother—I'm all right. Got upset, didn't I?"
he asked presently, eyeing the prostrate velocipede with
more anxiety about its damages than his own.

"I knew you'd hurt yourself with that horrid thing. Just let
it be and come home, for your head bleeds dreadfully and
everybody is looking at us," whispered Polly, trying to tie the
little handkerchief over the ugly cut.

"Come on, then. Jove! How queer my head feels! Give us
a boost, please. Stop howling, Maud, and come home. You
bring the machine, and I'll pay you, Pat." As he spoke Tom
slowly picked himself up and, steadying himself by Polly's
shoulder, issued his commands, and the procession fell into
line. First, the big dog, barking at intervals; then the good-
natured Irishman, trundling "that divil of a whirligig," as he
disrespectfully called the idolized velocipede; then the
wounded hero, supported by the faithful Polly, and Maud
brought up the rear in tears, bearing Tom's cap.

Unfortunately, Mrs. Shaw was out driving with Grandma,
and Fanny was making calls, so that there was no one but
Polly to stand by Tom, for the parlor maid turned faint at
the sight of blood, and the chamber maid lost her wits in the
flurry. It was a bad cut and must be sewed up at once, the
doctor said as soon as he came. "Somebody must hold his
head," he added as he threaded his queer little needle.

"I'll keep still, but if anybody must hold me, let Polly. You
ain't afraid, are you?" asked Tom with an imploring look, for
he didn't like the idea of being sewed a bit.

Polly was just going to shrink away, saying, "Oh, I can't!"
when she remembered that Tom once called her a coward.
Here was a chance to prove that she wasn't; besides, poor

Tom had no one else to help him, so she came up to the sofa where he lay and nodded reassuringly as she put a soft little hand on either side of the damaged head.

"You are a trump, Polly," whispered Tom. Then he set his teeth, clenched his hands, lay quite still, and bore it like a man. It was all over in a minute or two, and when he had had a glass of wine, and was nicely settled on his bed, he felt pretty comfortable in spite of the pain in his head and being ordered to keep quiet, he said, "Thank you ever so much, Polly," and watched her with a grateful face as she crept away.

He had to keep to the house for a week, and lay about looking very interesting with a great black patch on his forehead. Everyone petted him, for the doctor said that if the blow had been an inch nearer the temple, it would have been fatal, and the thought of losing him so suddenly made bluff old Tom very precious all at once. His father asked him how he was a dozen times a day, his mother talked continually of "that dear boy's narrow escape," Grandma cockered him up with every delicacy she could invent, and the girls waited on him like devoted slaves. This new treatment had an excellent effect, for when neglected Tom got over his first amazement at this change of base, he blossomed out delightfully, as sick people do sometimes, and surprised his family by being unexpectedly patient, grateful, and amiable. Nobody ever knew how much good it did him, for boys seldom have confidences of this sort except with their mothers, and Mrs. Shaw had never found the key to her son's heart. But a little seed was sowed then that took root, and though it grew very slowly, it came to something in the end. Perhaps Polly helped it a little. Evening was his hardest time, for want of exercise made him as restless and nervous as it was possible for a hearty lad to be on such a short notice. He couldn't sleep, so the girls amused him: Fanny played and read aloud; Polly sang and told stories, and did the latter so well that it got to be a regular thing for her to begin as soon as twilight came and Tom was settled in his favorite place on Grandma's sofa.

"Fire away, Polly," said the young sultan one evening as his little Scheherazade sat down in her low chair after stirring up the fire till the room was bright and cozy.

"I don't feel like stories tonight, Tom. I've told all I know, and can't make up any more," answered Polly, leaning her head on her hand with a sorrowful look that Tom had never seen before. He watched her a minute, and then asked curiously, "What were you thinking about just now, when you sat staring at the fire and getting soberer and soberer every minute?"

"I was thinking about Jimmy."

"Would you mind telling about him? You know you said you would sometime, but don't if you'd rather not," said Tom, lowering his rough voice respectfully.

"I like to talk about him, but there isn't much to tell," began Polly, grateful for his interest. "Sitting here with you reminded me of the way I used to sit with him when he was sick. We used to have such happy times, and it's so pleasant to think about them now."

"He was awfully good, wasn't he?"

"No, he wasn't, but he tried to be, and Mother says that is half the battle. We used to get tired of trying, but we kept making resolutions, and working hard to keep 'em. I don't think I got on much, but Jimmy did, and everyone loved him."

"Didn't you ever squabble, as we do?"

"Yes, indeed, sometimes, but we couldn't stay mad, and always made it up again as soon as we could. Jimmy used to come round first and say, 'All serene, Polly,' so kind and jolly that I couldn't help laughing and being friends right away."

"Did he not know a lot?"

"Yes, I think he did, for he liked to study and wanted to get on so he could help Father. People used to call him a fine boy, and I felt so proud to hear it, but they didn't know half how wise he was because he didn't show off a bit. I suppose sisters always are grand of their brothers, but I don't believe many girls had as much right to be as I had."

"Most girls don't care two pins about their brothers, so that shows you don't know much about it."

"Well, they ought to if they don't, and they would if the boys were as kind to them as Jimmy was to me."

"Why, what did he do?"

"Loved me dearly, and wasn't ashamed to show it," cried Polly with a sob in her voice that made her answer very eloquent.

"What made him die, Polly?" asked Tom soberly after a little pause.

"He got hurt coasting last winter, but he never told which boy did it, and he only lived a week. I helped take care of him, and he was so patient, I used to wonder at him, for he was in dreadful pain all the time. He gave me his books, and his dog, and his speckled hens, and his big knife, and said, 'Good-bye, Polly'—and kissed me the last thing—and then —oh, Jimmy! Jimmy! If he only could come back!"

Poor Polly's eyes had been getting fuller and fuller, her lips trembling more and more as she went on, and when she came to that "good-bye" she couldn't get any further, but covered up her face and cried as if her heart would break. Tom was full of sympathy, but didn't know how to show it, so he sat shaking up the camphor bottle and trying to think

of something proper and comfortable to say, when Fanny
came to the rescue and cuddled Polly in her arms, with
soothing little pats and whispers and kisses, till the tears
stopped and Polly said she "didn't mean to, and wouldn't
anymore. I've been thinking about my dear boy all the evening, for Tom reminds me of him," she added with a sigh.

"Me? How can I, when I ain't a bit like him?" cried Tom,
amazed.

"But you are in some ways."

"Wish I was, but I can't be, for he was good, you know."

"So are you, when you choose. Hasn't he been good and
patient, and don't we all like to pet him when he's clever,
Fan?" said Polly, whose heart was still aching for her brother
and ready for his sake to find virtues even in tormenting
Tom.

"Yes, I don't know the boy lately, but he'll be as bad as
ever when he's well," returned Fanny, who hadn't much
faith in sickbed repentances.

"Much you know about it," growled Tom, lying down
again, for he had sat bolt upright when Polly made the as-
tounding declaration that *he* was like the well-beloved
Jimmy. That simple little history had made a deep impression on Tom, and the tearful ending touched the tender spot
that most boys hide so carefully. It is very pleasant to be
loved and admired, very sweet to think we shall be missed
and mourned when we die, and Tom was seized with a sudden desire to imitate this boy, who hadn't done anything
wonderful yet was so dear to his sister that she cried for him
a whole year after he was dead, so studious and clever, the
people called him "a fine fellow," and so anxious to be good
that he kept on trying till he was better even than Polly,
whom Tom privately considered a model of virtue, as girls
go.

"I just wish I had a sister like you," he broke out all of a sudden.

"And I just wish I had a brother like Jim," cried Fanny, for she felt the reproach in Tom's words and knew she deserved it.

"I shouldn't think you'd envy anybody, for you've got one another," said Polly, with such a wistful look that it suddenly set Tom and Fanny to wondering why they didn't have better times together and enjoy themselves as Polly and Jim had.

"Fan don't care for anybody but herself," said Tom.

"Tom is such a bear," retorted Fanny.

"I wouldn't say such things, for if anything should happen to either of you, the other one would feel so sorry. Every cross word I ever said to Jimmy comes back now and makes me wish I hadn't."

Two great tears rolled down Polly's cheeks and were quietly wiped away, but I think they watered that sweet sentiment called fraternal love, which till now had been neglected in the hearts of this brother and sister. They didn't say anything then, or make any plans, or confess any faults, but when they parted for the night Fanny gave the wounded head a gentle pat (Tom never would have forgiven her if she had kissed him) and said, in a whisper, "I hope you'll have a good sleep, Tommy, dear."

And Tom nodded back at her, with a hearty "Same to you, Fan."

That was all, but it meant a good deal, for the voices were kind and the eyes met full of that affection which makes words of little consequence. Polly saw it, and though she didn't know that she had made the sunshine, it shone back upon her so pleasantly that she fell happily asleep, though her Jimmy wasn't there to say "good night."

Chapter 5

Scrapes

*A*fter being unusually good, children are apt to turn short round and refresh themselves by acting like Sancho.* For a week after Tom's mishap the young folks were quite angelic, so much so that Grandma said she was afraid "something was going to happen to them." The dear old lady needn't have felt anxious, for such excessive virtue doesn't last long enough to lead to translation, except with little prigs in the goody storybooks, and no sooner was Tom on his legs again when the whole party went astray, and much tribulation was the consequence.

It all began with "Polly's stupidity," as Fan said afterward. Just as Polly ran down to meet Mr. Shaw one evening, and was helping him off with his coat, the bell rang, and a fine bouquet of hothouse flowers was left in Polly's hands, for she never could learn city ways and opened the door herself.

---

* In *Don Quixote*, by Miguel de Cervantes (1547–1616), Sancho Panza was the peasant who served as the idealistic don's down-to-earth squire.

"Hey! What's this? My little Polly is beginning early, after all," said Mr. Shaw, laughing as he watched the girl's face dimple and flush as she smelt the lovely nosegay and glanced at a note half hidden in the heliotrope.

Now, if Polly hadn't been "stupid," as Fan said, she would have had her wits about her and let it pass, but, you see, Polly was an honest little soul, and it never occurred to her that there was any need of concealment, so she answered in her straightforward way, "Oh, they ain't for me, sir, they are for Fan, from Mr. Frank, I guess. She'll be so pleased."

"That puppy sends her things of this sort, does he?" And Mr. Shaw looked far from pleased as he pulled out the note and coolly opened it.

Polly had her doubts about Fan's approval of that "sort of thing," but dared not say a word, and stood thinking how she used to show her father the funny valentines the boys sent her, and how they laughed over them together. But Mr. Shaw did not laugh when he had read the sentimental verses accompanying the bouquet, and his face quite scared Polly as he asked, angrily, "How long has this nonsense been going on?"

"Indeed, sir, I don't know. Fan doesn't mean any harm. I wish I hadn't said anything!" stammered Polly, remembering the promise given to Fanny the day of the concert. She had forgotten all about it, and had become accustomed to see the "big boys," as she called Mr. Frank and his friends, with the girls on all occasions. Now it suddenly occurred to her that Mr. Shaw didn't like such amusements and had forbidden Fan to indulge in them. "Oh, dear! How mad she will be. Well, I can't help it. Girls shouldn't have secrets from their fathers, then there wouldn't be any fuss," thought Polly as she watched Mr. Shaw twist up the pink note and poke it back among the flowers, which he took from her, saying, shortly, "Send Fanny to me in the library."

"Now you've done it, you stupid thing!" cried Fanny, both angry and dismayed when Polly delivered the message.

"Why, what else *could* I do?" asked Polly, much disturbed.

"Let him think the bouquet was for you, then there'd have been no trouble."

"But that would have been doing a lie, which is most as bad as telling one."

"Don't be a goose. You've got me into a scrape, and you ought to help me out."

"I will if I can, but I won't tell lies for anybody!" cried Polly, getting excited.

"Nobody wants you to. Just hold your tongue, and let me manage."

"Then I'd better not go down," began Polly when a stern voice from below called, like Bluebeard, "Are you coming down?"

"Yes, sir," answered a meek voice, and Fanny clutched Polly, whispering, "You *must* come. I'm frightened out of my wits when he speaks like that. Stand by me, Polly, there's a dear."

"I will," whispered "sister Ann," and down they went with fluttering hearts.

Mr. Shaw stood on the rug, looking rather grim. The bouquet lay on the table, and beside it a note directed to "Frank Moore, Esq.," in a very decided hand, with a fierce-looking flourish after the "Esq." Pointing to this impressive epistle, Mr. Shaw said, knitting his black eyebrows as he looked at Fanny, "I'm going to put a stop to this nonsense at once, and if I see any more of it, I'll send you to school in a Canadian convent."

This awful threat quite took Polly's breath away, but

Fanny had heard it before, and having a temper of her own, she said, pertly, "I'm sure I haven't done anything so very dreadful. I can't help it if the boys send me philopena* presents, as they do to the other girls."

"There was nothing about philopenas in the note. But that's not the question. I forbid you to have anything to do with this Moore. He's not a boy, but a fast fellow, and I won't have him about. You knew this, and yet disobeyed me."

"I hardly ever see him," began Fanny.

"Is that true?" asked Mr. Shaw, turning suddenly to Polly.

"Oh, please, sir, don't ask me. I promised I wouldn't— that is—Fanny will tell you," cried Polly, quite red with distress at the predicament she was in.

"No matter about your promise, tell me all you know of this absurd affair. It will do Fanny more good than harm." And Mr. Shaw sat down looking more amiable, for Polly's dismay touched him.

"May I?" she whispered to Fanny.

"I don't care," answered Fan, looking both angry and ashamed as she stood sullenly tying knots in her handkerchief.

So Polly told, with much reluctance and much questioning, all she knew of the walks, the lunches, the meetings, and the notes. It wasn't much, and evidently less serious than Mr. Shaw expected, for as he listened his eyebrows smoothed themselves out, and more than once his lips twitched as if he wanted to laugh, for, after all, it *was* rather comical to see how the young people aped their elders, play-

---

* Philopena is a party game similar to forfeits, in which the players are a boy and a girl. The loser is required to present the winner with a gift.

ing the new-fashioned game, quite unconscious of its real beauty, power, and sacredness.

"Oh, please, sir, don't blame Fan much, for she truly isn't half as silly as Trix and the other girls. She wouldn't go sleigh riding, though Mr. Frank teased, and she wanted to ever so much. She's sorry, I know, and won't forget what you say anymore, if you'll forgive her this once," cried Polly, very earnestly, when the foolish little story was told.

"I don't see how I can help it when you plead so well for her. Come here, Fan, and mind this one thing. Drop all this nonsense and attend to your books, or off you go, and Canada is no joke in wintertime, let me tell you."

As he spoke Mr. Shaw stroked his sulky daughter's cheek, hoping to see some sign of regret, but Fanny felt injured and wouldn't show that she was sorry, so she only said, pettishly, "I suppose I can have my flowers, now the fuss is over."

"They are going straight back where they came from, with a line from me which will keep that puppy from ever sending you any more." Ringing the bell, Mr. Shaw dispatched the unfortunate posy and then turned to Polly, saying, kindly but gravely, "Set this silly child of mine a good example, and do your best for her, won't you?"

"Me? What can I do, sir?" asked Polly, looking ready, but quite ignorant how to begin.

"Make her as like yourself as possible, my dear. Nothing would please me better. Now go, and let us hear no more of this folly."

They went without a word, and Mr. Shaw heard no more of the affair, but poor Polly did, for Fan scolded her till Polly thought seriously of packing up and going home next day. I really haven't the heart to relate the dreadful lectures she got, the snubs she suffered, or the cold shoulders turned upon her for several days after this. Polly's heart was full, but she told no one and bore her trouble silently, feeling her friend's ingratitude and injustice deeply.

Tom found out what the matter was and sided with Polly, which proceeding led to scrape number two.

"Where's Fan?" asked the young gentleman, strolling into his sister's room, where Polly lay on the sofa, trying to forget her troubles in an interesting book.

"Downstairs, seeing company."

"Why didn't you go too?"

"I don't like Trix, and I don't know her fine New York friends."

"Don't want to, neither, why don't you say?"

"Not polite."

"Who cares? I say, Polly, come and have some fun."

"I'd rather read."

"That isn't polite."

Polly laughed and turned a page. Tom whistled a minute, then sighed deeply and put his hand to his forehead, which the black plaster still adorned.

"Does your head ache?" asked Polly.

"Awfully."

"Better lie down, then."

"Can't, I'm fidgety, and want to be 'amoosed,' as Pug says."

"Just wait till I finish my chapter, and then I'll come," said pitiful Polly.

"All right," returned the perjured boy, who had discovered that a broken head was sometimes more useful than a whole one, and exulting in his base stratagem, he roved about the room till Fan's bureau arrested him. It was covered with all sorts of finery, for she had dressed in a hurry and left everything topsy-turvy. A well-conducted boy would have let things alone, or a moral brother would have put things to rights. Being neither, Tom rummaged to his heart's content till Fan's drawers looked as if someone had been making hay in them. He tried the effect of earrings, ribbons, and collars; wound up the watch, though it wasn't time; burnt his inquisite nose with smelling salts; deluged his grimy handkerchief with Fan's best cologne; anointed his curly crop with her hair oil; powdered his face with her violet powder, and finished off by pinning on a bunch of false ringlets, which Fanny tried to keep a profound secret. The ravages committed by this bad boy are beyond the power of language to describe as he reveled in the interesting drawers, boxes, and cases which held his sister's treasures.

When the curls had been put on, with much pricking of fingers, and a blue ribbon added, à la Fan, he surveyed himself with satisfaction and considered the effect so fine that he was inspired to try a still greater metamorphosis. The dress Fan had taken off lay on a chair, and into it got Tom, chuckling with suppressed laughter, for Polly was absorbed and the bed curtains hid his iniquity. Fan's best velvet jacket and hat, ermine muff, and a sofa pillow for a pannier finished off the costume, and tripping along with elbows out, Tom appeared before the amazed Polly just as the chapter ended. She enjoyed the joke so heartily that Tom forgot consequences and proposed going down into the parlor to surprise the girls.

"Goodness no! Fanny never would forgive us if you showed her curls and things to those people. There are gentlemen among them, and it wouldn't be proper," said Polly, alarmed at the idea.

"All the more fun. Fan hasn't treated you well, and it will serve her right if you introduce me as your dear friend, Miss Shaw. Come on, it will be a jolly lark."

"I wouldn't for the world, it would be so mean. Take 'em off, Tom, and I'll play anything else you like."

"I ain't going to dress up for nothing. I look so lovely, someone must admire me. Take me down, Polly, and see if they don't call me 'a sweet creature.' "

Tom looked so unutterably ridiculous as he tossed his curls and pranced that Polly went off into another gale of merriment, but even while she laughed she resolved not to let him mortify his sister.

"Now, then, get out of the way if you won't come. I'm going down," said Tom.

"No, you're not."

"How will you help it, Miss Prim?"

"So." And Polly locked the door, put the key in her pocket, and nodded at him defiantly.

Tom was a pepper pot as to temper, and anything like opposition always had a bad effect. Forgetting his costume, he strode up to Polly, saying, with a threatening wag of the head, "None of that. I won't stand it."

"Promise not to plague Fan, and I'll let you out."

"Won't promise anything. Give me that key, or I'll make you."

"Now, Tom, don't be savage. I only want to keep you out of a scrape, for Fan will be raging if you go. Take off her things, and I'll give up."

Tom vouchsafed no reply, but marched to the other door, which was fast, as Polly knew, looked out of the three-story window, and finding no escape possible, came back with a wrathful face. "Will you give me that key?"

"No, I won't," said Polly valiantly.

"I'm stronger than you are, so you'd better hand over."

"I know you are, but it's cowardly for a great boy like you to rob a girl."

"I don't want to hurt you, but, by George, I won't stand this!"

Tom paused as Polly spoke, evidently ashamed of himself, but his temper was up, and he wouldn't give in. If Polly had cried a little just here, he would have yielded; unfortunately she giggled, for Tom's fierce attitude was such a funny contrast to his dress that she couldn't help it. That settled the matter. No girl that ever lived should giggle at him, much less lock him up like a small child. Without a word, he made a grab at Polly's arm, for the hand holding the key was still in her pocket. With her other hand she clutched her frock, and for a minute held on stoutly. But Tom's strong fingers were irresistible. Rip went the pocket, out came the hand, and with a cry of pain from Polly, the key fell on the floor.

"It's your own fault if you're hurt. I didn't mean to," muttered Tom as he hastily departed, leaving Polly to groan over her sprained wrist. He went down, but not into the parlor, for somehow the joke seemed to have lost its relish, so he made the girls in the kitchen laugh, and then crept up the back way, hoping to make it all right with Polly. But she had gone to Grandma's room, for, though the old lady was out, it seemed a refuge. He had just time to get things in order when Fanny came up, crosser than ever, for Trix had been telling her of all sorts of fun in which she might have had a share if Polly had held her tongue.

"Where is she?" asked Fan, wishing to vent her vexation on her friend.

"Moping in her room, I suppose," replied Tom, who was discovered reading studiously.

Now, while this had been happening, Maud had been getting into hot water also, for when her maid left her, to see a friend below, Miss Maud paraded into Polly's room and solaced herself with mischief. In an evil hour Polly had let her play boat in her big trunk, which stood empty. Since then Polly had stored some of her most private treasures in the upper tray, so that she might feel sure they were safe from all eyes. She had forgotten to lock the trunk, and when Maud raised the lid to begin her voyage, several objects of interest met her eyes. She was deep in her researches when Fan came in and looked over her shoulder, feeling too cross with Polly to chide Maud.

As Polly had no money for presents, she had exerted her ingenuity to devise all sorts of gifts, hoping by quantity to atone for any shortcomings in quality. Some of her attempts were successful, others were failures, but she kept them all, fine or funny, knowing the children at home would enjoy anything new. Some of Maud's cast-off toys had been neatly mended for Kitty; some of Fan's old ribbons and laces were converted into dolls' finery, and Tom's little figures, whittled out of wood in idle minutes, were laid away to show Will what could be done with a knife.

"What rubbish!" said Fanny.

"Queer girl, isn't she?" added Tom, who had followed to see what was going on.

"Don't you laugh at Polly's things. She makes nicer dolls than you, Fan, and she can wite and dwar ever so much better than Tom," cried Maud.

"How do you know? I never saw her draw," said Tom.

"Here's a book with lots of pictures in it. I can't wead the witing, but the pictures are so funny."

Eager to display her friend's accomplishments, Maud pulled out a fat little book, marked "Polly's Journal," and spread it in her lap.

"Only the pictures, no harm in taking a look at 'em," said Tom.

"Just one peep," answered Fanny, and the next minute

both were laughing at a droll sketch of Tom in the gutter, with the big dog howling over him and the velocipede running away. Very rough and faulty, but so funny that it was evident that Polly's sense of humor was strong. A few pages farther back came Fanny and Mr. Frank, caricatured; then Grandma, carefully done; Tom reciting his battle piece; Mr. Shaw and Polly in the park; Maud being borne away by Katy, and all the schoolgirls turned into ridicule with an unsparing hand.

"Sly little puss, to make fun of us behind our backs," said Fan, rather nettled by Polly's quiet retaliation for many slights from herself and friends.

"She does draw well," said Tom, looking critically at the sketch of a boy with a pleasant face, round whom Polly had drawn rays like the sun and under which was written "My dear Jimmy."

"You wouldn't admire her if you knew what she wrote here about you," said Fanny, whose eyes had strayed to the written page opposite and lingered there long enough to read something that excited her curiosity.

"What is it?" asked Tom, forgetting his honorable resolves for a minute.

"She says, 'I try to like Tom, and when he is pleasant we do very well, but he don't stay so long. He gets cross and rough, and disrespectful to his father and mother, and plagues us girls, and is so horrid I almost hate him. It's very wrong, but I can't help it.' How do you like that?" asked Fanny.

"Go ahead, and see how she comes down on you, ma'am," retorted Tom, who had read on a bit.

"Does she?" And Fanny continued, rapidly, "As for Fan, I don't think we can be friends anymore, for she told her father a lie and won't forgive me for not doing so too. I used to think her a very fine girl, but I don't now. If she would be as she was when I first knew her, I should love her just the same, but she isn't kind to me, and though she is always talking about politeness, I don't think it *is* polite to treat company as she does me. She thinks I am odd and countrified, and I daresay I am, but I shouldn't laugh at a girl's clothes because she was poor, or keep her out of the way because she didn't do just as other girls do here. I see her make fun of me, and I can't feel as I did, and I'd go home, only it would seem ungrateful to Mr. Shaw and Grandma, and I do love them dearly."

"I say, Fan, you've got it now. Shut the book and come away," cried Tom, enjoying this broadside immensely, but feeling guilty, as well he might.

"Just one bit more," whispered Fanny, turning on a page or two and stopping at a leaf that was blurred here and there, as if tears had dropped on it.

"Sunday morning, early. Nobody is up to spoil my quiet time, and I must write my journal, for I've been so bad lately, I couldn't bear to do it. I'm glad my visit is most done, for things worry me here, and there isn't anyone to help me get right when I get wrong. I used to envy Fanny, but I don't now, for her father and mother don't take care of her as mine do of me. She is afraid of her father, and makes her mother do as she likes. I'm glad I came though, for I see money don't give people everything, but I'd like a little all the same, for it is *so* comfortable to buy nice things. I read over my journal just now, and I'm afraid it's not a good one, for I have said all sorts of things about the people here, and it isn't kind. I should tear it out, only I promised to keep my diary, and I want to talk over things that puzzle me with Mother. I see now that it is my fault a good deal, for I haven't been half as patient and pleasant as I ought to be. I will truly try for the rest of the time, and be as good and grateful as I can, for I want them to like me, though I'm only 'an old-fashioned country girl.' "

That last sentence made Fanny shut the book with a face full of self-reproach, for she had said those words herself, in a fit of petulance, and Polly had made no answer, though her eyes filled and her cheeks burned. Fan opened her lips to say something, but not a sound followed, for there stood Polly looking at them with an expression they had never seen before.

"What are you doing with my things?" she demanded in a low tone while her eyes kindled and her color changed.

"Maud showed us a book she found, and we were just looking at the pictures," began Fanny, dropping it as if it burnt her fingers.

"And reading my journal, and laughing at my presents, and then putting the blame on Maud. It's the meanest thing I ever saw, and I'll never forgive you as long as I live!"

Polly said this all in one indignant breath, and then as if afraid of saying too much, ran out of the room with such a look of mingled contempt, grief, and anger that the three culprits stood dumb with shame. Tom hadn't even a whistle at his command; Maud was so scared at gentle Polly's outbreak that she sat as still as a mouse, while Fanny, conscience-stricken, laid back the poor little presents with a respectful hand, for somehow the thought of Polly's poverty came over her as it never had done before, and these odds and ends, so carefully treasured up for those at home, touched Fanny and grew beautiful in her eyes. As she laid back the little book, the confessions in it reproached her more sharply than any words Polly could have spoken, for she *had* laughed at her friend, *had* slighted her sometimes, and been unforgiving for an innocent offense. The last page, where Polly took the blame on herself and promised to "truly try" to be more kind and patient, went to Fanny's heart, melting all the coldness away, and she could only lay her head on the trunk, sobbing, "It wasn't Polly's fault, it was all mine."

Tom, still red with shame at being caught in such a scrape, left Fanny to her tears and went manfully away to find the injured Polly and confess his manifold transgressions. But Polly couldn't be found. He searched high and low in every room, yet no sign of the girl appeared, and Tom began to get anxious. "She can't have run away home, can she?" he said to himself as he paused before the hat tree. There was the little round hat, and Tom gave it a remorseful smooth, remembering how many times he had tweaked it half off or poked it over poor Polly's eyes. "Maybe she's gone down to the office, to tell Pa. 'T isn't a bit like her, though. Anyway, I'll take a look round the corner."

Eager to get his boots, Tom pulled the door of a dark closet under the stairs and nearly tumbled over backward with surprise, for there on the floor, with her head pillowed on a pair of rubbers, lay Polly in an attitude of despair. This mournful spectacle sent Tom's penitent speech straight out of his head, and with an astonished "Hullo!" he stood and stared in impressive silence. Polly wasn't crying, and lay so still that Tom began to think she might be in a fit or a faint and bent anxiously down to inspect the pathetic bunch. A glimpse of wet eyelashes, a round cheek redder than usual, and lips parted by quick breathing relieved his mind upon that point; so, taking courage, he sat down on the bootjack and begged pardon like a man.

Now, Polly was very angry, and I think she had a right to be, but she was not resentful, and after the first flash was over she soon began to feel better about it. It wasn't easy to forgive, but as she listened to Tom's honest voice, getting gruff with remorse now and then, she couldn't harden her heart against him or refuse to make up when he so frankly owned that it "was confounded mean to read her book that way." She liked his coming and begging pardon at once; it was a handsome thing to do. She appreciated it and forgave him in her heart some time before she did with her lips, for, to tell the truth, Polly had a spice of girlish malice and rather liked to see domineering Tom eat humble-pie, just enough to do him good, you know. She felt that atonement was proper, and considered it no more than just that Fan should drench a handkerchief or two with repentant tears and that Tom should sit on a very uncomfortable seat and call himself hard names for five or ten minutes before she relented.

"Come, now, do say a word to a fellow. I'm getting the worst of it, anyway, for there's Fan, crying her eyes out upstairs, and here are you stowed away in a dark closet as dumb as a fish, and nobody but me to bring you both round. I'd have cut over to the Smythes and got Ma home to fix things, only it looked like backing out of the scrape, so I didn't," said Tom as a last appeal.

Polly was glad to hear that Fan was crying. It would do her good, but she couldn't help softening to Tom, who did seem in a predicament between two weeping damsels. A little smile began to dimple the cheek that wasn't hidden, and then a hand came slowly out from under the curly head and was stretched toward him silently. Tom was just going to give it a hearty shake when he saw a red mark on the wrist and knew what had made it. His face changed, and he took the chubby hand so gently that Polly peeped to see what it meant.

"Will you forgive that too?" he asked in a whisper, stroking the red wrist.

"Yes, it don't hurt much now." And Polly drew her hand away, sorry he had seen it.

"I was a beast, that's what I was!" said Tom in a tone of great disgust, and just at that awkward minute down tumbled his father's old beaver over his head and face, putting a comical quencher on his self-reproaches.

Of course neither could help laughing at that, and when he emerged Polly was sitting up, looking as much better for her shower as he did for his momentary eclipse.

"Fan feels dreadfully. Will you kiss and be friends if I trot her down?" asked Tom, remembering his fellow sinner.

"I'll go to her." And Polly whisked out of the closet as suddenly as she had whisked in, leaving Tom sitting on the bootjack with a radiant countenance.

How the girls made it up no one ever knew, but after much talking and crying, kissing and laughing, the breach was healed and peace declared. A slight haze still lingered in the air after the storm, for Fanny was very humble and tender that evening; Tom a trifle pensive but distressingly polite, and Polly magnanimously friendly to every one, for generous natures like to forgive, and Polly enjoyed the petting after the insult, like a very human girl.

As she was brushing her hair at bedtime there came a tap on her door, and, opening it, she beheld nothing but a tall black bottle with a strip of flannel tied around it like a cravat and a cocked-hat note on the cork. Inside were these lines, written in a sprawling hand with very black ink:

> Dear Polly—Opydilldock is first-rate for sprains.
> You put a lot on the flannel and do up your wrist,

and I guess it will be all right in the morning. Will you come a sleigh-ride tomorrow? I'm awful sorry I hurt you.

Tom

Chapter 6

Grandma

"**W**here's Polly?" asked Fan one snowy afternoon as she came into the dining room, where Tom was reposing on the sofa with his boots in the air, absorbed in one of those delightful books in which boys are cast away on desert islands, where every known fruit, vegetable, and flower is in its prime all the year round, or, lost in boundless forests, where the young heroes have thrilling adventures, kill impossible beasts, and, when the author's invention gives out, suddenly find their way home laden with tiger skins, tame buffaloes, and other pleasing trophies of their prowess.

"Dun no," was Tom's brief reply, for he was just escaping from an alligator of the largest size.

"Do put down that stupid book and let's do something," said Fanny after a listless stroll round the room.

"Hi, they've got him!" was the only answer vouchsafed by the absorbed reader.

"Where's Polly?" asked Maud, joining the party with her hands full of paper dolls all suffering for ball dresses.

"Do get along and don't bother me," cried Tom, exasperated at the interruption.

"Then tell us where she is. I'm sure you know, for she was down here a little while ago," said Fanny.

"Up in Grandma's room, maybe."

"Provoking thing! You knew it all the time and didn't tell, just to plague us," scolded Maud.

But Tom was now underwater stabbing his alligator and took no notice of the indignant departure of the young ladies.

"Polly's always poking up in Grandma's room. I don't see what fun there is in it," said Fanny as they went upstairs.

"Polly's a verwy queer girl, and Gwandma pets her a great deal more than she does me," observed Maud with an injured air.

"Let's peek and see what they are doing," whispered Fan, pausing at the half-open door.

Grandma was sitting before a quaint old cabinet, the doors of which stood wide open, showing glimpses of the faded relics treasured there. On a stool at the old lady's feet sat Polly, looking up with intent face and eager eyes, quite absorbed in the history of a high-heeled brocade shoe which lay in her lap.

"Well, my dear," Grandma was saying, "she had it on the very day that Uncle Joe came in as she sat at work and said, 'Dolly, we must be married at once.' 'Very well, Joe,' says Aunt Dolly, and down she went to the parlor, where the minister was waiting, never stopping to change the dimity dress she wore, and was actually married with her scissors and pinball at her side and her thimble on. That was in wartimes, 1812, my dear, and Uncle Joe was in the army, so he had to go, and he took that very little pinball with him.

Here it is, with the mark of a bullet through it, for he always said his Dolly's cushion saved his life."

"How interesting that is!" cried Polly as she examined the faded cushion with the hole in it.

"Why, Grandma, you never told me that story," said Fanny, hurrying in, finding the prospect was a pleasant one for a stormy afternoon.

"You never asked me to tell you anything, my dear, so I kept my old stories to myself," answered Grandma quietly.

"Tell some now, please. May we stay and see the funny things?" said Fan and Maud, eyeing the open cabinet with interest.

"If Polly likes. She is my company, and I am trying to entertain her, for I love to have her come," said Grandma with her old-time politeness.

"Oh, yes! Do let them stay and hear the stories. I've often told them what good times we have up here and teased them to come, but they think it's too quiet. Now, sit down, girls, and let Grandma go on. You see I pick out something in the cabinet that looks interesting, and then she tells me about it," said Polly, eager to include the girls in her pleasures and glad to get them interested in Grandma's reminiscences, for Polly knew how happy it made the lonely old lady to live over her past and to have the children round her.

"Here are three drawers that have not been opened yet. Each take one and choose something from it for me to tell about," said Madam, quite excited at the unusual interest in her treasures.

So the girls each opened a drawer and turned over the contents till they found something they wanted to know about. Maud was ready first, and holding up an oddly shaped linen bag, with a big blue F embroidered on it, de-

manded her story. Grandma smiled as she smoothed the old
thing tenderly and began her story with evident pleasure.

"My sister Nelly and I went to visit an aunt of ours when
we were little girls, but we didn't have a very good time, for
she was extremely strict. One afternoon when she had gone
out to tea and old Debby, the maid, was asleep in her room,
we sat on the doorstep feeling homesick and ready for anything to amuse us.

" 'What *shall* we do?' said Nelly.

"Just as she spoke a ripe plum dropped with a bounce on
the grass before us, as if answering her question. It was all
the plum's fault, for if it hadn't fallen at that minute, I never
should have had the thought which popped into my mischievous mind.

" 'Let's have as many as we want and plague Aunt Betsey,
to pay her for being so cross,' I said, giving Nelly half the
great purple plum.

" 'It would be dreadful naughty,' began Nelly, 'but I guess
we will,' she added as the sweet mouthful slipped down her
throat.

" 'Debby's asleep. Come on, then, and help me shake,' I
said, getting up, eager for the fun.

"We shook and shook till we got red in the face, but not
one dropped, for the tree was large and our little arms were
not strong enough to stir the boughs. Then we threw stones,
but only one green and one half-ripe one came down, and
my last stone broke the shed window, so there was an end of
that.

" 'It's as provoking as Aunt Betsey herself,' said Nelly as
we sat down, out of breath.

" 'I wish the wind would come and blow 'em down for us,'
panted I, staring up at the plums with longing eyes.

" 'If wishing would do any good, I should wish 'em in my lap at once,' added Nelly.

" 'You might as well wish 'em in your mouth and be done with it if you are too lazy to pick 'em up. If the ladder wasn't too heavy, we could try that,' said I, determined to have them.

" 'You know we can't stir it, so what is the use of talking about it? You proposed getting the plums, now let's see you do it,' answered Nelly rather crossly, for she had bitten the green plum and it had puckered her mouth.

" 'Wait a minute, and you *will* see me do it,' cried I as a new thought came into my naughty head.

" 'What are you taking your shoes and socks off for? You can't climb the tree, Fan.'

" 'Don't ask questions, but be ready to pick 'em up when they fall, Miss Lazybones.'

"With this mysterious speech I pattered into the house barefooted and full of my plan. Upstairs I went to a window opening on the shed roof. Out I got, and creeping carefully along till I came near the tree, I stood up and suddenly crowed like the little rooster. Nelly looked up, and stared, and laughed, and clapped her hands when she saw what I was going to do.

" 'I'm afraid you'll slip and get hurt.'

" 'Don't care if I do. I'll have those plums if I break my neck doing it,' and half sliding, half walking, I went down the sloping roof till the boughs of the tree were within my reach.

" 'Hurrah!' cried Nelly, dancing down below as my first shake sent a dozen plums rattling round her.

" 'Hurrah!' cried I, letting go one branch and trying to reach another. But as I did so my foot slipped, I tried to catch something to hold by, but found nothing, and with a cry, down I fell, like a very big plum on the grass below.

"Fortunately the shed was low, the grass was thick, and the tree broke my fall, but I got a bad bump and a terrible shaking. Nelly thought I was killed and began to cry with her mouth full. But I picked myself up in a minute, for I was used to such tumbles and didn't mind the pain half as much as the loss of the plums.

" 'Hush! Debby will hear and spoil all the fun. I said I'd get 'em and I have. See what lots have come down with me.'

"So there had, for my fall shook the tree almost as much as it did me, and the green and purple fruit lay all about us.

"By the time the bump on my forehead had swelled as big as a nut, our aprons were half full, and we sat down to enjoy ourselves. But we didn't. Oh, dear, no! For many of the plums were not ripe, some were hurt by the birds, some crushed in falling, and many as hard as stones. Nelly got stung by a wasp, my head began to ache, and we sat looking at one another rather dismally when Nelly had a bright idea.

" 'Let's cook 'em, then they'll be good, and we can put some away in our little pails for tomorrow.'

" 'That will be splendid! There's a fire in the kitchen, Debby always leaves the kettle on, and we can use her saucepan, and I know where the sugar is, and we'll have a grand time.'

"In we went, and fell to work very quietly. It was a large, open fireplace, with the coals nicely covered up, and the big kettle simmering on the hook. We raked open the fire, put on the saucepan, and in it the best of our plums, with water enough to spoil them. But we didn't know that, and felt very important as we sat waiting for it to boil, each armed with a big spoon, while the sugar box stood between us ready to be used.

"How slow they were, to be sure! I never knew such obstinate things, for they wouldn't soften, though they danced about in the boiling water and bobbed against the cover as if they were doing their best.

"The sun began to get low, and we were afraid Debby would come down, and still those dreadful plums wouldn't look like sauce. At last they began to burst, the water got a lovely purple, we put lots of sugar in, and kept tasting till our aprons and faces were red and our lips burnt with the hot spoons.

" 'There's too much juice,' said Nelly, shaking her head wisely. 'It ought to be thick and nice like mama's.'

" 'I'll pour off some of the juice, and we can drink it,' said I, feeling that I'd made a mistake in my cooking.

"So Nelly got a bowl, and I got a towel and lifted the big saucepan carefully off. It was heavy and hot, and I was a little afraid of it, but didn't like to say so. Just as I began to pour, Debby suddenly called from the top of the stairs, 'Children, what under the sun are you doing?'

"It startled us both. Nelly dropped the bowl and ran. I dropped the saucepan and didn't run, for a part of the hot juice splashed upon my bare feet and ankles and made me scream with dreadful pain.

"Down rushed Debby to find me dancing about the kitchen with a great bump on my forehead, a big spoon in my hand, and a pair of bright purple feet. The plums were lying all over the hearth, the saucepan in the middle of the room, the basin was broken, and the sugar swimming about as if the bowl had turned itself over trying to sweeten our mess for us.

"Debby was very good to me, for she never stopped to scold, but laid me down on the old sofa and bound up my poor little feet with oil and cotton wool. Nelly, seeing me lie white and weak, thought I was dying, and went over to the neighbor's for Aunt Betsey, and burst in upon the old ladies sitting primly at their tea, crying, distractedly:

" 'Oh, Aunt Betsey, come quick, for the saucepan fell off the shed, and Fan's feet are all boiled purple!'

"Nobody laughed at this funny message, and Aunt Betsey ran all the way home with a muffin in her hand and her ball in her pocket, though the knitting was left behind.

"I suffered a great deal, but I wasn't sorry afterward, for I learned to love Aunt Betsey, who nursed me tenderly and seemed to forget her strict ways in her anxiety for me.

"This bag was made for my special comfort, and hung on the sofa where I lay all those weary days. Aunt kept it full of pretty patchwork, or, what I liked better, ginger nuts and peppermint drops, to amuse me, though she didn't approve of cosseting children up, any more than I do now."

"I like that vewy well, and I wish I could have been there" was Maud's condescending remark as she put back the little bag after a careful peep inside, as if she hoped to find an ancient ginger nut or a well-preserved peppermint drop still lingering in some corner.

"We had plums enough that autumn, but didn't seem to care much about them after all, for our prank became a household joke and for years we never saw the fruit, but Nelly would look at me with a funny face and whisper, 'Purple stockings, Fan!' "

"Thank you, ma'am," said Polly. "Now, Fan, your turn next."

"Well, I've a bundle of old letters, and I'd like to know if there is any story about them," answered Fanny, hoping some romance might be forthcoming.

Grandma turned over the little packet tied up with a faded pink ribbon, a dozen yellow notes written on rough, thick paper, with red wafers still adhering to the folds, showing plainly that they were written before the day of initial notepaper and self-sealing envelopes.

"They are not love letters, deary, but notes from my mates after I left Miss Cotton's boarding school. I don't think there is any story about them," and Grandma turned them over with spectacles before the dim eyes, so young and bright when they first read the very same notes.

Fanny was about to say "I'll choose again" when Grandma began to laugh so heartily that the girls felt sure she had caught some merry old memory which would amuse them.

"Bless my heart, I haven't thought of that frolic this forty years. Poor, dear, giddy Sally Pomroy, and she's a great-grandmother now!" cried the old lady after reading one of the notes and clearing the mist off her glasses.

"Now, please tell about her. I know it's something funny to make you laugh so," said Polly and Fan together.

"Well, it *was* droll, and I'm glad I remembered it, for it's just the story to tell you young things.

"It was years ago," began Grandma briskly, "and teachers were very much stricter than they are now. The girls at Miss Cotton's were not allowed lights in their rooms after nine o'clock, never went out alone, and were expected to behave like models of propriety from morning till night.

"As you may imagine, ten young girls, full of spirits and fun, found these rules hard to keep, and made up for good behavior in public by all sorts of frolics in private.

"Miss Cotton and her brother sat in the back parlor after school was over, and the young ladies were sent to bed. Mr. John was very deaf, and Miss Priscilla very nearsighted—two convenient afflictions for the girls on some occasions, but once they proved quite the reverse, as you shall hear.

"We had been very prim for a week, and our bottled-up

spirits could no longer be contained, so we planned a revel after our own hearts and set our wits to work to execute it.

"The first obstacle was surmounted in this way. As none of us could get out alone, we resolved to lower Sally from the window, for she was light and small and very smart.

"With our combined pocket money she was to buy nuts and candy, cake and fruit, pie, and a candle, so that we might have a light after Betsey took ours away as usual.

"We were to darken the window of the inner chamber, set a watch in the little entry, light up, and then for a good time.

"At eight o'clock on the appointed evening, several of us professed great weariness and went to our rooms, leaving the rest sewing virtuously with Miss Cotton, who read Hannah More's *Sacred Dramas** aloud in a way that fitted the listeners for bed as well as a dose of opium would have done.

"I am sorry to say I was one of the ringleaders, and as soon as we got upstairs, produced the rope provided for the purpose, and invited Sally to be lowered. It was an old-fashioned house, sloping down behind, and the closest window chosen by us was not many feet from the ground.

"It was a summer evening, so that at eight o'clock it was still light, but we were not afraid of being seen, for the street was a lonely one and our only neighbors two old ladies who put down their curtains at sunset and never looked out till morning.

"Sally had been bribed by promises of as many 'goodies' as she could eat, and being a regular madcap, she was ready for anything.

---

* Hannah More (1745–1833) was an English writer whose early works were clever and witty but whose later works—beginning with *Sacred Dramas* (1782)—were devoted to social and religious reform.

"Tying the rope round her waist, she crept out, and we let her safely down, sent a big basket after her, and saw her slip round the corner in my big sunbonnet and another girl's shawl so that she should not be recognized.

"Then we put our nightgowns over our dresses and were laid peacefully in bed when Betsey came up, earlier than usual, for it was evident that Miss Cotton felt a little suspicious at our sudden weariness.

"For half an hour we lay laughing and whispering as we waited for the signal from Sally. At last we heard a cricket chirp shrilly under the window, and flying up, saw a little figure below in the twilight.

" 'Oh, quick! quick!' cried Sally, panting with haste. 'Draw up the basket and then get me in, for I saw Mr. Cotton in the market and ran all the way home so that I might get in before he came.'

"Up came the heavy basket, bumping and scraping on the way and smelling, oh, so nice! Down went the rope, and with a long pull, a strong pull, and a pull altogether, we hoisted poor Sally halfway up to the window when, sad to tell, the rope slipped and down she fell, only being saved from broken bones by the haycock under the window.

" 'He's coming! he's coming! Oh, pull me up, for mercy sake!' cried Sally, scrambling to her feet unhurt, but a good deal shaken.

"We saw a dark figure approaching, and dragged her in with more bumping and scraping, and embraced her with rapture, for we had just escaped being detected by Mr. John, whose eyes were as sharp as his ears were dull.

"We heard the front door shut, then a murmur of voices, and then Betsey's heavy step coming upstairs.

"Under the bed went the basket, and into the beds went the conspirators, and nothing could have been more decorous than the appearance of the room when Betsey popped her head in.

" 'Master's an old fidget to send me traveling up again, just because he fancied he saw something amiss at the window. Nothing but a curtain flapping, or a shadder, for the poor dears is sleeping like lambs.'

"We heard her say this to herself, and a general titter agitated the white coverlets as she departed.

"Sally was in high feather at the success of her exploit and danced about like an elf as she put her nightgown on over her frock, braided her hair in funny little tails all over her head, and fastened the great red pin cushion on her bosom for a breastpin in honor of the feast.

"The other girls went to their rooms as agreed upon, and all was soon dark and still upstairs while Miss Cotton began to enjoy herself below, as she always did when 'her young charges' were safely disposed of.

"Then ghosts began to walk, and the mice scuttled back to their holes in alarm, for white figures glided from room to room, till all were assembled in the little chamber.

"The watch was set at the entry door, the signal agreed upon, the candle lighted, and the feast spread forth upon a newspaper on the bed, with the coverlet arranged so that it could be whisked over the refreshments at a moment's notice.

"How good everything was, to be sure! I don't think I've eaten any pies since that had such a delicious flavor as those broken ones, eaten hastily, in that little oven of a room, with Sally making jokes and the others enjoying stolen sweets with true girlish relish. Of course it was very wicked, but I must tell the truth.

"We were just beginning on the cake when the loud scratching of a rat disturbed us.

" 'The signal! Fly! Run! Hide! Hush, don't laugh!' cried several voices, and we scuttled into bed as rapidly and noiselessly as possible, with our mouths and hands full.

"A long pause, broken by more scratching, but as no one came, we decided on sending to inquire what it meant. I went and found Mary, the picket guard, half asleep and longing for her share of the feast.

" 'It was a real rat. I've not made a sound. Do go and finish. I'm tired of this,' said Mary, slapping away at the mosquitoes.

"Back I hurried with the good news. Everyone flew up briskly. We lighted the candle again and returned to our revel. The refreshments were somewhat injured by Sally's bouncing in among them, but we didn't care and soon finished the cake.

" 'Now let's have the nuts,' I said, groping for the paper bag.

" 'They are almonds and peanuts, so we can crack them with our teeth. Be sure you get the bag by the right end,' said Sally.

" 'I know what I'm about,' and to show her that it was all right, I gave the bag a little shake when out flew the nuts, rattling like a hailstorm all over the uncarpeted floor.

" 'Now you've done it,' cried Sally as Mary scratched like a mad rat and a door creaked below, for Miss Cotton was not deaf.

"Such a flurry as we were in! Out went the candle, and each one rushed away with as much of the feast as she could seize in her haste. Sally dived into her bed, recklessly demolishing the last pie and scattering the candy far and wide.

"Poor Mary was nearly caught, for Miss Cotton was quicker than Betsey, and our guard had to run for her life.

"Our room was the first, and was in good order, though

the two flushed faces on the pillows were rather suspicious. Miss Cotton stood staring about her, looking so funny without her cap that my bedfellow would have gone off in a fit of laughter if I had not pinched her warningly.

" 'Young ladies, what is this unseemly noise?'

"No answer from us but a faint snore. Miss Cotton marched into the next room, put the same question, and received the same reply.

"In the third chamber lay Sally, and we trembled as the old lady went in. Sitting up, we peeped and listened breathlessly.

" 'Sarah, I command you to tell me what this all means?'

"But Sally only sighed in her sleep and muttered wickedly, 'Ma, take me home. I'm starved at Cotton's.'

" 'Mercy on me! Is the child going to have a fever?' cried the old lady, who did not observe the telltale nuts at her feet.

" 'So dull, so strict! Oh, take me home!' moaned Sally, tossing her arms and gurgling like a naughty little gypsy.

"That last bit of acting upset the whole concern, for as she tossed her arms she showed the big red cushion on her breast. Nearsighted as she was, that ridiculous object could not escape Miss Cotton, neither did the orange that rolled out from the pillow, nor the boots appearing at the foot of the bed.

"With sudden energy the old lady plucked off the cover, and there lay Sally with her hair dressed *à la* Topsy, her absurd breastpin and her dusty boots among papers of candy, bits of pie and cake, oranges and apples, and a candle upside down burning a hole in the sheet.

"At the sound of Miss Cotton's horrified exclamation, Sally woke up and began laughing so merrily that none of us could resist following her example, and the rooms rang with merriment for many minutes. I really don't know when we

should have stopped if Sally had not got choked with the
nut she had in her mouth and so frightened us nearly out of
our wits."

"What became of the things, and how were you pun-
ished?" asked Fan in the middle of her laughter.

"The remains of the feast went to the pig, and we were
kept on bread and water for three days."

"Did that cure you?"

"Oh, dear, no! We had half a dozen other frolics that very
summer, and although I cannot help laughing at the remem-
brance of this, you must not think, child, that I approve of
such conduct or excuse it. No, no, my dear, far from it."

"I call that a tip-top story! Drive on, Grandma, and tell
one about boys," broke in a new voice, and there was Tom
astride of a chair, listening and laughing with all his might,
for his book had come to an end and he had joined the party
unobserved.

"Wait for your turn, Tommy. Now, Polly, dear, what will
you have?" said Grandma, looking so lively and happy that
it was very evident "reminiscing" did her good.

"Let mine come last, and tell one for Tom next," said
Polly, looking round and beckoning him nearer.

He came and sat himself cross-legged on the floor before
the lower drawer of the cabinet, which Grandma opened for
him, saying, with a benign stroke of the curly head:

"There, dear, that's where I keep the little memorials of
my brother Jack. Poor lad, he was lost at sea, you know.
Well, choose anything you like, and I'll try to remember a
story about it."

Tom made a rapid rummage and fished up a little broken
pistol.

"There, that's the chap for me! Wish it wasn't spoilt, then

we'd have fun popping away at the cats in the yard. Now, then, Grandma."

"I remember one of Jack's pranks when that was used with great effect," said Grandma after a thoughtful pause, during which Tom teased the girls by snapping the lock of the pistol in their faces.

"Once upon a time," continued Madam, much flattered by the row of interested faces before her, "my father went away on business, leaving Mother, Aunt, and us girls to Jack's care. Very proud he was, to be sure, of the responsibility, and the first thing he did was to load that pistol and keep it by his bed, to our great worriment, for we feared he'd kill himself with it. For a week all went well. Then we were startled by the news that robbers were about. All sorts of stories flew through the town—we were living in the country then. Some said that certain houses were marked with a black cross, and those were always robbed; others, that there was a boy in the gang, for windows so small that they were considered safe were entered by some little rogue. At one place the thieves had a supper and left ham and cake in the front yard. Mrs. Jones found Mrs. Smith's shawl in her orchard, with a hammer and an unknown teapot near it. One man reported that someone tapped at his window in the night, saying softly, 'Is anyone here?' and when he looked out, two men were seen to run down the road.

"We lived just out of town, in a lonely place. The house was old, with convenient little back windows and five outside doors. Jack was the only man about the place, and he was barely thirteen. Mother and Aunt were very timid, and the children weren't old enough to be of any use, so Jack and I were the home guard and vowed to defend the family manfully."

"Good for you! Hope the fellows came!" cried Tom, charmed with this opening.

"One day an ill-looking man came in and asked for food," continued Grandma with a mysterious nod, "and while he ate I saw him glance sharply about, from the wooden buttons on the back doors to the silver urn and tankards on the dining-room sideboard. A strong suspicion took possession of me, and I watched him as a cat does a mouse.

" 'He came to examine the premises, I'm sure of it, but we will be ready for him,' I said fiercely as I told the family about him.

"This fancy haunted us all, and our preparations were very funny. Mother borrowed a rattle and kept it under her pillow. Aunt took a big bell to bed with her. The children had little Jip, the terrier, to sleep in their room, while Jack and I mounted guard, he with the pistol and I with a hatchet, for I didn't like firearms. Biddy, who slept in the attic, practiced getting out on the shed roof so that she might run away at the first alarm. Every night we arranged pitfalls for the robbers, and all filed up to bed bearing plate, money, weapons, and things to barricade with, as if we lived in wartimes.

"We waited a week and no one came, so we began to feel rather slighted, for other people got 'a scare,' as Tom says, and after all our preparations we really felt a trifle disappointed that we had had no chance to show our courage. At last a black mark was found upon *our* door, and a great panic ensued, for we felt that now our time *had* come.

"That night we put a tub of water at the bottom of the back stairs and a pile of tin pans at the top of the front stairs so that any attempt to come up would produce a splash or a rattle. Bells were hung on door handles, sticks of wood piled up in dark corners for robbers to fall over, and the family retired, all armed and all provided with lamps and matches.

"Jack and I left our doors open and kept asking one another if we didn't hear something till he fell asleep. I was wakeful and lay listening to the crickets till the clock struck twelve, then I got drowsy and was just dropping off when the sound of steps outside woke me up staring wide awake. Creeping to the window, I was in time to see by the dim moonlight a shadow glide round the corner and disappear. A queer little thrill went over me, but I resolved to keep quiet till I was sure something was wrong, for I had given so many false alarms, I didn't want Jack to laugh at me again. Popping my head out of the door, I listened, and presently heard a scraping sound near the shed.

" 'There they are, but I won't rouse the house till the bell rings or the pans fall. The rogues can't go far without a clatter of some sort, and if we could only catch one of them, we should get the reward and a deal of glory,' I said to myself, grasping my hatchet firmly.

"A door closed softly below, and a step came creeping toward the back stairs. Sure now of my prey, I was just about to scream 'Jack!' when something went splash into the tub at the foot of the back stairs.

"In a minute everyone was awake and up, for Jack fired his pistol before he was half out of bed and roared 'Fire!' so loud it roused the house. Mother sprung her rattle, Aunt rang her bell, Jip barked like mad, and we all screamed while from below came up a regular Irish howl.

"Someone brought a lamp, and we peeped anxiously down, to see our own stupid Biddy sitting in the tub wringing her hands and wailing dismally.

" 'Ouch, murther, and it's kilt I am! The saints be about us! How iver did I come forninst this say iv wather, just crapin in quiet afther a bit iv sthroll wid Mike Mahoney, me own b'y, that's to marry me intirely, come Saint Patrick's day nixt.'

"We laughed so we could hardly fish the poor thing up or listen while she explained that she had slipped out of her window for a word with Mike and found it fastened when she wanted to come back, so she had sat on the roof, trying to discover the cause of this mysterious barring out, till she was tired, when she prowled round the house till she found a cellar window unfastened, after all our care, and got in quite cleverly, she thought, but the tub was a new arrangement which she knew nothing about, and when she fell into the 'say' she was bewildered and could only howl.

"This was not all the damage either, for Aunt fainted with the fright, Mother cut her hand with a broken lamp, the children took cold hopping about on the wet stairs, Jip barked himself sick, I sprained my ankle, and Jack not only smashed a looking glass with his bullets but spoilt his pistol by the heavy charge put in it. After the damages were repaired and the flurry was well over, Jack confessed that he had marked the door for fun and shut Biddy out as a punishment for 'gallivanting,' of which he didn't approve. Such a rogue as that boy was!"

"But didn't the robbers ever come?" cried Tom, enjoying the joke, but feeling defrauded of the fight.

"Never, my dear, but we had our 'scare,' and tested our courage, and that was a great satisfaction, of course," answered Grandma placidly.

"Well, I think you were the bravest of the lot. I'd like to have seen you flourishing round there with your hatchet," added Tom admiringly, and the old lady looked as much pleased with the compliment as if she had been a girl.

"I choose this," said Polly, holding up a long white kid

glove, shrunken and yellow with time, but looking as if it had a history.

"Ah, that now has a story worth telling!" cried Grandma, adding proudly, "Treat that old glove respectfully, my children, for Lafayette's honored hand has touched it."

"Oh, Grandma, did you wear it? Did you see him? Do tell us all about it, and that will be the best of the whole," cried Polly, who loved history and knew a good deal about the gallant Frenchman and his brave life.

Grandma loved to tell this story and always assumed her most imposing air to do honor to her theme. Drawing herself up, therefore, she folded her hands, and after two or three little "hems" began with an absent look, as if her eyes beheld a faraway time which brightened as she gazed.

"The first visit of Lafayette was before my time, of course, but I heard so much about it from my grandfather that I really felt as if I'd seen it all. Our Aunt Hancock lived in the governor's house, on Beacon Hill, at that time." Here the old lady bridled up still more, for she was very proud of "our aunt." "Ah, my dears, those were the good old times!" she continued with a sigh. "Such dinners and tea parties, such damask table cloths and fine plate, such solid, handsome furniture and elegant carriages. Aunt's was lined with red silk velvet, and when the coach was taken away from her at the governor's death, she just ripped out the lining, and we girls had spencers* made of it. Dear heart, how well I remember playing in Aunt's great garden, and chasing Jack up and down those winding stairs, and my blessed father, in his plum-colored coat and knee buckles, and the queue I used to

---

* Spencer: a short, close-fitting jacket named for the second Earl Spencer (1758–1834).

tie up for him every day, handing Aunt in to dinner, looking so dignified and splendid."

Grandma seemed to forget her story for a minute and become a little girl again, among the playmates dead and gone so many years. Polly motioned the others to be quiet, and no one spoke till the old lady, with a long sigh, came back to the present and went on.

"Well, as I was saying, the governor wanted to give a breakfast to the French officers, and madam, who was a hospitable soul, got up a splendid one for them. But by some mistake, or accident, it was discovered at the last minute that there was no milk.

"A great deal was needed, and very little could be bought or borrowed, so despair fell upon the cooks and maids, and the great breakfast would have been a failure if madam, with the presence of mind of her sex, had not suddenly bethought herself of the cows feeding on the common.

"To be sure, they belonged to her neighbors, and there was no time to ask leave, but it was a national affair, our allies *must* be fed, and feeling sure that her patriotic friends would gladly lay their cows on the altar of their country, Madam Hancock covered herself with glory by calmly issuing the command, 'Milk 'em!'

"It was done, to the great astonishment of the cows, and the entire satisfaction of the guests, among whom was Lafayette.

"This milking feat was such a good joke that no one seems to have remembered much about the great man, though one of his officers, a count, signalized himself by getting very tipsy and going to bed with his boots and spurs on—which caused the destruction of Aunt's best yellow damask coverlet, for the restless sleeper kicked it into rags by morning.

"Aunt valued it very much, even in its tattered condition,

and kept it a long while as a memorial of her distinguished guests.

"The time when *I* saw Lafayette was in 1825, and there were no tipsy counts then. Uncle Hancock—a sweet man, my dears, though some call him mean nowadays—was dead, and Aunt had married Captain Scott.

"It was not at all the thing for her to do. However, that's neither here nor there. She was living in Federal Street at the time, a most aristocratic street then, children, and we lived close by.

"Old Josiah Quincy was mayor of the city, and he sent Aunt word that the Marquis Lafayette wished to pay his respects to her.

"Of course she was delighted, and we all flew about to make ready for him. Aunt was an old lady, but she made a grand toilet and was as anxious to look well as any girl."

"What did she wear?" asked Fan with interest.

"She wore a steel-colored satin, trimmed with black lace, and on her cap was pinned a Lafayette badge of white satin.

"I never shall forget how *b-e-a-utifully* she looked as she sat in state on the front parlor *sophy*, right under a great portrait of her first husband, and on either side of her sat Madam Storer and Madam Williams, elegant to behold in their stiff silks, rich lace, and stately turbans. We don't see such splendid old ladies nowadays—"

"I think we do sometimes," said Polly slyly.

Grandma shook her head, but it pleased her very much to be admired, for she had been a beauty in her day.

"We girls had dressed the house with flowers. Old Mr. Coolidge sent in a clothes-basketful. Joe Joy provided the badges, and Aunt got out some of the Revolutionary wine from the old Beacon Street cellar.

"I wore my green and white palmyrine, my hair bowed

high, the beautiful leg-o'-mutton sleeves that were so becoming, and these very gloves.

"Well, by and by the general, escorted by the mayor, drove up. Dear me, I see him now! A little old man in nankeen trousers and vest, a long blue coat and ruffled shirt, leaning on his cane, for he was lame, and smiling and bowing like a true Frenchman.

"As he approached, the three old ladies rose and curtsied with the utmost dignity. Lafayette bowed first to the governor's picture, then to the governor's widow, and kissed her hand.

"That was droll, for on the back of her glove was stamped Lafayette's likeness, and the gallant old gentleman kissed his own face.

"Then some of the young ladies were presented, and, as if to escape any further self-salutations, the marquis kissed the pretty girls on the cheek.

"Yes, my dears, here is just the spot where the dear old man saluted me. I'm quite as proud of it now as I was then, for he was a brave, good man and helped us in our trouble.

"He did not stay long, but we were very merry, drinking his health, receiving his compliments, and enjoying the honor he did us.

"Down in the street there was a crowd, of course, and when he left they wanted to take out the horses and drag him home in triumph. But he didn't wish it, and while that affair was being arranged we girls had been pelting him with the flowers which we tore from the vases, the walls, and our own topknots to scatter over him.

"He liked that, and laughed, and waved his hand to us while we ran, and pelted, and begged him to come again.

"We young folks quite lost our heads that night, and I haven't a very clear idea of how I got home. The last thing I remember was hanging out of the window with a flock of girls watching the carriage roll away while the crowd cheered as if they were mad.

"Bless my heart, it seems as if I heard 'em now! 'Hurrah for Lafayette and Mayor Quincy! Hurrah for Madam Hancock and the pretty girls! Hurrah for Colonel May!' 'Three cheers for Boston! Now, then! Hurrah! Hurrah! Hurrah!' "

And here the old lady stopped, out of breath, with her cap askew, her spectacles on the end of her nose, and her knitting much the worse for being waved enthusiastically in the air while she hung over the arm of her chair shrilly cheering an imaginary Lafayette.

The girls clapped their hands, and Tom hurrahed with all his might, saying, when he got his breath:

"Lafayette was a regular old trump. I always liked him."

"My dear! What a disrespectful way to speak of that great man," said Grandma, shocked at Young America's irreverence.

"Well, he *was* a trump, anyway, so why not call him one?" asked Tom, feeling that the objectionable word was all that could be desired.

"What queer gloves you wore then," interrupted Fanny, who had been trying on the much-honored glove and finding it a tight fit.

"Much better and cheaper than we have now," returned Grandma, ready to defend "the good old times" against every insinuation. "You are an extravagant set nowadays, and I really don't know what you are coming to. By the way, I've got somewhere two letters written by two young ladies, one in 1517 and the other in 1868. The contrast between the two will amuse you, I think."

After a little search, Grandma produced an old portfolio, and selecting the papers, read the following letter, written by

Anne Boleyn before her marriage to Henry VIII, and now in
the possession of a celebrated antiquarian:

> DEAR MARY—I have been in town almost a
> month, yet I cannot say I have found anything in
> London extremely agreeable. We rise so late in the
> morning—seldom before six o'clock—and sit up so
> late at night—being scarcely in bed before ten—
> that I am quite sick of it, and was it not for the
> abundance of fine things I am every day getting, I
> should be impatient of returning into the country.
>
> My indulgent mother bought me, yesterday, at a
> merchant's in Cheapside, three new shifts, that
> cost fourteen pence an ell, and I am to have a pair
> of new stuff shoes, for my Lord of Norfolk's ball,
> which will be three shillings.
>
> The irregular life I have led since my coming to
> this place has quite destroyed my appetite. You
> know I could manage a pound of bacon and a tan-
> kard of good ale for my breakfast in the country,
> but in London I find it difficult to get through half
> the quantity, though I must own I am generally
> eager enough for the dinner hour, which is here
> delayed till twelve in your polite society.
>
> I played at hot cockles last night at my Lord of
> Leicester's. The Lord of Surrey was there, a very
> elegant young man who sung a song of his own
> composition on the "Lord of Kildare's Daughter."
> It was much approved, and my brother whispered
> me that the fair Geraldine, for so my Lord of Sur-
> rey calls his sweetheart, is the finest woman of the
> age. I should be glad to see her, for I hear she is
> good as she is beautiful.

Pray take care of the poultry during my absence. Poor things! I always fed them myself, and if Margery has knitted me the crimson worsted mittens, I should be glad if they were sent up the first opportunity.

Adieu, dear Mary. I am just going to mass, and you shall speedily have the prayers, as you have now the kindest love of your own.

ANNE BOLEYN

"Up before six, and think it late to go to bed at ten! What a countrified thing Anne must have been. Bacon and ale for breakfast and dinner at twelve. How very queer to live so!" cried Fanny. "Lord Surrey and Lord Leicester sound fine, but hot cockles and red mittens, and shoes for three shillings, are horrid."

"I like it," said Polly thoughtfully, "and I'm glad poor Anne had a little fun before her troubles began. May I copy that letter sometime, Grandma?"

"Yes, dear, and welcome. Now, here's the other, by a modern girl on her first visit to London. This will suit you better, Fan," and Grandma read what a friend had sent her as a pendant to Anne's little picture of London life long ago:

MY DEAREST CONSTANCE—After three months of intense excitement I snatch a leisure moment to tell you how much I enjoy my first visit to London. Having been educated abroad, it really seems like coming to a strange city. At first the smoke, dirt, and noise were very disagreeable, but I soon got used to these things, and now find all I see perfectly charming.

We plunged at once into a whirl of gaiety, and I

have had no time to think of anything but pleasure. It is the height of the season, and every hour
is engaged either in going to balls, concerts, the-
atres, fêtes, and church, or in preparing for them.
We often go to two or three parties in an evening,
and seldom get home till morning, so of course we
don't rise till noon next day. This leaves very little
time for our drives, shopping, and calls before dinner at eight, and then the evening gaieties begin
again.

At a ball at Lady Russell's last night, I saw the
Prince of Wales, and danced in the set with him. He
is growing stout, and looks dissipated. I was disappointed in him, for neither in appearance nor conversation was he at all princely. I was introduced to
a very brilliant and delightful young gentleman
from America. I was charmed with him, and rather
surprised to learn that he wrote the poems which
were so much admired last season, also that he is
the son of a rich tailor. How odd these Americans
are, with their money, and talent, and independence!

Oh, my dear, I must not forget to tell you the
great event of my first season. I am to be presented
at the next Drawing Room! Think how absorbed I
must be in preparation for this grand affair. Mama
is resolved that I shall do her credit, and we have
spent the last two weeks driving about from milli-
ners to mantua-makers, from merchants to jewel-
lers. I am to wear white satin and plumes, pearls
and roses. My dress will cost a hundred pounds or
more, and is very elegant.

My cousins and friends lavish lovely things upon

me, and you will open your unsophisticated eyes when I display my silks and laces, trinkets and French hats, not to mention *billets doux*, photographs, and other relics of a young belle's first season.

You ask if I ever think of home. I really haven't time, but I do sometimes long a little for the quiet, the pure air and the girlish amusements I used to enjoy so much. One gets pale, and old, and sadly fagged out with all this dissipation, pleasant as it is. I feel quite *blasé* already.

If you could send me the rosy cheeks, bright eyes, and gay spirits I always had at home, I'd thank you. As you cannot do that, please send me a bottle of June rainwater, for my maid tells me it is better than any cosmetic for the complexion, and mine is getting ruined by late hours.

I fancy some fruit off our own trees would suit me, for I have no appetite, and Mama is quite *désolée* about me. One cannot live on French cookery without dyspepsia, and one can get nothing simple here, for food, like everything else, is regulated by the fashion.

Adieu, *ma chère*, I must dress for church. I only wish you could see my new hat and go with me, for Lord Rockingham promised to be there.

Adieu, yours eternally,

FLORENCE

"Yes, I do like that better, and I wish I had been in this girl's place, don't you, Polly?" said Fan as Grandma took off her glasses.

"I should love to go to London and have a good time, but

I don't think I should care about spending ever so much money or going to Court. Maybe I might when I got there, for I *do* like fun and splendor," added honest Polly, feeling that pleasure was a very tempting thing.

"Grandma looks tired, let's go and play in the dwying woom," said Maud, who found the conversation getting beyond her depth.

"Let us all kiss and thank Grandma for amusing us so nicely before we go," whispered Polly. Maud and Fanny agreed, and Grandma looked so gratified by their thanks that Tom followed suit, merely waiting till "those girls" were out of sight to give the old lady a hearty hug and a kiss on the very cheek Lafayette had saluted.

When he reached the playroom Polly was sitting in the swing, saying, very earnestly, "I always told you it was nice up in Grandma's room, and now you see it is. I wish you'd go oftener. She admires to have you, and likes to tell stories and do pleasant things, only she thinks you don't care for her quiet sort of fun. *I* do, anyway, and *I* think she's the kindest, best old lady that ever lived, and I love her dearly!"

"I didn't say she wasn't, only old people are sort of tedious and fussy, so I keep out of their way," said Fanny.

"Well, you ought not to, and you miss lots of pleasant times. My mother says we ought to be kind and patient and respectful to all old folks just because they *are* old, and I always mean to be."

"Your mother's everlastingly preaching," muttered Fan, nettled by the consciousness of her own shortcomings with regard to Grandma.

"She don't preach!" cried Polly, firing up like a flash. "She only explains things to us, and helps us be good, and never scolds, and I'd rather have her than any other mother in the world, though she don't wear velvet cloaks and splendid bonnets—so now!"

"Go it, Polly!" called Tom, who was gracefully hanging head downward from the bar put up for his special benefit.

"Polly's mad! Polly's mad!" sung Maud, skipping rope round the room.

"If Mr. Sydney could see you now, he wouldn't think you such an angel anymore," added Fanny, tossing a bean bag and her head at the same time.

Polly *was* mad, her face was very red, her eyes very bright, and her lips twitched, but she held her tongue and began to swing as hard as she could, fearing to say something she would be sorry for afterward. For a few minutes no one spoke, Tom whistled, and Maud hummed, but Fan and Polly were each soberly thinking of something, for they had reached an age when children, girls especially, begin to observe, contrast, and speculate upon the words, acts, manners, and looks of those about them. A good deal of thinking goes on in the heads of these shrewd little folks, and the elders should mind their ways, for they get criticized pretty sharply and imitated very closely.

Two little things had happened that day, and the influence of a few words, a careless action, was still working in the active minds of the girls.

Mr. Sydney had called, and while Fanny was talking with him she saw his eye rest on Polly, who sat apart watching the faces round her with the modest, intelligent look which many found so attractive. At that minute Madam Shaw came in and stopped to speak to the little girl. Polly rose at once and remained standing till the old lady passed on.

"Are you laughing at Polly's prim ways?" Fanny had asked as she saw Mr. Sydney smile.

"No, I am admiring Miss Polly's fine manners," he an-

swered in a grave, respectful tone, which had impressed
Fanny very much, for Mr. Sydney was considered by all the
girls as a model of good breeding and that indescribable
something which they called "elegance."

Fanny wished *she* had done that little thing and won that
approving look, for she valued the young man's good opinion because it was so hard to win, by her set at least. So
when Polly talked about old people it recalled this scene and
made Fan cross.

Polly was remembering how, when Mrs. Shaw came home
that day in her fine visiting costume, and Maud ran to welcome her with unusual affection, she gathered up her lus-
trous silk and pushed the little girl away, saying, impatiently,
"Don't touch me, child, your hands are dirty." Then the
thought had come to Polly that the velvet cloak didn't cover
a right motherly heart, that the fretful face under the nodding purple plumes was not a tender motherly face, and that
the hands in the delicate primrose gloves had put away
something very sweet and precious. She thought of another
woman, whose dress never was too fine for little wet cheeks
to lie against or loving little arms to press; whose face, in
spite of many lines and the gray hairs above it, was never
sour or unsympathetic when children's eyes turned toward
it, and whose hands never were too busy, too full, or too
nice to welcome and serve the little sons and daughters who
freely brought their small hopes and fears, sins and sorrows,
to her, who dealt out justice and mercy with such wise love.
"Ah, that's a mother!" thought Polly as the memory came
warm into her heart, making her feel very rich and pity
Maud for being so poor.

This it was that caused such sudden indignation at Fanny's dreadful speech, and this it was that made quick-tem-
pered Polly try to calm her wrath before she used toward

Fanny's mother the disrespectful tone she so resented toward her own. As the swing came down after some dozen quick journeys to and fro, Polly seemed to have found a smile somewhere up aloft, for she looked toward Fan, saying pleasantly, as she paused a little in her airy exercise, "I'm not mad now, shall I come and toss with you?"

"No, I'll come and swing with you," answered Fanny, quick to feel the generous spirit of her friend. "You *are* an angel, and I'll never be so rude again," she added as Polly's arm came round her and half the seat was gladly offered.

"No, I ain't, but if I ever get at all like one, it will be 'mother's preaching' that did it," said Polly with a happy laugh.

"Good for you, Polly Peacemaker," cried Tom, quoting his father and giving them a grand push as the most appropriate way of expressing his approbation of the sentiment.

Nothing more was said, but from that day there slowly crept into the family more respect for Grandma, more forbearance with her infirmities, more interest in her little stories, and many a pleasant gossip did the dear old lady enjoy with the children as they gathered round her fire, solitary so long.

Chapter 7

Good-Bye

"*O*h, dear! Must you really go home Saturday?" said Fan, some days after what Tom called the "grand scrimmage."

"I really must, for I only came to stay a month, and here I've been nearly six weeks," answered Polly, feeling as if she had been absent a year.

"Make it two months, and stay over Christmas. Come, do, now," urged Tom heartily.

"You are very kind, but I wouldn't miss Christmas at home for anything. Besides, Mother says they can't possibly do without me."

"Neither can we. Can't you tease your mother and make up your mind to stay?" began Fan.

"Polly never teases. She says it's selfish, and I don't do it now much," put in Maud with a virtuous air.

"Don't you bother Polly. She'd rather go, and I don't wonder. Let's be just as jolly as we can while she stays and finish up with your party, Fan," said Tom in a tone that settled the matter.

Polly had expected to be very happy in getting ready for the party, but when the time came she was disappointed, for somehow that naughty thing called envy took possession of her and spoiled her pleasure. Before she left home she thought her new white muslin dress, with its fresh blue ribbons, the most elegant and proper costume she could have, but now, when she saw Fanny's pink silk, with a white tarlatan tunic and innumerable puffings, bows, and streamers, her own simple little toilet lost all its charms in her eyes and looked very babyish and old-fashioned.

Even Maud was much better dressed than herself and looked very splendid in her cherry-colored and white suit, with a sash so big she could hardly carry it, and little white boots with red buttons. They both had necklaces and bracelets, earrings and brooches, but Polly had no ornament except the plain locket on a bit of blue velvet. Her sash was only a wide ribbon tied in a simple bow, and nothing but a blue snood in the pretty curls. Her only comfort was the knowledge that the modest tucker drawn up round the plump shoulders was real lace and that her bronze boots cost nine dollars.

Poor Polly, with all her efforts to be contented, and not to mind looking unlike other people, found it hard work to keep her face bright and her voice happy that night. No one dreamed what was going on under the muslin frock till Grandma's wise old eyes spied out the little shadow on Polly's spirits and guessed the cause of it. When dressed, the three girls went to show themselves to the elders, who were in Grandma's room, where Tom was being helped into an agonizingly stiff collar.

Maud pranced like a small peacock, and Fan made a splendid curtsy as everyone turned to survey them, but Polly stood still and her eyes went from face to face with an anxious, wistful air which seemed to say, "I know I'm not right, but I hope I don't look very bad."

Grandma read the look in a minute, and when Fanny said, with a satisfied smile, "How do we look?" she answered, drawing Polly toward her so kindly.

"Very like the fashion plates you got the patterns of your dresses from. But this little costume suits me best."

"Do you really think I look nice?" And Polly's face brightened, for she valued the old lady's opinion very much.

"Yes, my dear, you look just as I like to see a child of your age look. What particularly pleases me is that you have kept your promise to your mother and haven't let anyone persuade you to wear borrowed finery. Young things like you don't need any ornaments but those you wear tonight—youth, health, intelligence, and modesty."

As she spoke Grandma gave a tender kiss that made Polly glow like a rose, and for a minute she forgot that there were such things as pink silk and coral earrings in the world. She only said "Thank you, ma'am," and heartily returned the kiss, but the words did her good, and her plain dress looked charming all of a sudden.

"Polly's so pretty, it don't matter what she wears," observed Tom, surveying her over his collar with an air of calm approval.

"She hasn't got any bwetelles to her dwess, and I have," said Maud, settling her ruffled bands over her shoulders, which looked like cherry-colored wings on a stout little cherub.

"I did wish she'd just wear my blue set, ribbon is so very plain, but, as Tom says, it don't much matter." And Fanny gave an effective touch to the blue bow above Polly's left temple.

"She might wear flowers, they always suit young girls,"

said Mrs. Shaw, privately thinking that her own daughters looked much the best, yet conscious that blooming Polly had the most attractive face.

"Bless me! I forgot my posies in admiring the belles. Hand them out, Tom." And Mr. Shaw nodded toward an interesting-looking box that stood on the table.

Seizing them wrong side up, Tom produced three little bouquets, all different in color, size, and construction.

"Why, Papa! How very kind of you," cried Fanny, who had not dared to receive even a geranium leaf since the late scrape.

"Your father used to be a very gallant young gentleman, once upon a time," said Mrs. Shaw with a simper.

"Ah, Tom, it's a good sign when you find time to think of giving pleasure to your little girls!" And Grandma patted her son's bald head as if he wasn't more than eighteen.

Thomas, Jr. had given a somewhat scornful sniff at first, but when Grandma praised his father the young man thought better of the matter and regarded the flowers with more respect as he asked, "Which is for which?"

"Guess," said Mr. Shaw, pleased that his unusual demonstration had produced such an effect.

The largest was a regular hothouse bouquet of tea rosebuds, scentless heath, and smilax; the second was just a handful of sweet peas and mignonette, with a few cheerful pansies and one fragrant little rose in the middle; the third, a small posy of scarlet verbenas, white feverfew, and green leaves.

"Not hard to guess. The smart one for Fan, the sweet one for Polly, and the gay one for Pug. Now, then, catch hold, girls." And Tom proceeded to deliver the nosegays with as much grace as could be expected from a youth in a new suit of clothes and very tight boots.

"That finishes you off just right, and is a very pretty attention of Papa's. Now run down, for the bell has rung, and remember not to dance too often, Fan, be as quiet as you can, Tom, and, Maud, don't eat too much supper. Grandma will attend to things, for my poor nerves won't allow me to come down."

With that Mrs. Shaw dismissed them, and the four descended to receive the first batch of visitors, several little girls who had been asked for the express purpose of keeping Maud out of her sister's way. Tom had likewise been propitiated by being allowed to bring his three bosom friends, who went by the schoolboy names of Rumple, Sherry, and Spider.

"They will do to make up sets, as gentlemen are scarce and the party is for Polly, so I must have some young folks on her account," said Fanny when sending out her invitations.

Of course the boys came early and stood about in corners, looking as if they had more arms and legs than they knew what to do with. Tom did his best to be a good host, but ceremony oppressed his spirits, and he was forced to struggle manfully with the wild desire to propose a game of leapfrog, for the long drawing rooms, cleared for dancing, tempted him sorely.

Polly sat where she was told, and suffered bashful agonies as Fan introduced very fine young ladies and very stiff young gentlemen, who all said about the same civil things and then appeared to forget all about her. When the first dance was called, Fanny cornered Tom, who had been dodging her, for he knew what she wanted, and said, in an earnest whisper:

"Now, Tom, you must dance this with Polly. You are the young gentleman of the house, and it's only proper that you should ask your company first."

"Polly don't care for manners. I hate dancing, don't know how. Let go my jacket and don't bother, or I'll cut away altogether," growled Tom, daunted by the awful prospect of opening the ball with Polly.

"I'll never forgive you if you do. Come, be clever, and help me, there's a dear. You know we both were dreadfully rude to Polly and agreed that we'd be as kind and civil to her as ever we could. I shall keep my word and see that she isn't slighted at my party, for I want her to love me and go home feeling all right."

This artful speech made an impression on the rebellious Thomas, who glanced at Polly's happy face, remembered his promise, and, with a groan, resolved to do his duty.

"Well, I'll take her, but I shall come to grief, for I don't know anything about your old dances."

"Yes, you do. I've taught you the steps a dozen times. I'm going to begin with a redowa, because the girls like it and it's better fun than square dances. Now, put on your gloves and go and ask Polly like a gentleman."

"Oh, thunder!" muttered Tom. And having split the detested gloves in dragging them on, he nerved himself for the effort, walked up to Polly, made a stiff bow, stuck out his elbow, and said solemnly, "May I have the pleasure, Miss Milton?"

He did it as much like the big fellows as he could, and expected that Polly would be impressed. But she wasn't a bit, for after a surprised look she laughed in his face and took him by the hand, saying, heartily:

"Of course you may, but don't be a goose, Tommy."

"Well, Fan told me to be elegant, so I tried to," whispered Tom, adding, as he clutched his partner with a somewhat desperate air, "Hold on tight, and we'll get through somehow."

The music struck up, and away they went, Tom hopping one way and Polly the other in a most ungraceful manner.

"Keep time to the music," gasped Polly.

"Can't, never could," returned Tom.

"Keep step with me, then, and don't tread on my toes," pleaded Polly.

"Never mind. Keep bobbing, and we'll come right by and by," muttered Tom, giving his unfortunate partner a sudden whisk, which nearly landed both on the floor.

But they did not "get right by and by," for Tom, in his frantic efforts to do his duty, nearly annihilated poor Polly. He tramped, he bobbed, he skated, he twirled her to the right, dragged her to the left, backed her up against people and furniture, trod on her feet, rumpled her dress, and made a spectacle of himself generally. Polly was much disturbed, but as everyone else was flying about also, she bore it as long as she could, knowing that Tom had made a martyr of himself and feeling grateful to him for the sacrifice.

"Oh, do stop now. This is dreadful!" cried Polly breathlessly after a few wild turns.

"Isn't it?" said Tom, wiping his red face with such an air of intense relief that Polly had not the heart to scold him, but said, "Thank you," and dropped into a chair exhausted.

"I know I've made a guy* of myself, but Fan insisted on it for fear you'd be offended if I didn't go the first dance with you," said Tom remorsefully, watching Polly as she settled the bow of her crushed sash, which Tom had used as a sort of handle by which to turn and twist her. "I can do the Lancers tip-top, but you won't ever want to dance with me

---

* *Guy* in nineteenth-century slang meant "fool" (from the English custom of dressing in bizarre clothing on Guy Fawkes Day).

anymore," he added as he began to fan her so violently that her hair flew about as if in a gale of wind.

"Yes, I will. I'd like to, and you shall put your name down here on the sticks of my fan. That's the way, Trix says, when you don't have a ball book."

Looking much gratified, Tom produced the stump of a lead pencil and wrote his name with a flourish, saying, as he gave it back:

"Now I'm going to get Sherry, or some of the fellows that do the redowa well, so you can have a real good go before the music stops."

Off went Tom, but before he could catch any eligible partner, Polly was provided with the best dancer in the room. Mr. Sydney had seen and heard the whole thing, and though he had laughed quietly, he liked honest Tom and good-natured Polly all the better for their simplicity. Polly's foot was keeping time to the lively music, and her eyes were fixed wistfully on the smoothly gliding couples before her, when Mr. Sydney came to her, saying, in the pleasant yet respectful way she liked so much:

"Miss Polly, can you give me a turn?"

"Oh, yes, I'm dying for another." And Polly jumped up, with both hands out and such a grateful face that Mr. Sydney resolved she should have as many turns as she liked.

This time all went well, and Tom, returning from an unsuccessful search, was amazed to behold Polly circling gracefully about the room, guided by a most accomplished partner.

"Ah, that's something like," he thought as he watched the bronze boots retreating and advancing in perfect time to the music. "Don't see how Sydney does the steering so well, but it must be fun, and, by Jupiter, I'll learn it!" added Shaw,

Jr., with an emphatic gesture which burst the last button off his gloves.

Polly enjoyed herself till the music stopped, and before she had time to thank Mr. Sydney as warmly as she wished, Tom came up to say, with his most lordly air:

"You dance splendidly, Polly. Now, you just show me anyone you like the looks of and I'll get him for you, no matter who he is."

"I don't want any of the gentlemen, they are so stiff, and don't care to dance with me, but I like those boys over there and I'll dance with any of them if they are willing," said Polly after a survey.

"I'll trot out the whole lot." And Tom gladly brought up his friends, who all admired Polly immensely and were proud to be chosen instead of the "big fellows."

There was no sitting still for Polly after that, for the lads kept her going at a great pace, and she was so happy, she never saw or suspected how many little maneuvers, heart burnings, displays of vanity, affectation, and nonsense were going on all round her. She loved dancing, and entered into the gaiety of the scene with a heartiness that was pleasant to see. Her eyes shone, her face glowed, her lips smiled, and the brown curls waved in the air as she danced with a heart as light as her feet.

"Are you enjoying yourself, Polly?" asked Mr. Shaw, who looked in now and then to report to Grandma that all was going well.

"Oh, such a splendid time!" cried Polly with an enthusiastic little gesture as she *chasséed* into the corner where he stood.

"She is a regular belle among the boys," said Fanny as she promenaded by.

"They are so kind in asking me, and I'm not afraid of

them," explained Polly, prancing simply because she couldn't keep still.

"So you *are* afraid of the young gentlemen, hey?" And Mr. Shaw held her by one curl.

"All but Mr. Sydney. He don't put on airs and talk nonsense, and, oh, he does 'dance like an angel,' as Trix says."

"Papa, I wish you'd come and waltz with me. Fan told me not to go near her 'cause my wed dwess makes her pink one look ugly, and Tom won't, and I want to dwedfully."

"I've forgotten how, Maudie. Ask Polly. She'll spin you round like a teetotum."

"Mr. Sydney's name is down for that," answered Polly, looking at her fan with a pretty little air of importance. "But I guess he wouldn't mind my taking poor Maud instead. She hasn't danced hardly any, and I've had more than my share. Would it be very improper to change my mind?" And Polly looked up at her tall partner with eyes which plainly showed that the change was a sacrifice.

"Not a bit. Give the little dear a good waltz, and we will look on," answered Mr. Sydney, with a nod and smile.

"That is a refreshing little piece of nature," said Mr. Shaw as Polly and Maud whirled away.

"She will make a charming little woman if she isn't spoilt."

"No danger of that. She has got a sensible mother."

"I thought so." And Sydney sighed, for he had lately lost his own good mother.

When supper was announced Polly happened to be talking, or trying to talk, to one of the "poky" gentlemen whom Fan had introduced. He took Miss Milton down, of course, put her in a corner, and having served her to a dab of ice and one macaroon, he devoted himself to his own supper with such interest that Polly would have fared badly if Tom had not come and rescued her.

"I've been looking everywhere for you. Come with me, and don't sit starving here," said Tom with a scornful look from her empty plate to that of her recreant escort, which was piled with good things.

Following her guide, Polly was taken to the big china closet, opening from the dining room to the kitchen, and here she found a jovial little party feasting at ease. Maud and her bosom friend "Gwace" were seated on tin cake boxes; Sherry and Spider adorned the refrigerator, while Tom and Rumple foraged for the party.

"Here's fun," said Polly as she was received with a clash of spoons and a waving of napkins.

"You just perch on that cracker keg and I'll see that you get enough," said Tom, putting a dumbwaiter before her and issuing his orders with a fine air of authority.

"We are a band of robbers in our cave, and I'm the captain, and we pitch into the folks passing by, and go out and bring home plunder. Now, Rumple, you go and carry off a basket of cake, and I'll watch here till Katy comes by with a fresh lot of oysters. Polly must have some. Sherry, cut into the kitchen and bring a cup of coffee. Spider, scrape up the salad and poke the dish through the slide for more. Eat away, Polly, and my men will be back with supplies in a jiffy."

Such fun as they had in that closet; such daring robberies of jelly pots and cake boxes; such successful raids into the dining room and kitchen; such base assaults upon poor Katy and the colored waiter, who did his best, but was helpless in the hands of the robber horde. A very harmless little revel, for no wine was allowed, and the gallant band were so busy skirmishing to supply the ladies that they had not time to eat too much. No one missed them, and when they emerged the feast was over, except for a few voracious young gentlemen who still lingered among the ruins.

"That's the way they always do—poke the girls in corners, give 'em just one taste of something, and then go and stuff like pigs," whispered Tom with a superior air, forgetting certain private banquets of his own after company had departed.

The rest of the evening was to be devoted to the German, and, as Polly knew nothing about it, she established herself in a window recess to watch the mysteries. For a time she enjoyed it, for it was all new to her, and the various pretty devices were very charming, but, by and by, that bitter weed, envy, cropped up again, and she could not feel happy to be left out in the cold while the other girls were getting gay tissue-paper suits, droll bonbons, flowers, ribbons, and all manner of tasteful trifles in which girlish souls delight. Everyone was absorbed: Mr. Sydney was dancing, Tom and his friends were discussing baseball on the stairs, and Maud's set had returned to the library to play.

Polly tried to conquer the bad feeling, but it worried her till she remembered something her mother once said to her:

"When you feel out of sorts, try to make someone else happy, and you will soon be so yourself."

"I will try it," thought Polly, and looked round to see what she could do. Sounds of strife in the library led her to enter. Maud and the young ladies were sitting on the sofa, talking about each other's clothes, as they had seen their mamas do.

"Was your dress imported?" asked Grace.

"No, was yours?" returned Blanche.

"Yes, and it cost—oh, ever so much."

"I don't think it is as pretty as Maud's."

"Mine was made in New York," said Miss Shaw, smoothing her skirts complacently.

"I can't dress much now, you know, 'cause Mama's in black for somebody," observed Miss Alice Lovett, feeling the importance which affliction conferred upon her when it took the form of a jet necklace.

"Well, I don't care if my dress isn't imported, my cousin had three kinds of wine at her party, so, now," said Blanche.

"Did she?" And all the little girls looked deeply impressed till Maud observed, with a funny imitation of her father's manner:

"My papa said it was scan-dill-us, for some of the little boys got tipsy and had to be tooked home. He wouldn't let us have any wine, and Gwandma said it was vewy impwoper for childwen to do so."

"My mother says your mother's *coupé* isn't half so stylish as ours," put in Alice.

"Yes, it is too. It's all lined with gween silk, and that's nicer than old web cloth," cried Maud, ruffling up like an insulted chicken.

"Well, my brother don't wear a horrid old cap and he's got nice hair. I wouldn't have a brother like Tom. He's horrid rude, my sister says," retorted Alice.

"He isn't. Your brother is a pig."

"You're a fib!"

"So are you!"

Here, I regret to say, Miss Shaw slapped Miss Lovett, who promptly returned the compliment, and both began to cry.

Polly, who had paused to listen to the edifying chat, parted the belligerents, and finding the poor things tired, cross, and sleepy, yet unable to go home till sent for, proposed to play games. The young ladies consented, and Puss in the Corner proved a peacemaker. Presently, in came the boys, and being exiles from the German, gladly joined in the games, which soon were lively enough to wake the sleepiest. Blindman's Buff was in full swing when Mr. Shaw peeped in, and seeing Polly flying about with bandaged eyes, joined in the fun to puzzle her. He got caught directly, and great merriment was caused by Polly's bewilderment, for she couldn't guess who he was till she felt the bald spot on his head.

This frolic put everyone in such spirits that Polly forgot her trouble, and the little girls kissed each other good night as affectionately as if such things as imported frocks, *coupés*, and rival brothers didn't exist.

"Well, Polly, do you like parties?" asked Fan when the last guest was gone.

"Very much, but I don't think it would be good for me to go to many," answered Polly slowly.

"Why not?"

"I shouldn't enjoy them if I didn't have a fine dress, and dance all the time, and be admired, and—all the rest of it."

"I didn't know you cared for such things," cried Fanny, surprised.

"Neither did I till tonight, but I do, and as I can't have 'em, it's lucky I'm going home tomorrow."

"Oh, dear! So you are! What shall I do without my 'sweet P.,' as Sydney calls you?" sighed Fanny, bearing Polly away to be cuddled.

Everyone echoed the exclamation next day, and many loving eyes followed the little figure in the drab frock as it went quietly about, doing for the last time the small services which would help to make its absence keenly felt. Polly was to go directly after an early dinner, and having packed her trunk, all but one tray, she was told to go and take a run while Grandma finished. Polly suspected that some pleasant surprise was going to be put in, for Fan didn't offer to go with her, Maud kept dodging about with something under her apron, and Tom had just whisked into his mother's room in a mysterious manner. So Polly took the hint and went away, rejoicing in the thought of the unknown treasures she was to carry home.

Mr. Shaw had not said he should come home so early, but Polly thought he might, and went to meet him. Mr. Shaw didn't expect to see Polly, for he had left her very busy, and now a light snow was falling, but as he turned into the mall there was the round hat, and under it the bright face, looking all the rosier for being powdered with snowflakes as Polly came running to meet him.

"There won't be anyone to help the old gentleman safely home tomorrow," he said as Polly took his hand in both hers with an affectionate squeeze.

"Yes, there will, see if there isn't," cried Polly, nodding and smiling, for Fan had confided to her that she meant to try it after her friend had gone.

"I'm glad of it. But, my dear, I want you to promise that you will come and make us a visit every winter—a good long one," said Mr. Shaw, patting the blue mittens folded round his hand.

"If they can spare me from home, I'd love to come dearly."

"They must lend you for a little while, because you do us all good, and we need you."

"Do I? I don't see how, but I'm glad to hear you say so," cried Polly, much touched.

"I can't tell you how, exactly, but you brought something into my house that makes it warmer and pleasanter and won't quite vanish, I hope, when you go away, my child."

Polly had never heard Mr. Shaw speak like that before and didn't know what to say, she felt so proud and happy at this proof of the truth of her mother's words when she said "even a little girl could exert an influence and do some good in this big, busy world." She only gave her friend a grateful look, sweeter than any words, and they went on together, hand in hand, through the "soft-falling snow."

If Polly could have seen what went into that top tray, she would have been entirely overcome, for Fanny had told Grandma about the poor little presents she had once laughed at and they had all laid their heads together to provide something really fine and appropriate for every member of the Milton family. Such a mine of riches! And so much goodwill, affection, and kindly forethoughts were packed away in the tempting bundles that no one could feel offended but would find an unusual charm about the pretty gifts that made them doubly welcome. I only know that if Polly had suspected that a little watch was ticking away in a little case, with her name on it, inside that trunk, she never could have left it locked, as Grandma advised, or have eaten her dinner so quietly. As it was, her heart was very full, and the tears rose to her eyes more than once, everyone was so kind and so sorry to have her go.

Tom didn't need any urging to play escort now, and both Fan and Maud insisted on going too. Mrs. Shaw forgot her nerves and put up some gingerbread with her own hands; Mr. Shaw kissed Polly as if she had been his dearest daughter; Grandma held her close, whispering in a tremulous tone, "My little comfort, come again soon," while Katy waved her apron from the nursery window, crying, as they drove away, "The saints bless ye, Miss Polly, dear, and sind ye the best of lucks!"

But the crowning joke of all was Tom's good-bye, for, when Polly was fairly settled in the car, the last "All aboard!" uttered, and the train in motion, Tom suddenly produced a knobby little bundle and, thrusting it in at the window while he hung on in some breakneck fashion, said, with a droll mixture of fun and feeling in his face:

"It's horrid, but you wanted it, so I put it in to make you laugh. Good-bye, Polly. Good-bye, good-bye!"

The last adieu was a trifle husky, and Tom vanished as it was uttered, leaving Polly to laugh over his parting souvenir till the tears ran down her cheeks. It was a paper bag of peanuts, and poked down at the very bottom was a photograph of Tom. It was "horrid," for he looked as if taken by a flash of lightning, so black, wild, and staring was it, but Polly liked it, and whenever she felt a little pensive at parting with her friends, she took a peanut or a peep at Tom's funny picture, which made her merry again.

So the short journey came blithely to an end, and in the twilight she saw a group of loving faces at the door of a humble little house, which was more beautiful than any palace in her eyes, for it was home.

Chapter 8

Six Years Afterward

"**W**hat *do* you think Polly is going to do this winter?" exclaimed Fanny, looking up from the letter she had been eagerly reading.

"Going to deliver lectures on Woman's Rights," said the young gentleman who was carefully examining his luxuriant crop of decidedly auburn hair as he lounged with both elbows on the chimneypiece.

"Going to set her cap for some young minister and marry him in the spring," added Mrs. Shaw, whose mind ran a good deal upon matchmaking just now.

"I think she is going to stay at home and do *all* the work, 'cause servants cost so much. It would be just like her," observed Maud, who could pronounce the letter *r* now.

"It's my opinion she is going to open a school, or something of that sort, to help those brothers of hers along," said Mr. Shaw, who had put down his paper at the sound of Polly's name.

"Every one of you wrong, though Papa comes nearest the truth," cried Fanny. "She is going to give music lessons and support herself so that Will may go to college. He is the studious one, and Polly is very proud of him. Ned, the other brother, has a business talent and don't care for books, so he has gone out West and will make his own way anywhere. Polly says she isn't needed at home now, the family is so small, and Kitty can take her place nicely, so she is actually going to earn her own living and hand over her share of the family income to Will. What a martyr that girl does make of herself." And Fanny looked as solemn as if Polly had proposed some awful self-sacrifice.

"She is a sensible, brave-hearted girl, and I respect her for doing it," said Mr. Shaw emphatically. "One never knows what may happen, and it does no harm for young people to learn to be independent."

"If she is as pretty as she was last time I saw her, she'll get pupils fast enough. I wouldn't mind taking lessons myself," was the gracious observation of Shaw, Jr., as he turned from the mirror with the soothing certainty that his objectionable hair actually *was* growing darker.

"She wouldn't take you at any price," said Fanny, remembering Polly's look of disappointment and disapproval when she came on her last visit and found him an unmistakable dandy.

"You just wait and see," was the placid reply.

"If Polly does carry out her plan, I wish Maud to take lessons of her. Fanny can do as she likes, but it would please me very much to have one of my girls sing as Polly sings. It suits old people better than your opera things, and Mother used to enjoy it so much."

As he spoke Mr. Shaw's eye turned toward the corner of the fire where Grandma used to sit. The easy chair was empty now, the kind old face was gone, and nothing but a very tender memory remained.

"I'd like to learn, Papa, and Polly is a splendid teacher, I know. She's always so patient, and makes everything so pleasant. I do hope she will get scholars enough to begin right away," said Maud.

"When is she coming?" asked Mrs. Shaw, quite willing to help Polly, but privately resolving that Maud should be finished off by the most fashionable master in the city.

"She doesn't say. She thanks me for asking her here, as usual, but says she shall go right to work and had better begin with her own little room at once. Won't it seem strange to have Polly in town and yet not with us?"

"We'll get her somehow. The little room will cost something, and she can stay with us just as well as not, even if she does teach. Tell her I say so," said Mr. Shaw.

"She won't come, I know, for if she undertakes to be independent, she'll do it in the most thorough manner," answered Fanny, and Mrs. Shaw sincerely hoped she would. It was all very well to patronize the little music teacher, but it was not so pleasant to have her settled in the family.

"I shall do what I can for her among my friends, and I daresay she will get on very well with young pupils to begin with. If she starts right, puts her terms high enough, and gets a few good names to give her the *entrée* into our first families, I don't doubt she will do nicely, for I must say Polly has the manners of a lady," observed Mrs. Shaw.

"She's a mighty taking little body, and I'm glad she's to be in town, though I'd like it better if she didn't bother about teaching but just stayed here and enjoyed herself," said Tom lazily.

"I've no doubt she would feel highly honored to be allowed to devote her time to your amusement, but she can't afford expensive luxuries, and she don't approve of flirting, so you will have to let her go her own way and refresh herself with such glimpses of you as her engagements permit," answered Fanny in the sarcastic tone which was becoming habitual to her.

"You are getting to be a regular old maid, Fan, as sharp as a lemon and twice as sour," returned Tom, looking down at her with an air of calm superiority.

"Do be quiet, children, you know I can't bear anything like contention. Maud, give me my Shetland shawl and put a cushion at my back."

As Maud obeyed her mother, with a reproving look at her erring brother and sister, a pause followed, for which everyone seemed grateful. They were sitting about the fire after dinner, and all looked as if a little sunshine would do them good. It had been a dull November day, but all of a sudden the clouds lifted and a bright ray shot into the room. Everyone turned involuntarily to welcome it, and everyone cried out, "Why, Polly!" for there on the threshold stood a bright-faced girl, smiling as if there was no such thing as November weather in the world.

"You dear thing, when did you come?" cried Fanny, kissing both the blooming cheeks with real affection while the rest hovered near, waiting for a chance.

"I came yesterday, and have been getting my nest in order, but I couldn't keep away any longer, so I ran up to say 'How do you do?' " answered Polly in the cheery voice that did one's heart good to hear.

"My Polly always brings the sunshine with her." And Mr. Shaw held out his hands to his little friend, for she was his favorite still.

It was good to see her put both arms about his neck and give him a tender kiss, that said a great deal, for Grandma had died since Polly met him last and she longed to comfort him, seeing how gray and old he had grown.

If Tom had had any thoughts of following his father's example, something in Polly's manner made him change his mind and shake hands with a hearty "I'm very glad to see you, Polly," adding to himself, as he looked at the face in the modest little bonnet, "Prettier than ever, by Jove!"

There was something more than mere prettiness in Polly's face, though Tom had not learned to see it yet. The blue eyes were clear and steady, the fresh mouth frank and sweet, the white chin was a very firm one in spite of the dimple, and the smooth forehead under the little curls had a broad, benevolent arch, while all about the face were those unmistakable lines and curves which can make even a plain countenance comely by breathing into it the beauty of a lovely character. Polly had grown up, but she had no more style now than in the days of the round hat and rough coat, for she was all in gray, like a young Quakeress, with no ornament but a blue bow at the throat and another in the hair. Yet the plain suit became her excellently, and one never thought of the dress, looking at the active figure that wore it, for the freedom of her childhood gave to Polly that good gift, health, and every movement was full of the vigor, grace, and ease which nothing else can so surely bestow. A happy soul in a healthy body is a rare sight in these days, when doctors flourish and everyone is ill, and this pleasant union was the charm which Polly possessed without knowing it.

"It does seem *so* good to have you here again," said Maud, cuddling Polly's cold hand as she sat at her feet when she was fairly established between Fanny and Mr. Shaw, while Tom leaned on the back of his mother's chair and enjoyed the prospect.

"How do you get on? When do you begin? Where is your nest? Now tell all about it," began Fanny, who was full of curiosity about the new plan.

"I shall get on very well, I think, for I've got twelve scholars to begin with, all able to pay a good price, and I shall give my first lesson on Monday."

"Don't you dread it?" asked Fanny.

"Not much, why should I?" answered Polly stoutly.

"Well, I don't know, it's a new thing and must be a little bit hard at first," stammered Fanny, not liking to say that working for one's living seemed a dreadful hardship to her.

"It will be tiresome, of course, but I shall get used to it. I shall like the exercise, and the new people and places I must see will amuse me. Then the independence will be delightful, and if I can save a little to help Kitty along with, that will be best of all."

Polly's face shone as if the prospect was full of pleasure instead of work, and the hearty goodwill with which she undertook the new task seemed to signify her humble hopes and plans and make them interesting in the sight of others.

"Who have you got for pupils?" asked Mrs. Shaw, forgetting her nerves for a minute.

Polly named her list and took a secret satisfaction in seeing the impression which certain names made upon her hearers.

"How in the world did you get the Davenports and the Greys, my dear?" said Mrs. Shaw, sitting erect in her surprise.

"Mrs. Davenport and mother are relations, you know."

"You never told us that before!"

"The Davenports have been away some years, and I forgot all about them. But when I was making my plan I knew I must have a good name or two to set me going, so I just wrote and asked Mrs. D. if she would help me. She came and saw us and was very kind, and has got these pupils for me, like a dear, good woman as she is."

"Where did you learn so much worldly wisdom, Polly?" asked Mr. Shaw as his wife fell back in her chair and took out her salts, as if this discovery had been too much for her.

"I learnt it here, sir," answered Polly, laughing. "I used to think patronage and things of that sort very disagreeable and not worth having, but I've got wiser, and to a certain extent I'm glad to use whatever advantages I have in my power, if they can be honestly got."

"Why didn't you let us help you in the beginning? We should have been very glad to, I'm sure," put in Mrs. Shaw, who quite burned to be known as a joint patroness with Mrs. Davenport.

"I know you would, but you have all been so kind to me I didn't want to trouble you with my little plans till the first steps were taken. Besides, I didn't know as you would like to recommend me as a teacher though you like me well enough as plain Polly."

"My dear, of course I would, and we want you to take Maud at once and teach her your sweet songs. She has a fine voice, and is really suffering for a teacher."

A slight smile passed over Polly's face as she returned her thanks for the new pupil, for she remembered a time when Mrs. Shaw considered her "sweet songs" quite unfit for a fashionable young lady's *repertoire*.

"Where is your room?" asked Maud.

"My old friend Miss Mills has taken me in, and I am nicely settled. Mother didn't like the idea of my going to a strange boardinghouse, so Miss Mills kindly made a place for me. You know she lets her rooms without board, but she is going to give me my dinners, and I'm to get my own breakfast and tea, quite independently. I like that way, and it's very little trouble, my habits are so simple—a bowl of bread and milk night and morning, with baked apples or something of that sort, is all I want, and I can have it when I like."

"Is your room comfortably furnished? Can we lend you anything, my dear? An easy chair now, or a little couch, so necessary when one comes in tired," said Mrs. Shaw, taking unusual interest in the affair.

"Thank you, but I don't need anything, for I brought all sorts of home comforts with me. Oh, Fan, you ought to have seen my triumphal entry into the city, sitting among my goods and chattels in a farmer's cart." Polly's laugh was so infectious that everyone smiled and forgot to be shocked at her performance. "Yes," she added, "I kept wishing I could meet you, just to see your horrified face when you saw me sitting on my little sofa, with boxes and bundles all round me, a bird cage on one side, a fishing basket, with a kitten's head popping in and out of the hole, on the other side, and jolly old Mr. Brown, in his blue frock, perched on a keg of apples in front. It was a lovely bright day, and I enjoyed the ride immensely, for we had all sorts of adventures."

"Oh, tell about it," begged Maud when the general laugh at Polly's picture had subsided.

"Well, in the first place, we forgot my ivy, and Kitty came running after me with it. Then we started again, but were soon stopped by a great shouting, and there was Will racing down the hill, waving a pillow in one hand and a squash pie in the other. How we did laugh when he came up and explained that our neighbor, old Mrs. Dodd, had sent in a hop pillow* for me, in case of headache, and a pie to begin housekeeping with. She seemed so disappointed at being too late that Will promised to get them to me if he ran all the

---

* A pillow filled with hops, an herb that induces sleep.

way to town. The pillow was easily disposed of, but that pie! I do believe it was stowed in every part of the wagon and never stayed anywhere. I found it in my lap, then on the floor, next, upside down among the books, then just on the point of coasting off a trunk into the road, and at last it landed in my rocking chair. Such a remarkable pie as it was, too, for in spite of all its wanderings, it never got spilt or broken, and we finally ate it for lunch in order to be left in peace. Next, my kitty got away, and I had a chase over walls and brooks before I got her while Mr. Brown sat shaking with fun to see me run. We finished off by having the bookshelves tumble on our heads as we went down a hill, and losing my chair off behind as we went up a hill. A shout made us pause, and, looking back, there was the poor little chair rocking all by itself in the middle of the road while a small boy sat on the fence and whooped. It was great fun, I do assure you."

Polly had run on in her lively way, not because she thought her adventures amounted to much, but from a wish to cheer up her friends, who had struck her as looking rather dull and out of sorts, especially Mr. Shaw, and when she saw him lean back in his chair with the old hearty laugh, she was satisfied, and blessed the unlucky pie for amusing him.

"Oh, Polly, you do tell such interesting things!" sighed Maud, wiping her eyes.

"I wish I'd met you. I'd have given you three cheers and a tiger, for it must have been an imposing spectacle," said Tom.

"No, you wouldn't, you'd have whisked round the corner when you saw me coming or have stared straight before you, utterly unconscious of the young woman in the baggage wagon."

Polly laughed in his face just as she used to do when she said that, and in spite of the doubt cast upon his courtesy, Tom rather liked it, though he had nothing to say for himself but a reproachful:

"Now, Polly, that's too bad."

"True, nevertheless. You must come and see my pets, Maud, for my cat and bird live together as happily as brother and sister," said Polly, turning to Maud, who devoured every word she said.

"That's not saying much for them," muttered Tom, feeling that Polly ought to address more of her conversation to him.

"Polly knows what she's talking about. *Her* brothers appreciate their sisters," observed Fanny in her sharp tone.

"And Polly appreciates *her* brothers, don't forget to add that, ma'am," answered Tom.

"Did I tell you that Will was going to college?" broke in Polly to avert the rising storm.

"Hope he'll enjoy himself," observed Tom with the air of a man who had passed through all the mysteries and reached that state of sublime indifference which juniors seem to pride themselves upon.

"I think he will, he is so fond of study, and is so anxious to improve every opportunity. I only hope he won't overwork and get sick, as so many boys do," said simple Polly with such a respectful belief in the eager thirst for knowledge of collegians as a class that Tom regarded the deluded girl with a smile of lofty pity from the heights of his vast and varied experience.

"Guess he won't hurt himself. I'll see that he don't study too hard." And Tom's eyes twinkled as they used to do when he planned his boyish pranks.

"I'm afraid you can't be trusted as a guide, if various rumors I've heard are true," said Polly, looking up at him with a wistful expression that caused his face to assume the sobriety of an owl's.

"Base slanders. I'm as steady as a clock, an ornament to my class, and a model young man, ain't I, Mother?" And Tom patted her thin cheek with a caressing hand, sure of one firm friend in her, for when he ceased to be a harumscarum boy, Mrs. Shaw began to take great pride in her son, and he, missing Grandma, tried to fill her place with his feeble mother.

"Yes, dear, you are all I could ask." And Mrs. Shaw looked up at him with such affection and confidence in her eyes that Polly gave Tom the first approving look she had vouchsafed him since she came.

Why Tom should look troubled and turn grave all at once, she couldn't understand, but she liked to see him stroke his mother's cheek so softly as he stood with his head resting on the high back of her chair, for Polly fancied that he felt a man's pity for her weakness and was learning a son's patient love for a mother who had had much to bear with him.

"I'm so glad you are going to be here all winter, for we are to be very gay, and I shall enjoy taking you round with me," began Fanny, forgetting Polly's plan for a moment.

Polly shook her head decidedly. "It sounds very nice, but it can't be done, Fan, for I've come to work, not play, to save, not spend, and parties will be quite out of the question for me."

"You don't intend to work all the time, without a bit of fun, I hope," cried Fanny, dismayed at the idea.

"I mean to do what I've undertaken and not to be tempted away from my purpose by anything. I shouldn't be fit to give lessons if I was up late, should I? And how far would my earnings go toward dress, carriages, and all the little expenses which would come if I set up for a young lady in society? I can't do both, and I'm not going to try, but I can pick up bits of fun as I go along and be contented with free concerts and lectures, seeing you pretty often, and every Sunday Will is to spend with me, so I shall have quite as much dissipation as is good for me."

"If you don't come to my parties, I'll never forgive you," said Fanny as Polly paused, while Tom chuckled inwardly at the idea of calling visits from a brother "dissipation."

"Any small party, where it will do to wear a plain black silk, I can come to, but the big ones mustn't be thought of, thank you."

It was charming to see the resolution of Polly's face when she said that, for she knew her weakness, and beyond that black silk she had determined *not* to go. Fanny said no more, for she felt quite sure that Polly would relent when the time came, and she planned to give her a pretty dress for a Christmas present so that one excuse should be removed.

"I say, Polly, won't you give some of us fellows music lessons? Somebody wants me to play, and I'd rather learn of you than any Senor Twankydillo," said Tom, who didn't find the conversation interesting.

"Oh, yes, if any of you boys honestly want to learn, and will behave yourselves, I'll take you, but I shall charge extra," answered Polly with a wicked sparkle of the eye, though her face was quite sober and her tone delightfully businesslike.

"Why, Polly, Tom isn't a boy, he's twenty, and he says I must treat him with respect. Besides, he's engaged, and does put on such airs," broke in Maud, who regarded her brother as a venerable being.

"Who is the little girl?" asked Polly, taking the news as a joke.

"Trix. Why, didn't you know it?" answered Maud as if it had been an event of national importance.

"No! Is it true, Fan?" And Polly turned to her friend with a face full of surprise while Tom struck an imposing attitude and affected absence of mind.

"I forgot to tell you in my last letter, it's just out, and we don't like it very well," observed Fanny, who would have preferred to be engaged first herself.

"It's a very nice thing, and *I* am perfectly satisfied," announced Mrs. Shaw, rousing from a slight doze.

"Polly looks as if she didn't believe it. Haven't I the appearance of 'the happiest man alive'?" asked Tom, wondering if it could be pity which he saw in the steady eyes fixed on him.

"No, I don't think you have," she said slowly.

"How the deuce should a man look, then?" cried Tom, rather nettled at her sober reception of the grand news.

"As if he had learned to care for someone a great deal more than for himself," answered Polly, with sudden color in her cheeks and a sudden softening of the voice as her eyes turned away from Tom, who was the picture of a complacent dandy, from the topmost curl of his auburn head to the tips of his aristocratic boots.

"Tommy's quenched,* I agree with you, Polly. I never liked Trix, and I hope it's only a boy-and-girl fancy that will soon die a natural death," said Mr. Shaw, who seemed to find it difficult to help falling into a brown study in spite of the lively chatter going on about him.

---

* The word *quenched* here means "squelched." Miss Alcott used the word in a similar way in *Little Women:* "Jo quenched her by slamming down the window" (vol. 1, ch. 6).

Shaw, Jr., being highly incensed at the disrespectful manner in which his engagement was treated, tried to assume a superb air of indifference, and finding that a decided failure, was about to stroll out of the room with a comprehensive nod when his mother called after him.

"Where are you going, dear?"

"To see Trix, of course. Good-bye, Polly." And Mr. Thomas departed, hoping that by the skillful change of tone, from ardent impatience to condescending coolness, he had impressed one hearer at least with the fact that he regarded Trix as the star of his existence and Polly as a presuming little chit.

If he could have heard her laugh, and Fanny's remarks, his wrath would have boiled over. Fortunately he was spared the trial and went away hoping that the coquetries of his Trix would make him forget Polly's look when she answered his question.

"My dear, that boy is the most deluded creature you ever saw," began Fanny as soon as the front door banged. "Belle and Trix both tried to catch him, and the slyest got him, for, in spite of his airs, he is as soft-hearted as a baby. You see Trix has broken off two engagements already, and the third time she got jilted herself. Such a fuss as she made! I declare, it really was absurd. But I do think she felt it very much, for she wouldn't go out at all, and got thin and pale and blue, and was really quite touching. I pitied her, and had her here a good deal, and Tom took her part. He always does stand up for the crushed ones, and that's good of him, I allow. Well, she did the forsaken very prettily, let Tom amuse her, and led him on till the poor fellow lost his wits, and finding her crying one day—about her hat, which wasn't becoming —he thought she was mourning for Mr. Banks, and so, to comfort her, the goose proposed. That was all she wanted.

She snapped him up at once, and there he is in a nice scrape, for since her engagement she is as gay as ever, flirts awfully with anyone who comes along, and keeps Tom in a fume all the time. I really don't think he cares for her half as much as he makes believe, but he'll stand by her through thick and thin rather than do as Banks did."

"Poor Tom!" was all Polly said when Fan had poured the story into her ear as they sat whispering in the sofa corner.

"My only consolation is that Trix will break off the affair before spring. She always does so that she may be free for the summer campaign. It won't hurt Tom, but I hate to have him make a fool of himself out of pity, for he is more of a man than he seems, and I don't want anyone to plague him."

"No one but yourself," said Polly, smiling.

"Well, that's all fair, he *is* a torment sometimes, but I'm rather fond of him in spite of it. I get so tired of the other fellows, they *are* such absurd things, and when Tom is in his good mood he is very nice and quite refreshing."

"I'm glad to hear it," said Polly, making a mental note of the fact.

"Yes, and when Grandma was ill he was perfectly devoted. I didn't know the boy had so much gentleness in him. He took her death sadly to heart, for, though he didn't say much, he was very grave and steady for a long time. I tried to comfort him, and we had two or three real sweet little talks together and seemed to get acquainted for the first time. It was very nice, but it didn't last. Good times never do with us. We soon got back into the old way, and now we hector one another just as before."

Fanny sighed, then yawned, and fell into her usual listless attitude, as if the brief excitement of Polly's coming had begun to subside.

"Walk home with me and see my funny little room. It's bright now, and the air will do you good. Come, both of you, and have a frolic as we used to," said Polly, for the red sunset now burning in the west seemed to invite them out.

They agreed, and soon the three were walking briskly away to Polly's new home in a quiet street where a few old trees rustled in the summer and the morning sun shone pleasantly in wintertime.

> "The way into my parlor
> Is up a winding stair,"

sang Polly, running up two flights of broad, old-fashioned steps and opening the door of a back room, out of which streamed the welcome glow of firelight.

"These are my pets, Maud," she added, pausing on the threshold and beckoning the girls to look in quietly.

On the rug, luxuriously basking in the warmth, lay a gray kitten, and close by, meditatively roosting on one leg, stood a plump canary, who cocked his bright eye at the newcomers, gave a loud chirp as if to wake his comrade, and then flew straight to Polly's shoulder, where he broke into a joyful song to welcome his mistress home.

"Allow me to introduce my family," said Polly. "This noisy little chap the boys named Nicodemus, and this dozy cat is called Ashputtel because the joy of her life is to get among the cinders. Now, take off your things and let me do the honors, for you are to stop to tea and the carriage is to come for you at eight. I arranged it with your mother while you were upstairs."

"I want to see *everything*," said Maud when the hats were off and the hands warmed.

"So you shall, for I think my housekeeping arrangements will amuse you."

Then Polly showed her kingdom, and the three had a merry time over it. The big piano took up so much room there was no place for a bed, but Polly proudly displayed the resources of her chintz-covered couch, for the back let down, the seat lifted up, and inside were all the pillows and blankets. "So convenient, you see, and yet out of the way in the daytime, for two or three of my pupils come to me," explained Polly.

Then there was a bright drugget over the faded carpet, the little rocking chair and sewing table stood at one window, the ivy ran all over the other and hid the banqueting performances which went on in that corner. Bookshelves hung over the sofa, a picture or two on the walls, and a great vase of autumn leaves and grasses beautified the low chimney-piece. It was a very humble little room, but Polly had done her best to make it pleasant, and it already had a homelike look, with the cheery fire and the household pets chirping and purring confidingly on the rug.

"How nice it is!" exclaimed Maud as she emerged from the big closet where Polly kept her stores. "Such a cunning teakettle and saucepan, and a tête-à-tête set, and lots of good things to eat. Do have toast for tea, Polly, and let me make it with the new toasting fork. It's such fun to play cook."

Fanny was not so enthusiastic as her sister, for her eyes saw many traces of what seemed like poverty to her, but Polly was so gay, so satisfied with her small establishment, so full of happy hopes and plans that her friend had not the heart to find a fault or suggest an improvement and sat where she was told, laughing and talking while the others got tea.

"This will be a country supper, girls," said Polly, bustling about. "Here is real cream, brown bread, homemade cake, and honey from my own beehives. Mother fitted me out with such a supply, I'm glad to have a party, for I can't eat it all quick enough. Butter the toast, Maudie, and put that little cover over it. Tell me when the kettle boils, and don't step on Nicodemus, whatever you do."

"What a capital housekeeper you will make someday," said Fanny as she watched Polly spread her table with a neatness and dispatch which was pleasant to behold.

"Yes, it's good practice," laughed Polly, filling her tiny teapot and taking her place behind the tray with a matronly air, which was the best joke of the whole.

"This is the most delicious party I ever went to," observed Maud, with her mouth full of honey, when the feast was well under way. "I do wish I could have a nice room like this, and a cat and a bird that wouldn't eat each other up, and a dear little teakettle, and make just as much toast as I like."

Such a peal of laughter greeted Maud's pensive aspiration that Miss Mills smiled over her solitary cup of tea, and little Nick burst into a perfect ecstasy of song as he sat on the sugar bowl helping himself.

"I don't care for the toast and the kettle, but I do envy you your good spirits, Polly," said Fanny as the merriment subsided. "I'm so tired of everybody and everything, it seems sometimes as if I should die of *ennui*. Don't you ever feel so?"

"Things worry me sometimes, but I just catch up a broom and sweep, or wash hard, or walk, or go at something with all my might, and I usually find that by the time I get through the worry is gone, or I've got courage enough to bear it without grumbling," answered Polly, cutting the brown loaf energetically.

"I can't do those things, you know. There's no need of it, and I don't think they'd cure my worrying," said Fanny, languidly feeding Ashputtel, who sat decorously beside her at the table winking at the cream pot.

"A little poverty would do you good, Fan, just enough necessity to keep you busy till you find how good work is, and when you once learn that, you won't complain of *ennui* anymore," returned Polly, who had taken kindly the hard lesson which twenty years of cheerful poverty had taught her.

"Mercy, no, I should hate that, but I wish someone would invent a new amusement for rich people. I'm dead sick of parties and flirtations, trying to outdress my neighbors, and going the same round year after year, like a squirrel in a cage."

Fanny's tone was bitter as well as discontented, her face sad as well as listless, and Polly had an instinctive feeling that some trouble, more real than any she had ever known before, was lying heavy at her friend's heart. That was not the time to speak of it, but Polly resolved to stand ready to offer sympathy, if nothing more, whenever the confidential minute came, and her manner was so kind, so comfortable, that Fanny felt its silent magic, grew more cheerful in the quiet atmosphere of that little room, and when they said good night, after an old-time gossip by the fire, she kissed her hostess warmly, saying, with a grateful look:

"Polly, dear, I shall come often, you do me so much good."

Chapter 9

Lessons

*T*he first few weeks were hard ones, for Polly had not yet outgrown her natural shyness, and going among so many strangers caused her frequent panics. But her purpose gave her courage, and when the ice was once broken her little pupils quickly learned to love her. The novelty soon wore off, and though she thought she was prepared for drudgery, she found it very tedious to go on doing the same thing day after day. Then she was lonely, for Will could only come once a week, her leisure hours were Fanny's busiest, and the "bits of pleasure" were so few and far between that they only tantalized her. Even her small housekeeping lost its charms, for Polly was a social creature, and the solitary meals were often sad ones. Ashputtel and Nick did their best to cheer her, but they, too, seemed to pine for country freedom and home atmosphere. Poor Puttel, after gazing wistfully out of the window at the gaunt city cats skulking about the yard, would retire to the rug and curl herself up as if all hope of finding congenial society had failed, while little Nick would sing till he vibrated on his perch without receiving any response except an inquisitive chirp from the pert sparrows, who seemed to twit him with his captivity. Yes, by the time the little teakettle had lost its brightness, Polly had decided that getting one's living was no joke, and many of her brilliant hopes had shared the fate of the little kettle.

If one could only make the sacrifice all at once and be done with it, then it would seem easier, but to keep up a daily sacrifice of one's wishes, tastes, and pleasures is rather a hard task, especially when one is pretty, young, and gay. Lessons all day, a highly instructive lecture, books over a solitary fire, or music with no audience but a sleepy cat and a bird with his head tucked under his wing for evening entertainment was not exactly what might be called festive, so, in spite of her brave resolutions, Polly did long for a little fun sometimes, and after saying virtuously to herself at nine, "Yes, it is much wiser and better for me to go to bed early and be ready for work tomorrow," she would lie awake hearing the carriages roll to and fro and imagining the gay girls inside going to party, opera, or play till Mrs. Dodd's hop pillow might as well have been stuffed with nettles for any sleep it brought or any use it was, except to catch and hide the tears that dropped on it when Polly's heart was very full.

Another thorn that wounded our Polly in her first attempt to make her way through the thicket that always bars a woman's progress was the discovery that working for a living shuts a good many doors in one's face even in democratic America. As Fanny's guest she had been, in spite of poverty, kindly received wherever her friend took her, both as child and woman. Now, things were changed. The kindly people patronized, the careless forgot all about her, and even Fanny, with all her affection, felt that Polly the music teacher would not be welcome in many places where Polly the young lady had been accepted as "Miss Shaw's friend."

Some of the girls still nodded amiably, but never invited her to visit them; others merely dropped their eyelids and went by without speaking, while a good many ignored her as entirely as if she had been invisible. These things hurt Polly more than she would confess, for at home everyone worked, and everyone was respected for it. She tried not to care, but girls feel little slights keenly, and more than once Polly was severely tempted to give up her plan and run away to the safe shelter at home.

Fanny never failed to ask her to every sort of festivity in the Shaw mansion, but after a few trials Polly firmly declined everything but informal visits when the family were alone. She soon found that even the new black silk wasn't fine enough for Fanny's smallest party, and after receiving a few of the expressive glances by which women convey their opinion of their neighbor's toilet, and overhearing a joke or two "about that inevitable dress" and "the little blackbird," Polly folded away the once-treasured frock, saying, with a choke in her voice:

"I'll wear it for Will, he likes it, and clothes can't change his love for me."

I am afraid the wholesome sweetness of Polly's nature was getting a little soured by these troubles, but before lasting harm was done she received, from an unexpected source, some of the real help which teaches young people how to bear these small crosses by showing them the heavier ones they have escaped and by giving them an idea of the higher pleasures one may earn in the good old-fashioned ways that keep hearts sweet, heads sane, hands busy.

Everybody has their days of misfortune like little Rosa-

mond,* and Polly was beginning to think she had more than
her share. One of these ended in a way which influenced her
whole life, and so we will record it. It began early, for the
hard-hearted little grate wouldn't behave itself till she had
used up a ruinous quantity of kindling. Then she scalded
poor Puttel by upsetting her coffeepot, and instead of a leisurely, cozy meal had to hurry away uncomfortably, for everything went wrong even to the coming off of both bonnet
strings in the last dreadful scramble. Being late, she of course
forgot her music, and hurrying back for it, fell into a puddle,
which capped the climax of her despair.

Such a trying morning as that was! Polly felt out of tune
herself, and all the pianos seemed to need a tuner as much as
she did. The pupils were unusually stupid, and two of them
announced that their mama was going to take them to the
South, whither they were suddenly called. This was a blow,
for they had just begun, and Polly hadn't the face to send in
a bill for a whole quarter, though her plans and calculations
were sadly disturbed by the failure of that sum.

Trudging home to dinner, tired and disappointed, poor
Polly received another blow, which hurt her more than the
loss of all her pupils. As she went hurrying along with a big
music book in one hand and a paper bag of rolls for tea in
the other, she saw Tom and Trix coming. As she watched
them while they slowly approached, looking so gay and
handsome and happy, it seemed to Polly as if all the sunshine and good walking was on their side of the street, all the
wintry wind and mud on hers. Longing to see a friendly face
and receive a kind word, she crossed over, meaning to nod
and smile at least. Trix saw her first and suddenly became

---

* *Rosamond,* a novel by Irish writer Maria Edgeworth (1767–1849).

absorbed in the distant horizon. Tom apparently did not see her, for his eyes were fixed on a fine horse just prancing by. Polly thought that he *had* seen her and approached with a curious little flutter at her heart, for if Tom cut her she felt that her cup would be full.

On they came, Trix intent on the view, Tom staring at the handsome horse, and Polly, with red cheeks, expectant eyes, and the brown bundle, in full sight. One dreadful minute as they came parallel, and no one spoke or bowed—then it was all over, and Polly went on, feeling as if someone had slapped her in the face. "She wouldn't have believed it of Tom. It was all the doings of that horrid Trix. Well, she wouldn't trouble him anymore if he was such a snob as to be ashamed of her just because she carried bundles and worked for her bread." She clutched the paper bag fiercely as she said this to herself, then her eyes filled and her lips trembled as she added, "How could he do it, before her too?"

Now Tom was quite guiltless of this offense and had always nodded to Polly when they met, but it so happened he had always been alone till now, and that was why it cut so deeply, especially as Polly never had approved of Trix. Before she could clear her eyes or steady her face, a gentleman met her, lifted his hat, smiled, and said pleasantly:

"Good morning, Miss Polly, I'm glad to meet you." Then, with a sudden change of voice and manner, he added, "I beg pardon—is anything the matter—can I be of service?"

It was very awkward, but it couldn't be helped, and all Polly could do was to tell the truth and make the best of it.

"It's very silly, but it hurts me to be cut by my old friends. I shall get used to it presently, I daresay."

Mr. Sydney glanced back, recognized the couple behind them, and turned round with a disgusted expression. Polly was fumbling for her handkerchief, and without a word he took both book and bundle from her, a little bit of kindness that meant a good deal just then. Polly felt it, and it did her good. Hastily wiping the traitorous eyes, she laughed and said cheerfully:

"There, I'm all right again. Thank you, don't trouble yourself with my parcels."

"No trouble, I assure you, and this book reminds me of what I was about to say. Have you an hour to spare for my little niece? Her mother wants her to begin and desired me to make the inquiry."

"Did she, really?" And Polly looked up at him as if she suspected him of inventing the whole thing out of kindness.

Mr. Sydney smiled, and taking a note from his pocket, presented it, saying, with a reproachful look:

"Behold the proof of my truth, and never doubt again."

Polly begged pardon, read the note from the little girl's mother, which was to have been left at her room if she was absent, and gave the bearer a very grateful look as she accepted this welcome addition to her pupils. Well pleased at the success of his mission, Sydney artfully led the conversation to music, and for a time Polly forgot her woes, talking enthusiastically on her favorite theme. As she reclaimed her book and bag at her own door, she said, in her honest way:

"Thank you very much for trying to make me forget my foolish little troubles."

"Then let me say one thing more. Though appearances are against them, I don't believe Tom Shaw saw you. Miss Trix is equal to that sort of thing, but it isn't like Tom, for with all his foppery he is a good fellow at heart."

As Mr. Sydney said this Polly held out her hand with a hearty "Thank you for that." The young man shook the little hand in the gray woollen glove, gave her exactly the same bow which he did the Honorable Mrs. Davenport, and

went away, leaving Polly to walk upstairs and address Puttel
with the peculiar remark:

"You are a true gentleman! So kind to say that about
Tom. I'll think it's so, anyway, and won't I teach Minnie in
my very best style!"

Puttel purred, Nick chirped approvingly, and Polly ate her
dinner with a better appetite than she had expected. But at
the bottom of her heart there was a sore spot still, and the
afternoon lessons dragged dismally. It was dusk when she got
home, and as she sat in the firelight eating her bread and
milk, several tears bedewed the little rolls, and even the
home honey had a bitter taste.

"Now this won't do," she broke out all at once. "This is
silly and wicked, and can't be allowed. I'll try the old plan
and put myself right by doing some little kindness to somebody. Now what shall it be? Oh, I know! Fan is going to a
party tonight. I'll run up and help her dress. She likes to
have me, and I enjoy seeing the pretty things. Yes, and I'll
take her two or three clusters of my daphne, it's so sweet."

Up got Polly, and taking her little posy, trotted away to
the Shaws', determined to be happy and contented in spite
of Trix and hard work.

She found Fanny enduring torment under the hands of
the hairdresser, who was doing his best to spoil her hair and
distort her head with a mass of curls, braids, frizzles, and
puffs, for though I discreetly refrain from any particular description, still, judging from the present fashions, I think one
may venture to predict that six years hence they would be
something frightful.

"How kind of you, Polly. I was just wishing you were here
to arrange my flowers. These lovely daphnes will give odor to
my camellias, and you were a dear to bring them. There's my

dress. How do you like it?" said Fanny, hardly daring to lift
her eyes from under the yellow tower on her head.

"It's regularly splendid, but how do you ever get into it?"
answered Polly, surveying with girlish interest the cloud of
pink and white lace that lay upon the bed.

"It's fearfully and wonderfully made, but distractingly becoming, as you shall see. Trix thinks I'm going to wear blue,
so she has got a green one and told Belle it would spoil the
effect of mine, as we are much together, of course. Wasn't
that sweet of her? Belle came and told me in time, and I just
got pink so my amiable sister, that is to be, won't succeed in
her pretty little plot."

"I guess she has been reading the life of Josephine. You
know she made a pretty lady of whom she was jealous sit
beside her on a green sofa, which set off her own white dress
and spoilt the blue one of her guest," answered Polly, busy
with the flowers.

"Trix never reads anything. You are the one to pick up
clever little stories. I'll remember and use this one. Am I
done? Yes, that is charming, isn't it, Polly?" and Fan rose to
inspect the success of Monsieur's long labor.

"You know I don't appreciate a stylish coiffure as I ought,
so I like your hair in the old way best. But this is 'the thing,'
I suppose, and not a word must be said."

"Of course it is. Why, child, I have frizzed and burnt my
hair so that I look like an old maniac with it in its natural
state and have to repair damages as well as I can. Now put
the flowers just here." And Fanny laid a pink camellia in a
nest of fuzz and stuck a spray of daphne straight up at the
back of her head.

"Oh, Fan, don't, it looks horridly so!" cried Polly, longing
to add a little beauty to her friend's sallow face by a graceful
adjustment of the flowers.

"Can't help it, that's the way, and so it must be," answered Fan, planting another sprig halfway up the tower.

Polly groaned and offered no more suggestions as the work went on, but when Fan was finished from top to toe, she admired all she honestly could, and tried to keep her thoughts to herself. But her frank face betrayed her, for Fanny turned on her suddenly, saying:

"You may as well free your mind, Polly, for I see by your eyes that something don't suit."

"I was only thinking of what Grandma once said, that 'modesty had gone out of fashion,'" answered Polly, glancing at the waist of her friend's dress, which consisted of a belt, a bit of lace, and a pair of shoulder straps.

Fanny laughed good-naturedly, saying, as she clasped her necklace, "If I had such shoulders as yours, I shouldn't care what the fashion was. Now don't preach, but put my cloak on nicely and come along, for I'm to meet Tom and Trix and promised to be there early."

Polly was to be left at home after depositing Fan at Belle's.

"I feel as if I was going myself," she said as they rolled along.

"I wish you were, and you would be, Polly, if you weren't such a resolute thing. I've teased, and begged, and offered anything I have if you'll only break your absurd vow and come and enjoy yourself."

"Thank you, but I won't, so don't trouble your kind heart about me. I'm all right," said Polly stoutly.

But when they drew up before the lighted house, and she found herself in the midst of the pleasant stir of festivity, the coming and going of carriages, the glimpses of bright colors, forms, and faces, the bursts of music, and a general atmosphere of gaiety, Polly felt that she wasn't all right, and as she drove away for a dull evening in her lonely little room, she just cried as heartily as any child denied a stick of candy.

"It's dreadful wicked of me, but I can't help it," she sobbed to herself in the corner of the carriage. "That music sets me all in a twitter, and I should have looked nice in Fan's blue tarlatan, and I know I could behave as well as anyone, and have lots of partners, though I'm not in that set. Oh, just one good gallop with Mr. Sydney or Tom! No, Tom wouldn't ask me there, and I wouldn't accept if he did. Oh, me! Oh, me! I wish I was as old and homely and good and happy as Miss Mills!"

So Polly made her moan, and by the time she got home was just in the mood to go to bed and cry herself to sleep, as girls have a way of doing when their small affliction becomes unbearable.

But Polly didn't get a chance to be miserable very long, for as she went upstairs feeling like the most injured girl in the world, she caught a glimpse of Miss Mills, sewing away with such a bright face that she couldn't resist stopping for a word or two.

"Sit down, my dear, I'm glad to see you, but excuse me if I go on with my work, as I'm in a driving hurry to get these things done tonight," said the brisk little lady with a smile and a nod as she took a new needleful of thread and ran up a seam as if for a wager.

"Let me help you, then. I'm lazy and cross, and it will do me good," said Polly, sitting down with the resigned feeling. "Well, if I can't be happy, I can be useful, perhaps."

"Thank you, my dear. Yes, you can just hem the skirt while I put in the sleeves, and that will be a great lift."

Polly put on her thimble in silence, but as Miss Mills spread the white flannel over her lap she exclaimed, "Why, it looks like a shroud! Is it one?"

"No, dear, thank God, it isn't, but it might have been if we hadn't saved the poor little soul," cried Miss Mills with a sudden brightening of the face, which made it beautiful in spite of the stiff gray curl that bobbed on each temple, the want of teeth, and a crooked nose.

"Will you tell me about it? I like to hear your adventures and good works so much," said Polly, ready to be amused by anything that made her forget herself.

"Ah, my dear, it's a very common story, and that's the saddest part of it. I'll tell you all about it, for I think you may be able to help me. Last night I watched with poor Mary Floyd. She's dying of consumption, you know," began Miss Mills as her nimble fingers flew and her kind old face beamed over the work as if she put a blessing in with every stitch. "Mary was very low, but about midnight fell asleep, and I was trying to keep things quiet when Mrs. Finn—she's the woman of the house—came and beckoned me out with a scared face. 'Little Jane has killed herself, and I don't know what to do,' she said, leading me up to the attic."

"Who was little Jane?" broke in Polly, dropping her work.

"I only knew her as a pale, shy young girl who went in and out and seldom spoke to anyone. Mrs. Finn told me she was poor, but a busy, honest little thing who didn't mix with the other folks but lived and worked alone. 'She has looked so downhearted and pale for a week that I thought she was sick and asked her about it,' said Mrs. Finn, 'but she thanked me in her bashful way and said she was pretty well, so I let her alone. But tonight, as I went up late to bed, I was kind of impressed to look in and see how the poor thing did, for she hadn't left her room all day. I did look in, and here's what I found.' As Mrs. Finn ended she opened the door of the back attic and I saw about as sad a sight as these old eyes ever looked at."

"Oh, what?" cried Polly, pale now with interest.

"A bare room, cold as a barn, and on the bed a little dead, white face that almost broke my heart, it was so thin, so patient, and so young. On the table was a bottle half full of laudanum, an old pocketbook, and a letter. Read that, my dear, and don't think hard of little Jane."

Polly took the bit of paper Miss Mills gave her and read these words:

> DEAR MRS. FINN—Please forgive me for the trouble I make you, but I don't see any other way. I can't get work that pays enough to keep me. The Dr. says I can't be well unless I rest. I hate to be a burden, so I'm going away not to trouble anybody anymore. I've sold my things to pay what I owe you. Please let me be as I am, and don't let people come and look at me. I hope it isn't very wicked, but there don't seem any room for me in the world, and I'm not afraid to die now, though I should be if I stayed and got bad because I hadn't strength to keep right. Give my love to the baby, and so good-bye, good-bye.
>
> JANE BRYANT.

"Oh, Miss Mills, how dreadful!" cried Polly, with her eyes so full she could hardly read the little letter.

"Not so dreadful as it might have been, but a bitter, sad thing to see that child, only seventeen, lying there in her little clean, old nightgown waiting for death to come and take her because there didn't seem to be any room for her in the world. Ah, well, we saved her, for it wasn't too late, thank heaven, and the first thing she said was, 'Oh, why did you bring me back?' I've been nursing her all day, hearing her story, and trying to show her that there *is* room and a welcome for her. Her mother died a year ago, and since then she has been struggling along alone. She is one of the timid, innocent, humble creatures who can't push their way and so get put aside and forgotten. She has tried all sorts of poorly paid work, couldn't live on it decently, got discouraged, sick, frightened, and could see no refuge from the big, bad world but to get out of it while she wasn't afraid to die. A very old story, my dear, new and dreadful as it seems to you, and I think it won't do you any harm to see and help this little girl who has gone through dark places that you are never like to know."

"I will. Indeed, I will do all I can! Where is she now?" asked Polly, touched to the heart by the story, so simple yet so sad.

"There." And Miss Mills pointed to the door of her own little bedroom. "She was well enough to be moved tonight so I brought her home and laid her safely in my bed. Poor little soul! She looked about her for a minute, then the lost look went away, and she gave a great sigh and took my hand in both her thin bits of ones and said, "Oh, ma'am, I feel as if I'd been born into a new world. Help me to begin again, and I'll do better.' So I told her she was my child now and might rest here, sure of a home as long as I had one."

As Miss Mills spoke in her motherly tone, and cast a proud and happy look toward the warm and quiet nest in which she had sheltered this friendless little sparrow, feeling sure that God meant her to keep it from falling to the ground, Polly put both arms about her neck and kissed her withered cheek with as much loving reverence as if she had been a splendid saint, for in the likeness of this plain old maid she saw the lovely charity that blesses and saves the world.

"How good you are! Dear Miss Mills, tell me what to do, let me help you, I'm ready for anything," said Polly very humbly, for her own troubles looked so small and foolish beside the stern hardships which had nearly had so tragical an end that she felt heartily ashamed of herself and quite burned to atone for them.

Miss Mills stopped to stroke the fresh cheek opposite, to smile and say:

"Then, Polly, I think I'll ask you to go in and say a friendly word to my little girl. The sight of you will do her good, and you have just the right way of comforting people without making a fuss."

"Have I?" said Polly, looking much gratified by the words.

"Yes, dear, you've the gift of sympathy and the rare art of showing it without offending. I wouldn't let many girls in to see my poor Jenny because they'd only flutter and worry her, but you'll know what to do, so go, and take this wrapper with you, it's done now, thanks to your nimble fingers."

Polly threw the warm garment over her arm, feeling a thrill of gratitude that it was to wrap a living girl in and not to hide away a young heart that had grown cold too soon. Pushing open the door, she went quietly into the dimly lighted room and on the pillow saw a face that drew her to it with an irresistible power, for it was touched by a solemn shadow that made its youth pathetic. As she paused at the bedside, thinking the girl asleep, a pair of hollow, dark eyes opened wide and looked up at her, startled at first, then softening with pleasure at sight of the bonny face before them, and then a humble, beseeching expression filled them, as if asking pardon for the rash act nearly committed and pity for the hard fate that prompted it. Polly read the language of these eyes and answered their mute prayer with a simple eloquence that said more than any words, for she just stooped down and kissed the poor child, with her own eyes full and lips that trembled with the sympathy she could not tell. Jenny put both arms about her neck and began to shed the quiet tears that so refresh and comfort heavy hearts when a tender touch unseals the fountain where they lie.

"Everybody is so kind," she sobbed, "and I was so wicked, I don't deserve it."

"Oh, yes, you do, don't think of that, but rest and let us pet you. The old life was too hard for such a little thing as you, and we are going to try and make the new one ever so much easier and happier," said Polly, forgetting everything except that this was a girl like herself who needed heartening up.

"Do you live here?" asked Jenny when her tears were wiped away, still clinging to the newfound friend.

"Yes, Miss Mills lets me have a little room upstairs, and there I have my cat and bird, my piano and my posy pots, and live like a queen. You must come up and see me tomorrow if you are able. I'm often lonely, for there are no young people in the house to play with me," answered Polly, smiling hospitably.

"Do you sew?" asked Jenny.

"No, I'm a music teacher and trot round giving lessons all day."

"How beautiful it sounds, and how happy you must be, so strong and pretty, and able to go round making music all the time," sighed Jenny, looking with respectful admiration at the plump, firm hand held in both her thin and feeble ones.

It did sound pleasant even to Polly's ears, and she felt suddenly so rich, and so contented, that she seemed a different creature from the silly girl who cried because she couldn't go to the party. It passed through her mind like a flash, the contrast between her life and that of the wan creature lying before her, and she felt as if she could not give enough out of her abundance to this needy little sister who had nothing in the wide world but the life just saved to her. That minute did more for Polly than many sermons or the wisest books, for it brought her face-to-face with bitter truths, showed her the dark side of life, and seemed to blow away her little vanities, her frivolous desires, like a wintry wind that left a wholesome atmosphere behind. Sitting on the bedside, Polly listened while Jane told the story, which was so new to her listener that every word sank deep into her heart and never was forgotten.

"Now you must go to sleep. Don't cry nor think, nor do anything but rest. That will please Miss Mills best. I'll leave the doors open and play you a lullaby that you can't resist. Good night, dear." And with another kiss Polly went away to sit in the darkness of her own room, playing her softest airs till the tired eyes below were shut, and little Jenny seemed to float away on a sea of pleasant sounds into the happier life which had just dawned for her.

Polly had fully intended to be very miserable and cry herself to sleep, but when she lay down at last her pillow seemed very soft, her little room very lovely, with the firelight flickering on all the homelike objects and her new-blown roses breathing her a sweet good night. She no longer felt an injured, hardworking, unhappy Polly, but as if quite burdened with blessings for which she wasn't half grateful enough. She had heard of poverty and suffering, in the vague, far-off way which is all that many girls, safe in happy homes, ever know of it, but now she had seen it in a shape which she could feel and understand, and life grew more earnest to her from that minute. So much to do in the great, busy world, and she had done so little. Where should she begin? Then, like an answer came little Jenny's thoughts, now taking a new significance to Polly's mind: to be strong, and beautiful, and go round making music all the time. Yes, she could do that, and with a very earnest prayer Polly asked for the strength of an upright soul, the beauty of a tender heart, the power to make her life a sweet and stirring song, helpful while it lasted, remembered when it died.

Little Jenny's last thought had been to wish with all her might that "God would bless the dear, kind girl up there and give her all she asked." I think both prayers, although too humble to be put in words, went up together, for in the fullness of time they were beautifully answered.

Chapter 10

Brothers and Sisters

*P*olly's happiest day was Sunday, for Will never failed to spend it with her. Instead of sleeping later than usual that morning, she was always up bright and early, flying round to get ready for her guest, for Will came to breakfast and they made a long day of it. Will considered his sister the best and prettiest girl going, and Polly, knowing well that a time would come when he would find a better and a prettier, was grateful for his good opinion and tried to deserve it. So she made her room and herself as neat and inviting as possible and always ran to meet him with a bright face and a motherly greeting when he came tramping in, ruddy, brisk, and beaming, with the brown loaf and the little pot of beans from the bakehouse nearby.

They liked a good country breakfast, and nothing gave Polly more satisfaction than to see her big boy clear the dishes, empty the little coffeepot, and then sit and laugh at her across the ravaged table. Another pleasure was to let him help clear away, as they used to do at home, while the peals of laughter that always accompanied this performance

did Miss Mills's heart good to hear, for the room was so
small and Will so big that he seemed to be everywhere at
once, and Polly and Puttel were continually dodging his long
arms and legs. Then they used to inspect the flowerpots, pay
Nick a visit, and have a little music as a good beginning for
the day, after which they went to church and dined with
Miss Mills, who considered Will "an excellent young man."
If the afternoon was fair, they took a long walk together over
the bridges into the country or about the city streets full of
Sabbath quietude. Most people meeting them would have
seen only an awkward young man, with a boy's face atop of
his tall body, and a quietly dressed, fresh-faced little woman
hanging on his arm, but a few people, with eyes to read
romances and pleasant histories everywhere, found something very attractive in this couple and smiled as they
passed, wondering if they were young lovers or country cousins "looking round."

If the day was stormy, they stayed at home, reading, writing letters, talking over their affairs, and giving each other
good advice, for, though Will was nearly three years younger
than Polly, he couldn't for the life of him help assuming
amusingly venerable airs when he became a freshman. In the
twilight he had a good lounge on the sofa and Polly sung to
him, which arrangement he particularly enjoyed, it was so
"cozy and homey." At nine o'clock Polly packed his bag
with clean clothes, nicely mended, such remnants of the festive tea as were transportable, and kissed him "good night,"
with many injunctions to muffle up his throat going over the
bridge and be sure that his feet were dry and warm when he
went to bed. All of which Will laughed at, accepted graciously, and didn't obey, but he liked it, and trudged away
for another week's work, rested, cheered, and strengthened
by that quiet, happy day with Polly, for he had been brought

up to believe in home influences, and this brother and sister loved one another dearly and were not ashamed to own it.

One other person enjoyed the humble pleasures of these Sundays quite as much as Polly and Will. Maud used to beg to come to tea, and Polly, glad to do anything for those who had done a good deal for her, made a point of calling for the little girl as they came home from their walk or sending Will to escort her in the carriage, which Maud always managed to secure if bad weather threatened to quench her hopes. Tom and Fanny laughed at her fancy, but she did not tire of it, for the child was lonely and found something in that little room which the great house could not give her.

Maud was twelve now, a pale, plain child, with sharp, intelligent eyes and a busy little mind that did a good deal more thinking than anybody imagined. She was just at the unattractive, fidgety age when no one knew what to do with her and so let her fumble her way up as she could, finding pleasure in odd things and living much alone, for she did not go to school because her shoulders were growing round, and Mrs. Shaw would not "allow her figure to be spoiled." That suited Maud excellently, and whenever her father spoke of sending her again or getting a governess, she was seized with bad headaches, a pain in her back, or weakness of the eyes, at which Mr. Shaw laughed but let her holiday go on. Nobody seemed to care much for plain, pug-nosed little Maudie. Her father was busy, her mother nervous and sick, Fanny absorbed in her own affairs, and Tom regarded her as most young men do their younger sisters, as a person born for his amusement and convenience, nothing more. Maud admired Tom with all her heart, and made a little slave of herself to him, feeling well repaid if he merely said, "Thank you, chicken," or didn't pinch her nose or nip her ear, as he had a way of doing, "Just as if I was a doll, or a

dog, and hadn't got any feelings," she sometimes said to
Fanny when some service or sacrifice had been accepted
without gratitude or respect. It never occurred to Tom, when
Maud sat watching him with her face full of wistfulness, that
she wanted to be petted as much as ever he did in his neglected boyhood, or that when he called her "Pug" before
people her little feelings were as deeply wounded as his used
to be when the boys called him "Carrots." He was fond of
her in his fashion, but he didn't take the trouble to show it,
so Maud worshiped him afar off, afraid to betray the affection that no rebuff could kill or cool.

One snowy Sunday afternoon Tom lay on the sofa in his
favorite attitude, reading *Pendennis* for the fourth time and
smoking like a chimney as he did so. Maud stood at the
window watching the falling flakes with an anxious countenance, and presently a great sigh broke from her.

"Don't do that again, chicken, or you'll blow me away.
What's the matter?" asked Tom, throwing down his book
with a yawn that threatened dislocation.

"I'm afraid I can't go to Polly's," answered Maud disconsolately.

"Of course you can't. It's snowing hard and Father won't
be home with the carriage till this evening. What are you
always cutting off to Polly's for?"

"I like it. We have such nice times, and Will is there, and
we bake little johnnycakes in the baker before the fire, and
they sing, and it is *so* pleasant."

"Warbling johnnycakes must be interesting. Come and
tell me all about it."

"No, you'll only laugh at me."

"I give you my word I won't if I can help it, but I really am
dying of curiosity to know what you do down there. You like

to hear secrets, so tell me yours, and I'll be as dumb as an oyster."

"It isn't a secret, and you wouldn't care for it. Do you want another pillow?" she added as Tom gave his a thump.

"This will do, but why you women always stick tassels and fringe all over a sofa cushion to tease and tickle a fellow is what I don't understand."

"One thing that Polly does Sunday nights is to take Will's head in her lap and smooth his forehead. It rests him after studying so hard, she says. If you don't like the pillow, I could do that for you, 'cause you look as if you were more tired of studying than Will," said Maud with some hesitation but an evident desire to be useful and agreeable.

"Well, I don't care if you do try it, for I *am* confoundedly tired." And Tom laughed as he recalled the frolic he had been on the night before.

Maud established herself with great satisfaction, and Tom owned that a silk apron *was* nicer than a fuzzy cushion.

"Do you like it?" she asked after a few strokes over the hot forehead, which she thought was fevered by intense application to Greek and Latin.

"Not bad, play away," was the gracious reply as Tom shut his eyes and lay so still that Maud was charmed at the success of her attempt. Presently, she said softly:

"Tom, are you asleep?"

"Just turning the corner."

"Before you get quite round would you please tell me what a public admonition is?"

"What do you want to know for?" demanded Tom, opening his eyes very wide.

"I heard Will talking about publics and privates, and I meant to ask him but I forgot."

"What did he say?"

"I don't remember. It was about somebody who cut prayers and got a private, and had done all sorts of bad things, and had one or two publics. I didn't hear the name and didn't care. I only wanted to know what the words meant."

"So Will tells tales, does he?" And Tom's forehead wrinkled with a frown.

"No, he didn't. Polly knew about it and asked him."

"Will's a 'dig,' " growled Tom, shutting his eyes again as if nothing more could be said of the delinquent William.

"I don't care if he is, I like him very much, and so does Polly."

"Happy fresh!" said Tom with a comical groan.

"You needn't sniff at him, for he *is* nice, and treats me with respect," cried Maud with an energy that made Tom laugh in her face.

"He's good to Polly always, and puts on her cloak for her, and says 'my dear,' and kisses her 'good-night,' and don't think it's silly, and I wish I had a brother just like him, yes, I do!" And Maud showed signs of woe, for her disappointment about going was very great.

"Bless my boots! What's the chicken ruffling up her little feathers and pecking at me for? Is that the way Polly soothes the best of brothers?" said Tom, still laughing.

"Oh, I forgot! There, I won't cry, but I do want to go." And Maud swallowed her tears and began to stroke again.

Now, Tom's horse and sleigh were in the stable, for he meant to drive out to college that evening, but he didn't take Maud's hint. It was less trouble to lie still and say in a conciliatory tone:

"Tell me some more about this good boy, it's very interesting."

"No, I shan't, but I'll tell about Puttel's playing on the

piano," said Maud, anxious to efface the memory of her momentary weakness. "Polly points to the right key with a little stick, and Puttel sits on the stool and pats each key as it's touched, and it makes a tune. It's so funny to see her, and Nick perches on the rack and sings as if he'd kill himself."

"Very thrilling," said Tom in a sleepy tone.

Maud felt that her conversation was not as interesting as she hoped and tried again.

"Polly thinks you are handsomer than Mr. Sydney."

"Much obliged."

"I asked which she thought had the nicest face, and she said yours was the handsomest and his the best."

"Does he ever go there?" asked a sharp voice behind them, and looking round, Maud saw Fanny in the big chair, cooking her feet over the register.

"I never saw him there. He sent up some books one day, and Will teased her about it."

"What did she do?" demanded Fanny.

"Oh, she shook him."

"What a spectacle!" And Tom looked as if he would have enjoyed seeing it, but Fanny's face grew so forbidding that Tom's little dog, who was approaching to welcome her, put his tail between his legs and fled under the table.

"Then there isn't any 'Sparking Sunday Night'?" sang Tom, who appeared to have waked up again.

"Of course not. Polly isn't going to marry anybody, she's going to keep house for Will when he's a minister, I heard her say so," cried Maud with importance.

"What a fate for pretty Polly!" ejaculated Tom.

"She likes it, and I'm sure I should think she would. It's beautiful to hear 'em plan it all out."

"Any more gossip to retail, Pug?" asked Tom a minute after, as Maud seemed absorbed in visions of the future.

"He told a funny story about blowing up one of the professors. You never told us, so I suppose you didn't know it. Some bad fellow put a torpedo, or some sort of powder thing, under the chair, and it went off in the midst of the lesson, and the poor man flew up, frightened most to pieces, and the boys ran with pails of water to put the fire out. But the thing that made Will laugh most was that the very fellow who did it got his trousers burned trying to put out the fire, and he asked the—is it faculty or president?"

"Either will do," murmured Tom, who was shaking with suppressed laughter.

"Well, he asked 'em to give him some new ones, and they did give him money enough for a nice pair, but he got some cheap ones, with horrid great stripes on 'em, and always wore 'em to that particular class, 'which was one too many for the fellows,' Will said, and with the rest of the money he had a punch party. Wasn't it dreadful?"

"Awful!" And Tom exploded into a great laugh that made Fanny cover her ears and the little dog bark wildly.

"Did you know that bad boy?" asked innocent Maud.

"Slightly," gasped Tom, in whose wardrobe at college those identical trousers were hanging at that moment.

"Don't make such a noise, my head aches dreadfully," said Fanny fretfully.

"Girls' heads always do ache," answered Tom, subsiding from a roar into a chuckle.

"What pleasure you boys can find in such ungentlemanly things, I don't see," said Fanny, who was evidently out of sorts.

"As much a mystery to you as it is to us how you girls can

like to gabble and prink from one week's end to the other," retorted Tom.

There was a pause after this little passage-at-arms, but Fan wanted to be amused, for time hung heavily on her hands, so she asked, in a more amiable tone:

"How's Trix?"

"As sweet as ever," answered Tom gruffly.

"Did she scold you, as usual?"

"She just did."

"What was the matter?"

"Well, I'll leave it to you if this isn't unreasonable. She won't dance with me herself, yet don't like me to go it with anybody else. I said I thought if a fellow took a girl to a party, she ought to dance with him once, at least, especially if they were engaged. She said that was the very reason why she shouldn't do it, so at the last hop I let her alone, and had a gay time with Belle, and today Trix gave it to me hot and heavy, coming home from church."

"If you go and engage yourself to a girl like that, I don't know what you can expect. Did she wear her Paris hat today?" added Fan with sudden interest in her voice.

"She wore some sort of a blue thing, with a confounded bird of paradise in it, that kept whisking into my face every time she turned her head."

"Men never know a pretty thing when they see it. That hat is perfectly lovely."

"They know a lady when they see her, and Trix don't look like one. I can't say where the trouble is, but there's too much fuss and feathers for my taste. You are twice as stylish, yet you never look loud or fast."

Touched by this unusual compliment, Fanny drew her chair nearer as she replied with complacency:

"Yes, I flatter myself I do know how to dress well. Trix

never did. She's fond of gay colors and generally looks like a walking rainbow."

"Can't you give her a hint? Tell her not to wear blue gloves anyway, she knows I hate 'em."

"I've done my best for your sake, Tom, but she is a perverse creature and don't mind a word I say, even about things much more objectionable than blue gloves."

"Maudie, run and bring me my other cigar case, it's lying round somewhere."

Maud went, and as soon as the door was shut Tom rose on his elbow, saying in a cautiously lowered voice:

"Fan, does Trix paint?"

"Yes, and draws too," answered Fanny with a sly laugh.

"Come, you know what I mean. I've a right to ask and you ought to tell," said Tom soberly, for he was beginning to find that being engaged was not unmitigated bliss.

"What makes you think she does?"

"Well, between ourselves," said Tom, looking a little sheepish, but anxious to set his mind at rest, "she never will let me kiss her on her cheek, nothing but an unsatisfactory peck at her lips. Then the other day, as I took a bit of heliotrope out of a vase to put in my buttonhole, I whisked a drop of water into her face. I was going to wipe it off, but she pushed my hand away and ran to the glass, where she carefully dabbed it dry, and came back with one cheek redder than the other. I didn't say anything, but I had my suspicions. Come now, does she?"

"Yes, she does, but don't say a word to her, for she'll never forgive my telling if she knew it."

"I don't care for that. I don't like it and I won't have it," said Tom decidedly.

"You can't help yourself. Half the girls do it, either paint or powder, darken their lashes with burnt hairpins, or take cologne on lumps of sugar or belladonna to make their eyes bright. Clara tried arsenic for her complexion, but her mother stopped it," said Fanny, betraying the secrets of the prison house in the basest manner.

"I knew you girls were a set of humbugs, and very pretty ones, too, some of you, but I can't say I like to see you painted up like a lot of actresses," said Tom with an air of disgust.

"*I* don't do anything of the sort, or need it, but Trix does, and having chosen her, you must abide your choice for better or worse."

"It hasn't come to that yet," muttered Tom as he lay down again with a rebellious air.

Maud's return put an end to these confidences, though Tom excited her curiosity by asking the mysterious question: "I say, Fan, is Polly up to that sort of thing?"

"No, she thinks it's awful. When she gets pale and dragged out she will probably change her mind."

"I doubt it," said Tom.

"Polly says it isn't proper to talk secrets before people who ain't in 'em," observed Maud with dignity.

"Do, for mercy sake, stop talking about Polly. I'm sick to death of it," cried Fanny snappishly.

"Hullo!" And Tom sat up to take a survey. "I thought you were bosom friends and as spoony as ever."

"Well, I am fond of Polly, but I get tired of hearing Maud sing her praises everlastingly. Now don't go and repeat that, chatterbox."

"My goodness, isn't she cross?" whispered Maud to Tom.

"As two sticks. Let her be. There's the bell. See who it is, Pug," answered Tom as a tinkle broke the silence of the house.

Maud went to peep over the banisters and came flying back in a rapture.

"It's Will come for me! Can't I go? It don't snow hard, and I'll bundle up, and you can send for me when Papa comes."

"I don't care what you do," answered Fan, who was in a very bad temper.

Without waiting for any other permission, Maud rushed away to get ready. Will wouldn't come up, he was so snowy, and Fanny was glad, because with her he was bashful, awkward, and silent, so Tom went down and entertained him with Maud's report. They were very good friends, but led entirely different lives, Will being a "dig" and Tom a "bird," or, in plain English, one was a hard student and the other a jolly young gentleman. Tom had rather patronized Will, who didn't like it, and showed that he didn't by refusing to borrow money of him or accept any of his invitations to join the clubs and societies to which Tom belonged. So Shaw let Milton alone, and he got on very well in his own way, doggedly sticking to his books and resisting all temptations but those of certain libraries, athletic games, and such inexpensive pleasures as were within his means, for this benighted youth had not yet discovered that college nowadays is a place in which to "skylark," not to study.

When Maud came down and trotted contentedly away holding Will's hand, Tom watched them out of sight and then strolled about the house whistling and thinking till he went to sleep in his father's armchair for want of something better to do. He awoke to the joys of a solitary tea, for his mother never came down and Fanny had shut herself and her headache up in her own room.

"Well, this is cheerful," he said as the clock struck eight and his fourth cigar came to an end. "Trix is mad and Fan in the dumps, so I'll take myself off. Guess I'll go round to

Polly's and ask Will to drive out with me and save him the walk, poor chap. Might bring Midget home, it will please her, and there's no knowing when the governor will be back."

With these thoughts in his head, Tom leisurely got under way and left his horse at a neighboring stable, for he meant to make a little call and see what it was Maud enjoyed so much.

"Polly is holding forth," he said to himself as he went quietly upstairs and the steady murmur of a pleasant voice came down to him. Tom laughed at Polly's earnest way of talking when she was interested in anything. But he liked it because it was so different from the coquettish clatter of most of the girls with whom he talked. Young men often laugh at the sensible girls whom they secretly respect, and affect to admire the silly ones whom they secretly despise because earnestness, intelligence, and womanly dignity are not the fashion.

The door was ajar, and pausing in the dark entry, Tom took a survey before he went in. The prospect was not dazzling but homelike and pleasant. The light of a bright fire filled the little room, and down on a stool before it was Maud tending Puttel and watching with deep interest the roasting of an apple intended for her special benefit. On the couch lounged Will, his thoughtful eyes fixed on Polly, who, while she talked, smoothed the broad forehead of her "yellow-haired laddie" in a way that Tom thought an immense improvement on Maud's performance. They had evidently been building castles in the air, for Polly was saying in her most impressive manner:

"Well, whatever you do, Will, don't have a great, costly church that takes so much money to build and support it that you have nothing to give away. I like the plain, old-fashioned churches, built for use, not show, where people met for hearty praying and preaching, and where everybody made their own music instead of listening to opera singers as we do now. I don't care if the old churches were bare and cold, and the seats hard, there was real piety in them, and the sincerity of it was felt in the lives of the people. I don't want a religion that I put away with my Sunday clothes and don't take out till the day comes round again. I want something to see and feel and live by day by day, and I hope you'll be one of the true ministers who can teach by precept and example how to get and keep it."

"I hope I shall be, Polly, but you know they say that in families if there is a boy who can't do anything else, they make a minister of him. I sometimes think I ain't good for much, and that seems to me the reason why I shouldn't even try to be a minister," said Will, smiling, yet looking as if with all his humility he did have faith in the aspirations that came to him in his best moments.

"Someone said that very thing to Father once, and I remember he answered, 'I am glad to give my best and brightest son to the service of God.' "

"Did he say that?" And Will's color rose, for the big, book-loving fellow was as sensitive as a girl to the praise of those dearest to him.

"Yes," said Polly, unconsciously giving the strongest stimulus to her brother's hope and courage. "Yes, and he added, 'I shall let my boys follow the guide that is in them, and only ask of them to use their gifts conscientiously, and be honest, useful men.' "

"So we will! Ned is doing well out West, and I'm hard at it here. If Father does his best to give us the chance we each want, the least we can do is to work with a will."

"Whatever you do, you can't help working with a Will,"

cried Tom, who had been so interested that he forgot he was playing eavesdropper.

Polly flew up, looking so pleased and surprised that Tom reproached himself for not having called oftener.

"I've come for Maud," he announced in a paternal tone, which made that young lady open her eyes.

"I can't go till my apple is done. Besides, it isn't nine yet, and Will is going to take me along when he goes. I'd rather have him."

"I'm going to take you both in the cutter. The storm is over, but it is heavy walking, so you'll drive out with me, old man?" said Tom with a nod at Will.

"Of course he will, and thank you very much. I've been trying to keep him all night. Miss Mills always manages to find a corner for stray people, but he insists on going so as to get to work early tomorrow," said Polly, delighted to see that Tom was taking off his coat as if he meant to wait for Maud's apple, which Polly blessed for being so slow to cook.

Putting her guest into the best chair, Polly sat down and beamed at him with such hospitable satisfaction that Tom went up several pegs in his own estimation.

"You don't come very often, so we are rather overpowered when you do honor us," she said demurely.

"Well, you know we fellows are so busy, we haven't much time to enjoy ourselves," answered Tom.

"Ahem!" said Will loudly.

"Take a troche," said Tom.

Then they both burst out laughing, and Polly, fully understanding the joke, joined them, saying:

"Here are some peanuts, Tom. Do enjoy yourself while you can."

"Now I call that a delicate compliment!" And Tom, who had not lost his early relish for this sort of refreshment, though he seldom indulged his passion nowadays, because peanuts are considered vulgar, fell to cracking and munching with great satisfaction.

"Do you remember the first visit I made at your house, how you gave me peanuts coming from the depot and frightened me out of my wits pretending the coachman was tipsy?" asked Polly.

"Of course I do, and how we coasted one day," answered Tom, laughing.

"Yes, and the velocipede. You've got the scar of that yet, I see."

"I remembered how you stood by me while it was sewed up. That was very plucky, Polly."

"I was dreadfully afraid, but I remember I wanted to seem very brave because you'd called me a coward."

"Did I? Ought to have been ashamed of myself. I used to rough you shamefully, Polly, and you were so good-natured, you let me do it."

"Couldn't help myself," laughed Polly. "I did use to think you were an awful boy, but seems to me I rather liked it."

"She had so much of it at home, she got used to it," put in Will, pulling the little curl behind Polly's ear.

"You boys never teased me as Tom did, that's the reason it amused me, I suppose. Novelty hath charms, you know."

"Grandma used to lecture Tom for plaguing you, Polly, and he used to say he'd be a tip-top boy, but he wasn't," observed Maud with a venerable air.

"Dear old Grandma, she did her best, but I'm a bad lot," said Tom with a shake of the head and a sober face.

"It always seems as if she must be up in her rooms, and I can't get used to finding them empty," added Polly softly.

"Father wouldn't have anything moved, and Tom sits up there sometimes. It makes him feel good, he says," said

Maud, who had a talent for betraying trifles which people preferred should not be mentioned in public.

"You'd better hurry up your apple, for if it isn't done pretty soon, you'll have to leave it, Pug," said Tom, looking annoyed.

"How is Fan?" asked Polly with tact.

"Well, Fan is rather under the weather, says she's dyspeptic, which means cross."

"She is cross, but she's sick, too, for I found her crying one day and she said nobody cared about her and she might as well be dead," added Maud, having turned her apple with tender care.

"We must try to cheer her up, among us. If I wasn't so busy, I'd like to devote myself to her, she has done so much for me," said Polly gratefully.

"I wish you could. I can't understand her, for she acts like a weathercock, and I never know how I'm going to find her. I hate to have her mope so, but, upon my life, I don't know what to do," said Tom, but as he uttered the words something was suggested by the sight before him. Chairs were few, and Polly had taken half of Will's when they drew round the fire. Now she was leaning against him, in a cozy, confiding way, delightful to behold, while Will's strong arm went round her with a protecting air, which said, as plainly as any words, that this big brother and small sister knew how to love and help one another. It was a pleasant little picture, all the pleasanter for its unconsciousness, and Tom found it both suggestive and agreeable.

"Poor old Fan, she don't get much petting, maybe that's what she wants. I'll try it and see, for she stands by me like a trump. If she was a rosy, cozy little woman, like Polly, it would come easier, though," thought Tom as he meditatively ate his last nut, feeling that fraternal affection could not be very difficult of demonstration to brothers blessed with pretty, good-tempered sisters.

"I told Tom about the bad fellow who blew up the professor, and he said he knew him slightly, and I was *so* relieved, because I had a kind of a feeling that it was Tom himself, you and Will laughed so about it."

Maud had a queer way of going on with her own thoughts and suddenly coming out with whatever lay uppermost, regardless of time, place, or company. As this remark fell from her there was a general smile, and Polly said, with mock solemnity:

"It was a sad thing, and I've no doubt that misguided young man is very sorry for it now."

"He looked perfectly bowed down with remorse last time I saw him," said Will, regarding Tom with eyes full of fun, for Will was a boy as well as a bookworm and relished a joke as well as scatterbrained Tom.

"He always is remorseful after a scrape, I've understood, for he isn't a very bad fellow, only his spirits are one too many for him, and he isn't as fond of his book as another fellow I know."

"I'm afraid he'll be expelled if he don't mind," said Polly warningly.

"Shouldn't wonder if he was, he's such an unlucky dog," answered Tom rather soberly.

"I hope he'll remember that his friends will be very much disappointed if he is. He might make them so proud and happy that I guess he will, for he isn't half as thoughtless as he makes himself out," said Polly, looking across at Tom with such friendly eyes that he was quite touched, though of course he didn't show it.

"Thank you, Polly. He may pull through, but I have my doubts. Now, old man, let us 'pud' along, it's getting late for the chicken," he added, relapsing into the graceful diction with which a classical education gifts its fortunate possessor.

Taking advantage of the moment while Will was wrestling with his boots in the closet, and Maud was absorbed in packing her apple into a large basket, Polly said to Tom in a low tone:

"Thank you very much for being so kind to Will."

"Bless your heart, I haven't done anything. He's such a proud fellow he won't let me," answered Tom.

"But you do in many little ways—tonight, for example. Do you think I don't know that the suit of clothes he's just got would have cost a good deal more if your tailor hadn't made them? He's only a boy and don't understand things yet, but I know your way of helping proud people so that they don't find it out, and I do thank you, Tom, so much."

"Oh, come, Polly, that won't do. What do you know about tailors and college matters?" said Tom, looking as much confused as if she had found him out in something reprehensible.

"I don't know much, and that's the reason why I'm grateful for your kindness to Will. I don't care what stories they tell about you, I'm sure you won't lead *him* into trouble, but keep him straight, for my sake. You know I've lost one brother, and Will takes Jimmy's place to me now."

The tears in Polly's eyes as she said that made Tom vow a tremendous vow within himself to stand by Will through thick and thin and "keep him straight for Polly's sake," feeling all the time how ill-fitted he was for such a task.

"I'll do my best," he said heartily as he pressed the hand Polly gave him with a look which assured her that he felt the appeal to his honor, and that henceforth the country lad was safe from all the temptations Tom could have offered him.

"There! Now I shall give that to Mama to take her pills in,

it's just what she likes, and it pleases her to be thought of," said Maud, surveying her gift with complacency as she put on her things.

"You're a good little soul to remember poor Mum," said Tom with an approving nod.

"Well, she was so pleased with the grapes you brought her, I thought I'd try something, and maybe she'd say 'Thank you, darling' to me too. Do you think she will?" whispered Maud with the wistful look so often seen on her little plain face.

"See if she don't." And to Maud's great surprise, Tom didn't laugh at her project.

"Good night, dear, take care of yourself, and keep your muffler round your mouth going over the bridge or you'll be as hoarse as a crow tomorrow," said Polly as she kissed her brother, who returned it without looking, as if he thought it "girl's nonsense." Then the three piled into the sleigh and drove off, leaving Polly nodding on the doorstep.

Maud found the drive altogether too short, but was consoled by the promise of a longer one if the sleighing lasted till next Saturday, and when Tom ran up to bid his mother good-bye and give her a hint about Maud's gift, she stayed below to say, at the last minute, in unconscious imitation of Polly:

"Good night, take care of yourself, my dear."

Tom laughed and was about to pinch the much-enduring little nose, but, as if the words reminded him of something, he gave her a kiss instead, a piece of forbearance which almost took Maud's breath away with surprise and gratification.

It was rather a silent drive, for Will obediently kept his muffler up and Tom fell into a brown study.

He was not much given to reflection, but occasionally indulged when something gave him a turn in that direction, and at such times he was as sober and sincere as could be desired. Anyone might have lectured him for an hour without doing as much good as that little call and the chat that grew out of it, for, though nothing very wise or witty was said, many things were suggested, and everyone knows that persuasive influences are better than any amount of moralizing. Neither Polly nor Will *tried* to do anything of the sort, and that was the charm of it. Nobody likes to be talked to, but nobody can resist the eloquence of unconscious preaching. With all his thoughtlessness, Tom was quick to see and feel these things, and was not spoilt enough yet to laugh at them. The sight of Will and Polly's simple affection for one another reminded him of a neglected duty so pleasantly that he could not forget it. Talking of early days made him wish he could go back and start again, doing better. Grandma's name recalled the tender memory that always did him good, and the thought that Polly trusted her dearest brother to his care stirred up a manful desire to deserve the confidence. Tortures wouldn't have drawn a word of all this from him, but it had its effect, for boys don't leave their hearts and consciences behind them when they enter college, and little things of this sort do much to keep both from being damaged by the four years' scrimmage which begins the battle of life for most of them.

Chapter 11

Needles and Tongues

DEAR POLLY—The Sewing Circle meets at our house this P.M. This is in your line, so do come and help me through. I shall depend on you.

Yours ever,

FAN

"*B*ad news, my dear?" asked Miss Mills, who had just handed the note to Polly as she came in one noon a few weeks after Jenny's arrival.

Polly told her what it was, adding, "I suppose I ought to go and help Fanny, but I can't say I want to. The girls talk about things I have nothing to do with, and I don't find their gossip very amusing. I'm an outsider, and they only accept me on Fan's account, so I sit in a corner and sew while they chatter and laugh."

"Wouldn't it be a good chance to say a word for Jenny? She wants work, and these young ladies probably have quantities done somewhere. Jenny does fine work exquisitely and begins to feel anxious to be earning something. I don't want her to feel dependent and unhappy, and a little well-paid sewing would be all she needs to do nicely. I can get it for her by running round to my friends, but I really haven't the time till I get the Mullers off. They are paupers here, but out West they can take care of themselves, so I've begged the money to send them, and as soon as I can get them some clothes, off they go. That's the way to help people help themselves." And Miss Mills clashed her big scissors energetically as she cut out a little red flannel shirt.

"I know it is, and I want to help, but I don't know where to begin," said Polly, feeling quite oppressed with the immensity of the work.

"We can't any of us do *all* we would like, but we can do our best for every case that comes to us, and that helps amazingly. Begin with Jenny, my dear. Tell those girls about her, and if I'm not much mistaken, you will find them ready to help, for half the time it isn't hardness of heart but ignorance or thoughtlessness on the part of the rich that makes them seem so careless of the poor."

"To tell the truth, I'm afraid of being laughed at if I try to talk seriously about such things to the girls," said Polly frankly.

"You believe that 'such things' *are* true? You are sincere in your wish to help better them, and you respect those who work for that end?"

"Yes, I do."

"Then, my dear, can't you bear a little ridicule for the sake of a good cause? You said yesterday that you were going to make it a principle of your life to help up your sex as far and as fast as you could. It did my heart good to hear you say it, for I was sure that in time you would keep your word. But,

Polly, a principle that can't bear being laughed at, frowned on, and cold-shouldered isn't worthy of the name."

"I want to *be* strong-minded in the real sense of the word, but I don't like to be called so by people who don't understand my meaning, and I shall be if I try to make the girls think soberly about anything sensible or philanthropic. They call me old-fashioned now, and I'd rather be thought that, though it isn't pleasant, than be set down as a rampant woman's rights reformer," said Polly, in whose memory many laughs and snubs and sarcasms still lingered, forgiven but not forgotten.

"This love and thought and care for those weaker, poorer, or worse than ourselves, which we call Christian charity, is a very old fashion, my dear. It began eighteen hundred years ago, and only those who honestly follow the beautiful example set us then learn how to get genuine happiness out of life. *I'm* not a 'rampant women's rights reformer,'" added Miss Mills, with a smile at Polly's sober face, "but I think that women can do a great deal for each other if they will only stop fearing what 'people will think' and take a hearty interest in whatever is going to fit their sisters and themselves to deserve and enjoy the rights God gave them. There are so many ways in which this can be done that I wonder they don't see and improve them. I don't ask you to go and make speeches, only a few have the gift for that, but I do want every girl and woman to feel this duty, and make any little sacrifice of time or feeling that may be asked of them, because there is so much to do, and no one can do it as well as ourselves if we only think so."

"I'll try!" said Polly, influenced more by her desire to keep Miss Mills's good opinion than any love of self-sacrifice for her sex. It was rather a hard thing to ask of a shy, sensitive girl, and the kind old lady knew it, for in spite of the gray hair and withered face, her heart was very young and her own girlish trials not forgotten. But she knew also that Polly had more influence over others than she herself suspected, simply because of her candid, upright nature, and that while she tried to help others, she was serving herself in a way that would improve heart and soul more than any mere social success she might gain by following the rules of fashionable life, which drill the character out of girls till they are as much alike as pins in a paper and have about as much true sense and sentiment in their little heads. There was good stuff in Polly, unspoiled as yet, and Miss Mills was only acting out of her principle of women helping each other. The wise old lady saw that Polly had reached that point where the girl suddenly blooms into a woman, asking something more substantial than pleasure to satisfy the new aspirations that are born, a time as precious and important to the afterlife as the hour when the apple blossoms fall and the young fruit waits for the elements to ripen or destroy the harvest.

Polly did not know this, and was fortunate in possessing a friend who knew what influences would serve her best and who could give her what all women should desire to give each other, the example of a sweet, good life, more eloquent and powerful than any words, for this is a right no one can deny us.

Polly turned the matter over in her mind as she dressed while Jenny played waiting maid, little dreaming what this new friend was meaning to do for her, if she dared.

"Is it going to be a tea party, miss?" asked Jenny as the black silk went rustling on, to her great admiration, for she considered Polly a beauty.

"Well, no, I think it will probably be a lecture," answered Polly, laughing, for Jenny's grateful service and affectionate eyes confirmed the purpose which Miss Mills's little homily had suggested.

As she entered the Shaws' parlor an hour or two later, an appalling array of well-dressed girls appeared, each provided with a dainty reticule, basket, or bag, and each tongue going a good deal faster than the needle while the white fingers stitched sleeves in upside down, put flannel jackets together hind part before, or gobbled buttonholes with the best intentions in life.

"You are a dear to come so early. Here's a nice place for you between Belle and Miss Perkins, and here's a sweet little dress to make, unless you like something else better," said Fanny, receiving her friend with warmth and placing her where she thought she would enjoy herself.

"Thank you, I'll take an unbleached cotton shirt if you have such a thing, for it is likely to be needed before a cambric frock," replied Polly, subsiding into her corner as quickly as possible, for at least six eyeglasses were up and she didn't enjoy being stared at.

Miss Perkins, a grave, cold-looking young lady with an aristocratic nose, bowed politely and then went on with her work, which displayed two diamond rings to great advantage. Belle, being of the demonstrative sort, smiled and nodded, drew up her chair, and began a whispered account of Trix's last quarrel with Tom. Polly listened with interest while she sewed diligently, occasionally permitting her eyes to study the elegant intricacies of Miss Perkins's dress, for that young lady sat like a statue, quirking her delicate fingers and accomplishing about two stitches a minute.

In the midst of Belle's story a more exciting bit of gossip caught her ear, and she plunged into the conversation going on across the table, leaving Polly free to listen and admire the wit, wisdom, and charitable spirit of the accomplished young ladies about her. There was a perfect babel of tongues, but out of the confusion Polly gathered scraps of fashionable intelligence which somewhat lessened her respect for the dwellers in high places. One fair creature asserted that Joe Somebody took so much champagne at the last German that he had to be got away and sent home with two servants. Another divulged the awful fact that Carrie P.'s wedding presents were half of them hired for the occasion. A third circulated a whisper to the effect that though Mrs. Buckminster wore a thousand-dollar cloak, her boys were not allowed but one sheet to their beds. And a fourth young gossip assured the company that a certain person *never* had offered himself to a certain other person, though the report was industriously spread by interested parties. This latter remark caused such a clamor that Fanny called the meeting to order in a most unparliamentary fashion.

"Girls! Girls! You really must talk less and sew more or our society will be disgraced. Do you know our branch sent in less work than any of the others last month, and Mrs. Fitz George said she didn't see how fifteen young ladies *could* manage to do so little?"

"We don't talk a bit more than the old ladies do. I just wish you could have heard them go on last time. The way they get so much done is they take work home and make their seamstresses do it, and then they take credit for vast industry," said Belle, who always spoke her mind with charming candor.

"That reminds me that Mama says they want as many things as we can make, for it's a hard winter and the poor are suffering very much. Do any of you wish to take articles home to do at odd times?" said Fan, who was president of this energetic Dorcas Society.*

"Mercy, no! It takes all my leisure time to mend my gloves and refresh my dresses," answered Belle.

"I think if we meet once a week, it is all that should be expected of us, with our other engagements. Poor people *always* complain that the winter is a hard one and *never* are satisfied," remarked Miss Perkins, making her diamonds sparkle as she sewed buttons on the wrong side of a pink calico apron which would hardly survive one washing.

"Nobody can ask me to do any more if they remember all I've got to attend to before summer," said Trix with an important air. "I've got three women hard at work and want another, but everyone is so busy and ask such abominable prices that I'm in despair and shall have to take hold myself, I'm afraid."

"There's a chance for Jane," thought Polly, but hadn't courage "to speak out loud in meeting" just then and resolved to ask Trix for work in private.

"Prices *are* high, but you forget how much more it costs to live now than it used to do. Mama never allows us to beat down workwomen but wishes us to pay them well and economize in some other way if we must," said Emma Davenport, a quiet, bright-eyed girl who was called "odd" among the young ladies because she dressed simply when her father was a millionaire.

"Just hear that girl talk about economy! I beg your par-

---

* Dorcas: a woman mentioned in the Bible (Acts 9:36).
Dorcas Society: a church group formed for the purpose of providing clothing for the poor.

don, she's some relation of yours, I believe!" said Belle in a low tone.

"Very distant, but I'm proud of it, for, with her, economy doesn't mean scrimping in one place to make a show in another. If everyone would follow the Davenports' example, workwomen wouldn't starve or servants be such a trouble. Emma is the plainest dressed girl in the room, next to me, yet anyone can see she is a true gentlewoman," said Polly warmly.

"And you are another," answered Belle, who had always loved Polly, in her scatterbrained way.

"Hush. Trix has the floor."

"If they spent their wages properly, I shouldn't mind so much, but they think they must be as fine as anybody and dress so well that it is hard to tell mistress from maid. Why, our cook got a bonnet just like mine—the materials were cheaper, but the effect was the same—and had the impertinence to wear it before my face. I forbid it, and she left, of course, which made Papa so cross he wouldn't give me the camel's-hair shawl he promised this year."

"It's perfectly shameful!" said Miss Perkins as Trix paused, out of breath. "Servants ought to be made to dress like servants, as they do abroad, then we should have no more trouble," observed Miss Perkins, who had just made the grand tour and had brought home a French maid.

"Perky don't practice as she preaches," whispered Belle to Polly as Miss P. became absorbed in the chat of her other neighbors. "She pays her chamber girl with old finery, and the other day, when Betsey was out parading in her Miss's cast-off purple plush suit, Mr. Curtis thought she was mademoiselle and bowed to her. He is as blind as a bat, but recognized the dress and pulled off his hat to it in the most elegant style. Perky adores him and was mad enough to beat

Betsey when she told the story and giggled over it. Betsey is quite as stylish and ever so much prettier than Perky and she knows it, which is an aggravation."

Polly couldn't help laughing, but grew sober a minute after as Trix said pettishly:

"Well, I'm sick of hearing about beggars. I believe half of them are humbugs, and if we let them alone they'd go to work and take care of themselves. There's altogether too much fuss made about charity. I do wish we could be left in peace."

"There can't be *too much* charity!" burst out Polly, forgetting her shyness all at once.

"Oh, indeed! Well, I take the liberty to differ from you," returned Trix, putting up her glass and bestowing upon Polly her most "toploftical stare," as the girls called it.

I regret to say that Polly never could talk with or be near Trix without feeling irritated and combative. She tried to conquer this feeling, but she couldn't, and when Trix put on airs Polly felt an intense desire to box her ears. That eyeglass was her especial aversion, for Trix was no more nearsighted than herself but pretended to be because it was the fashion, and at times used the innocent glass as a weapon with which to put down anyone who presumed to set themselves up. The supercilious glance which accompanied her ironically polite speech roused Polly, who answered with sudden color and the kindling of the eyes that always betrayed a perturbed spirit:

"I don't think many of us would enjoy that selfish sort of peace while little children starve and girls no older than us kill themselves because their dreadful poverty leaves them no choice but sin or death."

A sudden lull took place, for, though Polly did not raise her voice, it was full of indignant emotion, and the most frivolous girl there felt a little thrill of sympathy, for the most utterly fashionable life does not kill the heart out of women till years of selfish pleasure have passed over their heads. Trix was ashamed of herself, but she felt the same antagonism toward Polly that Polly did toward her, and, being less generous, took satisfaction in plaguing her. Polly did not know that the secret of this was the fact that Tom often held her up as a model for his fiancée to follow, which caused that young lady to dislike her more than ever.

"Half the awful stories in the papers are made up for a sensation, and it's absurd to believe them unless one likes to be harrowed up. I don't, and as for peace, I'm not likely to get much while I have Tom to look after," said Trix with an aggravating laugh.

Polly's needle snapped in two, but she did not mind it as she said, with a look that silenced even sharp-tongued Trix:

"I can't help believing what my own eyes and ears have seen and heard. You lead such safe and happy lives, you can't imagine the misery that is all round you, but if you *could* get a glimpse of it, it would make your hearts ache, as it has mine."

"Do you suffer from heartache? Someone hinted as much to me, but you looked so well, I couldn't believe it."

Now that was cruel in Trix, more cruel than anyone guessed, but girls' tongues can deal wounds as sharp and sudden as the slender stiletto Spanish women wear in their hair, and Polly turned pale as those words stabbed her. Belle saw it and rushed to the rescue with more goodwill than wisdom.

"Nobody ever accused *you* of having any heart to ache with. Polly and I are not old enough yet to get tough and cool, and we are still silly enough to pity unhappy people, Tom Shaw especially," added Belle under her breath.

That was a two-edged thrust, for Trix was decidedly an old girl and Tom was generally regarded as a hapless victim. Trix turned red, but before she could load and fire again, Emma Davenport, who labored under the delusion that this sort of skirmishing was ill-natured, and therefore ill-bred, spoke up in her pleasant way:

"Speaking of pitying the poor, I always wonder why it is that we all like to read and cry over their troubles in books, but when we have the real thing before us we think it is uninteresting and disagreeable."

"It's the genius that gets into the books which makes us like the poverty, I fancy. But I don't quite agree that the real thing isn't interesting. I think it would be if we knew how to look at and feel it," said Polly very quietly as she pushed her chair out of the arctic circle of Miss Perkins into the temperate one of friendly Emma.

"But how shall we learn that? I don't see what we girls can do, more than we do now. We haven't much money for such things, shouldn't know how to use it if we had, and it isn't proper for us to go poking into dirty places to hunt up the needy. 'Going about doing good in pony phaetons,' as somebody says, may succeed in England, but it won't work here," said Fanny, who had begun lately to think a good deal of someone beside herself and so found her interest in her fellow beings increasing daily.

"We can't do much, perhaps, just yet, but still there are things left undone that naturally fall to us. I know a house," said Polly, sewing busily as she talked, "where every servant who enters it becomes an object of interest to the mistress and her daughters. These women are taught good habits, books are put where they can get them, sensible amusements are planned for them sometimes, and they soon feel that they are not considered mere scrubs, to do as much work as possible, for as little money as possible, but helpers in the family who are loved and respected in proportion to their faithfulness. This lady feels her duty to them, owns it, and does it as conscientiously as she wants them to do theirs by her, and that is the way it ought to be, I think."

As Polly paused several keen eyes discovered that Emma's cheeks were very red and saw a smile lurking in the corners of the mouth that tried to look demure, which told them who Polly meant.

"Do the biddies all turn out saints in that well-regulated family?" asked the irrepressible Trix.

"No, few of us do that, even in the parlor, but every one of the biddies is better for being there, whether they are grateful or not. I ought not to have mentioned this, perhaps, but I wanted to show you one thing that we girls can do. We all complain about bad servants, most as much as if we were housekeepers ourselves, but it never occurs to us to try and mend the matter by getting up a better spirit between mistress and maid. Then there's another thing we can do," added Polly, warming up. "Most of us find money enough for our little vanities and pleasures but feel dreadfully poor when we come to pay for work, sewing especially. Couldn't we give up a few of the vanities and pay the seamstresses better?"

"I declare I will!" cried Belle, whose conscience suddenly woke and smote her for beating down the woman who did her plain sewing in order that she might have an extra flounce on a new dress.

"Belle has got a virtuous fit. Pity it won't last a week," said Trix.

"Wait and see," retorted Belle, resolving that it should last just to disappoint "that spiteful minx," as she sweetly called her old schoolmate.

"Now we shall behold Belle galloping away at a great pace on her new hobby. I shouldn't be surprised to hear of her preaching in the jail, adopting a nice dirty little orphan, or passing round tracts at a Woman's Rights meeting," said Trix, who never could forgive Belle for having a lovely complexion and so much hair of her own that she never patronized either rats, mice, waterfalls, switches, or puff combs.

"Well, I might do worse, and I think of the two I'd rather amuse myself so than as some young ladies do who get into the papers for their pranks," returned Belle with a moral air.

"Suppose we have a little recess and rest while Polly plays to us. Will you, Polly? It will do us good, they all want to hear you and begged I'd ask."

"Then I will, with pleasure." And Polly went to the piano with such obliging readiness that several reproachful glances fell upon Trix, who didn't need her glass to see them.

Polly was never too sad, perturbed, or lazy to sing, for it was almost as easy to her as breathing and seemed the most natural outlet for her emotions. For a minute her hands wandered over the keys as if uncertain what to play, then, falling into a sad, sweet strain, she sang "The Bridge of Sighs." Polly didn't know why she chose it, but the instinct seemed to have been a true one, for, old as the song was, it went straight to the hearts of the hearers, and Polly sang it better than she ever had before, for now the memory of little Jane lent it a tender pathos which no art could give. It did them all good, for music is a beautiful magician and few can resist its power. The girls were touched by the appeal, Polly was lifted out of herself, and when she turned round the softened look on all the faces told her that for the moment foolish differences and frivolous beliefs were forgotten in the one womanly sentiment of pity for the wrongs and woes of which the listeners' happy lives were ignorant.

"That song always makes me cry and feel as if I had no right to be so comfortable," said Belle, openly wiping her eyes on a crash towel.

"Fortunately such cases are very rare," said another young lady, who seldom read the newspapers.

"I wish they were, but I'm afraid they are not, for only three weeks ago I saw a girl younger than any of us, and no worse, who tried to destroy herself simply because she was so discouraged, sick, and poor," said Polly.

"Do tell about her," cried Belle eagerly.

Feeling that the song had paved the way for the story and given her courage to tell it, Polly did tell it, and must have done it well, for the girls stopped work to listen, and when she ended, other eyes besides warmhearted Belle's were wet. Trix looked quite subdued. Miss Perkins thawed to such a degree that something glittered on her hand as she bent over the pink pinafore again, better and brighter than her biggest diamond. Emma got up and went to Polly with a face full of affectionate respect, while Fanny, moved by a sudden impulse, caught up a costly Sèvres plate that stood on the *etagère* and, laying a five-dollar bill in it, passed it around, quoting Polly's words:

"Girls, I know you'll like to help poor little Jenny 'begin again, and do better this time.' "

It was good to see how quickly the pretty purses were out, how generously each gave of its abundance, and what hearty applause broke from the girls as Belle laid down her gold thimble, saying with an April face:

"There, take that. I never have any money, somehow it won't stay with me, but I can't let the plate pass me this time."

When Fanny brought the contributions to Polly she just

gathered it up in her two hands with such a glad, grateful face, the girls wished they had had more to give.

"I can't thank you enough," she said with an eloquent little choke in her voice. "This will help Jenny very much, but the way in which it was done will do her more good than double the money because it will prove to her that she isn't without friends and make her feel that there *is* a place in the world for her. Let her work for you in return for this. She don't ask alms, she only wants employment and a little kindness, and the best charity we can bestow is to see that she has both."

"I'll give her as much sewing as she wants, and she can stay at our house while she does it if she needs a home," said Trix in a spasm of benevolence.

"She doesn't need a home, thank you. Miss Mills has given half of hers and considers Jane her child," answered Polly with proud satisfaction in the fact.

"What an old dear!" cried Belle.

"I want to know her. May I?" whispered Emma.

"Oh, yes, I'm glad to make her known to anyone. She is a quiet little old lady, but she does one heaps of good and shows you how to be charitable in the wisest way."

"Do tell us about it. I'm sure I want to do my duty, but it's such a muddle, I don't know how," said Belle.

Then, quite naturally, the conversation fell upon the great work that none should be too busy to think of and which few are too young or too poor to help on with their mite. The faces grew more earnest, the fingers flew faster as the quick young hearts and brains took in the new facts, ideas, and plans that grew out of the true stories, the sensible hints, the successful efforts which Polly told them, fresh from the lips of Miss Mills, for, of late, Polly had talked much with the good lady and learned quickly the lessons her unselfish life conveyed. The girls found this more interesting than gossip, partly owing to its novelty, doubtless, but the enthusiasm was sincere while it lasted and did them good. Many of them forgot all about it in a week, but Polly's effort was not lost, for Emma, Belle, and Fanny remained firm friends to Jane, so kindly helping her that the poor child felt as if she had indeed been born again into a new and happy world.

Not till long afterward did Polly see how much good this little effort had done her, for the first small sacrifice of this sort leads the way to others, and a single hand's turn given heartily to the world's great work helps one amazingly with one's own small tasks. Polly found this out as her life slowly grew easier and brighter, and the beautiful law of compensation gave her better purposes and pleasures than any she had lost. The parents of some of her pupils were persons of real refinement, and such are always quick to perceive the marks of culture in others, no matter where they find them. These, attracted first by Polly's cheerful face, modest manners, and faithful work, soon found in her something more than a good teacher. They found a real talent for music, an eager desire for helpful opportunities, and a heart grateful for the kindly sympathy that makes rough places smooth. Fortunately, those who have the skill to detect these traits also possess the spirit to appreciate and often the power to serve and develop them. In ways so delicate that the most sensitive pride could not resent the favor, these true gentlefolk showed Polly their respect and regard, put many pleasures in her way, and when they paid her for her work gave her also the hearty thanks that takes away all sense of degradation even from the humblest service, for money so earned and paid sweetens the daily bread it buys and makes the mutual obligation a mutual benefit and pleasure.

A few such patrons did much for Polly, and the music she

gave them had an undertone of gratitude that left blithe echoes in those great houses which money could not buy.

Then, as her butterfly acquaintances deserted her, she found her way into a hive of friendly bees who welcomed her and showed her how to find the honey that keeps life sweet and wholesome. Through Miss Mills, who was the counselor and comforter of several, Polly came to know a little sisterhood of busy, happy, independent girls who each had a purpose to execute, a talent to develop, an ambition to achieve, and brought to the work patience and perseverance, hope and courage. Here Polly found her place at once, for in this little world love and liberty prevailed; talent, energy, and character took the first rank; money, fashion, and position were literally nowhere, for here, as in the big world outside, genius seemed to blossom best when poverty was head gardener. Young teachers, doing much work for little pay; young artists, trying to pencil, paint, or carve their way to Rome; young writers, burning to distinguish themselves; young singers, dreaming of triumphs, great as those of Jenny Lind, and some who tried to conquer independence, armed only with a needle, like poor Jane. All these helped Polly as unconsciously as she helped them, for purpose and principle are the best teachers we can have, and the want of them makes half the women of America what they are: restless, aimless, frivolous, and sick.

To outsiders that was a very hardworking and uneventful winter to Polly. She thought so herself, but as spring came on, the seed of new virtues, planted in the wintertime and ripened by the sunshine of endeavor, began to bud in Polly's nature, betraying their presence to others by the added strength and sweetness of her character long before she herself discovered these May flowers that had blossomed for her underneath the snow.

Chapter 12

Forbidden Fruit

"*I*'m perfectly aching for some fun," said Polly to herself as she opened her window one morning and the sunshine and frosty air set her blood dancing and her eyes sparkling with youth, health, and overflowing spirits. "I really must break out somewhere and have a good time. It's quite impossible to keep steady any longer. Now what will I do?" Polly sprinkled crumbs to the doves, who came daily to be fed, and while she watched the gleaming necks and rosy feet, she racked her brain to devise some unusually delightful way of enjoying herself, for she really had bottled up her spirits so long, they were in a state of uncontrollable effervescence.

"I'll go to the opera," she suddenly announced to the doves. "It's expensive, I know, but it's remarkably good, and music is such a treat to me. Yes, I'll get two tickets as cheap as I can, send a note to Will—poor lad, he needs fun as much as I do—and we'll go and have a nice time in some corner, as Charles Lamb and his sister used to."

With that Polly slammed down the window, to the dismay

of her gentle little pensioners, and began to fly about with great energy, singing and talking to herself as if it was impossible to keep quiet. She started early to her first lesson that she might have time to buy the tickets, hoping, as she put a five-dollar bill into her purse, that they wouldn't be very high, for she felt that she was not in a mood to resist temptation. But she was spared any struggle, for when she reached the place the ticket office was blocked up by eager purchasers and the disappointed faces that turned away told Polly there was no hope for her.

"Well, I don't care, I'll go somewhere, for I will have my fun," she said with great determination, for disappointment only seemed to whet her appetite. But the playbills showed her nothing inviting and she was forced to go away to her work with the money burning her pocket and all manner of wild schemes floating in her head. At noon, instead of going home to dinner, she went and took an ice, trying to feel very gay and festive all by herself. It was rather a failure, however, and after a tour of the picture shops she went to give Maud a lesson, feeling that it was very hard to quench her longings and subside into a prim little music teacher.

Fortunately she did not have to do violence to her feelings very long, for the first thing Fanny said to her was:

"Can you go?"

"Where?"

"Didn't you get my note?"

"I didn't go home to dinner."

"Tom wants us to go to the opera tonight and—" Fan got no further, for Polly uttered a cry of rapture and clasped her hands.

"Go? Of course I will. I've been dying to go all day, tried to get tickets this morning and couldn't, been fuming about it ever since, and now—oh, how splendid!" And Polly could not restrain an ecstatic skip, for this burst of joy rather upset her.

"Well, you come to tea, and we'll dress together, and go all comfortable with Tom, who is in a heavenly frame of mind today."

"I must run home and get my things," said Polly, resolving on the spot to buy the nicest pair of gloves the city afforded.

"You shall have my white cloak and any other little rigging you want. Tommy likes to have his ladies a credit to him, you know," said Fanny, departing to take a beauty sleep.

Polly instantly decided that she wouldn't borrow Becky's best bonnet, as she at first intended, but get a new one, for in her present excited state no extravagance seemed too prodigal in honor of this grand occasion. I am afraid that Maud's lesson was not as thorough as it should have been, for Polly's head was such a chaos of bonnets, gloves, opera cloaks, and fans that Maud blundered through, murdering time and tune at her own sweet will. The instant it was over Polly rushed away and bought not only the kids but a bonnet frame, a bit of illusion, and a pink crape rose, which had tempted her for weeks in a certain shop window, then home and to work with all the skill and speed of a distracted milliner.

"I'm rushing madly into expense, I'm afraid, but the fit is on me and I'll eat bread and water for a week to make up for it. I *must* look nice, for Tom seldom takes me and ought to be gratified when he does. I want to do like other girls, just for once, and enjoy myself without thinking about right and wrong. Now a bit of pink ribbon to tie it with, and I shall be done in time to do up my best collar," she said, turning her boxes topsy-turvy for the necessary ribbon in that delightful flurry which young ladies feel on such occasions.

It is my private opinion that the little shifts and struggles we poor girls have to undergo beforehand give a peculiar relish to our fun when we get it. This fact will account for the rapturous mood in which Polly found herself when, after making her bonnet, washing and ironing her best set, blacking her boots and mending her fan, she at last, like Consuelo, "put on a little dress of black silk" and, with the smaller adornments pinned up in a paper, started for the Shaws', finding it difficult to walk decorously when her heart was dancing in her bosom.

Maud happened to be playing a redowa up in the parlor, and Polly came prancing into the room so evidently spoiling for a dance that Tom, who was there, found it impossible to resist catching her about the waist and putting her through the most intricate evolutions till Maud's fingers gave out.

"That was splendid! Oh, Tom, thank you so much for asking me tonight. I feel just like having a regular good time," cried Polly when she stopped, with her hat hanging round her neck and her hair looking as if she had been out in a high wind.

"Glad of it. I felt so myself and thought we'd have a jolly little party all in the family," said Tom, looking much gratified at her delight.

"Is Trix sick?" asked Polly.

"Gone to New York for a week."

"Ah, when the cat's away the mice will play."

"Exactly. Come and have another turn."

Before they could start, however, the awful spectacle of a little dog trotting out of the room with a paper parcel in his mouth made Polly clasp her hands with the despairing cry:

"My bonnet! Oh, my bonnet!"

"Where? What? Which?" And Tom looked about him, bewildered.

"Snip's got it. Save it! Save it!"

"I will!" And Tom gave chase with more vigor than discretion.

Snip, evidently regarding it as a game got up for his special benefit, enjoyed the race immensely and scampered all over the house, shaking the precious parcel like a rat while his master ran and whistled, commanded and coaxed, in vain. Polly followed, consumed with anxiety, and Maud laughed till Mrs. Shaw sent down to know who was in hysterics. A piteous yelp from the lower regions at last announced that the thief was captured, and Tom appeared bearing Snip by the nape of the neck in one hand and Polly's cherished bonnet in the other.

"The little scamp was just going to worry it when I grabbed him. I'm afraid he has eaten one of your gloves. I can't find it, and this one is pretty well chewed up," said Tom, bereaving Snip of the torn kid, to which he still pertinaciously clung.

"Serves me right," said Polly with a groan. "I'd no business to get a new pair, but I wanted to be extra gorgeous tonight and this is my punishment for such mad extravagance."

"Was there anything else?" asked Tom.

"Only my best cuffs and collar. You'll probably find them in the coal bin," said Polly with the calmness of despair.

"I saw some little white things on the dining-room floor as I raced through. Go get them, Maud, and we'll repair damages," said Tom, shutting the culprit into the boot closet, where he placidly rolled himself up and went to sleep.

"They ain't hurt a bit," proclaimed Maud, restoring the lost treasures.

"Neither is my bonnet, for which I'm deeply grateful,"

said Polly, who had been examining it with a solicitude which made Tom's eyes twinkle.

"So am I, for it strikes me that is an uncommonly 'nobby' little affair," he said approvingly. Tom had a weakness for pale pink roses, and perhaps Polly knew it.

"I'm afraid it's too gay," said Polly, with a dubious look.

"Not a bit. Sort of bridal, you know. Must be becoming. Put it on and let's see."

"I wouldn't for the world, with my hair all tumbling down. Don't look at me till I'm respectable, and don't tell anyone how I've been acting. I think I must be a little crazy tonight," said Polly, gathering up her rescued finery and preparing to go and find Fan.

"Lunacy is mighty becoming, Polly. Try it again," answered Tom, watching her as she went laughing away, looking all the prettier for her dishevelment. "Dress that girl up and she'd be a raving, tearing beauty," added Tom to Maud in a lower tone as he took her into the parlor under his arm.

Polly heard it and instantly resolved to be as "raving and as tearing" as her means would allow, "just for one night," she said as she peeped over the banisters, glad to see that the dance and the race had taken the "band-boxy" air out of Tom's elegant array.

I deeply regret being obliged to shock the eyes and ears of such of my readers as have a prejudice in favor of pure English by expressions like the above, but, having rashly undertaken to write a little story about Young America, for Young America, I feel bound to depict my honored patrons as faithfully as my limited powers permit. Otherwise I must expect the crushing criticism, "Well, I daresay it's all very prim and proper, but it isn't a bit like us," and never hope to arrive at the distinction of finding the covers of "An Old-Fashioned Girl" the dirtiest in the library.

The friends had a social "cup o' tea" upstairs, which Polly considered the height of luxury, and then each took a mirror and proceeded to prink to her heart's content. The earnestness with which Polly made her toilet that night was delightful to behold. Feeling in a daring mood, she released her pretty hair from the braids in which she usually wore it and permitted the curls to display themselves in all their brown abundance, especially several dangerous little ones about the temples and forehead. The putting on of the rescued collar and cuffs was a task which absorbed her whole mind. So was the settling of a minute bit of court plaster just to the left of the dimple in her chin, an unusual piece of coquetry in which Polly would not have indulged if an almost invisible scratch had not given her an excuse for doing it. The white, down-trimmed cloak, with certain imposing ornaments on the hood, was assumed with becoming gravity and draped with much advancing and retreating before the glass as its wearer practiced the true Boston gait, elbows back, shoulders forward, a bend and a slide, occasionally varied by a slight skip. But when that bonnet went on, Polly actually held her breath till it was safely landed and the pink rose bloomed above the smooth waves of hair with what Fanny called "a ravishing effect." At this successful stage of affairs Polly found it impossible to resist the loan of a pair of gold bands for the wrists and Fanny's white fan with the little mirror in the middle.

"I can put them in my pocket if I feel too much dressed," said Polly as she snapped on the bracelets, but after a wave or two of the fan she felt that it would be impossible to take them off till the evening was over, so enticing was their glitter.

Fanny also lent her a pair of three-button gloves, which completed her content, and when Tom greeted her with an approving "Here's a sight for gods and men! Why, Polly, you're gorgeous!" she felt that her "fun" had decidedly be-gun.

"Wouldn't Polly make a lovely bride?" said Maud, who was revolving about the two girls, trying to decide whether she would have a blue or a white cloak when she grew up and went to operas.

"Faith, and she would! Allow me to congratulate you, Mrs.—Sydney," added Tom, advancing with his wedding-reception bow and a wicked look at Fanny.

"Go away! How dare you?" cried Polly, growing much redder than her rose.

"If we are going to the opera tonight, perhaps we'd better start, as the carriage has been waiting some time," observed Fan coolly, and sailed out of the room in an unusually lofty manner.

"Don't you like it, Polly?" whispered Tom as they went downstairs together.

"Very much."

"The deuce you do!"

"I'm so fond of music, how can I help it?"

"I'm talking about Syd."

"Well, I'm not."

"You'd better try for him."

"I'll think of it."

"Oh, Polly, Polly, what are you coming to?"

"A tumble into the street, apparently," answered Polly as she slipped a little on the step, and Tom stopped in the middle of his laugh to pilot her safely into the carriage, where Fanny was already seated.

"Here's richness!" said Polly to herself as she rolled away, feeling as Cinderella probably did when the pumpkin coach bore her to the first ball, only Polly had two princes to think about, and poor Cinderella, on that occasion, had not even one. Fanny didn't seem inclined to talk much, and Tom would go on in such a ridiculous manner that Polly told him she wouldn't listen and began to hum bits of the opera. But she heard every word, nevertheless, and resolved to pay him for his impertinence as soon as possible by showing him what he had lost.

Their seats were in the balcony, and hardly were they settled when, by one of those remarkable coincidences which are continually occurring in our youth, Mr. Sydney and Fanny's old friend Frank Moore took their places just behind them.

"Oh, you villain! You did it on purpose," whispered Polly as she turned from greeting their neighbors and saw a droll look on Tom's face.

"I give you my word I didn't. It's the law of attraction, don't you see?"

"If Fan likes it, I don't care."

"She looks resigned, I think."

She certainly did, for she was talking and laughing in the gayest manner with Frank while Sydney was covertly survey-ing Polly as if he didn't quite understand how the gray grub got so suddenly transformed into a white butterfly. It is a well-known fact that dress plays a very important part in the lives of most women, and even the most sensible cannot help owning sometimes how much happiness they owe to a becoming gown, gracefully arranged hair, or a bonnet which brings out the best points in their faces and puts them in a good humor. A great man was once heard to say that what first attracted him to his well-beloved wife was seeing her in a white muslin dress with a blue shawl on the chair behind her. The dress caught his eye, and, stopping to admire that, the wearer's intelligent conversation interested his mind, and in time the woman's sweetness won his heart. It is not the finest dress which does the most execution, I fancy, but that which best interprets individual taste and character. Wise people understand this, and everybody is more influenced by it than they know, perhaps. Polly was not very wise, but she felt that everyone about her found something more attractive than usual in her and modestly attributed Tom's devotion, Sydney's interest, and Frank's undisguised admiration to the new bonnet or, more likely, to that delightful combination of cashmere, silk, and swan's down, which, like Charity's mantle, seemed to cover a multitude of sins in other people's eyes and exalt the little music teacher to the rank of a young lady.

Polly scoffed at this sort of thing sometimes, but tonight she accepted it without a murmur—rather enjoyed it in fact, let her bracelets shine before the eyes of all men, and felt that it was good to seem comely in their sight. She forgot one thing, however: that her own happy spirits gave the crowning charm to a picture which everyone liked to see—a blithe young girl enjoying herself with all her heart. The music and the light, costume and company, excited Polly and made many things possible which at most times she would never have thought of saying or doing. She did not mean to flirt, but somehow "it flirted itself" and she couldn't help it, for, once started, it was hard to stop, with Tom goading her on and Sydney looking at her with that new interest in his eyes. Polly's flirting was such a very mild imitation of the fashionable thing that Trix & Co. would not have recognized it, but it did very well for a beginner, and Polly understood that night wherein the fascination of it lay, for she felt as if she had found a new gift all of a sudden and was learning how to use it, knowing that it was dangerous, yet finding its chief charm in that very fact.

Tom didn't know what to make of her at first, though he thought the change uncommonly becoming and finally decided that Polly had taken his advice and was "setting her cap for Syd," as he gracefully expressed it. Sydney, being a modest man, thought nothing of the kind but simply fancied that little Polly was growing up to be a very charming woman. He had known her since her first visit and had always liked the child. This winter he had been interested in the success of her plans and had done what he could to help them, but he never thought of falling in love with Polly till that night. Then he began to feel that he had not fully appreciated his young friend; that she was such a bright and lovable girl, it was a pity she should not always be gay and pretty and enjoy herself; that she would make a capital wife for somebody, and perhaps it *was* about time to think of "settling," as his sister often said. These thoughts came and went as he watched the white figure in front, felt the enchantment of the music, and found everybody unusually blithe and beautiful. He had heard the opera many times, but it had never seemed so fine before, perhaps because he had never happened to have had an ingenuous young face so near him in which the varying emotions born of the music, and the romance it portrayed, came and went so eloquently that it was impossible to help reading them. Polly did not know that this was why he leaned down so often to speak to her, with an expression which she did not understand but liked very much nevertheless.

"Don't shut your eyes, Polly. They are so full of mischief tonight, I like to see them," said Tom, after idly wondering for a minute if she knew how long and curly her lashes were.

"I don't wish to look affected, but the music tells the story so much better than the acting that I don't care to look on half the time," answered Polly, hoping Tom wouldn't see the tears she had so cleverly suppressed.

"Now I like the acting best. The music is all very fine, I know, but it does seem so absurd for people to go round telling tremendous secrets at the top of their voices. I can't get used to it."

"That's because you've more common sense than romance. I don't mind the absurdity, and quite long to go and comfort that poor girl with the broken heart," said Polly with a sigh as the curtain fell on a most affecting tableau.

"What's-his-name is a great jack not to see that she adores him. In real life we fellows ain't such bats as all that," observed Tom, who had decided opinions on many subjects that he knew very little about and expressed them with great candor.

A curious smile passed over Polly's face and she put up her glass to hide her eyes as she said:

"I think you are bats sometimes, but women are taught to wear masks, and that accounts for it, I suppose."

"I don't agree. There's precious little masking nowadays. Wish there was a little more sometimes," added Tom, thinking of several blooming damsels whose beseeching eyes had begged him not to leave them to wither on the parent stem.

"I hope not, but I guess there's a good deal more than anyone would suspect."

"What can you know about broken hearts and blighted beings?" asked Sydney, smiling at the girl's pensive tone.

Polly glanced up at him and her face dimpled and shone again as she answered, laughing:

"Not much. My time is to come."

"I can't imagine you walking about the world with your back hair down, bewailing a hard-hearted lover," said Tom.

"Neither can I. That wouldn't be my way."

"No, Miss Polly would let concealment prey on her damask cheeks and still smile on in the novel fashion, or turn sister of charity and nurse the heartless lover through smallpox, or some other contagious disease, and die seraphically, leaving him to the agonies of remorse and tardy love."

Polly gave Sydney an indignant look as he said that in a slow satirical way that nettled her very much, for she hated to be thought sentimental.

"That's not my way either," she said decidedly. "I'd try to outlive it, and if I couldn't, I'd try to be the better for it. Disappointment needn't make a woman a fool."

"Nor an old maid, if she's pretty and good. Remember that, and don't visit the sins of one blockhead on all the rest of mankind," said Tom, laughing at her earnestness.

"I don't think there is the slightest possibility of Miss Polly's being either," added Sydney with a look which made it evident that concealment had not seriously damaged Polly's damask cheek as yet.

"There's Clara Bird. I haven't seen her but once since she was married. How pretty she looks!" And Polly retired behind the big glass again, thinking the chat was becoming rather personal.

"Now, there's a girl who tried a different cure for unrequited affection from any you mention. People say she was fond of Belle's brother. He didn't reciprocate but went off to India to spoil his constitution, so Clara married a man twenty years older than she is and consoles herself by being the best-dressed woman in the city."

"That accounts for it," said Polly when Tom's long whisper ended.

"For what?"

"The tired look in her eyes."

"I don't see it," said Tom, after a survey through the glass.

"Didn't expect you would."

"I see what you mean. A good many women have it nowa-days," said Sydney over Polly's shoulder.

"What's she tired of? The old gentleman?" asked Tom.

"And herself," added Polly.

"You've been reading French novels, I know you have. That's just the way the heroines go on," cried Tom.

"I haven't read one, but it's evident you have, young man, and you'd better stop."

"I don't care for 'em, only do it to keep up my French. But how came you to be so wise, ma'am?"

"Observation, sir. I like to watch faces, and I seldom see a grown-up one that looks perfectly happy."

"True for you, Polly. No more you do, now I think of it. I don't know but one that always looks so, and there it is."

"Where?" asked Polly with interest.

"Look straight before you and you'll see it."

Polly did look, but all she saw was her own face in the little mirror of the fan which Tom held up and peeped over with a laugh in his eyes.

"Do I look happy? I'm glad of that." And Polly surveyed herself with care.

Both young men thought it was girlish vanity and smiled at its naïve display, but Polly was looking for something deeper than beauty and was glad not to find it.

"Rather a pleasant little prospect, hey, Polly?"

"My bonnet is straight, and that's all I care about. Did you ever see a picture of Beau Brummel?" asked Polly quickly.

"No."

"Well, there he is, modernized." And turning the fan, she showed him himself.

"Any more portraits in your gallery?" asked Sydney, as if he liked to share all the nonsense going.

"One more."

"What do you call it?"

"The portrait of a gentleman." And the little glass reflected a gratified face for the space of two seconds.

"Thank you. I'm glad I don't disgrace my name," said Sydney, looking down into the merry blue eyes that thanked him silently for many of the small kindnesses that women never can forget.

"Very good, Polly, you are getting on fast," whispered Tom, patting his yellow kids approvingly.

"Be quiet! Dear me, how warm it is!" And Polly gave him a frown that delighted his soul.

"Come out and have an ice, we shall have time."

"Fan is so absorbed, I couldn't think of disturbing her," said Polly, fancying that her friend was enjoying the evening as much as she was—a great mistake, by the way, for Fan was acting for effect, and though she longed to turn and join them, wouldn't do it unless a certain person showed signs of missing her. He didn't, and Fanny chatted on, raging inwardly over her disappointment and wondering how Polly could be so gay and selfish.

It was delicious to see the little airs Polly put on, for she felt as if she were somebody else and acting a part. She leaned back, as if quite oppressed by the heat, permitted Sydney to fan her, and paid him for the service by giving him a flower from her bouquet—proceedings which amused Tom immensely, even while it piqued him a little to be treated like an old friend who didn't count.

"Go in and win, Polly, I'll give you my blessing," he whispered as the curtain rose again.

"It's only part of the fun, so don't you laugh, you disrespectful boy," she whispered back in a tone never used toward Sydney.

Tom didn't quite like the different way in which she treated them, and the word "boy" disturbed his dignity, for he was almost twenty-one and Polly ought to treat him with more respect. Sydney, at the same moment, was wishing he was in Tom's place—young, comely, and such a familiar friend that Polly would scold and lecture him in the delightful way she did Tom, while Polly forgot them both when the music began and left them ample time to look at her and think about themselves.

While they waited to get out when all was over, Polly heard Fan whisper to Tom:

"What do you think Trix will say to this?"

"What do you mean?"

"Why, the way you've been going on tonight."

"Don't know and don't care. It's only Polly."

"That's the very thing. She can't bear P."

"Well, I can, and I don't see why I shouldn't enjoy myself as well as Trix."

"You'll get to enjoying yourself too much if you aren't careful. Polly's waked up."

"I'm glad of it and so's Syd."

"I only spoke for your good."

"Don't trouble yourself about me. I get lecturing enough in another quarter and can't stand any more. Come, Polly."

She took the arm he offered her, but her heart was sore and angry, for that phrase "It's only Polly" hurt her sadly. "As if I wasn't anybody, hadn't any feelings, and was only made to amuse or work for people! Fan and Tom are both mistaken, and I'll show them that Polly *is* awake," she thought indignantly. "Why shouldn't I enjoy myself as well

as the rest? Besides, it's only Tom," she added with a bitter
smile as she thought of Trix.

"Are you tired, Polly?" asked Tom, bending down to look
into her face.

"Yes, of being nobody."

"Ah, but you ain't nobody, you're Polly, and you couldn't
better that if you tried ever so hard," said Tom warmly, for
he really was fond of Polly and felt uncommonly so just then.

"I'm glad you think so, anyway. It's so pleasant to be
liked." And she looked up with her face quite bright again.

"I always did like you, don't you know, ever since that first
visit."

"But you teased me shamefully, for all that."

"So I did, but I don't now."

Polly did not answer, and Tom asked, with more anxiety
than the occasion required:

"Do I, Polly?"

"Not in the same way, Tom," she answered in a tone that
didn't sound quite natural.

"Well, I never will again."

"Yes, you will, you can't help it." And Polly's eye glanced
at Sydney, who was in front with Fan.

Tom laughed and drew Polly closer as the crowd pressed,
saying, with mock tenderness:

"Didn't she like to be chaffed about her sweethearts? Well,
she shan't be if I can help it. Poor dear, did she get her little
bonnet knocked into a cocked hat and her little temper riled
at the same time?"

Polly couldn't help laughing and, in spite of the crush,
enjoyed the slow journey from seat to carriage, for Tom took
such excellent care of her, she was rather sorry when it was
over.

They had a merry little supper after they got home, and

Polly gave them a burlesque opera that convulsed her hearers, for her spirits rose again and she was determined to get the last drop of fun before she went back to her humdrum life again.

"I've had a regularly splendid time, and thank you ever so much," she said when the "good nights" were being exchanged.

"So have I. Let's go and do it again tomorrow," said Tom, holding the hand from which he had helped to pull a refractory glove.

"Not for a long while, please. Too much pleasure would soon spoil me," answered Polly, shaking her head.

"I don't believe it. Good night, 'sweet Mistress Milton,' as Syd called you. Sleep like an angel, and don't dream of—I forgot, no teasing allowed." And Tom took himself off with a theatrical farewell.

"Now it's all over and done with," thought Polly as she fell asleep after a long vigil. But it was not, and Polly's fun cost more than the price of gloves and bonnet, for, having nibbled at forbidden fruit, she had to pay the penalty. She only meant to have a good time, and there was no harm in that, but unfortunately she yielded to the various small temptations that beset pretty young girls and did more mischief to others than to herself. Fanny's friendship grew cooler after that night. Tom kept wishing Trix was half as satisfactory as Polly, and Mr. Sydney began to build castles that had no foundation.

Chapter 13

The Sunny Side

"*I*'ve won the wager, Tom."

"Didn't know there was one."

"Don't you remember you said Polly would be tired of her teaching and give it up in three months and I said she wouldn't?"

"Well, isn't she?"

"Not a bit of it. I thought she was at one time, and expected every day to have her come in with a long face and say she couldn't stand it. But somehow, lately, she is always bright and happy, seems to like her work, and don't have the tired, worried look she used to at first. The three months are out, so pay up, Tommy."

"All right, what will you have?"

"You may make it gloves. I always need them, and Papa looks sober when I want money."

There was a minute's pause as Fan returned to her practicing and Tom relapsed into the reverie he was enjoying seated astride of a chair with his chin on his folded arms.

"Seems to me Polly don't come here as often as she used to," he said presently.

"No, she seems to be very busy, got some new friends, I believe—old ladies, sewing girls, and things of that sort. I miss her, but know she'll get tired of being goody and will come back to me before long."

"Don't be too sure of that, ma'am." Something in Tom's tone made Fan turn round and ask:

"What do you mean?"

"Well, it strikes me that Sydney is one of Polly's new friends. Haven't you observed that she is uncommonly jolly, and don't that sort of thing account for it?"

"Nonsense!"

"Hope it is," coolly returned Tom.

"What put it into your head?" demanded Fanny, twirling round again so that her face was hidden.

"Oh, well, I keep meeting Syd and Polly circulating in the same directions. She looks as if she had found something uncommonly nice, and he looks as if all creation was getting Pollyfied pretty rapidly. Wonder you haven't observed it."

"I have."

It was Tom's turn to look surprised now, for Fanny's voice sounded strange to him. He looked at her steadily for a minute, but saw only a rosy ear and a bent head. A cloud passed over his face, and he leaned his chin on his arm again with a despondent whistle as he said to himself:

"Poor Fan! Both of us in a scrape at once."

"Don't you think it would be a good thing?" asked Fanny after playing a bar or two very badly.

"Yes, for Syd."

"Not for Polly? Why, he's rich, and clever, and better than most of you good-for-nothing fellows. What can the girl expect?"

"Can't say, but I don't fancy the match myself."

"Don't be a dog in the manger, Tom."

"Bless your little heart, I only take a brotherly sort of interest in Polly. She's a capital girl, and she ought to marry a missionary or one of your reformer fellows and be a shining light of some sort. I don't think setting up for a fine lady would suit her."

"I think it would, and I hope she'll have the chance," said Fanny, evidently making an effort to speak kindly.

"Good for you, Fan!" And Tom gave an emphatic nod, as if her words meant more than she suspected. "Mind you," he added, "I don't know anything and only fancied there might be some little flirtation going on. But I daresay it's nothing."

"Time will show." Then Fan began to sing, and Tom's horse came, so he departed with the very unusual demonstration of a gentle pat on the head as he said kindly:

"That's right, my dear, keep jolly." It wasn't an elegant way of expressing sympathy, but it was hearty, and Fan thanked him for it, though she only said:

"Don't break your neck, Tommy."

When he was gone Fan's song ended as suddenly as it began, and she sat thinking, with varying expressions of doubt and trouble passing rapidly across her face.

"Well, I can't do anything but wait!" she said at last, slamming the music book together with a desperate look. "Yes, I can," she added a minute after. "It's Polly's holiday. I can go and see her, and if there is anything in it, I shall find it out."

Fanny dropped her face into her hands with a little shiver as she said that. Then she got up, looking as pale and resolute as if going to meet some dreadful doom, and putting on her things, went away to Polly's as fast as her dignity would allow.

Saturday morning was Polly's clearing-up day, and Fan found her with a handkerchief tied over her head and a big apron on, just putting the last touches to the tidy little room, which was as fresh and bright as water, air, and a pair of hands could make it.

"All ready for company. I'll just whisk off my regimentals and Polly the maid becomes Polly the missis. It was lovely of you to come early. Take off your things. Another new bonnet? You extravagant wretch! How is your mother and Maudie? It's a nice day, and we'll have a walk, won't we?"

By the time Polly's welcome was uttered, she had got Fan on the little sofa beside her and was smiling at her in such an infectious manner that Fan couldn't help smiling back.

"I came to see what you have been doing with yourself lately. You don't come and report, and I got anxious about you," said Fanny, looking into the clear eyes before her.

"I've been so busy, and I knew you wouldn't care to hear about my doings, for they aren't the sort you like," answered Polly.

"Your lessons didn't use to take up all your time. It's my private opinion that you are taking as well as giving lessons, miss," said Fan, putting on a playfully stern air to hide her real anxiety.

"Yes, I am," answered Polly soberly.

"In what? Love?"

A quick color came to Polly's cheeks as she laughed and said, looking away:

"No, friendship and good works."

"Oh, indeed! May I ask who is your teacher?"

"I've more than one, but Miss Mills is head teacher."

"She instructs in good works. Who gives the friendship lessons?"

"Such pleasant girls! I wish you knew them, Fan. So clever

and energetic and kind and happy, it always does me good to see them," cried Polly, with a face full of enthusiasm.

"Is that all?" And Fan gave her a curious look of mingled disappointment and relief.

"There, I told you my doings would not interest you, and they don't. They sound flat and prosy after your brilliant adventures. Let's change the subject," said Polly, looking relieved herself.

"Dear me, which of our sweethearts sends us dainty bouquets of violets so early in the morning?" asked Fanny, suddenly spying the purple cluster in a graceful little vase on the piano.

"He sends me one every week, he knows I love them so." And Polly's eyes turned that way full of pride and pleasure.

"I'd no idea he was so devoted," said Fanny, stooping to smell the flowers and at the same time read a card that lay near them.

"You needn't plague me about it, now you know it. I never speak of our fondness for one another because such things seem silly to other people. Will isn't all that Jimmy was to me, but he tries to be, and I love him dearly for it."

"Will?" Fanny's voice quite startled Polly, it was so sharp and sudden, and her face grew red and pale all in a minute as she upset the little vase with the start she gave.

"Yes, of course. Who did you think I meant?" asked Polly, sopping up the water before it damaged her piano.

"Never mind. I thought you might be having a quiet little flirtation with somebody. I feel responsible, you know, because I told your mother I'd look after you. The flowers are all right. My head aches so, I hardly know what I'm doing this morning."

Fanny spoke fast and laughed uncomfortably as she went back to the sofa, wondering if Polly had told her a lie. Polly seemed to guess at her thoughts as she saw the card, and turning toward her, she held it up, saying, with a conscious look in her eyes:

"You thought Mr. Sydney sent them? Well, you are mistaken, and the next time you want to know anything, please ask straight out. I like it better than talking at cross purposes."

"Now, my dear, don't be angry, I was only teasing you in fun. Tom took it into his foolish head that something was going on, and I felt a natural interest, you know."

"Tom! What does he know or care about my affairs?" demanded Polly.

"He met you two in the street pretty often, and being in a sentimental mood himself, got up a romance for you and Sydney."

"I'm much obliged to him for his interest, but it's quite wasted, thank you."

Fan's next proceeding gave her friend another surprise, for, being rather ashamed of herself, very much relieved, and quite at a loss what to say, she took refuge in an hysterical fit of tears, which changed Polly's anger into tenderness at once.

"Is that the trouble she has been hiding all winter? Poor dear, I wish I'd known it sooner," thought Polly as she tried to soothe her with comfortable pats, sniffs of cologne, and sympathizing remarks upon the subject of headache, carefully ignoring that other feminine affliction, the heartache.

"There, I feel better. I've been needing a good cry for some time, and now I shall be all right. Never mind it, Polly, I'm nervous and tired. I've danced too much lately, and dyspepsia makes me blue." And Fanny wiped her eyes and laughed.

"Of course it does. You need rest and petting, and here

I've been scolding you when I ought to have been extra kind. Now tell me what I can do for you," said Polly, with a remorseful face.

"Talk to me, and tell me all about yourself. You don't seem to have as many worries as other people. What's the secret, Polly?" And Fan looked up with wet eyes and a wistful face at Polly, who was putting little dabs of cologne all over her head.

"Well," said Polly slowly, "I just try to look on the bright side of things—that helps one amazingly. Why, you've no idea how much goodness and sunshine you can get out of the most unpromising things if you make the best of them."

"I don't know how," said Fan despondently.

"You can learn. I did. I used to croak and fret dreadfully and get so unhappy, I wasn't fit for anything. I do it still more than I ought, but I try not to, and it gets easier, I find. Get a-top of your troubles and then they are half cured, Miss Mills says."

"Everything is so contrary and provoking," said Fanny petulantly.

"Now what in the world have you to fret about?" asked Polly rather anxiously.

"Quantities of things," began Fan, and then stopped, for somehow she felt ashamed to own that she was afflicted because she couldn't have a new set of furs, go to Paris in the spring, and make Mr. Sydney love her. She hunted up something more presentable and said in a despairing tone:

"Well, Mother is very poorly, Tom and Trix quarrel all the time, Maud gets more and more willful every day, and Papa is worried about his affairs."

"A sad state of things, but nothing very desperate. Can't you lend a hand anywhere? That might do good all round."

"No, I haven't the talent for managing people, but I see what ought to be done."

"Well, don't wail about it. Keep *yourself* happy if you can. It will help other people to see you cheerful."

"Just what Tom said, 'Keep jolly,' but, dear me, how can one when everything is so stupid and tiresome?"

"If ever a girl needed work, it's you!" cried Polly. "You began to be a young lady so early that you are tired of everything at twenty-two. I wish you'd go at something, then you'd find how much talent and energy you really have."

"I know ever so many girls who are just like me, sick to death of fashionable life, but don't know what to take in its place. I'd like to travel, but Papa says he can't afford it, so I can only drag about and get on as I may."

"I pity you rich girls so much, you have so many opportunities and don't seem to know how to use them. I suppose I should do just the same in your place, but it seems now as if I could be very happy and useful with plenty of money."

"You are that without it. There, I won't croak anymore. Let us go and take a good walk, and don't you tell anyone how I came and cried like a baby."

"Never!" said Polly, putting on her bonnet.

"I ought to go and make calls," said Fanny, "but I don't feel now as if I ever want to see any of the girls again. Dreadful state of mind, isn't it?"

"Suppose you come and see some of my friends instead! They are not fine or ceremonious, but lively, odd, and pleasant. Come, it will amuse you."

"I will," cried Fanny, whose spirits seemed improved by the shower. "Nice little old lady, isn't she?" added Fan as she caught sight of Miss Mills on their way out sitting at a table piled with work and sewing away with an energy that made the gray curls vibrate.

"St. Mehitable, I call her. Now, there is a rich woman who knew how to get happiness out of her money," said Polly as they walked away. "She was poor till she was nearly fifty, then a comfortable fortune was left her, and she knew just how to use it. That house was given her, but instead of living in it all alone, she filled it with poor gentlefolks who needed neat, respectable homes but couldn't get anything comfortable for their little money. I'm one of them, and I know the worth of what she does for me. Two old widow ladies live below me, several students overhead, poor Mrs. Kean and her lame boy have the back parlor, and Jenny the little bedroom next Miss Mills. Each pays what they can. That's independent and makes us feel better, but that dear woman does a thousand things that money can't pay for, and we feel her influence all through the house. I'd *rather* be married and have a home of my own, but next to that, I should like to be an old maid like Miss Mills."

Polly's sober face and emphatic tone made Fanny laugh, and at the cheery sound a young girl pushing a baby carriage looked round and smiled.

"What lovely eyes!" whispered Fanny.

"Yes, that's little Jane," returned Polly, adding, when she had passed with a nod and a friendly "Don't get tired, Jenny," "we help one another at our house, and every fine morning Jenny takes Johnny Kean out when she goes for her own walk. That gives his mother time to rest, does both the children good, and keeps things neighborly. Miss Mills suggested it, and Jenny is so glad to do anything for anybody, it's a pleasure to let her."

"I've heard of Miss Mills before. But I should think she would get tired to death, sitting there making hoods and petticoats day after day," said Fanny after thinking over Jenny's story for a few minutes, for seeing the girl seemed to bring it nearer and make it more real to her.

"But she don't sit there all the time. People come to her with their troubles and she goes to them with all sorts of help, from soap to soup, to shrouds for the dead and comfort for the living. I go with her sometimes, and it is more exciting than any play to see and hear the lives and stories of the poor."

"How can you bear the dreadful sights and sounds, the bad air, and the poverty that can't be cured?"

"But it isn't all dreadful. There are good and lovely things among them if one only has eyes to see them. It makes me grateful and contented, shows me how rich I am, and keeps me ready to do all I can for these poor souls."

"My good Polly!" And Fanny gave her friend's arm an affectionate squeeze, wondering if it was this alone that had worked the change in Polly.

"You have seen two of my new friends, Miss Mills and Jenny, now I'll show you two more," said Polly presently as they reached a door and she led the way up several flights of public stairs. "Rebecca Jeffrey is a regularly splendid girl, full of talent. She won't let us call it genius. She will be famous someday, I know. She is so modest and yet so intent on her work. Lizzie Small is an engraver and designs the most delightful little pictures. Becky and she live together and take care of one another in true Damon and Pythias style. This studio is their home—they work, eat, sleep, and live here, going halves in everything. They are all alone in the world, but as happy and independent as birds—real friends, whom nothing will part."

"Let a lover come between them and their friendship won't last long," said Fanny.

"I think it will. Take a look at them and you'll change

your mind," answered Polly, tapping at a door on which two modest cards were tacked.

"Come in!" said a voice, and obeying, Fanny found herself in a large, queerly furnished room, lighted from above and occupied by two girls. One stood before a great clay figure in a corner. This one was tall, with a strong face, keen eyes, short curly hair, and a fine head. Fanny was struck at once by this face and figure, though the one was not handsome, and the other half hidden by a great pinafore covered with clay. At a table where the light was clearest sat a frail-looking girl with a thin face, big eyes, and pale hair—a dreamy, absorbed little person who bent over a block, skillfully wielding her tools.

"Becky and Bess, how do you do? This is my friend Fanny Shaw. We are out on a rampage, so go on with your work and let us lazy ones look on and admire."

As Polly spoke both girls looked up and nodded smilingly. Bess gave Fan the one easy chair. Becky took an artistic survey of the newcomer with eyes that seemed to see everything, then each went on with her work and all began to talk.

"You are just what I want, Polly. Pull up your sleeve and give me an arm while you sit. The muscles here aren't right, and you've got just what I want," said Becky, slapping the round arm of the statue at which Fan was gazing with awe.

"How do you get on?" asked Polly, throwing off her cloak and rolling up her sleeves as if going to washing.

"Slowly. The idea is working itself clear, and I follow as fast as my hands can. Is the face better, do you think?" said Becky, taking off a wet cloth and showing the head of the statue.

"How beautiful it is!" cried Fanny, staring at it with increased respect.

"What does it mean to you?" asked Rebecca, turning to her with a sudden shine in her keen eyes.

"I don't know whether it is meant for a saint or a muse, a goddess or a fate, but to me it is only a beautiful woman, bigger, lovelier, and more imposing than any woman I ever saw," answered Fanny slowly, trying to express the impression the statue made upon her.

Rebecca smiled brightly, and Bess looked round to nod approvingly, but Polly clapped her hands and said:

"Well done, Fan! I didn't think you'd get the idea so well, but you have, and I'm proud of your insight. Now I'll tell you, for Becky will let me, since you have paid her the compliment of understanding her work. Some time ago we got into a famous talk about what women should be, and Becky said she'd show us her idea of the coming woman. There she is, as you say, bigger, lovelier, and more imposing than any we see nowadays, and at the same time, she is a true woman. See what a fine forehead, yet the mouth is both firm and tender, as if it could say strong, wise things as well as teach children and kiss babies. We couldn't decide what to put in the hands as the most appropriate symbol. What do you say?"

"Give her a scepter. She would make a fine queen," answered Fanny.

"No, we have had enough of that. Women have been called queens a long time, but the kingdom given them isn't worth ruling," answered Rebecca.

"I don't think it is nowadays," said Fanny with a tired sort of sigh.

"Put a man's hand in hers to help her along, then," said Polly, whose happy fortune it had been to find friends and helpers in fathers and brothers.

"No, my woman is to stand alone and help herself," said Rebecca decidedly.

"She's to be strong-minded, is she?" And Fanny's lip curled a little as she uttered the misused words.

"Yes, strong-minded, strong-hearted, strong-souled, and strong-bodied. That is why I made her larger than the miserable, pinched-up woman of our day. Strength and beauty must go together. Don't you think these broad shoulders can bear burdens without breaking down, these hands work well, these eyes see clearly, and these lips do something besides simper and gossip?"

Fanny was silent, but a voice from Bess's corner said:

"Put a child in her arms, Becky."

"Not that even, for she is to be something more than a nurse."

"Give her a ballot box," cried a new voice, and turning round, they saw an odd-looking woman perched on a sofa behind them.

"Thank you for the suggestion, Kate. I'll put that with the other symbols at her feet, for I'm going to have needle, pen, palette, and broom somewhere to suggest the various talents she owns, and the ballot box will show that she has earned the right to use them. How goes it?" And Rebecca offered a clay-daubed hand, which the newcomer cordially shook.

"Great news, girls! Anna is going to Italy!" cried Kate, tossing up her bonnet like a schoolboy.

"Oh, how splendid! Who takes her? Has she had a fortune left her? Tell all about it," exclaimed the girls, gathering round the speaker.

"Yes, it *is* splendid, just one of the beautiful things that do everybody heaps of good, it is so generous and so deserved. You know Anna has been longing to go, working and hoping for a chance and never getting it, till all of a sudden Miss

Burton is inspired to invite the girl to go with her for several years to Italy. Think of the luck of that dear soul, the advantages she'll have, the good it will do her, and, best of all, the lovely way in which it comes to her. Miss Burton wants her as a friend, asks nothing of her but her company, and Anna will go through fire and water for her, of course. Now, isn't that fine?"

It was good to see how heartily these girls sympathized in their comrade's good fortune. Polly danced all over the room, Bess and Becky hugged one another, and Kate laughed with her eyes full, while even Fanny felt a glow of pride and pleasure at the kind act.

"Who is that?" she whispered to Polly, who had subsided into a corner.

"Why it's Kate King, the authoress. Bless me, how rude not to introduce you! Here, my King, is an admirer of yours, Fanny Shaw, and my well-beloved friend," cried Polly, presenting Fan, who regarded the shabby young woman with as much respect as if she had been arrayed in velvet and ermine, for Kate had written a successful book by accident and happened to be the fashion just then.

"It's time for lunch, girls, and I brought mine along with me, it's so much jollier to eat in sisterhood. Let's club together and have a revel," said Kate, producing a bag of oranges and several big, plummy buns.

"We've got sardines, crackers, and cheese," said Bess, clearing off a table with all speed.

"Wait a bit and I'll add my share," cried Polly, and catching up her cloak, she ran off to the grocery store nearby.

"You'll be shocked at our performances, Miss Shaw, but you can call it a picnic, and never tell what dreadful things you saw us do," said Rebecca, polishing a paint knife by rubbing it up and down in a pot of ivy while Kate spread forth the feast in several odd plates and a flat shell or two.

"Let us have coffee to finish off with. Put on the pot, Bess, and skim the milk," added Becky as she produced cups, mugs, and a queer little vase to supply drinking vessels for the party.

"Here's nuts, a pot of jam, and some cake. Fan likes sweet things, and we want to be elegant when we have company," said Polly, flying in again and depositing her share on the table.

"Now, then, fall to, ladies, and help yourselves. Never mind if the china don't hold out. Take the sardines by their little tails and wipe your fingers on my brown-paper napkins," said Kate, setting the example with such a relish that the others followed it in a gale of merriment.

Fanny had been to many elegant lunches, but never enjoyed one more than that droll picnic in the studio, for there was a freedom about it that was charming, an artistic flavor to everything, and such a spirit of goodwill and gaiety that she felt at home at once. As they ate the others talked and she listened, finding it as interesting as any romance to hear these young women discuss their plans, ambitions, successes, and defeats. It was a new world to her, and they seemed a different race of creatures from the girls whose lives were spent in dress, gossip, pleasure, or *ennui*. They were girls still, full of spirits, fun, and youth, but below the lightheartedness each cherished a purpose, which seemed to ennoble her womanhood, to give her a certain power, a sustaining satisfaction, a daily stimulus that led her on to daily effort and in time to some success in circumstance or character, which was worth all the patience, hope, and labor of her life.

Fanny was just then in the mood to feel the beauty of this, for the sincerest emotion she had ever known was beginning to make her dissatisfied with herself and the aimless life she led. "Men must respect such girls as these," she thought. "Yes, and love them, too, for in spite of their independence, they are womanly. I wish I had a talent to live for, if it would do as much for me as it does for them. It is this sort of thing that is improving Polly, that makes her society interesting to Sydney, and herself so dear to everyone. Money can't buy these things for me, and I want them very much."

As these thoughts were passing through her mind, Fanny was hearing all sorts of topics discussed with feminine enthusiasm and frankness. Art, morals, politics, society, books, religion, housekeeping, dress, and economy, for the minds and tongues roved from subject to subject with youthful rapidity and seemed to get something from the dryest and the dullest.

"How does the new book come on?" asked Polly, sucking her orange in public with a composure which would have scandalized the good ladies of Cranford.*

"Better than it deserves. My children, beware of popularity; it is a delusion and a snare; it puffeth up the heart of man, and especially of woman; it blindeth the eyes to faults; it exalteth unduly the humble powers of the victim; it is apt to be capricious, and just as one gets to liking the taste of this intoxicating draught, it suddenly faileth, and one is left gasping, like a fish out of water." And Kate emphasized her speech by spearing a sardine with a penknife and eating it with a groan.

"It won't hurt you much, I guess. You have worked and waited so long, a large dose will do you good," said Rebecca, giving her a generous spoonful of jam, as if eager to add as

---

* *Cranford:* a novel by Elizabeth Cleghorn Gaskell (1810–1865).

much sweetness as possible to a life that had not been an easy one.

"When are you and Becky going to dissolve partnership?" asked Polly, eager for news of all.

"Never! George knows he can't have one without the other, and has not suggested such a thing as parting us. There is always room in my house for Becky, and she lets me do as she would if she was in my place," answered Bess with a look which her friend answered by a smile.

"The lover won't separate this pair of friends, you see," whispered Polly to Fan. "Bess is to be married in the spring, and Becky is to live with her."

"By the way, Polly, I've got some tickets for you. People are always sending me such things, and as I don't care for them, I'm glad to make them over to you young and giddy infants. There are passes for the statuary exhibition, Becky shall have those. Here are the concert tickets for you, my musical girl, and this is for a course of lectures on literature, which I'll keep for myself."

As Kate dealt out the colored cards to the grateful girls, Fanny took a good look at her, wondering if the time would ever come when women could earn a little money and success without paying such a heavy price for them, for Kate looked sick, tired, and too early old. Then her eye went to the unfinished statue and she said impulsively:

"I hope you'll put that in marble and show us what we ought to be."

"I wish I could!" And an intense desire shone in Rebecca's face as she saw her faulty work and felt how fair her model was.

For a minute the five young women sat silent, looking up at the beautiful, strong figure before them, each longing to see it done and each unconscious that she was helping, by her individual effort and experience, to bring the day when their noblest ideal of womanhood should be embodied in flesh and blood, not clay.

The city bells rang one, and Polly started up.

"I must go, for I promised a neighbor of mine a lesson at two."

"I thought this was a holiday," said Fanny.

"So it is, but this is a little labor of love and doesn't spoil the day at all. The child has talent, loves music, and needs help. I can't give her money, but I *can* teach her, so I do, and she is the most promising pupil I have. 'Help one another' is part of the religion of our sisterhood, Fan."

"I must put you in a story, Polly. I want a heroine, and you will do," said Kate.

"Me! Why there never was such a humdrum, unromantic thing as I am," cried Polly, amazed.

"I've booked you, nevertheless, so in you go, but you may add as much romance as you like, it's time you did."

"I'm ready for it when it comes, but it can't be forced, you know." And Polly blushed and smiled as if some little spice of that delightful thing *had* stolen into her life, for all its prosaic seeming.

Fanny was amused to see that the girls did not kiss at parting but shook hands in a quiet, friendly fashion, looking at one another with eyes that said more than the most "gushing" words.

"I like your friends very much, Polly. I was afraid I should find them mannish and rough, or sentimental and conceited. But they are simple, sensible creatures full of talent and all sorts of fine things. I admire and respect them, and want to go again, if I may."

"Oh, Fan, I *am* so glad! I hoped you'd like them, I knew they'd do you good, and I'll take you anytime, for you stood the test better than I expected. Becky asked me to bring you again, and she seldom does that for fashionable young ladies, let me tell you."

"I want to be ever so much better, and I think you and they might show me how," said Fanny with a traitorous tremble in her voice.

"We'll show you the sunny side of poverty and work, and that is a useful lesson for anyone, Miss Mills says," answered Polly, hoping that Fan *would* learn how much the poor can teach the rich and what helpful friends girls may be to one another.

Chapter 14

Nipped in the Bud

*O*n the evening of Fan's visit Polly sat down before her fire with a resolute and thoughtful aspect. She pulled her hair down, turned her skirt back, put her feet on the fender, and took Puttel into her lap, all of which arrangements signified that something very important had got to be thought over and settled. Polly did not soliloquize aloud, as heroines on the stage and in books have a way of doing, but the conversation she held with herself was very much like this:

"I'm afraid there *is* something in it. I've tried to think it's nothing but vanity or imagination, yet I can't help seeing a difference and feeling as if I ought not to pretend that I don't. I know it's considered proper for girls to shut their eyes and let things come to a crisis, no matter how much mischief is done. But I don't think it's doing as we'd be done by, and it seems a great deal more honest to show a man that you don't love him before he has entirely lost his heart. The girls laughed at me when I said so, and they declared that it would be a very improper thing to do, but I've observed that *they* don't hesitate to snub 'ineligible parties,' as they call poor, very young, or unpopular men. It's all right then, but when a nice person comes it's part of the fun to let him go on to the very end, whether the girls care for him or not. The more proposals, the more credit. Fan says Trix always asks when she comes home after the summer excursions, 'How many birds have you bagged?' as if men were partridges. What wicked creatures we are, some of us at least. I wonder why such a love of conquest was put into us? Mother says a great deal of it is owing to bad education nowadays, but some girls seem born for the express purpose of making trouble and would manage to do it if they lived in a howling wilderness. I'm afraid I've got a spice of it, and if I had the chance, should be as bad as any of them. I've tried it and liked it, and maybe this is the consequence of that night's fun."

Here Polly leaned back and looked up at the little mirror over the chimneypiece, which was hung so that it reflected the faces of those about the fire. In it Polly saw a pair of telltale eyes looking out from a tangle of bright brown hair, cheeks that flushed and dimpled suddenly as the fresh mouth smiled with an expression of conscious power, half proud, half ashamed, and as pretty to see as the coquettish gesture with which she smoothed back her curls and flourished a white hand. For a minute she regarded the pleasant picture while visions of girlish romances and triumphs danced through her head, then she shook her hair all over her face and pushed her chair out of range of the mirror, saying, with a droll mixture of self-reproach and self-approval in her tone:

"Oh, Puttel, Puttel, what a fool I am!"

Puss appeared to endorse the sentiment by a loud purr

and a graceful wave of her tail, and Polly returned to the subject from which these little vanities had beguiled her.

"Just suppose it *is* true, that he *does* ask me, and I say yes! What a stir it would make, and what fun it would be to see the faces of the girls when it came out! They all think a great deal of him because he is so hard to please, and almost any of them would feel immensely flattered if he liked them, whether they chose to marry him or not. Trix has tried for years to fascinate him, and he can't bear her, and I'm so glad! What a spiteful thing I am. Well, I can't help it, she does aggravate me so!" And Polly gave the cat such a tweak of the ear that Puttel bounced out of her lap in high dudgeon.

"It don't do to think of her, and I won't!" said Polly to herself, setting her lips with a grim look that was not at all becoming. "What an easy life I should have—plenty of money, quantities of friends, all sorts of pleasures, and no work, no poverty, no cold shoulders or patched boots. I could do so much for all at home—how I should enjoy that!" And Polly let her thoughts revel in the luxurious future her fancy painted. It was a very bright picture, but something seemed amiss with it, for presently she sighed and shook her head, thinking sorrowfully, "Ah, but I don't love him, and I'm afraid I never can as I ought! He's very good, and generous, and wise, and would be kind, I know, but somehow I can't imagine spending my life with him. I'm so afraid I should get tired of him, and then what should I do? Polly Sydney don't sound well, and Mrs. Arthur Sydney don't seem to fit me a bit. Wonder how it would seem to call him 'Arthur'?" And Polly said it under her breath, with a look over her shoulder to be sure no one heard it. "It's a pretty name, but rather too fine, and I shouldn't dare to say 'Syd,' as his sister does. I like short, plain, homelike names, such as

Will, Ned, or Tom. No, no, I can never care for him, and it's no use to try!" The exclamation broke from Polly as if a sudden trouble had seized her, and laying her head down on her knees, she sat motionless for many minutes.

When she looked up her face wore an expression which no one had ever seen on it before, a look of mingled pain and patience, as if some loss had come to her and left the bitterness of regret behind.

"I won't think of myself or try to mend one mistake by making another," she said with a heavy sigh. "I'll do what I can for Fan and not stand between her and a chance of happiness. Let me see, how can I begin? I won't walk with him anymore. I'll dodge and go roundabout ways, so that we can't meet. I never had much faith in the remarkable coincidence of his always happening home to dinner just as I go to give the Roths their lesson. The fact is, I like to meet him, I'm glad to be seen with him, and put on airs, I daresay, like a vain goose as I am. Well, I won't do it anymore, and that will spare Fan one affliction. Poor dear, how I must have worried her all this time and never guessed it. She hasn't been quite as kind as ever, but when she got sharp I fancied it was dyspepsia. Oh, me! I wish the other trouble could be cured as easily as this."

Here puss showed an amiable desire to forgive and forget, and Polly took her up, saying aloud:

"Puttel, when missis abuses you, play it's dyspepsia and don't bear malice, because it's a very trying disease, my dear."

Then, going back to her thoughts, she rambled on again:

"If he doesn't take that hint, I will give him a stronger one, for I *will not* have matters come to a crisis, though I can't deny that my wicked vanity strongly tempts me to try and 'bag a bird' just for the excitement and credit of the thing. Polly, I'm ashamed of you! What would your blessed mother say to hear such expressions from you? I'd write and tell her all the worry, only it wouldn't do any good and would only trouble her. I've no right to tell Fan's secrets, and I'm ashamed to tell mine. No, I'll leave Mother in peace and fight it out alone. I do think Fan would suit him excellently by and by. He has known her all her life and has a good influence over her. Love would do so much toward making her what she might be, it's a shame to have the chance lost just because he happens to see me. I should think she'd hate me, but I'll show her that she needn't and do all I can to help her, for she has been so good to me nothing shall ever make me forget that. It is a delicate and dangerous task, but I guess I can manage it. At any rate I'll try, and have nothing to reproach myself with if things do go 'contrary.' "

What Polly thought of as she lay back on her chair, with her eyes shut and a hopeless look on her face, is none of our business, though we might feel a wish to know what caused a tear to gather slowly from time to time under her lashes and roll down on Puttel's Quaker-colored coat. Was it regret for the conquest she relinquished, was it sympathy for her friend, or was it an uncontrollable overflow of feeling as she read some sad or tender passage of the little romance which she kept hidden away in her own heart?

On Monday, Polly began the "delicate and dangerous task." Instead of going to her pupils by way of the park and the pleasant streets adjoining, she took a roundabout route through back streets and thus escaped Mr. Sydney, who, as usual, came home to dinner very early that day and looked disappointed because he nowhere saw the bright face in the modest bonnet. Polly kept this up for a week, and by carefully avoiding the Shaws' house during calling hours, she saw nothing of Mr. Sydney, who, of course, didn't visit her at

Miss Mills's. Minnie happened to be poorly that week and took no lesson, so Uncle Syd was deprived of his last hope and looked as if his allowance of sunshine had been suddenly cut off.

Now, as Polly was by no means a perfect creature, I am free to confess that the old temptation assailed her more than once that week, for, when the first excitement of the dodging reform had subsided, she missed the pleasant little interviews that used to put a certain flavor of romance into her dull, hardworking days. She liked Mr. Sydney very much, for he had always been kind and friendly since the early times when he had treated the little girl with a courtesy which the young woman gratefully remembered. I don't think it was his wealth, accomplishments, or position that most attracted Polly, though these doubtless possessed a greater influence than she suspected. It was that indescribable something which women are quick to see and feel in men who have been blessed with wise and good mothers. This had an especial charm to Polly, for she soon found that this side of his character was not shown to everyone. With most girls he was very like the other young men of his set, except perhaps in a certain grace of manner which was as natural to him as his respect for all womankind. But with Fanny and Polly he showed the domestic traits and virtues which are more engaging to womanly women than any amount of cool intellect or worldly wisdom.

Polly had seen a good deal of him during her visits at the Shaws', where he was intimate, owing to the friendship between Madam and his mother, but she had never thought of him as a possible lover for either Fanny or herself because he was six or eight years older than they and still sometimes assumed the part of a venerable mentor, as in the early days. Lately this had changed, especially toward Polly, and it flattered her more than she would confess even to herself. She knew he admired her one talent, respected her independence, and enjoyed her society, but when something warmer and more flattering than admiration, respect, or pleasure crept into his manner, she could not help seeing that one of the good gifts of this life was daily coming more and more within her reach and began to ask herself if she could honestly receive the gift and reward the giver.

At first she tried to think she could, but unfortunately hearts are so "contrary" that they won't be obedient to reason, will, or even gratitude. Polly felt a very cordial friendship for Mr. Sydney, but not one particle of the love which is the only coin in which love can be truly paid. Then she took a fancy into her head that she ought to accept this piece of good fortune for the sake of the family and forget herself. But this false idea of self-sacrifice did not satisfy, for she was not a fashionable girl trained to believe that her first duty was to make "a good match" and never mind the consequences, though they rendered her miserable for life. Polly's creed was very simple: "If I don't love him, I ought not to marry him, especially when I do love somebody else, though everything is against me." If she had read as many French novels as some young ladies, she might have considered it interesting to marry under the circumstances and suffer a secret anguish to make herself a romantic victim. But Polly's education had been neglected, and after a good deal of natural indecision she did what most women do in such cases—thought she would "wait and see."

The discovery of Fanny's secret seemed to show her something to do, for if the "wait and see" decision was making her friend unhappy, it must be changed as soon as possible. This finished Polly's indecision, and after that night she never allowed herself to dwell upon the pleasant temptation

which came in a guise particularly attractive to a young girl
with a spice of the old Eve in her composition. So day after
day she trudged through the dull back streets, longing for
the sunny park, the face that always brightened when it saw
her coming, and most of all the chance of meeting—well, it
wasn't Trix.

When Saturday came Polly started as usual for a visit to
Beck and Bess, but couldn't resist stopping at the Shaws' to
leave a little parcel for Fan, though it *was* calling time. As
she stepped in, meaning to run up for a word if Fanny
should chance to be alone, two hats on the table arrested
her.

"Who is here, Katy?"

"Only Mr. Sydney and Master Tom. Won't you stop a bit,
Miss Polly?"

"Not this morning, I'm rather in a hurry." And away
went Polly as if a dozen eager pupils were clamoring for her
presence. But as the door shut behind her she felt so left out
in the cold that her eyes filled, and when Nep, Tom's great
Newfoundland, came blundering after her she stopped and
hugged his shaggy head, saying softly, as she looked into the
brown, benevolent eyes, full of almost human sympathy:

"Now, go back, old dear, you mustn't follow me. Oh,
Nep, it's *so* hard to put love away when you want it very
much and it isn't right to take it."

A foolish little speech to make to a dog, but you see Polly
was only a tender-hearted girl trying to do her duty.

"Since he is safe with Fanny, I may venture to walk where
I like. It's such a lovely day, all the babies will be out, and it
always does me good to see them," thought Polly, turning
into the wide, sunny street where West End-dom promenaded at that hour.

The babies *were* out in full force, looking as gay and deli-

cate and sweet as the snowdrops, hyacinths, and daffodils on
the banks whence the snow had melted. But somehow the
babies didn't do Polly the good she expected, though they
smiled at her from their carriages and kissed their chubby
hands as she passed them, for Polly had the sort of face that
babies love. One tiny creature in blue plush was casting despairing glances after a very small lord of creation who was
walking away with a toddling belle in white while a second
young gentleman in gorgeous purple gaiters was endeavoring
to console the deserted damsel.

"Take hold of Master Charley's hand, Miss Mamie, and
walk pretty, like Willy and Flossy," said the maid.

"No, no, I want to do wid Willy, and he won't let me. Do
'way, Tarley, I don't lite you," cried little Blue Bonnet, casting down her ermine muff and sobbing into a microscopic
handkerchief, the thread-lace edging on which couldn't miti-
gate her woe as it might have done that of an older sufferer.

"Willy likes Flossy best, so stop crying and come right
along, you naughty child."

As poor little Dido was jerked away by the unsympathetic
maid, and Purple Gaiters essayed in vain to plead his cause,
Polly said to herself, with a smile and a sigh:

"How early the old story begins!"

It seemed as if the spring weather had brought out all
manner of tender things besides fresh grass and the first
dandelions, for as she went down the street Polly kept seeing
different phases of the sweet old story which she was trying
to forget.

At a street corner a black-eyed schoolboy was parting
from a rosy-faced schoolgirl whose music roll he was reluc-
tantly surrendering.

"Don't you forget, now," said the boy, looking bashfully

into the bright eyes that danced with pleasure as the girl blushed and smiled and answered reproachfully:

"Why, of course I shan't!"

"That little romance runs smoothly so far. I hope it may to the end," said Polly heartily as she watched the lad tramp away, whistling as blithely as if his pleasurable emotions must find a vent or endanger the buttons on the round jacket while the girl pranced on her own doorstep as if practicing for the joyful dance which she had promised not to forget.

A little farther on Polly passed a newly engaged couple whom she knew, walking arm in arm for the first time, both wearing that proud yet conscious look which is so delightful to behold upon the countenances of these temporarily glorified beings.

"How happy they seem. Oh, dear!" said Polly, and trudged on, wondering if her turn would ever come and fearing that it was impossible.

A glimpse of a motherly-looking lady entering a door, received by a flock of pretty children who cast themselves upon mama and her parcels with cries of rapture, did Polly good, and when a minute after she passed a gray old couple walking placidly together in the sunshine, she felt better still, and was glad to see such a happy ending to the romance she had read all down the street.

As if the mischievous little god wished to take Polly at a disadvantage, or perhaps to give her another chance, just at that instant Mr. Sydney appeared at her side. How he got there was never very clear to Polly, but there he was, flushed and a little out of breath, but looking so glad to see her that she hadn't the heart to be stiff and cool, as she had fully intended to be when they met.

"Very warm, isn't it?" he said when he had shaken hands and fallen into step, just in the old way.

"You seem to find it so." And Polly laughed, with a sudden sparkle in her eyes. She really couldn't help it, it was so pleasant to see him again, just when she was feeling so lonely.

"Have you given up teaching the Roths?" asked Sydney, changing the subject.

"No."

"Do you go as usual?"

"Yes."

"Well, it's a mystery to me how you get there."

"As much as it is to me how *you* got here so suddenly."

"I saw you from the Shaws' window and took the liberty of running after you by the back street," he said, laughing.

"That is the way I get to the Roths," answered Polly. She did not mean to tell, but his frankness was so agreeable she forgot herself.

"It's not nearly so pleasant or so short for you as the park."

"I know it, but people sometimes get tired of old ways and like to try new ones."

Polly didn't say that quite naturally, and Sydney gave her a quick look as he asked:

"Do you get tired of old friends, too, Miss Polly?"

"Not often, but—" And there she stuck, for the fear of being ungrateful or unkind made her almost hope that he wouldn't take the hint which she had been carefully preparing for him.

There was a dreadful little pause, which Polly broke by saying abruptly:

"How is Fan?"

"Dashing as ever. Do you know I'm rather disappointed

in Fanny, for she don't seem to improve with her years,"
said Sydney, as if he accepted the diversion and was glad of
it.

"Ah, you never see her at her best. She puts on that
dashing air before people to hide her real self. But I know
her better, and I assure you that she *does* improve. She tried
to mend her faults, though she won't own it, and will surprise you someday by the amount of heart and sense and
goodness she has got."

Polly spoke heartily now, and Sydney looked at her as if
Fanny's defender pleased him more than Fanny's defense.

"I'm very glad to hear it and willingly take your word for
it. Everybody shows you their good side, I think, and that is
why you find the world such a pleasant place."

"Oh, but I don't! It often seems like a very hard and
dismal place, and I croak over my trials like an ungrateful
raven."

"Can't we make the trials lighter for you?"

The voice that put the question was so very kind that
Polly dared not look up, because she knew what the eyes
were silently saying.

"Thank you, no. I don't get more tribulation than is good
for me, I fancy, and we are apt to make mistakes when we try
to dodge troubles."

"Or people," added Sydney in a tone that made Polly
color up to her forehead.

"How lovely the park looks," she said in great confusion.

"Yes, it's the pleasantest walk we have, don't you think
so?" asked the artful young man, laying a trap into which
Polly immediately fell.

"Yes, indeed! It's always so refreshing to me to see a little
bit of the country, as it were, especially at this season."

Oh, Polly, Polly, what a stupid speech to make when you

had just given him to understand that you were tired of the park! Not being a fool or a coxcomb, Sydney put this and that together, and taking various trifles into the account, he had by this time come to the conclusion that Polly had heard the same bits of gossip that he had, which linked their names together, that she didn't like it, and tried to show she didn't in this way. He was quicker to take a hint than she had expected, and being both proud and generous, resolved to settle the matter at once, for Polly's sake as well as his own. So when she made her last brilliant remark, he said quietly, watching her face keenly all the while:

"I thought so. Well, I'm going out of town on business for several weeks, so you can enjoy your 'little bit of country' without being annoyed by me."

"Annoyed? Oh, no!" cried Polly earnestly, then stopped short, not knowing what to say for herself.

She thought she had a good deal of the coquette in her, and I've no doubt that with time and training she would have become a very dangerous little person, but now she was far too transparent and straightforward by nature even to tell a white lie cleverly. Sydney knew this and liked her for it, but he took advantage of it nevertheless by asking suddenly:

"Honestly, now, wouldn't you go the old way and enjoy it as much as ever if I wasn't anywhere about to set the busybodies gossiping?"

"Yes," said Polly before she could stop herself, and then could have bitten her tongue out for being so rude. Another awful pause seemed impending, but just at that moment a horseman clattered by with a smile and a salute, which caused Polly to exclaim, "Oh, there's Tom!" with a tone and a look that silenced the words hovering on Sydney's lips and caused him to hold out his hand with a look which made

Polly's heart flutter then and ache with pity for a good while afterward, though he only said, "Good-bye, Polly."

He was gone before she could do anything but look up at him with a remorseful face and she walked on, feeling that the first and perhaps the only lover she would ever have had read his answer and accepted it in silence. She did not know what else he had read and comforted herself with the thought that he did not care for her very much, since he took the first rebuff so quickly.

Polly did not return to her favorite walk till she learned from Minnie that "Uncle" had really left town, and then she found that his friendly company and conversation was what had made the way so pleasant after all. She sighed over the perversity of things in general and croaked a little over her trials in particular, but on the whole got over her loss better than she expected, for soon she had other sorrows besides her own to comfort, and such work does a body more good than floods of regretful tears or hours of sentimental lamentation.

She shunned Fanny for a day or two, but gained nothing by it, for that young lady, hearing of Sydney's sudden departure, could not rest till she discovered the cause of it and walked in upon Polly one afternoon just when the dusk made it a propitious hour for tender confidences.

"What have you been doing with yourself lately?" asked Fanny, composing herself, with her back toward the rapidly waning light.

"Wagging to and fro as usual. What's the news with you?" answered Polly, feeling that something was coming and rather glad to have it over and done with.

"Nothing particular. Trix treats Tom shamefully, and he bears it like a lamb. I tell him to break his engagement and not to be worried so, but he won't because she has been jilted once and he thinks it's such a mean thing to do."

"Perhaps she'll jilt him."

"I've no doubt she will if anything better comes along. But Trix is getting *passée*, and I shouldn't wonder is she kept him to his word just out of perversity if nothing else."

"Poor Tom, what a fate!" said Polly with what was meant to be a comical groan, but it sounded so tragical that she saw it wouldn't pass and hastened to hide the failure by saying, with a laugh, "If you call Trix *passée* at twenty-three, what shall we all be at twenty-five?"

"Utterly done with and laid upon the shelf. I feel so already, for I don't get half the attention I used to have, and the other night I heard Maud and Grace wondering why those old girls 'didn't stay at home and give them a chance.' "

"How is Maudie?"

"Pretty well, but she worries me by her queer tastes and notions. She loves to go into the kitchen and mess, she hates to study, and said right before the Vincents that she should think it would be great fun to be a beggar girl, to go round with a basket, it must be so interesting to see what you'd get."

"Minnie said the other day she wished she was a pigeon so she could paddle in the puddles and not fuss about rubbers."

"By the way, when is her uncle coming back?" asked Fanny, who couldn't wait any longer and joyfully seized the opening Polly made for her.

"I'm sure I don't know."

"Nor care, I suppose, you hard-hearted thing."

"Why, Fan, what do you mean?"

"I'm not blind, my dear, neither is Tom, and when a

young gentleman cuts a call abruptly short, and races after a young lady, and is seen holding her hand at the quietest corner of the park, and then goes traveling all of a sudden, *we* know what it means if you don't."

"Who got up that nice idea I should like to know?" demanded Polly as Fanny stopped for breath.

"Now don't be affected, Polly, but just tell me, like a dear, hasn't he proposed?"

"No, he hasn't."

"Don't you think he means to?"

"I don't think he'll ever say a word to me."

"Well, I *am* surprised!" And Fanny drew a long breath, as if a load was off her mind. Then she added, in a changed tone:

"But don't you love him, Polly?"

"No."

"Truly."

"Truly, Fan."

Neither spoke for a minute, but the heart of one of them beat joyfully and the dusk hid a very happy face.

"Don't you think he cared for you, dear?" asked Fanny presently. "I don't mean to be prying, but I really thought he did."

"That's not for me to say, but if it is so, it's only a passing fancy and he'll soon get over it."

"Do tell me all about it. I'm *so* interested, and I know something has happened, I hear it in your voice, for I can't see your face."

"Do you remember the talk we once had after reading one of Miss Edgeworth's stories about not letting one's lovers come to a declaration if one didn't love them?"

"Yes."

"And you girls said it wasn't proper, and I said it was

honest, anyway. Well, I always meant to try it if I got a chance, and I have. Mind you, I don't say Mr. Sydney loved me, for he never said so, and never will now, but I did fancy he rather liked me and might do more if I didn't show him that it was of no use."

"And you did?" cried Fanny, much excited.

"I just gave him a hint and he took it. He meant to go away before that, so don't think his heart is broken or mind what silly tattlers say. I didn't like his meeting me so much and told him so by going another way. He understood, and being a gentleman, made no fuss. I daresay he thought I was a vain goose and laughed at me for my pains, like Churchill in *Helen*."

"No, he wouldn't. He'd like it and respect you for doing it. But, Polly, it would have been a grand thing for you."

"I can't sell myself for an establishment."

"Mercy! What an idea!"

"Well, that's the plain English of half your fashionable matches. I'm 'odd,' you know, and prefer to be an independent spinster and teach music all my days."

"Ah, but you won't. You were made for a nice, happy home of your own, and I hope you'll get it, Polly, dear," said Fanny warmly, feeling so grateful to Polly that she found it hard not to pour out all her secret at once.

"I hope I may, but I doubt it," answered Polly in a tone that made Fanny wonder if she, too, knew what heartache meant.

"Something troubles you, Polly, what is it? Confide in me, as I do in you," said Fanny tenderly, for all the coldness she had tried to hide from Polly had melted in the sudden sunshine that had come to her.

"Do you always?" asked her friend, leaning forward with an irresistible desire to win back the old-time love and confidence, too precious to be exchanged for a little brief excitement or the barren honor of "bagging a bird," to use Trix's elegant expression. Fanny understood it then, and threw herself into Polly's arms, crying, with a shower of grateful tears:

"Oh, my dear, my dear, did you do it for my sake?"

And Polly held her close, saying, in that tender voice of hers, "I didn't mean to let a lover part this pair of friends if I could help it."

Chapter 15

Breakers Ahead

*G*oing into the Shaws' one evening, Polly found Maud sitting on the stairs with a troubled face.

"Oh, Polly, I'm so glad you've come!" cried the little girl, running to hug her.

"What's the matter, deary?"

"I don't know. Something dreadful must have happened, for Mama and Fan are crying together upstairs, Papa is shut up in the library, and Tom is raging round like a bear in the dining room."

"I guess it isn't anything very bad. Perhaps Mama is sicker than usual, or Papa worried about business, or Tom in some new scrape. Don't look so frightened, Maudie, but come into the parlor and see what I've got for you," said Polly, feeling that there was trouble of some sort in the air, but trying to cheer the child, for her little face was full of a sorrowful anxiety that went to Polly's heart.

"I don't think I *can* like anything till I know what the matter is," answered Maud. "It's something horrid, I'm sure, for when Papa came home he went up to Mama's room and talked ever so long, and Mama cried very loud, and when I tried to go in Fan wouldn't let me and she looked scared and strange. I wanted to go to Papa when he came down, but the door was locked, and he said, 'Not now, my little girl,' and then I sat here waiting to see what would happen and Tom came home. But when I ran to tell him, he said, 'Go away and don't bother,' and just took me by the shoulders and put me out. Oh, dear! Everything is so queer and horrid, I don't know what to do.''

Maud began to cry, and Polly sat down on the stairs beside her, trying to comfort her while her own thoughts were full of a vague fear. All at once the dining-room door opened and Tom's head appeared. A single glance showed Polly that something *was* the matter, for the care and elegance which usually marked his appearance were entirely wanting. His tie was under one ear, his hair in a toss, the cherished mustache had a neglected air, and his face an expression both excited, ashamed, and distressed. Even his voice betrayed disturbance, for instead of the affable greeting he usually bestowed upon the young lady, he seemed to have fallen back into the bluff tone of his boyish days and all he said was:

"Hullo, Polly."

"How do you do?" answered Polly.

"I'm in a devil of a mess, thank you. Send that chicken up stairs and come in and hear about it," he said, as if he had been longing to tell someone and welcomed prudent Polly as a special providence.

"Go up, deary, and amuse yourself with this book and these gingersnaps that I made for you, there's a good child," whispered Polly as Maud rubbed away her tears and stared at Tom with round, inquisitive eyes.

"You'll tell me all about it, by and by, won't you?" she whispered, preparing to obey.

"If I may," answered Polly.

Maud departed with unexpected docility, and Polly went into the dining room, where Tom was wandering about in a restless way. If he *had* been "raging like a bear," Polly wouldn't have cared, she was so pleased that he wanted her and so glad to be a *confidante,* as she used to be in the happy old days, that she would joyfully have faced a much more formidable person than reckless Tom.

"Now, then, what is it?" she said, coming straight to the point.

"Guess."

"You've killed your horse racing."

"Worse than that."

"You are suspended again."

"Worse than that."

"Trix has run away with somebody," cried Polly with a gasp.

"Worse still."

"Oh, Tom, you haven't horsewhipped or shot anyone?"

"Came pretty near blowing my own brains out, but you see I didn't."

"I can't guess. Tell me, quick."

"Well, I'm expelled."

Tom paused on the rug as he gave the answer and looked at Polly to see how she took it. To his surprise, she seemed almost relieved, and after a minute's silence said soberly:

"That's bad, very bad, but it might have been worse."

"It *is* worse." And Tom walked away again with a despairing sort of groan.

"Don't knock the chairs about, but come and sit down and tell me quietly."

"Can't do it."

"Well, go on, then. Are you truly expelled? Can't it be made up? What did you do?"

"It's a true bill this time. I just had a row with the chapel watchman and knocked him down. If it was a first offense, I might have got off, but you see I've had no end of narrow escapes and this was my last chance. I've lost it, and now there'll be the dickens to pay. I knew it was all up with me, so I didn't wait to be turned out, but just took myself off."

"What *will* your father say?"

"It will come hard on the governor, but the worst of it is—" There Tom stopped and stood a minute in the middle of the room with his head down, as if he didn't find it easy to tell even kind little Polly. Then out came the truth all in a breath, just as he used to bolt out his boyish misdemeanors and then back up against the wall ready to take the consequences.

"I owe an awful lot of money that the governor don't know about."

"Oh, Tom, how could you?"

"I've been an extravagant rascal, I know it, and I'm thundering sorry, but that don't help a fellow. I've got to tell the dear old buffer, and there's where it cuts."

At another time Polly would have laughed at the contrast between Tom's face and his language, but there was a sincere remorse which made even the dreadful word "buffer" rather touching than otherwise.

"He will be very angry, I daresay, but he'll help you, won't he? He always does, Fan says."

"That's the worst of it, you see. He's paid up so often that the last time he said his patience couldn't stand it, nor his pocket either, and if I got into any more scrapes of that sort, I must get out as I could. I meant to be as steady as Bunker Hill Monument, but here I am again, worse than ever, for

last quarter I didn't say anything to Father, he was so both-
ered by the loss of those ships just then, so things have
mounted up confoundedly."

"What have you done with all your money?"

"Hanged if I know."

"Can't you pay it anyway?"

"Don't see how, as I haven't a cent of my own and no way
of getting it, unless I try gambling."

"Oh, mercy, no! Sell your horse," cried Polly after a minute of deep meditation.

"I have, but he didn't bring half I gave for him. I lamed
him last winter, and the beggar won't get over it."

"And that didn't pay up the debts?"

"Only about a half of 'em."

"Why, Tom, how much do you owe?"

"I have dodged figuring it up till yesterday, then things
were so desperate I thought I might as well face the truth so I
overhauled my accounts, and there's the result."

Tom threw a blotted, crumpled paper into Polly's lap and
tramped up and down again, faster than ever. Polly took one
look at the total and clasped her hands, for to her inexperi-
enced eyes it looked appalling.

"Tidy little sum, isn't it?" asked Tom, who couldn't bear
the silence or the startled, grieved look in Polly's eyes.

"It's awful! I don't wonder you dread telling your father."

"I'd rather be shot. I say, Polly, suppose we break it to him
easy!" added Tom after another turn.

"How do you mean?"

"Why, suppose Fan, or, better still, you go and sort of
pave the way. I can't bear to come down on him with the
whole truth at once."

"So you'd like to have me go and tell him for you?" Polly's
lip curled a little as she said that, and she gave Tom a look

that would have shown him how blue eyes can flash if he
had seen it. But he was at the window and didn't turn as he
said slowly:

"Well, you see, he's so fond of you, we all confide in you,
and you are so like one of the family that it seems quite
natural. Just tell him I'm expelled, you know, and as much
more as you like, then I'll come in and we'll have it out."

Polly rose and went to the door without a word. In doing
so, Tom caught a glimpse of her face and said hastily:

"Don't you think it would be a good plan?"

"No, I don't."

"Why not? Don't you think he'd rather have it told him
nicely by you than blurted out as I always do blurt things?"

"I *know* he'd rather have his son go to him and tell the
truth, like a man, instead of sending a girl to do what he is
afraid to do himself."

If Polly had suddenly boxed his ears, Tom couldn't have
looked more taken aback than by that burst. He looked at
her excited face, seemed to understand the meaning of it,
and remembered all at once that he *was* trying to hide behind a girl. He turned scarlet, said shortly, "Come back,
Polly," and walked straight out of the room, looking as if
going to instant execution, for poor Tom had been taught to
fear his father and had not entirely outgrown the dread.

Polly sat down, looking both satisfied and troubled. "I
hope I did right," she said to herself. "I couldn't bear to
have him shirk and seem cowardly. He isn't, only he didn't
think how it seemed to me, and I don't wonder he *was* a
little afraid, Mr. Shaw is *so* severe with the poor fellow. Oh,
dear, what should we do if Will got into such scrapes. Thank
goodness he's poor and can't. I'm so glad of that!"

Then she sat silent beside the half-open door, hearing the
murmur of Tom's voice across the hall and hoping with all

her heart that he wouldn't have a very hard time. He seemed
to tell his story rapidly and steadily, without interruption, to
the end. Then Polly heard Mr. Shaw's deeper voice say a few
words, at which Tom uttered a loud exclamation, as if taken
by surprise. Polly couldn't distinguish a word, so she kept
her seat, wondering anxiously what was going on between
the two men. A sudden pause seemed to follow Tom's ejacu-
lation. Then Mr. Shaw talked a long time in a low, earnest
tone, so different from the angry one Polly had expected to
hear that it made her nervous, for Mr. Shaw usually "blew
Tom up first and forgave him afterward," as Maud said.
Presently Tom's voice was heard, apparently asking eager
questions to which brief replies were given. Then a dead
silence fell upon the room and nothing was heard but the
spring rain softly falling out-of-doors. All of a sudden she
heard a movement and Tom's voice say audibly:

"Let me bring Polly." And he appeared, looking so pale
and miserable that Polly was frightened.

"Go and say something to him. I can't. Poor old Father, if
I'd only known." And to Polly's utter dismay, Tom threw
himself into a chair and laid his head down on the table, as if
he had got a blow that was too much for him.

"Oh, Tom, what is it?" cried Polly, hurrying to him full of
fears she dared not speak.

Without looking up, Tom answered, in a smothered voice:

"Failed, all gone to smash, and tomorrow everyone will
know it."

Polly held on to the back of Tom's chair for a minute, for
the news took her breath away, and she felt as if the world
was coming to an end. "Failed" was such a vaguely dreadful
word to her.

"Is it very bad?" she asked softly, feeling as if anything was
better than to stand still and see Tom so wretched.

"Yes, he means to give up everything. He's done his best, but it can't be staved off any longer, and it's all up with him."

"Oh, I wish I had a million to give him!" cried Polly, clasping her hands, with the tears running down her cheeks. "How does he bear it, Tom?"

"Like a man, Polly, and I'm proud of him," said Tom, looking up, all red and excited with the emotions he was trying to keep under. "Everything has been against him, and he has fought all alone to stand the pressure, but it's too much for him and he's given in. It's an honorable failure, mind you, and no one can say a word against him. I'd like to see 'em try it!" And Tom clenched his hands, as if it would be an immense relief to him to thrash half a dozen aspersers of his father's honest name.

"Of course they can't! This is what poor Maud was troubled about. He had told your mother and Fan before you came, and that is why they are so unhappy, I suppose."

"They are safe enough. Father hasn't touched Mother's money, he 'couldn't rob his girls,' he said, and that's all safe for 'em. Isn't he a trump, Polly?" And Tom's face shone with pride, even while his lips would twitch with a tenderer feeling.

"If I could only do anything to help," cried Polly, oppressed with her own powerlessness.

"You can. Go and be good to him, you know how, he needs it enough, all alone there. I can't do it, for I'm only a curse instead of a comfort to him."

"How did he take *your* news?" asked Polly, who, for a time, had forgotten the lesser trouble in the greater.

"Like a lamb, for when I'd done he only said, 'My poor lad, we must bear with one another,' and then told his story."

"I'm glad he was kind," began Polly in a soothing tone, but Tom cried out remorsefully:

"That's what knocks me over! Just when I ought to be a pride and a prop to him, I bring him my debts and disgrace and he never says a word of blame. It's no use, I can't stand it!" And Tom's head went down again with something very like a sob, that would come in spite of manful efforts to keep it back, for the poor fellow had the warmest heart that ever was, and all the fine waistcoats outside couldn't spoil it.

That sound gave Polly more pain than the news of a dozen failures and expulsions, and it was as impossible for her to resist putting her hand tenderly on the bent head as it was for her to help noticing with pleasure how brown the little curls were growing and how soft they were. In spite of her sorrow, she enjoyed that minute very much, for she was a born consoler and, it is hardly necessary for me to add, loved this reprehensible Tom with all her heart. It was a very foolish thing for her to do, she quite agreed to that. She couldn't understand it, explain it, or help it, she only felt that she did care for him very much, in spite of his faults, his indifference, and his engagement. You see, she learned to love him one summer when he made them a visit. That was before Trix caught him, and when she heard that piece of news Polly couldn't unlove him all at once, though she tried very hard, as was her duty. That engagement was such a farce that she never had much faith in it, so she put her love away in a corner of her heart and tried to forget it, hoping it would either die or have a right to live. It didn't make her very miserable because patience, work, and common sense lent her a hand, and hope would keep popping up its bright face from the bottom of her Pandora box of troubles. Now and then, when anyone said Trix wouldn't jilt Tom, or that Tom did care for Trix more than he should, Polly had a pang and thought she couldn't possibly bear it. But she always found she could, and so came to the conclusion that it was a merciful provision of nature that girls' hearts could stand so much and their appetites continue good when unrequited love was starving.

Now, she could not help yearning over this faulty, well-beloved scapegrace Tom or help thinking, with a little thrill of hope, "If Trix only cared for his money, she may cast him off now he's lost it, but I'll love him all the better because he's poor." With this feeling warm at her heart, I don't wonder that Polly's hand had a soothing effect, and that after a heave or two Tom's shoulders were quiet, and certain smothered sniffs suggested that he would be all right again if he could only wipe his eyes without anyone's seeing him do it.

Polly seemed to divine his wish, and tucking a little clean handkerchief into one of his half-open hands, she said, "I'm going to your father now," and with a farewell smooth, so comforting that Tom wished she'd do it again, she went away.

As she paused a minute in the hall to steady herself, Maud called her from above, and thinking that the women might need her more than the men, she ran up to find Fanny waiting for her in her own room.

"Mama's asleep, quite worn out, poor dear, so we can talk in here without troubling her," said Fanny, receiving her friend so quietly that Polly was amazed.

"Let me come, too, I won't make any fuss. It's so dreadful to be shut out everywhere, and have people crying and talking, and locked up, and I not know what it means," said Maud beseechingly.

"You do know, now. I've told her, Polly," said Fan as they sat down together and Maud perched herself on the bed so that she might retire among the pillows if her feelings were too much for her.

"I'm glad you take it so well, dear. I was afraid it might upset you," said Polly, seeing now that in spite of her quiet manner, Fan's eyes had an excited look and her cheeks a feverish color.

"I shall groan and moan by and by, I daresay, but at first it sort of dazed me, and now it begins to excite me. I ought to be full of sorrow for poor Papa, and I am truly sorry, but, wicked as it may seem, it's a fact, Polly, that I'm half glad it's happened, for it takes me out of myself and gives me something to do."

Fanny's eyes fell and her color rose as she spoke, but Polly understood why she wanted to forget herself and put her arm round her with a more tender sympathy than Fanny guessed.

"Perhaps things are not as bad as they seem. I don't know much about such matters, but I've seen people who have failed and they seemed just as comfortable as before," said Polly.

"It won't be so with us, for Papa means to give up everything and not have a word said against him. Mama's little property is settled upon her and hasn't been risked. That touched her so much! She dreads poverty even more than I do, but she begged him to take it if it would help him. That pleased him, but he said nothing would induce him to do it, for it wouldn't help much and was hardly enough to keep her comfortable."

"Do you know what he means to do?" asked Polly anxiously.

"He said his plans were not made, but he meant to go into the little house that belonged to Grandma as soon as he could, for it wasn't honest for a bankrupt to keep up an establishment like this."

"I shan't mind that at all. I like the little house 'cause it's got a garden and there's a cunning room with a three-cornered closet in it that I always wanted. If that's all, I don't think bankrupting is so very bad," said Maud, taking a cheerful view of things.

"Ah, just wait till the carriage goes and the nice clothes and the servants and we have to scratch along as we can. You'll change your mind then, poor child," said Fanny, whose ideas of failure were decidedly tragical.

"Will they take all my things away?" cried Maud in dismay.

"I daresay I don't know what we are allowed to keep, but not much, I fancy." And Fan looked as if strung up to sacrifice everything she possessed.

"They shan't have my new earrings—I'll hide 'em—and my best dress and my gold smelling bottle. Oh, oh, oh! I think it's mean to take a little girl's things away!" And Maud dived among the pillows to smother a wail of anguish at the prospect of being bereft of her treasures.

Polly soon lured her out again by assurances that she wouldn't be utterly despoiled and promises to try and soften the hard hearts of her father's creditors if the earrings and the smelling bottle were attached.

"I wonder if we shall be able to keep one servant, just till we learn how to do the work," said Fanny, looking at her white hands with a sigh.

But Maud clapped hers and gave a joyful bounce as she cried:

"Now I can learn to cook! I love so to beat eggs! I'll have an apron with a bib to it, like Polly's, and a feather duster, and sweep the stairs, maybe, with my head tied up, like Katy. Oh, what fun!"

"Don't laugh at her or discourage her. Let her find comfort in bibs and dustpans if she can," whispered Polly to Fan while Maud took a joyful "header" among the pillows and came up smiling and blowzy, for she loved housework and often got lectured for stolen visits to the kitchen and surreptitious sweepings and dustings when the coast was clear.

"Mama is so feeble, I shall have to keep house, I suppose, and you must show me how, Polly," said Fan.

"Good practice, ma'am, as you'll find out someday," answered Polly, laughing significantly.

Fanny smiled, then grew both grave and sad. "This changes everything. The old set will drop me, as we did the Mertons when their father failed, and my 'prospects,' as we say, are quite ruined."

"I don't believe it. Your real friends won't drop you, and you'll find out which the true ones are now. I know one friend who will be kinder than ever."

"Oh, Polly, do you think so?" And Fanny's eyes softened with sudden tears.

"I know who she means," cried Maud, always eager to find out things. "It's herself. Polly won't mind if we are poor 'cause she likes beggars."

"Is that who you meant?" asked Fan wistfully.

"No, it's a much better and dearer friend than I am," said Polly, pinching Fanny's cheek as it reddened prettily under her eyes. "You'll never guess, Maud, so I wouldn't try, but be planning what you will put in your cunning three-cornered closet when you get it."

Having got rid of "Miss Paulina Pry," as Tom called Maud, who was immediately absorbed by her cupboard, the older girls soberly discussed the sudden change which had

come, and Polly was surprised to see what unexpected
strength and sense Fanny showed. Polly was too unconscious
of the change which love had made in herself to understand
at first the cause of her friend's new patience and fortitude,
but she rejoiced over it and felt that her prophecy would yet
be fulfilled. Presently Maud emerged from her new closet
bringing a somewhat startling idea with her.

"Do bankrupting men"—Maud liked that new word—
"always have fits?"

"Mercy, no! What put that into your head, child?" cried
Polly.

"Why, Mr. Merton did, and I was thinking perhaps Papa
had got one down there and it kind of frightened me."

"Mr. Merton's was a bad, disgraceful failure, and I don't
wonder he had a fit. Ours isn't, and Papa won't do anything
of that sort, you may be sure," said Fanny with as proud an
air as if "our failure" was rather an honor than otherwise.

"Don't you think you and Maud had better go down and
see him?" asked Polly.

"Perhaps he wouldn't like it, and I don't know what to
say, either," began Fan, but Polly said eagerly:

"I know he *would* like it. Never mind what you say, just
go, and show him that you don't doubt or blame him for
this but love him all the more and are ready and glad to help
him bear the trouble."

"I'm going, I ain't afraid. I'll just hug him and say I'm ever
so glad we are going to the little house," cried Maud, scrambling off the bed and running downstairs.

"Come with me, Polly, and tell me what to do," said
Fanny, drawing her friend after her.

"You'll know what to do when you see him better than I
can tell you," answered Polly, readily yielding, for she knew
they considered her "quite one of the family," as Tom said.

At the study door they found Maud, whose courage had given out, for Mr. Merton's fit rather haunted her. Polly opened the door, and the minute Fanny saw her father she *did* know what to do. The fire was low, the gas dim, and Mr. Shaw was sitting in his easy chair, his gray head in both his hands, looking lonely, old, and bowed down with care. Fanny gave Polly one look, then went and took the gray head in both her arms, saying, with a tender quiver in her voice:

"Father, dear, we've come to help you bear it."

Mr. Shaw looked up, and seeing in his daughter's face something that never had been there before, put his arm about her and leaned his tired head against her as if, when least expected, he had found the consolation he most needed. In that minute Fanny felt, with mingled joy and self-reproach, what a daughter might be to her father, and Polly, thinking of feeble, selfish Mrs. Shaw, asleep upstairs, saw with sudden clearness what a wife should be to her husband —a helpmeet, not a burden. Touched by these unusual demonstrations, Maud crept quietly to her father's knee and whispered, with a great tear shining on her little pug nose:

"Papa, we don't mind it much, and I'm going to help Fan keep house for you. I'd like to do it, truly."

Mr. Shaw's other arm went round the child, and for a minute no one said anything, for Polly had slipped behind his chair, that nothing should disturb the three, who were learning from misfortune how much they loved one another. Presently Mr. Shaw steadied himself and asked:

"Where is my other daughter, where's my Polly?"

She was there at once, gave him one of the quiet kisses that had more than usual tenderness in it, for she loved to hear him say "my other daughter," and then she whispered:

"Don't you want Tom too?"

"Of course I do. Where is the poor fellow?"

"I'll bring him." And Polly departed with most obliging alacrity.

But in the hall she paused a minute to peep into the glass and see if she was all right, for somehow she was more anxious to look neat and pretty to Tom in his hour of trouble than she had ever been in his prosperous days. In lifting her arms to perk up the bow at her throat, she knocked a hat off the bracket. Now, a shiny black beaver is not an object exactly calculated to inspire tender or romantic sentiments, one would fancy, but that particular "stove pipe" seemed to touch Polly to the heart, for she caught it up, as if its fall suggested a greater one, smoothed out a slight dint, as if it was symbolical of the hard knocks its owner's head was now in danger of receiving, and stood looking at it with as much pity and respect as if it had been the crown of a disinherited prince. Girls will do such foolish little things, and though we laugh at them, I think we like them the better for it after all.

Richard was himself again when Polly entered, for the handkerchief had disappeared, his head was erect, his face was steady, and his whole air had a dogged composure which seemed to say to fate, "Hit away, I'm ready." He did not hear Polly come in, for he was looking fixedly at the fire with eyes that evidently saw a very different future there from that which it used to show him, but when she said, "Tom, dear, your father wants you," he got up at once, held out his hand to her, saying, "Come, too, we can't get on without you," and took her back into the study with him.

Then they had a long talk, for the family troubles seemed to warm and strengthen the family affection and confidence, and as the young people listened while Mr. Shaw told them as much of his business perplexities as they could understand, every one of them blamed him or herself for going on so gaily and blindly while the storm was gathering and the poor man was left to meet it all alone. Now, however, the thunderclap had come, and after the first alarm, finding they were not killed, they began to discover a certain half-anxious, half-pleasant excitement in talking it over, encouraging one another, and feeling unusually friendly, as people do when a sudden shower drives two or three to the shelter of one umbrella.

It was a sober talk, but not all sad, for Mr. Shaw felt inexpressibly comforted by his children's unexpected sympathy, and they, trying to take the downfall cheerfully for his sake, found it easier to bear themselves. They even laughed occasionally, for the girls, in their ignorance, asked queer questions; Tom made ludicrously unbusinesslike propositions, and Maud gave them one hearty peal, that did a world of good, by pensively remarking when the plans for the future had been explained to her:

"I'm so relieved, for when Papa said we must give up everything, and Mama called us all beggars, I did think I'd got to go round asking for cold vittles with a big basket and an old shawl over my head. I said once I'd like that, but I'm afraid I shouldn't, for I can't bear Indian cake and cold potatoes—that's what the poor children always seem to get—and I *should* hate to have Grace and the rest see me scuffing round the back gates."

"My little girl shall never come to that if I can help it," said Mr. Shaw, holding her close, with a look that made Maud add, as she laid her cheek against his own:

"But I'd do it, Father, if you asked me to, for I truly want to help."

"So do I!" cried Fanny, wondering at the same minute how it would seem to wear turned silks and clean her gloves.

Tom said nothing, but drew toward him a paper of figures

which his father had drawn up and speedily reduced himself
to the verge of distraction by trying to understand them in
his ardent desire to prove his willingness to put his shoulder
to the wheel.

"We shall pull through, children, so don't borrow trouble,
only be ready for discomforts and annoyances. Put your
pride in your pockets, and remember poverty isn't disgraceful, but dishonesty is."

Polly had always loved kind Mr. Shaw, but now she respected him heartily and felt that she had not done him
justice when she sometimes thought that he only cared for
making money.

"I shouldn't wonder if this was a good thing for the whole
family, though it don't look so. Mrs. Shaw will take it the
hardest, but it may stir her up so she will forget her nerves
and be as busy and happy as Mother is," said Polly to herself
in a hopeful mood, for poverty was an old friend, and she
had learned long ago not to fear it but to take its bitter and
its sweet and make the best of both.

When they parted for the night Polly slipped away first to
leave them free, yet couldn't help lingering outside to see
how tenderly the girls parted from their father. Tom hadn't
a word to say for himself, for men don't kiss, caress, or cry
when they feel most, and all he could do to express his
sympathy and penitence was to wring his father's hand with
a face full of respect, regret, and affection and then bolt
upstairs as if the furies were after him, as they were, in a mild
and modern form.

Chapter 16

A Dress Parade

*T*he weeks that followed taught the Shaws, as many other families have been taught, how rapidly riches take to themselves wings and fly away when they once begin to go. Mr. Shaw carried out his plans with an energy and patience that worked wonders and touched the hearts of his hardest creditors. The big house was given up as soon as possible and the little house taken, being made comfortable with the furniture Madam left there when she went to live with her son. The old-fashioned things had been let with the house, and now seemed almost like a gift from Grandma, doubly precious in these troublous times. At the auction several persons tried to show the family that, though they had lost their fortune, friends still remained, for one bid on Fanny's piano and sent it to her; another secured certain luxurious articles for Mrs. Shaw's comfort, and a third saved such of Mr. Shaw's books as he valued most, for he had kept his word and given up everything with the most punctilious integrity. So the little house was not bare but made pleasant to their eyes by these waifs from the wreck, brought them by the tide of sympathy and goodwill which soon set in.

Everybody who knew them hastened to call, many from a real regard, but more from mere curiosity to "see how they took it." This was one of the hardest things they had to bear, and Tom used strong language more than once when some fine lady came to condole and went away to gossip. Polly's hopes of Mrs. Shaw were disappointed, for misfortune did not have a bracing effect. She took to her bed at once, received her friends in tears and a point-lace cap, and cheered her family by plaintively inquiring when she was to be taken to the almshouse. This was hard for Fanny, but after an interval of despair, she came to the conclusion that under the circumstances it was the best thing her mother could have done, and with something of her father's energy, Fanny shouldered the new burden, feeling that at last necessity had given her what she had long needed—something to do.

The poor girl knew as much of household affairs as Snip, but pride and the resolution "to stand by Father" kept up her courage and she worked away with feverish activity at whatever task came first till, just as strength and heart were about to fail, order began to emerge from chaos and the vision of a home made happy and comfortable by her skill and care came to repay and sustain her.

Maud, being relieved from the fear of back-door beggary, soon became reconciled to bankruptcy, thought it rather a good joke on the whole, for children like novelty and don't care much for Mrs. Grundy.* She regarded the new abode as a baby house on a large scale, where she was allowed to

---

* Mrs. Grundy is a character often mentioned but never seen in *Speed the Plough*, a play by Thomas Morton (1764–1838). She has become a proverbial guardian of social propriety.

play her part in the most satisfactory manner. From the moment when, on taking possession of the coveted room, she opened the doors of the three-cornered closet and found a little kettle just like Polly's standing there, she felt that a good time was coming for her and fell to dusting furniture, washing cups, and making toast, the happiest, fussiest little housewife in the city. For Maud inherited the notable gifts of her grandmother and would have made a capital farmer's daughter in spite of her city breeding.

Polly came and went through all these changes, faithful, helpful, and as cheery as she could be when her friends were in trouble. The parts seemed reversed now, and it was Polly who gave, Fanny who received, for where everything seemed strange and new to Fan, Polly was quite at home, and every one of the unfashionable domestic accomplishments now came into play, to the comfort of the Shaws and the great satisfaction of Polly. She could not do enough to prove her gratitude for former favors, and went toiling and moiling about, feeling that the hardest, most disagreeable tasks were her especial duty. In the moving nothing suited her better than to trot up and down lugging heavy things, to pound her fingers black and blue nailing carpets and curtains, and the day she nearly broke her neck tumbling down the cellar stairs, in her eagerness to see that Mrs. Shaw's wine was rightly stored, she felt that she was only paying her debts and told Tom she liked it when he picked her up looking as grimy as a chimney sweep.

"You can turn your hand to anything, you clever girl, so do come and give me some advice, for I am in the depths of despair," said Fanny when the "maid-of-all-work," as Polly called herself, found a leisure hour.

"What is it? Moths in the furs, a smoky chimney, or small-pox next door?" asked Polly as they entered Fan's room, where Maud was trying on old bonnets before the looking glass.

"Actually I have nothing to wear," began Fan impressively. "I've been too busy to think or care till now, but here it is nearly May and I have hardly a decent rag to my back. Usually, you know, I just go to Mrs. O'Grady and tell her what I want, she makes my spring wardrobe, Papa pays the bill, and there I am. Now I've looked into the matter and I declare to you, Polly, I'm frightened to see how much it costs to dress me."

"Not so much as some girls I know," said Polly encouragingly.

"Perhaps not, for I have a conscience, and taste is economy sometimes, but really, Polly, I haven't the heart to ask Papa for a cent just now, and yet I must have clothes. You are such a genius for planning and working wonders that I throw myself upon you and ask, 'How shall I make a spring wardrobe out of nothing?' "

"Let me see the 'nothing' before I advise. Bring out every rag you've got and we'll see what can be done," said Polly, looking as if she enjoyed the prospect, for she had a great deal of that feminine faculty which we call "knack," and much practice had increased it.

Fanny brought out her "rags" and was astonished to see how many she had, for chair, sofa, bed, and bureau were covered, and still Maud, who was burrowing in the closets, kept crying, "Here's another."

"There's a discouraging heap of rubbish for you!" said Fan as she added a faded muslin to the last pile.

"Now, to me your 'rubbish' looks very encouraging because there is good material there and not much worn-out finery—that's my detestation, for you can't do anything with it. Let me see, five bonnets. Put the winter ones away till autumn, rip up the summer ones, and out of three old ones we'll get a pretty new one if my eyes don't deceive me."

"I'll rip, and then do let me see you make a bonnet, it must be so interesting," said Maud, whipping out her scissors and eagerly beginning to reduce a shabby little bonnet to its original elements.

"Now the dresses," continued Polly, who had rapidly sorted out the piles.

"Will you have the goodness to look at this?" said Fan, holding up a gray street suit faded past cure.

Polly whisked it wrong side out, and showing the clean, bright fabric, said, with a triumphant wave:

"Behold your new suit! Fresh trimming and less of it will finish you off as smart as ever."

"I never wore a turned dress in my life. Do you suppose people will know it?" said Fan doubtfully.

"What if they do? It won't hurt you. Not one in a hundred will ever think anything about your dress except that it is pretty. I've worn turned and dyed gowns all my days and it don't seem to have alienated my friends or injured my constitution."

"That it hasn't. I'm a goose, Polly, and I'll get over the feeling that it's sort of disgraceful to be poor and have to economize. We'll turn the gray, and I'll wear it bravely."

"Then it will be more becoming than ever. Oh, here's the pretty violet silk. That will make a lovely suit," cried Polly, going on with the review.

"Don't see how two draggled skirts and a stained waist can be transformed into a whole rig," said Fan, sitting on the bed with her garments strewn about her in various attitudes of limp despondency.

"Well, ma'am, my plan is this," began Polly, imitating Mrs. O'Grady's important tone and bad grammar. "Gores is out, and plaits is in. Therefore, as the top of this skirt is quite fresh, we will take off the ruffles, turn it upside down, and leave it plain. The upper skirt will be made scanter and finished with a frill. Then the waist can be refreshed with the best parts of these wide flounces, and out of those new bits we will concoct a hat. The black lace Maud has just taken off the green one will do to edge the violet, and with your nice silk mantilla you are complete, don't you see?"

"I don't quite see it yet, but I have firm faith that I shall in time, and consider my calling costume finished," said Fanny, getting more and more interested as she saw her condemned wardrobe coming out fresh under Polly's magic knack.

"There are two. Then that piqué is all right if you cut the tail off the jacket and change the trimming a bit. The muslins only need mending and doing up to look as well as ever. You ought not to put them away torn and soiled, my child. The two black silks will be good stand-bys for years. If *I* were you, I'd have a couple of neat, pretty prints for home wear, and then I don't see why you aren't fixed well enough for our short season."

"Can't I do anything with this barege? It's one of my favorite dresses, and I hate to give it up."

"You wore that thoroughly out, and it's only fit for the ragbag. Yes, it was very pretty and becoming, I remember, but its day is over."

Fanny let the dress lie in her lap a minute as she absently picked at the fringe, smiling to herself over the happy time when she wore it last and Sydney said she only needed cowslips in her lap to look like spring. Presently she folded it up and put it away with a sigh, but it never went into the ragbag, and my sentimental readers can understand what saved it.

"The ball dresses had better be put nicely away till next year," began Polly, coming to a rainbow-colored heap.

"My day is over, I shall never use them again. Do what you like with them," said Fan calmly.

"Did you ever sell your cast-off finery, as many ladies do?" asked Polly.

"Never. I don't like the fashion. I give it away or let Maud have it for tableaux."

"I wonder if you would mind my telling you something Belle proposed?"

"If it's an offer to buy my clothes, I *should* mind," answered Fanny sharply.

"Then I won't." And Polly retired behind a cloud of arsenic-green gauze, which made her look as if she had the cholera.

"If she wanted to buy that horrid new 'gooseberry-colored gown,' as Tom calls it, I'd let her have it cheap," put in Maud, who was of a practical turn.

"Does she want it, Polly?" asked Fan, whose curiosity got the better of her pride.

"Well, she merely asked me if I thought you'd be mortally offended if she offered to take it off your hands, as you'd never worn it. You don't like it, and another season it will be all out of fashion," said Polly from her verdant retreat.

"What did you say?"

"I saw she meant it kindly, so I said I'd ask. Now between ourselves, Fan, the price of that dress would give you all you'll want for your spring fixings, that's one consideration. Then here's another, which may have some weight with you," added Polly slyly. "Trix told Belle she was going to ask you for the dress, as you wouldn't care to wear it now. That made Belle fire up and say it was a mean thing to do without offering some return for a costly thing like that, and then

Belle said, in her blunt way, 'I'll give Fan all she paid for it, and more, too, if it will be any help to her. I don't care for the dress, but I'd like to slip a little money into her pocket, for I know she needs it and is too good to ask dear Mr. Shaw for anything she can get on without.' "

"Did she say that? I'll *give* her the dress and not take a penny for it," cried Fan, flushing up with mingled anger toward Trix and gratitude to Belle.

"That won't suit her. You let me manage it and don't feel any shame or anxiety about it. You did many a kind and generous thing for Belle when you had the power, and you liked to do it. Now let her pay her debts and have the same pleasure."

"If she looks at it in that way, it makes a difference. Perhaps I'd better—the money *would* be an immense help—only I don't quite like to take it."

"Kings and queens sell their jewels when times are hard or they get turned off their thrones and no one thinks it anything amiss, so why need you? It's just a little transaction between two friends who exchange things they don't want for things which they do, and I'd do it if I were you."

"We'll see about it," said Fan, privately resolving to take Polly's advice.

"If I had lots of things like Fan, I'd have an auction and get all I could for them. Why don't you?" asked Maud, beginning on her third bonnet.

"We will," said Polly, and mounting a chair, she put up, bid in, and knocked down Fan's entire wardrobe to an imaginary group of friends, with such droll imitations of each one that the room rang with laughter.

"That's enough nonsense. Now we'll return to business," said Polly, descending breathless but satisfied with the effect of her fun.

"These white muslins and pretty silks will keep for years, so I should lay them by till they are needed. It will save buying, and you can go to your stock anytime and make over what you want. That's the way Mother does. We've always had things sent us from richer friends, and whatever wasn't proper for us to wear at the time, Mother put away to be used when we needed it. Such funny bundles as we used to have sometimes—odd shoes, bonnets without crowns, stockings without heels or toes, and old finery of all sorts. We used to rush when a bundle came and sit round while Mother opened it. The boys always made fun of the things, though they were as grateful, really, as any of us. Will made a verse one day which we thought pretty well for a little chap:

'To poor country folks
    Who haven't any clothes,
Rich folks, to relieve them,
    Send old lace gowns and satin bows.' "

"I think that Will is going to be as nice a poet as Mr. Shakespeare," remarked Maud in a tone of serious conviction.

"He is already a Milton, but I don't believe he will ever be anything but a poet in name," said Polly, working away while she talked.

"Didn't your mother ever let you wear the nice things that came?" asked Maud.

"No, she thought it wasn't the thing for a poor minister's girls to go flourishing about in secondhand finery, so she did what I'm doing now, put away what would be useful and proper for us by and by and let us play with the shabby silk bonnets and dirty flounced gowns. Such fun as we used to have up in our big garret! I remember one day we'd been playing have a ball and were all rigged up, even the boys. Some new neighbors came to call and expressed a wish to see us, having been told that we were pattern children. Mother called us, but we had paraded out into the garden after our ball and were having a concert, as we sat about on the cabbages for green satin seats, so we didn't hear the call, and just as the company was going a great noise arrested them on the doorstep, and round the corner of the house rattled Ned in full costume, wheeling Kitty in a barrow, while Jimmy, Will, and I ran screaming after, looking like Bedlamites, for we were playing that Lady Fitz Perkins had fainted and was being borne home senseless in a cab. I thought Mother would kill herself with laughing, and you can imagine what a fine impression the strangers received of the model children."

Maud was so tickled with this youthful prank that she unguardedly sat down to laugh on the edge of an open trunk, immediately doubled up, fell in, and was with difficulty extricated.

"People in the country have great deal nicer times than we do. I never rode in a wheelbarrow, I never sat on cabbages, and I don't think it's fair," she said with an injured expression. "You needn't save any old silk gowns for me. I don't mean to be a fine lady when I grow up, I'm going to be a farmer's wife, and make butter and cheese, and have ten children, and raise pigs," she added in one enthusiastic burst.

"I do believe she will if she can find a farmer anywhere," said Fanny.

"Oh, I'm going to have Will. I asked him and he said, 'All right.' He's going to preach Sundays and work on the farm the rest of the time. Well, he is, so you needn't laugh, for we've made all our plans," said Maud with comical dignity as she tried the effect of an old white bonnet, wondering if farmers' wives could wear ostrich feathers when they went to meeting.

"Blessed innocence! Don't you wish you were a child and dared tell what you want?" murmured Fanny.

"I wish I had seen Will's face when Maud proposed," answered Polly, with a nod which answered her friend's speech better than her words.

"Any news of anybody?" whispered Fan, affecting to examine a sleeve with care.

"Still at the South, don't think late events have been reported yet, that accounts for absence," answered Polly.

"I think Sir Philip was hit harder than was supposed," said Fan.

"I doubt it, but time cures wounds of that sort amazing quick."

"Wish it did!"

"Who is Sir Philip?" demanded Maud, pricking up her ears.

"A famous man who lived in the time of Queen Elizabeth," answered Fan, with a look at Polly.

"Oh!" And Maud seemed satisfied, but the sharp child had her suspicions nevertheless.

"There will be an immense deal of work in all this fixing over and I hate to sew," said Fanny to divert a certain person's thoughts.

"Jenny and I are going to help. We are your debtors, as well as Belle, and demand the privilege of paying up. Blessings, like curses, come home to roost, Fan."

"Mine come home a good deal bigger than they went," answered Fanny, looking pleased that little favors should be so faithfully remembered.

"The interest on that sort of investment rolls up beauti-

fully, you know. Now rip that dress for Jenny to put in order
and I'll· toss you up a bonnet in less than no time," said
Polly, determined to have things go smoothly, for she knew
Fan's feelings had been a good deal tried lately in many ways.

"I must have something to match my dress, and blue inside," said Fanny, bringing out her ribbon boxes.

"Anything you like, my dear. When it comes to bonnets, I
am usually inspired. I have it! There we are! And nothing
could be nicer," cried Polly, making a dive among the silks
Fan was turning over with a lost expression. "This bit of
silver-gray is all I ask, here's enough for a killing bonnet, and
those forget-me-nots are both pretty and appropriate."

"You wretch, be still!" cried Fanny as Polly looked up at
her with a wicked laugh in her eyes.

"It will be done in time, and the dress likewise, so look
your prettiest and accept my blessing," continued Polly, seeing that Fan liked her raillery.

"Time for what?" asked Paulina Pry.

"Your wedding, dear," sweetly answered Fan, for Polly's
pleasant hints and predictions put her in a charming humor
and even made old clothes of little consequence.

Maud gave an incredulous sniff and wondered why "big
girls need to be so dreadful mysterious about their old
secrets."

"This silk reminds me of Kitty's performance last summer.
A little checked silk was sent in our spring bundle from Mrs.
Davenport, and Mother said Kit might have it if she could
make it do. So I washed it nicely, and we fussed and
planned, but it came short by half of one sleeve. I gave it up,
but Kit went to work and matched every scrap that was left
so neatly that she got out the half sleeve, put it on the under
side, and no one was the wiser. How many pieces do you
think she put in, Maud?"

"Fifty," was the wise reply.

"No, only ten, but that was pretty well for a fourteen-year-old dressmaker. You ought to have seen the little witch laugh in her sleeve when anyone admired the dress, for she wore it all summer and looked as pretty as a pink in it. Such things are great fun when you get used to them. Besides, contriving sharpens your wits and makes you feel as if you had more hands than most people."

"I think we'll get a farm near your house. I should like to know Kitty," said Maud, feeling a curious interest in a girl who made such peculiar patchwork.

"The dress parade is over, and I'm ever so much obliged to you, Polly, for helping me through and showing me how to make the best of things. I hope in time to have as many hands as you," said Fan gratefully when the simple bonnet was done and everything planned out ready to be finished.

"I hope you will soon have two good, strong ones beside your own, my dear," answered Polly as she vanished with a parting twinkle that kept Fan's face bright all day.

Chapter 17

Playing Grandmother

I think Tom had the hardest time of all, for besides the family troubles, he had many of his own to perplex and harass him. College scrapes were soon forgotten in greater afflictions, but there were plenty of tongues to blame "that extravagant dog" and plenty of heads to wag ominously over prophecies of the good time Tom Shaw would now make on the road to ruin. As reporters flourish in this country, of course Tom soon heard all the friendly criticisms passed upon him and his career, and he suffered more than anybody guessed, for the truth that was at the bottom of the gossip filled him with the sharp regret and impotent wrath against himself, as well as others, which drives many a proud fellow, so placed, to destruction or the effort that redeems boyish folly and makes a man of him.

Now that he had lost his heritage, Tom seemed to see for the first time how goodly it had been, how rich in power, pleasure, and gracious opportunities. He felt its worth even while he acknowledged, with the sense of justice that is strong in manly men, how little he deserved a gift which he had so misused. He brooded over this a good deal, for, like the bat in the fable, he didn't seem to find any place in the new life which had begun for all. Knowing nothing of business, he was not of much use to his father, though he tried to be, and generally ended by feeling that he was a hindrance, not a help. Domestic affairs were equally out of his line, and the girls, more frank than their father, did not hesitate to tell him he was in the way when he offered to lend a hand anywhere. After the first excitement was over, and he had time to think, heart and energy seemed to die out, remorse got hold of him, and, as generous, thoughtless natures are apt to do when suddenly confronted with conscience, he exaggerated his faults and follies into sins of the deepest dye and fancied he was regarded by others as a villain and an outcast.

Pride and penitence made him shrink out of sight as much as possible, for he could not bear pity, even when silently expressed by a friendly hand or a kindly eye. He stayed at home a good deal and loafed about with a melancholy and neglected air, vanished when anyone came, talked very little, and was either pathetically humble or tragically cross. He wanted to do something, but nothing seemed to appear, and while he waited to get his poise after the downfall, he was so very miserable that I'm afraid, if it had not been for one thing, my poor Tom would have got desperate and been a failure. But when he seemed most useless, outcast, and forlorn, he discovered that one person needed him, one person never found him in the way, one person always welcomed and clung to him with the strongest affection of a very feeble nature. This dependence of his mother's was Tom's salvation at that crisis of his life, and the gossips, who said softly to one another over their muffins and tea, "It really would be a relief to that whole family if poor, dear Mrs. Shaw could be—ahem!—mercifully removed," did not know that the invalid's weak, idle hands were unconsciously keeping the son safe in that quiet room, where she gave him all that she had to give, mother love, till he took heart again and faced the world, ready to fight his battles manfully.

"Dear, dear! How old and bent poor Father does look. I hope he won't forget to order my sweetbread," sighed Mrs. Shaw one day as she watched her husband slowly going down the street.

Tom, who stood by her, idly spinning the curtain tassel, followed the familiar figure with his eye, and seeing how gray the hair had grown, how careworn the florid face, and how like a weary old man his once strong, handsome father walked, was smitten by a new pang of self-reproach, and with his usual impetuosity set about repairing the omission as soon as he discovered it.

"I'll see to your sweetbread, Mum. Good-bye, back to dinner," And with a hasty kiss, Tom was off.

He didn't know exactly what he meant to do, but it had suddenly come over him that he was hiding from the storm and letting his father meet it alone, for the old man went to his office every day with the regularity of a machine that would go its usual round until it stopped while the young man stayed at home with the women and let his mother comfort him.

"He has a right to be ashamed of me, but I act as if I was ashamed of him. Daresay people think so. I'll show them that I ain't. Yes, by the powers, I will!" And Tom drew on his gloves with the air of a man about to meet and conquer an enemy.

"Have an arm, sir? If you don't mind, I'll walk down with you. Little commission for Mother—nice day, isn't it?"

Tom rather broke down at the end of his speech, for the

look of pleased surprise with which his father greeted him, the alacrity with which he accepted and leaned on the strong arm offered him, proved that the daily walks *had* been solitary and doubtless sad ones. I think Mr. Shaw understood the real meaning of that little act of respect, and felt better for the hopeful change it seemed to foretell. But he took it quietly, and leaving his face to speak for him, merely said:

"Thanky, Tom. Yes, Mother will enjoy her dinner twice as much if you order it."

Then they began to talk business with all their might, as if they feared that some trace of sentiment might disgrace their masculine dignity. But it made no difference whether they discussed lawsuits or love, mortgages or mothers, the feeling was all right and they knew it, so Mr. Shaw walked straighter than usual, and Tom felt that he was in his proper place again. The walk was not without its trials, however, for while it did Tom's heart good to see the cordial respect paid to his father, it tried his patience sorely to see also inquisitive or disapproving glances fixed upon himself when hats were lifted to his father and to hear the hearty "Good day, Mr. Shaw" drop into a cool or careless "That's the son, it's hard on him. Wild fellow, do him good."

"Granted, but you needn't hit a man when he's down," muttered Tom to himself, feeling every moment a stronger desire to do something that should silence everybody. "I'd cut away to Australia if it wasn't for Mother—anything, anywhere, to get out of the way of people who know me. I never can right myself here, with all the fellows watching and laying wagers whether I sink or swim. Hang Greek and Latin! Wish I'd learned a trade and had something to fall back upon. Haven't a blessed thing now but decent French and my fists. Wonder if old Bell don't want a clerk for the Paris branch of the business? That wouldn't be bad. Faith, I'll try it."

And when Tom had landed his father safely at the office, to the great edification of all beholders, he screwed up his courage and went to prefer his request, feeling that the prospect brightened a little. But Mr. Bell was not in a good humor and only gave Tom a severe lecture on the error of his ways, which sent him home much depressed and caused the horizon to lower again.

As he roamed about the house that afternoon, trying to calculate how much an Australian outfit would cost, the sound of lively voices and clattering spoons attracted him to the kitchen. There he found Polly giving Maud lessons in cookery, for the "new help," not being a high-priced article, could not be depended on for desserts, and Mrs. Shaw would have felt as if the wolf was at the door if there was not "a sweet dish" at dinner. Maud had a genius for cooking, and Fanny hated it, so that little person was in her glory, studying receipt books and taking lessons whenever Polly could give them.

"Gracious me, Tom, don't come now, we are awful busy! Men don't belong in kitchens," cried Maud as her brother appeared in the doorway.

"Couldn't think what you were about. Mum is asleep, and Fan out, so I loafed down to see if there was any fun afoot," said Tom, lingering, as if the prospect was agreeable. He was a social fellow and very grateful just then to anyone who helped him to forget his worries for a time. Polly knew this, felt that his society would not be a great affliction to herself, at least, and whispering to Maud, "He won't know," she added, aloud:

"Come in if you like, and stir this cake for me. It needs a

strong hand and mine are tired. There, put on that apron to keep you tidy, sit here, and take it easy."

"I used to help Grandma bat up cake and rather liked it, if I remember right," said Tom, letting Polly tie a checked apron on him, put a big bowl into his hands, and settle him near the table, where Maud was picking raisins and she herself stirring busily about among spice boxes, rolling pins, and butter pots.

"You do it beautifully, Tom. I'll give you a conundrum to lighten your labor. 'Why are bad boys like cake?'" asked Polly, anxious to cheer him up.

"'Because a good beating makes them better.' I doubt that myself, though," answered Tom, nearly knocking the bottom of the bowl out with his energetic demonstrations, for it really was a relief to do something.

"Bright boy! Here's a plum for you." And Polly threw a plump raisin into his mouth.

"Put in lots, won't you? I'm rather fond of plum cake," observed Tom, likening himself to Hercules with the distaff and finding his employment pleasant if not classical.

"I always do, if I can. There's nothing I like better than to shovel in sugar and spice and make nice, plummy cake for people. It's one of the few things I have a gift for."

"You've hit it this time, Polly. You certainly have a gift for putting a good deal of both articles into your own and other people's lives, which is lucky, as we all have to eat that sort of cake whether we like it or not," observed Tom so soberly that Polly opened her eyes and Maud exclaimed:

"I do believe he's preaching."

"Feel as if I could sometimes," continued Tom. Then his eye fell upon the dimples in Polly's elbows and he added, with a laugh, "That's more in your line, ma'am. Can't you give us a sermon?"

"A short one. Life, my brethren, is like plum cake," began Polly, impressively folding her floury hands. "In some the plums are all on the top and we eat them gaily, till we suddenly find they are gone. In others the plums sink to the bottom and we look for them in vain as we go on, and often come to them when it is too late to enjoy them. But in the well-made cake the plums are wisely scattered all through, and every mouthful is a pleasure. We make our own cakes, in a great measure, therefore let us look to it, my brethren, that they are mixed according to the best receipt, baked in a well-regulated oven, and gratefully eaten with a temperate appetite."

"Good! Good!" cried Tom, applauding with the wooden spoon. "That's a model sermon, Polly—short, sweet, sensible, and not a bit sleepy. I'm one of your parish and will see that you get your 'celery punctooal,' as old Deacon Morse used to say."

" 'Thank you, brother, my wants is few, and ravens scurser than they used to be,' as dear old Parson Miller used to answer. Now, Maud, bring on the citron." And Polly began to put the cake together in what seemed a most careless and chaotic manner while Tom and Maud watched with absorbing interest till it was safely in the oven.

"Now make your custards, dear. Tom may like to beat the eggs for you, it seems to have a good effect upon his constitution."

"First-rate. Hand 'em along." And Tom smoothed his apron with a cheerful air. "By the way, Syd's got back. I met him yesterday and he treated me like a man and a brother," he added, as if anxious to contribute to the pleasures of the hour.

"I'm so glad!" cried Polly, clapping her hands, regardless of the egg she held, which dropped and smashed on the floor at her feet. "Careless thing! Pick it up, Maud, I'll get some more." And Polly whisked out of the room, glad of an excuse to run and tell Fan, who had just come in, lest, hearing the news in public, she might be startled out of the well-bred composure with which young ladies are expected to receive tidings, even of the most vital importance.

"You know all about history, don't you?" asked Maud suddenly.

"Not quite," modestly answered Tom.

"I just want to know if there really was a man named Sir Philip in the time of Queen Elizabeth."

"You mean Sir Philip Sidney? Yes, he lived then, and a fine old fellow he was too."

"There. I knew the girls didn't mean him," cried Maud with a chop that sent the citron flying.

"What mischief are you up to now, you little magpie?"

"I shan't tell you what they said because I don't remember much of it, but I heard Polly and Fan talking about someone dreadful mysterious, and when I asked who it was Fan said, 'Sir Philip.' Ho! She needn't think I believe it! I saw 'em laugh, and blush, and poke one another, and I *knew* it wasn't about any old Queen Elizabeth man," cried Maud, turning up her nose as far as that somewhat limited feature would go.

"Look here, you are letting cats out of the bag. Never mind, I thought so. They don't tell us their secrets, but we are so sharp, we can't help finding them out, can we?" said Tom, looking so much interested that Maud couldn't resist airing her knowledge a little.

"Well, I daresay it isn't proper for *you* to know, but *I* am old enough now to be told anything, and those girls better mind what they say, for I'm not a stupid chit like Blanche. I just wish you could have heard them go on. I'm sure there's something very nice about Mr. Sydney, they looked so pleased when they whispered and giggled on the bed and thought I was ripping bonnets and didn't hear a word."

"Which looked most pleased?" asked Tom, investigating the kitchen boiler with deep interest.

"Well, 'pears to me Polly did. She talked most and looked funny and very happy all the time. Fan laughed a good deal, but I guess Polly is the loveress," replied Maud after a moment's reflection.

"Hold your tongue, she's coming!" And Tom began to pump as if the house was on fire.

Down came Polly, with heightened color, bright eyes, and not a single egg. Tom took a quick look at her over his shoulder and paused as if the fire was suddenly extinguished. Something in his face made Polly feel a little guilty, so she fell to grating nutmeg with a vigor which made red cheeks the most natural thing in life. Maud, the traitor, sat demurely at work, looking very like what Tom had called her, a magpie with mischief in its head. Polly felt a change in the atmosphere, but merely thought Tom was tired, so she graciously dismissed him with a stick of cinnamon, as she had nothing else just then to lay upon the shrine.

"Fan's got the books and maps you wanted. Go and rest now. I'm much obliged. Here's your wages, Bridget."

"Good luck to your messes," answered Tom as he walked away meditatively crunching his cinnamon and looking as if he did not find it as spicy as usual. He got his books, but did not read them, for, shutting himself up in the little room called "Tom's den," he just sat down and brooded.

When he came down to breakfast the next morning, he was greeted with a general "Happy birthday, Tom!" and at his place lay gifts from every member of the family, not as costly as formerly, perhaps, but infinitely dearer, as tokens of the love that had outlived the change and only grown the warmer for the test of misfortune. In his present state of mind Tom felt as if he did not deserve a blessed thing, so when every one exerted themselves to make it a happy day for him, he understood what it means "to be nearly killed with kindness" and sternly resolved to be an honor to his family or perish in the attempt. Evening brought Polly to what she called a "festive tea," and when they gathered round the table another gift appeared, which, though not of a sentimental nature, touched Tom more than all the rest. It was a most delectable cake, with a nosegay atop, and round it on the snowy frosting there ran a pink inscription, just as it had been every year since Tom could remember.

"Name, age, and date, like a nice white tombstone," observed Maud complacently, at which funereal remark Mrs. Shaw, who was down in honor of the day, dropped her napkin and demanded her salts.

"Whose doing is that?" asked Tom, surveying the gift with satisfaction, for it recalled the happier birthdays, which seemed very far away now.

"I didn't know what to give you, for you've got everything a man wants, and I was in despair till I remembered that dear Grandma always made you a little cake like that, and that you once said it wouldn't be a happy birthday without it. So I tried to make it just like hers, and I do hope it will prove a good, sweet, plummy one."

"Thank you," was all Tom said as he smiled at the giver, but Polly knew that her present had pleased him more than the most elegant trifle she could have made.

"It ought to be good, for you beat it up yourself, Tom," cried Maud. "It was so funny to see you working away and never guessing who the cake was for. I perfectly trembled every time you opened your mouth for fear you'd ask some question about it. That was the reason Polly preached and I kept talking when she was gone."

"Very stupid of me, but I forgot all about today. Suppose we cut it? I don't seem to care for anything else," said Tom, feeling no appetite but bound to do justice to that cake if he fell a victim to his gratitude.

"I hope the plums won't all be at the bottom," said Polly as she rose to do the honors of the cake by universal appointment.

"I've had a good many at the top already, you know," answered Tom, watching the operation with as much interest as if he had faith in the omen.

Cutting carefully, slice after slice fell apart, each firm and dark, spicy and rich under the frosty rime above, and laying a specially large piece in one of Grandma's quaint little china plates, Polly added the flowers and handed it to Tom with a look that said a good deal, for, seeing that he remembered her sermon, she was glad to find that her allegory held good in one sense at least. Tom's face brightened as he took it, and after an inspection which amused the others very much, he looked up, saying, with an air of relief, "Plums all through. I'm glad I had a hand in it, but Polly deserves the credit and must wear the posy," and turning to her, he put the rose into her hair with more gallantry than taste, for a thorn pricked her head, the leaves tickled her ear, and the flower was upside down.

Fanny laughed at his want of skill, but Polly wouldn't have it altered, and everybody fell to eating cake as if indigestion was one of the lost arts. They had a lively tea, and were getting on famously afterward, when two letters were brought for Tom, who glanced at one and retired rather precipitately to his den, leaving Maud consumed with curiosity and the older girls slightly excited, for Fan thought she recognized the handwriting on one, and Polly, on the other.

One half an hour and then another elapsed, and Tom did not return. Mr. Shaw went out, Mrs. Shaw retired to her room escorted by Maud, and the two girls sat together wondering if anything dreadful had happened. All of a sudden a voice called, "Polly!" and that young lady started out of her chair as if the sound had been a thunderclap.

"Do run! I'm perfectly fainting to know what the matter is," said Fan.

"You'd better go," began Polly, wishing to obey yet feeling a little shy.

"He don't want me. Besides, I couldn't say a word for myself if that letter was from Sydney," cried Fanny, hustling her friend toward the door in a great flutter.

Polly went without another word, but she wore a curiously anxious look and stopped on the threshold of the den as if a little afraid of its occupant. Tom was sitting in his favorite attitude, astride a chair, with his arms folded and his chin on the top rail. Not an elegant posture, but the only one in which, he said, he could think well.

"Did you want me, Tom?"

"Yes. Come in, please, and don't look scared. I only want to show you a present I've had and ask your advice about accepting it."

"Why, Tom, you look as if you had been knocked down!" exclaimed Polly, forgetting all about herself as she saw his face when he rose and turned to meet her.

"I have, regularly floored, but I'm up again and steadier than ever. Just you read that and tell me what you think of it."

Tom snatched a letter off the table, put it into her hands, and began to walk up and down the little room like a verita-

ble bear in its cage. As Polly read that short note all the
color went out of her face and her eyes began to kindle.
When she came to the end she stood a minute, as if too
indignant to speak, then gave the paper a nervous sort of
crumple and dropped it on the floor, saying, all in one
breath:

"I think she is a mercenary, heartless, ungrateful girl!
That's what I think."

"Oh, the—deuce! I didn't mean to show that one, it's the
other." And Tom took up a second paper, looking half angry, half ashamed at his own mistake. "I don't care, though.
Everyone will know tomorrow, and perhaps you'll be good
enough to keep the girls from bothering me with questions
and gabble," he added, as if, on second thought, he *was*
relieved to have the communication made to Polly first.

"I don't wonder you looked upset. If the other letter is as
bad, I'd better have a chair before I read it," said Polly,
feeling that she began to tremble with excitement.

"It's a million times better, but it knocked me worse than
the other. Kindness always does." Tom stopped short there
and stood a minute, turning the letter about in his hand as if
it contained a sweet which neutralized the bitter in that
smaller note and touched him very much. Then he drew up
an armchair, and beckoning Polly to take it, said in a sober,
steady tone that surprised her greatly:

"Whenever I was in a quandary, I used to go and consult
Grandma, and she always had something sensible or comfortable to say to me. She's gone now, but somehow, Polly,
you seem to take her place. Would you mind sitting in her
chair and letting me tell you two or three things, as Will
does?"

Mind it? Polly felt that Tom had paid her the highest and
most beautiful compliment he could have devised. She had

often longed to do it, for, being brought up in the most affectionate and frank relations with her brothers, she had early learned what it takes most women some time to discover, that sex does not make nearly as much difference in hearts and souls as we fancy. Joy and sorrow, love and fear, life and death, bring so many of the same needs to all that the wonder is we do not understand each other better but wait till times of tribulation teach us that human nature is very much the same in men and women. Thanks to this knowledge, Polly understood Tom in a way that surprised and won him. She knew that he wanted womanly sympathy and that she could give it to him because she was not afraid to stretch her hand across the barrier which our artificial education puts between boys and girls and to say to him in all good faith, "If I can help you, let me."

Ten minutes sooner Polly could have done this almost as easily to Tom as to Will, but in that ten minutes something had happened which made this difficult. Reading that Trix had given Tom back his freedom changed many things for Polly and caused her to shrink from his confidence because she felt as if it would be harder now to keep self out of sight, for, in spite of maiden modesty, love and hope would wake and sing at the good news. Slowly she sat down, and hesitatingly she said, with her eyes on the ground, in a very humble voice:

"I'll do my best, but I can't fill Grandma's place or give you any wise, good advice. I wish I could!"

"You'll do it better than anyone else. Talk troubles Mother, Father has enough to think of without any of my worries. Fan is a good soul, but she isn't practical, and we always get into a snarl if we try to work together, so who have I but my other sister, Polly? The pleasure that letter will give you may make up for my boring you."

As he spoke Tom laid the other paper in her lap and went off to the window, as if to leave her free to enjoy it unseen, but he could not help a glance now and then, and as Polly's face brightened, his own fell.

"Oh, Tom, that's a birthday present worth having, for it's so beautifully given I don't see how you can refuse it. Arthur Sydney is a real nobleman!" cried Polly, looking up at last, with her face glowing and her eyes full of delight.

"So he is! I don't know another man living, except Father, who would have done such a thing or who I could bring myself to take it from. Do you see, he's not only paid the confounded debts, but has done it in my name, to spare me all he could?"

"I see, it's like him, and I think he must be very happy to be able to do such a thing."

"It *is* an immense weight off my shoulders, for some of those men couldn't afford to wait till I'd begged, borrowed, or earned the money. Sydney *can* wait, but he won't long if I know myself."

"You won't take it as a gift, then?"

"Would you?"

"No."

"Then don't think I will. I'm a pretty poor affair, Polly, but I'm not mean enough to do that while I've got a conscience and a pair of hands."

A rough speech, but it pleased Polly better than the smoothest Tom had ever made in her hearing, for something in his face and voice told her that the friendly act had roused a nobler sentiment than gratitude, making the canceled obligations of the boy debts of honor to the man.

"What will you do, Tom?"

"I'll tell you. May I sit here?" And Tom took the low footstool that always stood near Grandma's old chair. "I've had so many plans in my head lately that sometimes it seems as if it would split," continued the poor fellow, rubbing his tired forehead as if to polish up his wits. "I've thought seriously of going to California, Australia, or some out-of-the-way place where men get rich in a hurry."

"Oh, no!" cried Polly, putting out her hand as if to keep him, and then snatching it back again before he could turn round.

"It would be hard on Mother and the girls, I suppose. Besides, I don't quite like it myself, looks as if I shirked and ran away."

"So it does," said Polly decidedly.

"Well, you see I don't seem to find anything to do unless I turn clerk, and I don't think that would suit. The fact is, I couldn't stand it here, where I'm known. It would be easier to scratch gravel on a railroad with a gang of Paddies than to sell pins to my friends and neighbors. False pride, I daresay, but it's the truth, and there's no use in dodging."

"Not a bit, and I quite agree with you."

"That's comfortable. Now I'm coming to the point where I specially want your advice, Polly. Yesterday I heard you telling Fan about your brother Ned, how well he got on, how he liked his business and wanted Will to come and take some place near him. You thought I was reading, but I heard, and it struck me that perhaps I could get a chance out West somewhere. What do you think?"

"If you really mean work, I *know* you could," answered Polly quickly, as all sorts of plans and projects went sweeping through her mind. "I wish you could be with Ned, you'd get on together, I'm sure, and he'd be so glad to do anything he could. I'll write and ask straightaway if you want me to."

"Suppose you do, just for information, you know, then I shall have something to go upon. I want to have a feasible plan all ready before I speak to Father. There's nothing so convincing to business men as facts, you know."

Polly could not help smiling at Tom's new tone, it seemed so strange to hear him talking about anything but horses and tailors, dancing and girls. She liked it, however, as much as she did the sober expression of his face and the way he had lately of swinging his arms about, as if he wanted to do something energetic with them.

"That will be wise. Do you think your father will like this plan?"

"Pretty sure he will. Yesterday, when I told him I must go at something right off, he said, 'Anything honest, Tom, and don't forget that your father began the world as a shop boy.' You knew that, didn't you?"

"Yes, he told me the story once, and I always liked to hear it, because it was pleasant to see how well he had succeeded."

"I never did like the story, a little bit ashamed, I'm afraid, but when we talked it over last night, it struck me in a new light and I understood why Father took the failure so well and seems so contented with this poorish place. It is only beginning again, he says, and having worked his way up once, he feels as if he could again. I declare to you, Polly, that sort of confidence in himself, and energy and courage in a man of his years, makes me love and respect the dear old gentleman as I never did before."

"I'm so glad to hear you say that, Tom! I've sometimes thought you didn't quite appreciate your father any more than he knew how much of a man you were."

"Never was till today, you know," said Tom, laughing, yet looking as if he felt the dignity of his one and twenty years. "Odd, isn't it, how people live together ever so long and don't seem to find one another out till something comes to do it for them. Perhaps this smash-up was sent to introduce me to my own father."

"There's philosophy for you," said Polly, smiling even while she felt as if adversity was going to do more for Tom than years of prosperity.

They both sat quiet for a minute, Polly in the big chair looking at him with a new respect in her eyes, Tom on the stool nearby slowly tearing up a folded paper he had absently taken from the floor while he talked.

"Did this surprise you?" he asked as a little white shower fluttered from his hands.

"No."

"Well, it did me, for you know as soon as we came to grief I offered to release Trix from the engagement and she wouldn't let me," continued Tom, as if, having begun the subject, he wished to explain it thoroughly.

"That surprised me," said Polly.

"So it did me, for Fan always insisted it was the money and not the man she cared for. Her first answer pleased me very much, for I didn't expect it, and nothing touches a fellow more than to have a woman stand by him through thick and thin."

"She don't seem to have done it."

"Fan was right. Trix only waited to see how bad things really were, or rather her mother did. She's as cool, hard, and worldly-minded an old soul as I ever saw, and Trix is bound to obey. She gets round it very neatly in her note, 'won't be a burden,' 'will sacrifice her hopes,' 'and always remain my warm friend,' but the truth is, Tom Shaw rich was worth making much of, but Tom Shaw poor is in the way and may go to the devil as fast as he likes."

"Well, he isn't going!" cried Polly defiantly, for her wrath burned hotly against Trix, though she blessed her for setting the bondman free.

"Came within an ace of it," muttered Tom to himself, adding aloud, in a tone of calm resignation that assured Polly his heart would not be broken though his engagement was:

"It never rains but it pours, 'specially in hard times, but when a man is down, a rap or two more don't matter much, I suppose. It's the first blow that hurts most."

"Glad to see you take the last blow so well." There was an ironical little twang to that speech, and Polly couldn't help it. Tom colored up and looked hurt for a minute, then seemed to right himself with a shrug and said, in his outspoken way:

"To tell the honest truth, Polly, it wasn't a very hard one. I've had a feeling for some time that Trix and I were not suited to one another and it might be wiser to stop short. But she didn't or wouldn't see it, and I wasn't going to back out and leave her to wear any more willows, so here we are. I don't bear malice, but hope she'll do better and not be disappointed again, upon my word I do."

"That's very good of you, quite Sydneyesque and noble," said Polly, feeling rather ill at ease and wishing she could hide herself behind a cap and spectacles if she was to play Grandma to this confiding youth.

"It will be all plain sailing for Syd, I fancy," observed Tom, getting up as if the little cricket suddenly ceased to be comfortable.

"I hope so," murmured Polly, wondering what was coming next.

"He deserves the very best of everything, and I pray the Lord he may get it," added Tom, poking the fire in a destructive manner.

Polly made no answer, fearing to say too much, for she knew Fan had made no confidant of Tom, and she guarded her friend's secret as jealously as her own.

"You'll write to Ned tomorrow, will you? I'll take anything he's got, for I want to be off," said Tom, casting down the poker and turning round with a resolute air which was lost on Polly, who sat twirling the rose that had fallen into her lap.

"I'll write tonight. Would you like me to tell the girls about Trix and Sydney?" she asked as she rose, feeling that the council was over.

"I wish you would. I don't know how to thank you for all you've done for me. I wish to heaven I did," said Tom, holding out his hand with a look that Polly thought a great deal too grateful for the little she had done.

As she gave him her hand, and looked up at him with those confiding eyes of hers, Tom's gratitude seemed to fly to his head, for, without the slightest warning, he stooped down and kissed her—a proceeding which startled Polly so that he recovered himself at once and retreated into his den with the incoherent apology:

"I beg pardon—couldn't help it—Grandma always let me on my birthday."

While Polly took refuge upstairs, forgetting all about Fan as she sat in the dark with her face hidden, wondering why she wasn't very angry and resolving never again to indulge in the delightful but dangerous pastime of playing Grandmother.

Chapter 18

The Woman
Who Did Not Dare

*P*olly wrote enthusiastically, Ned answered satisfactorily, and after much corresponding, talking, and planning, it was decided that Tom should go West. Never mind what the business was—it suffices to say that it was a good beginning for a young man like Tom, who, having been born and bred in the most conservative class of the most conceited city in New England, needed just the healthy, hearty, social influences of the West to widen his views and make a man of him.

Of course there was much lamentation among the women, but everyone felt it was the best thing for him, so while they sighed, they sewed, packed visions of a brilliant future away with his new pocket handkerchiefs, and rejoiced that the way was open before him even in the act of bedewing his boots with tears. Sydney stood by him to the last, "like a man and a brother" (which expression of Tom's gave Fanny infinite satisfaction), and Will felt entirely consoled for Ned's disappointment at his refusal to go and join him, since Tom was to take the place Ned had kept for him.

Fortunately everyone was so busy with the necessary preparations that there was no time for romance of any sort, and the four young people worked together as soberly and sensibly as if all sorts of emotions were not bottled up in their respective hearts. But in spite of the silence, the work, and the hurry, I think they came to know one another better in that busy little space of time than in all the years that had gone before, for the best and bravest in each was up and stirring, and the small house was as full of the magnetism of love and friendship, self-sacrifice and enthusiasm, as the world outside was full of spring sunshine and enchantment. Pity that the end should come so soon, but the hour did its work and went its way, leaving a clearer atmosphere behind, though the young folks did not see it then, for their eyes were dim because of the partings that must be.

Tom was off to the West; Polly went home for the summer; Maud was taken to the seaside with Belle, and Fanny left alone to wrestle with housekeeping, "help," and heartache. If it had not been for two things, I fear she never would have stood a summer in town, but Sydney often called, till his vacation came, and a voluminous correspondence with Polly beguiled the long days. Tom wrote once a week to his mother, but the letters were short and not very satisfactory, for men never do tell the interesting little things that women best like to hear. Fanny forwarded her bits of news to Polly. Polly sent back all the extracts from Ned's letters concerning Tom, and by putting the two reports together, they gained the comfortable assurance that Tom was well, in good spirits, hard at work, and intent on coming out strong in spite of all obstacles.

Polly had a quiet summer at home, resting and getting

ready in mind and body for another winter's work, for in the
autumn she tried her plan again, to the satisfaction of her
pupils and the great joy of her friends. She never said much
of herself in her letters, and Fanny's first exclamation when
they met again was an anxious:

"Why, Polly, dear! Have you been sick and never told
me?"

"No, I'm only tired, had a good deal to do lately, and the
dull weather makes me just a trifle blue. I shall soon brighten
up when I get to my work again," answered Polly, bustling
about to put away her things.

"You don't look a bit natural. What have you been doing
to your precious little self?" persisted Fanny, troubled by the
change, yet finding it hard to say wherein it lay.

Polly did not look sick, though her cheeks were thinner
and her color paler than formerly, but she seemed spiritless,
and there was a tired look in her eyes that went to Fanny's
heart.

"I'm all right enough, as you'll see when I'm in order. I'm
proper glad to find *you* looking so well and happy. Does all
go smoothly, Fan?" asked Polly, beginning to brush her hair
industriously.

"Answer me one question first," said Fanny, looking as if
a sudden fear had come over her. "Tell me, truly, have you
never repented of your hint to Sydney?"

"Never!" cried Polly, throwing back the brown veil behind which she had half hidden her face at first.

"On your honor, as an honest girl?"

"On my honor, as anything you please. Why do you suspect me of it?" demanded Polly, almost angrily.

"Because something is wrong with you. It's no use to deny
it, for you've got the look I used to see in that very glass on
my own face when I thought he cared for you. Forgive me,

Polly, but I can't help saying it, for it *is* there, and I want to be as true to you as you were to me if I can."

Fanny's face was full of agitation, and she spoke fast and frankly, for she was trying to be generous and found it very hard. Polly understood now and put her fear at rest by saying, almost passionately:

"I tell you I *don't* love him! If he was the only man in the world, I wouldn't marry him, because I—don't want to."

The last three words were added in a different tone, for Polly had checked herself there with a half-frightened look and turned away to hide her face behind her hair again.

"Then if it's not him, it's someone else. You've got a secret, Polly, and I should think you might tell it, as you know mine," said Fanny, unable to rest till everything was told, for Polly's manner troubled her.

There was no answer to her question, but she was satisfied, and putting her arm round her friend, she said, in her most persuasive tone:

"My precious Polly, do I know him?"

"You have seen him."

"And is he very wise, good, and splendid, dear?"

"No."

"He ought to be if you love him. I hope he isn't bad?" cried Fan anxiously, still holding Polly, who kept her head obstinately turned.

"I'm suited, that's enough."

"Oh, please just tell me one thing more. Don't he love back again?"

"No. Now don't say another word, I can't bear it!" And Polly drew herself away as she spoke in a desperate sort of tone.

"I won't, but now I'm not afraid to tell you that I think, I hope, I do believe that Sydney cares a little for me. He's been very kind to us all, and lately he has seemed to like to see me always when he comes and miss me if I'm gone. I didn't dare to hope anything till Papa observed something in his manner and teased me about it. I try not to deceive myself, but it does seem as if there was a chance of happiness for me."

"Thank heaven for that!" cried Polly, with the heartiest satisfaction in her voice. "Now come and tell me all about it," she added, sitting down on the couch with the air of one who has escaped a great peril.

"I've got some notes and things I want to ask your opinion about, if they really mean anything, you know," said Fanny, getting out a bundle of papers from the inmost recesses of her desk. "There's a photograph of Tom, came in his last letter. Good, isn't it? He looks older, but that's the beard and the rough coat, I suppose. Dear old fellow, he is doing so well I really begin to feel quite proud of him."

Fan tossed her the photograph and went on rummaging for a certain note. She did not see Polly catch up the picture and look at it with hungry eyes, but she did hear something in the low tone in which Polly said:

"It don't do him justice." And glancing over her shoulder, Fan's quick eye caught a glimpse of the truth, though Polly was half turned away from her. Without stopping to think, Fan dropped her letters, took Polly by the shoulders, and cried in a tone full of astonishment:

"Polly, is it Tom?"

Poor Polly was so taken by surprise that she had not a word to say. None were needed; her telltale face answered for her, as well as the impulse which made her hide her head in the sofa cushion like a foolish ostrich when the hunters are after it.

"Oh, Polly, I *am* so glad! I never thought of it—you are so good, and he's such a wild boy—I can't believe it—but it *is* so dear of you to care for him."

"Couldn't help it—tried not to—but it was so hard—you know, Fan, you know," said a stifled voice from the depths of the very fuzzy cushion which Tom had once condemned.

The last words, and the appealing hand outstretched to her, told Fanny the secret of her friend's tender sympathy for her own love troubles and seemed so pathetic that she took Polly in her arms and cried over her, in the fond, foolish way girls have of doing when their hearts are full and tears can say more than tongues. The silence never lasts long, however, for the feminine desire to "talk it over" usually gets the better of the deepest emotion. So presently the girls were hard at it, Polly very humble and downcast, Fanny excited and overflowing with curiosity and delight.

"Really my sister! You dear thing, how heavenly that will be," she cried.

"It never will be," answered Polly in a tone of calm despair.

"What will prevent it?"

"Maria Bailey," was the tragic reply.

"What do you mean? Is she the Western girl? She shan't have Tom, I'll kill her first!"

"To late, let me tell you—is that door shut and Maud safe?"

Fanny reconnoitered, and returning, listened breathlessly while Polly poured into her ear the bitter secret which was preying on her soul.

"Hasn't he mentioned Maria in his letters?"

"Once or twice, but sort of jokingly, and I thought it was only some little flirtation. He can't have time for much of that fun, he's so busy.

"Ned writes good, gossipy letters—I taught him how—

and he tells me all that's going on. When he'd spoken of this girl several times—they board with her mother, you know—I asked about her, quite carelessly, and he told me she was pretty, good, and well educated, and he thought Tom was rather smitten. That was a blow, for you see, Fan, since Trix broke the engagement, and it wasn't wrong to think of Tom, I let myself hope, just a little, and was so happy! Now I must give it up, and now I see how much I hoped and what a dreadful loss it's going to be."

Two great tears rolled down Polly's cheeks, and Fanny wiped them away, feeling an intense desire to go West by the next train, wither Maria Bailey with a single look, and bring Tom back as a gift to Polly.

"It was so stupid of me not to guess before. But you see Tom always seems so like a boy, and you are more womanly for your age than any girl I know, so I never thought of your caring for him in that way. I knew you were very good to him, you are to everyone, my precious, and I knew that he was fond of you as he is of me, fonder if anything, because he thinks you are perfect, but still I never dreamed of his loving you as more than a dear friend."

"He doesn't," sighed Polly.

"Well, he ought, and if I could get hold of him, he should!"

Polly clutched Fan at that and held her tight, saying sternly:

"If you ever breathe a word, drop a hint, look a look that will tell him or anyone else about me, I'll—yes, as sure as my name is Mary Milton—I'll proclaim from the housetops that you like Ar—" Polly got no further, for Fan's hand was on her mouth and Fan's alarmed voice vehemently protested:

"I won't! I promise solemnly I'll never say a word to a

mortal creature. Don't be so fierce, Polly, you quite frighten me."

"It's bad enough to love someone who don't love you, but to have them told of it is perfectly awful. It makes me wild just to think of it. Oh, Fan, I'm getting so ill-tempered and envious and wicked, I don't know what will happen to me."

"I'm not afraid for you, my dear, and I do believe things will go right because you are so good to everyone. How Tom could help adoring you I don't see. I know he would if he had stayed at home longer after he got rid of Trix. It would be the making of him, but though he is my brother, I don't think he's good enough for you, Polly, and I don't quite see how you can care for him so much when you might have had a person so infinitely superior."

"I don't want a 'superior' person, he'd tire me if he was like A. S. Besides, I do think Tom *is* superior to him in many things. Well, you needn't stare, I *know* he is, or will be. He's so different, and very young, and has lots of faults, I know, but I like him all the better for it, and he's honest and brave, and has got a big, warm heart, and I'd rather have him care for me than the wisest, best, most accomplished man in the world, simply because I love him!"

If Tom could only have seen Polly's face when she said that! It was so tender, earnest, and defiant that Fanny forgot the defense of her own lover in admiration of Polly's loyalty to hers, for this faithful, all-absorbing love was a new revelation to Fanny, who was used to hearing her friends boast of two or three lovers a year and calculate their respective values with almost as much coolness as the young men discussed the fortunes of the girls they wished but "could not afford to marry." She had thought her love for Sydney very romantic because she did not really care whether he was rich or poor, though she never dared to say so, even to Polly, for fear of being laughed at. She began to see now what true love was, and to feel that the sentiment which she could not conquer was a treasure to be accepted with reverence and cherished with devotion.

"I don't know when I began to love Tom, but I found out that I did last winter, and was as much surprised as you are," continued Polly, as if glad to unburden her heart. "I didn't approve of him at all. I thought he was extravagant, reckless, and dandified. I was very much disappointed when he chose Trix, and the more I thought and saw of it, the worse I felt, for Tom was too good for her and I hated to see her do so little for him, when she might have done so much, because he is one of the men who can be led by their affections and the woman he marries can make or mar him."

"That's true!" cried Fan as Polly paused to look at the picture, which appeared to regard her with a grave, steady look which seemed rather to belie her assertions.

"I don't mean that he's weak or bad. If he was, I should hate him, but he does need someone to love him very much and make him happy, as a good woman best knows how," said Polly, as if answering the mute language of Tom's face. "I hope Maria Bailey is all he thinks her," she added softly, "for I couldn't bear to have him disappointed again."

"I daresay he don't care a fig for her, and you are only borrowing trouble. What do you say Ned answered when you asked about this inconvenient girl?" said Fanny, turning hopeful all at once.

Polly repeated it and added, "I asked him in another letter if he didn't admire Miss B. as much as Tom, and he wrote back that she was 'a nice girl, but he had no time for non-sense, and I needn't get my white kids ready for some years yet, unless to dance at Tom's wedding.' Since then he hasn't mentioned Maria, so I was sure there was something serious going on, and being in Tom's confidence, he kept quiet."

"It does look bad. Suppose I say a word to Tom, just inquire after his heart in a general way, you know, and give him a chance to tell me, if there is anything to tell."

"I'm willing, but you must let me see the letter. I can't trust you not to hint or say too much."

"You shall. I'll keep my promise in spite of everything, but it will be hard to see things going wrong when a word would set it right."

"You know what will happen if you do." And Polly looked so threatening that Fan trembled before her, discovering that the gentlest girls when roused are more impressive than any shrew, for even turtledoves peck gallantly to defend their nests.

"If it is true about Maria, what shall we do?" said Fanny after a pause.

"Bear it. People always do bear things, somehow," answered Polly, looking as if sentence had been passed upon her.

"But if it isn't?" cried Fan, unable to endure the sight.

"Then I shall wait." And Polly's face changed so beautifully that Fan hugged her on the spot, fervently wishing that Maria Bailey never had been born.

Then the conversation turned to lover number two, and after a long confabulation Polly gave it as her firm belief that A. S. had forgotten M. M. and was rapidly finding consolation in the regard of F. S. With this satisfactory decision the council ended, after the ratification of a Loyal League, by which the friends pledged themselves to stand staunchly by one another through the trials of the coming year.

It was a very different winter from the last for both the girls. Fanny applied herself to her duties with redoubled ardor, for A. S. was a domestic man and admired housewifely accomplishments. If Fanny wanted to show him what she could do toward making a pleasant home, she certainly succeeded better than she suspected, for in spite of many failures and discouragements behind the scenes, the little house became a most attractive place, to Mr. Sydney at least, for he was more the house friend than ever and seemed determined to prove that change of fortune made no difference to him.

Fanny had been afraid that Polly's return might endanger her hopes, but Sydney met Polly with the old friendliness and very soon convinced her that the nipping-in-the-bud process had been effectual, for being taken early, the sprouting affection had died easy and left room for an older friendship to blossom into a happier love.

Fanny seemed glad of this, and Polly soon set her heart at rest by proving that she had no wish to try her power. She kept much at home when the day's work was done, finding it pleasanter to sit dreaming over book or sewing alone than to exert herself even to go to the Shaws'.

"Fan don't need me, and Sydney don't care whether I come or not, so I'll keep out of the way," she would say, as if to excuse her seeming indolence.

Polly was not at all like herself that winter, and those nearest to her saw and wondered at it most. Will got very anxious, she was so quiet, pale, and spiritless, and distracted poor Polly by his affectionate stupidity till she completed his bewilderment by getting cross and scolding him. So he consoled himself with Maud, who, now being in her teens, assumed dignified airs and ordered him about in a style that afforded him continued amusement and employment.

Western news continued vague, for Fan's general inquiries produced only provokingly unsatisfactory replies from Tom, who sang the praises of "the beautiful Miss Bailey" and professed to be consumed by a hopeless passion for somebody in such half-comic, half-tragic terms that the girls could not decide whether it was "all that boy's mischief" or only a cloak to hide the dreadful truth.

"We'll have it out of him when he comes home in the spring," said Fanny to Polly as they compared the letters of their brothers and agreed that "men were the most uncommunicative and provoking animals under the sun." For Ned was so absorbed in business that he ignored the whole Bailey question and left them in utter darkness.

Hunger of any sort is a hard thing to bear, especially when the sufferer has a youthful appetite, and Polly was kept on such a short allowance of happiness for six months that she got quite thin and interesting, and often, when she saw how big her eyes were getting, and how plainly the veins on her temples showed, indulged the pensive thought that perhaps spring dandelions might blossom o'er her grave. She had no intention of dying till Tom's visit was over, however, and as the time drew near she went through such alternations of hope and fear, and lived in such a state of feverish excitement, that spirits and color came back and she saw that the interesting pallor she had counted on would be an entire failure.

May came at last, and with it a burst of sunshine which cheered even poor Polly's much-enduring heart. Fanny came walking in upon her one day, looking as if she brought tidings of such great joy that she hardly knew how to tell them.

"Prepare yourself—somebody is engaged!" she said in a solemn tone that made Polly put up her hand as if to ward off an expected blow. "No, don't look like that, my poor dear, it isn't Tom, it's—I!"

Of course there was a rapture, followed by one of the

deliciously confidential talks which bosom friends enjoy, interspersed with tears and kisses, smiles and sighs.

"Oh, Polly, though I've waited and hoped so long, I couldn't believe it when it came, and don't deserve it, but I will, for the knowledge that he loves me seems to make everything possible!" said Fanny, with an expression which made her really beautiful for the first time in her life.

"You happy girl!" sighed Polly, then smiled and added, "I think you deserve all that's coming to you, for you have truly tried to be worthy of it, and whether it ever came or not, that would have been a thing to be proud of."

"He says that is what made him love me," answered Fanny, never calling her lover by his name, but making the little personal pronoun a very sweet word by the tone in which she uttered it. "He was disappointed in me last year, he told me, but you said good things about me, and though he didn't care much then, yet, when he lost you and came back to me, he found that you were not altogether mistaken and he has watched me all this winter, learning to respect and love me better every day. Oh, Polly, when he said that, I couldn't bear it, because in spite of all my trying, I'm still so weak and poor and silly."

"We don't think so, and I know you'll be all he hopes to find you, for he's just the husband you ought to have."

"Thank you all the more, then, for not keeping him yourself," said Fanny, laughing the old blithe laugh again.

"That was only a slight aberration of his. He knew better all the time. It was your white cloak and my idiotic behavior the night we went to the opera that put the idea into his head," said Polly, feeling as if the events of that evening had happened some twenty years ago, when she was a giddy young thing fond of gay bonnets and girlish pranks.

"I'm not going to tell Tom a word about it, but keep it for

a surprise till he comes. He will be here next week, and then we'll have a grand clearing up of mysteries," said Fan, evidently feeling that the millennium was at hand.

"Perhaps," said Polly, as her heart fluttered and then sank, for this was a case where she could do nothing but hope and keep her hands busy with Will's new set of shirts.

There is a good deal more of this sort of silent suffering than the world suspects, for the "women who dare" are few, the women who "stand and wait" are many. But if work baskets were gifted with powers of speech, they could tell stories more true and tender than any we read. For women often sew the tragedy or comedy of life into their work as they sit, apparently safe and serene at home, yet thinking deeply, living whole heart histories and praying fervent prayers while they embroider pretty trifles or do the weekly mending.

Chapter 19

Tom's Success

"Come, Philander, let us be a-marching,
Everyone his true love a-searching,"

*W*ould be the most appropriate motto for this chapter, because, intimidated by the threats, denunciations, and complaints showered upon me in consequence of taking the liberty to end a certain story as I liked, I now yield to the amiable desire of giving satisfaction, and, at the risk of outraging all the unities, intend to pair off everybody I can lay my hands on.

Occasionally a matrimonial epidemic appears, especially toward spring, devastating society, thinning the ranks of bachelordom, and leaving mothers lamenting for their fairest daughters. That spring the disease broke out with great violence in the Shaw circle, causing paternal heads much bewilderment, as one case after another appeared with alarming rapidity. Fanny, as we have seen, was stricken first,

and hardly had she been carried safely through the crisis
when Tom returned to swell the list of victims. As Fanny was
out a good deal with her Arthur, who was sure that exercise
was necessary for the convalescent, Polly went every day to
see Mrs. Shaw, who found herself lonely, though much better than usual, for the engagement had a finer effect upon
her constitution than any tonic she ever tried. Some three
days after Fan's joyful call Polly was startled on entering the
Shaws' door by Maud, who came tumbling downstairs sending an avalanche of words before her:

"He's come before he said he should to surprise us! He's
up in Mama's room and was just saying 'How's Polly?' when
I heard you come, in your creep-mouse way, and you must go
right up. He looks so funny with whiskers, but he's ever so
nice, real big and brown, and he swung me right up when he
kissed me. Never mind your bonnet, I can't wait."

And pouncing upon Polly, Maud dragged her away like a
captured ship towed by a noisy little steam tug.

"The sooner it's over the better for me," was the only
thought Polly had time for before she plunged into the room
above, propelled by Maud, who cried triumphantly:

"There he is! Ain't he splendid?"

For a minute everything danced before Polly's eyes as a
hand shook hers warmly and a gruffish voice said heartily—

"How are you, Polly?" Then she slipped into a chair beside Mrs. Shaw, hoping that her reply had been all right and
proper, for she had not the least idea what she said.

Things got steady again directly, and while Maud expati-
ated on the great surprise, Polly ventured to look at Tom,
feeling glad that her back was toward the light and his was
not. It was not a large room, and Tom seemed to fill it entirely. Not that he had grown so very much, except broader
in the shoulders, but there was a brisk, genial, free-and-easy

air about him, suggestive of a stirring, out-of-door life with people who kept their eyes wide open and were not very particular what they did with their arms and legs. The rough-and-ready traveling suit, stout boots, brown face, and manly beard changed him so much that Polly could find scarcely a trace of elegant Tom Shaw in the hearty-looking young man who stood with one foot on a chair while he talked business to his father in a sensible way, which delighted the old gentleman. Polly liked the change immensely and sat listening to the state of Western trade with as much interest as if it had been the most thrilling romance, for, as he talked, Tom kept looking at her with a nod or a smile so like old times that for a little while she forgot Maria Bailey and was in bliss.

By and by Fanny came flying in and gave Tom a greater surprise than his had been. He had not the least suspicion of what had been going on at home, for Fan had said to herself, with girlish malice, "If he don't choose to tell me his secrets, I'm not going to tell mine," and had said nothing about Sydney, except an occasional illusion to his being often there and very kind. Therefore, when she announced her engagement Tom looked so staggered for a minute that Fan thought he didn't like it, but after the first surprise passed, he showed such an affectionate satisfaction that she was both touched and flattered.

"What do you think of this performance?" asked Tom, wheeling round to Polly, who still sat by Mrs. Shaw in the shadow of the bed curtains.

"I like it very much," she said in such a hearty tone that Tom could not doubt the genuineness of her pleasure.

"Glad of that. Hope you'll be as well pleased with another engagement that's coming out before long." And with an odd laugh, Tom carried Sydney off to his den, leaving the girls to telegraph to one another the awful message:

"It *is* Maria Bailey."

How she managed to get through that evening, Polly never knew, yet it was not a long one, for at eight o'clock she slipped out of the room, meaning to run home alone and not compel anyone to serve as escort. But she did not succeed, for as she stood warming her rubbers at the dining-room fire, wondering pensively as she did so if Maria Bailey had small feet, and if Tom ever put her rubbers on for her, the little overshoes were taken out of her hands and Tom's voice said reproachfully:

"Did you really mean to run away and not let me go home with you?"

"I'm not afraid. I didn't want to take you away," began Polly, secretly hoping that she didn't look *too* pleased.

"But I like to be taken away. Why, it's a whole year since I went home with you. Do you remember that?" said Tom, flapping the rubbers about without any signs of haste.

"Does it seem long?"

"Everlasting!"

Polly meant to say that quite easily and smile incredulously at his answer, but in spite of the coquettish little rose-colored hood she wore, and which she knew was very becoming, she did not look or speak gaily, and Tom saw something in the altered face that made him say hastily:

"I'm afraid you've been doing too much this winter. You look tired out, Polly."

"Oh, no! It suits me to be very busy." And she began to drag on her gloves as if to prove it.

"But it doesn't suit me to have you get thin and pale, you know."

Polly looked up to thank him, but never did, for there was

something deeper than gratitude in the honest blue eyes that
could not hide the truth entirely. Tom saw it, flushed all over
his brown face, and dropping the rubbers with a crash, took
her hands, saying, in his old impetuous way:

"Polly, I want to tell you something!"

"Yes, I know, we've been expecting it. I hope you'll be *very*
happy, Tom." And Polly shook his hands with a smile that
was more pathetic than a flood of tears.

"What!" cried Tom, looking as if he thought she had lost
her mind.

"Ned told us all about her, he thought it would be so, and
when you spoke of another engagement, we knew you meant
your own."

"But I didn't! Ned's the man, he told me to tell you. It's
just settled."

"Is it Maria?" cried Polly, holding on to a chair as if to be
prepared for anything.

"Of course. Who else should it be?"

"He didn't say—you talked about her most—and so we
thought—" stammered Polly, falling into a sudden flutter.

"That I was in love? Well, I am, but not with her."

"Oh!" And Polly caught her breath as if a dash of cold
water had fallen on her, for the more in earnest Tom grew,
the blunter he became.

"Do you want to know the name of the girl I've loved for
more than a year? Well, it's Polly!" As he spoke Tom
stretched out his arms to her with the sort of mute eloquence that cannot be resisted, and Polly went straight into
them without a word.

Never mind what happened for a little bit. Love scenes, if
genuine, are indescribable, for to those who have enacted
them, the most elaborate description seems tame, and to
those who have not, the simplest picture seems overdone. So

romancers had better let imagination paint for them that which is above all art and leave their lovers to themselves during the happiest minutes of their lives.

Before long Tom and Polly were sitting side by side enjoying the blissful state of mind which usually follows the first step out of our workaday world into the glorified region wherein lovers rapturously exist for a month or two. Tom just sat and looked at Polly as if he found it difficult to believe that the winter of his discontent had ended in this glorious spring. But Polly, being a true woman, asked questions even while she laughed and cried for joy.

"Now, Tom, how could I know you loved me when you went away and never said a word?" she began in a tenderly reproachful tone, thinking of the hard year she had spent.

"And how could I have the courage to say a word when I had nothing on the face of the earth to offer you but my worthless self?" answered Tom warmly.

"That was all I wanted!" whispered Polly in a tone which caused him to feel that the race of angels was not entirely extinct.

"I've always been fond of you, my Polly, but I never realized *how* fond till just before I went away. Besides I had a strong impression that you liked Sydney in spite of the damper which Fan hinted you gave him last winter. He's such a capital fellow, I really don't see how you could help it."

"It is strange. I don't understand it myself, but women are queer creatures, and there's no accounting for their tastes," said Polly with a sly look which Tom fully appreciated.

"You were so good to me those last days that I came very near speaking out, but couldn't bear to seem to be offering you a poor, disgraced sort of fellow, whom Trix wouldn't have and no one seemed to think worth much. 'No,' I said to myself, 'Polly ought to have the best. If Syd can get her, let him, and I won't say a word. I'll try to be better worthy of her friendship, anyway, and perhaps, when I've proved that I *can* do something and am not ashamed to work, then, if Polly is free, I shan't be afraid to try my chance.' So I held my tongue, worked like a horse, satisfied myself and others that I could get my living honestly, and then came home to see if there was any hope for me."

"And I was waiting for you all the time," said a soft voice close to his shoulder, for Polly was much touched by Tom's manly efforts to deserve her.

"I didn't mean to do it the first minute, but look about me a little and be sure Syd was all right. But Fan's news settled that point, and just now the look in my Polly's face settled the other. I couldn't wait another minute, or let you either, and I couldn't help stretching out my arms to my little wife, God bless her, though I know I don't deserve her."

Tom's voice got lower and lower as he spoke, and his face was full of an emotion of which he need not be ashamed, for a very sincere love ennobled him, making him humble, where a shallower affection would have been proud of its success. Polly understood this and found the honest, hearty speech of her lover more eloquent than poetry itself. Her hand stole up to his cheek and she leaned her own confidingly against the rough coat as she said in her frank, simple way:

"Tom, dear, don't say that as if I was the best girl in the world. I've got ever so many faults, and I want you to know them all and help me cure them, as you have your own. Waiting has not done us any harm, and I love you all the better for your trial. But I'm afraid your year has been harder than mine, you look so much older and graver than when you went away. You never would complain, but I've had a feeling that you were going through a good deal more than any of us guessed."

"Pretty tough work at first, I own. It was all so new and strange, I'm afraid I shouldn't have stood it if it had not been for Ned. He'd laugh and say, 'Pooh!' if he heard me say it, but it's true nevertheless that he's a grand fellow and helped me through the first six months like a—well, a brother as he is. There was no reason why he should go out of his way to back up a shiftless party like me, yet he did, and made many things easy and safe that would have been confoundedly hard and dangerous if I'd been left to myself. The only way I can explain it is that it's a family trait and as natural to the brother as it is to the sister."

"It's a Shaw trait to do the same. But tell me about Maria. Is Ned really engaged to her?"

"Very much so. You'll get a letter full of raptures tomorrow he hadn't time to send by me, I came off in such a hurry. Maria is a sensible, pretty girl, and Ned will be a happy old fellow."

"Why did you let us think it was you?"

"I only teased Fan a little. I did like Maria, for she reminded me of you sometimes, and was such a kind, cozy little woman I couldn't help enjoying her society after a hard day's work. But Ned got jealous, and then I knew that he was in earnest, so I left him a clear field and promised not to breathe a word to anyone till he had got a yes or no from his Maria."

"I wish I'd known it," sighed Polly. "People in love always do such stupid things!"

"So they do, for neither you nor Fan gave us poor fellows the least hint about Syd, and there I've been having all sorts of scares about you."

"Serves us right. Brothers and sisters shouldn't have secrets from each other."

"We never will again. Did you miss me very much?"

"Yes, Tom, very, very much."

"My patient little Polly!"

"Did you really care for me before you went?"

"See if I didn't." And with great pride Tom produced a portly pocketbook stuffed with businesslike documents of a most imposing appearance, opened a private compartment, and took out a worn-looking paper, unfolded it carefully, and displayed a small brown object which gave out a faint fragrance.

"That's the rose you put in the birthday cake, and next week we'll have a fresh one in another jolly little cake which you'll make me. You left it on the floor of my den the night we talked there, and I've kept it ever since. There's love and romance for you!"

Polly touched the little relic, treasured for a year, and smiled to read the words "My Polly's rose" scribbled under the crumbling leaves.

"I didn't know you could be so sentimental," she said, looking so pleased that he did not regret confessing his folly.

"I never was till I loved you, my dear, and I'm not very bad yet, for I don't wear my posy next my heart, but where I can see it every day, and so never forget for whom I am working. Shouldn't wonder if that bit of nonsense had kept me economical, honest, and hard at it, for I never opened my pocketbook that I didn't think of you."

"That's lovely, Tom." And Polly found it so touching that she felt for her handkerchief, but Tom took it away and made her laugh instead of cry by saying in a wheedlesome tone:

"I don't believe you did as much, for all your romance. Did you, now?"

"If you won't laugh, I'll show you my treasures. I began first, and I've worn them longest."

As she spoke Polly drew out the old locket, opened it, and showed the picture Tom gave her in the bag of peanuts, cut small and fitted in on one side. On the other was a curl of reddish hair and a black button. How Tom laughed when he saw them!

"You don't mean you've kept that frightful guy of a boy all this time? Polly! Polly! You are the most faithful 'loveress,' as Maud says, that was ever known."

"Don't flatter yourself that I've worn it all these years, sir. I only put it in last spring because I didn't dare to ask for one of the new ones. The button came off the old coat you insisted on wearing after the failure, as if it was your duty to look as shabby as possible, and the curl I stole from Maud. Aren't we silly?"

He did not seem to think so, and after a short pause for refreshments, Polly turned serious and said anxiously:

"When must you go back to your hard work?"

"In a week or two, but it won't seem drudgery now, for you'll write every day and I shall feel that I'm working to get a home for you. That will give me a forty-man power, and I'll pay up my debts and get a good start, and then Ned and I will both be married and go into partnership, and we'll all be the happiest, busiest people in the West."

"It sounds delightful, but won't it take a long time, Tom?"

"Only a few years, and we needn't wait a minute after Syd is paid if you don't mind beginning rather low down, Polly."

"I'd rather work up with you, than sit idle while you toil away all alone. That's the way Father and Mother did, and I think they were very happy in spite of the poverty and hard work."

"Then we'll do it by another year, for I must get more salary before I take you away from a good home here. I wish, oh, Polly, how I wish I had a half of the money I've wasted to make you comfortable now."

"Never mind, I don't want it. I'd rather have less and know you earned it all yourself," cried Polly as Tom struck his hand on his knee with an acute pang of regret at the power he had lost.

"It's like you to say it, and I won't waste any words bewailing myself because I was a fool. We will work up together, my brave Polly, and you shall yet be proud of your husband, though he is 'poor Tom Shaw.' "

She was as sure of that as if an oracle had foretold it, and was not deceived, for the loving heart that had always seen, believed, and tried to strengthen all good impulses in Tom was well repaid for its instinctive trust by the happiness of the years to come.

"Yes," she said hopefully, "I *know* you will succeed, for the best thing a man can have is work with a purpose in it and the will to do it heartily."

"There is one better thing, Polly," answered Tom, turning her face up a little that he might see his inspiration shining in her eyes.

"What is it, dear?"

"A good woman to love and help him all his life, as you will me, please God."

"Even though she *is* old-fashioned," whispered Polly, with happy eyes, the brighter for their tears, as she looked up at the young man who, through her, had caught a glimpse of the truest success and was not ashamed to owe it to love and labor, two beautiful old fashions that began long ago, with the first pair in Eden.

Lest any of my young readers who have honored Maud with their interest should suffer the pangs of unsatisfied curiosity as to her future, I will add for their benefit that she did *not* marry Will but remained a busy, lively spinster all her days and kept house for her father in the most delightful manner.

Will's ministerial dream came to pass in the course of time, however, and a gentle, bright-eyed lady ruled over the parsonage, whom the Reverend William called his "little Jane."

Farther into futurity even this rash pen dares not proceed, but pauses here, concluding in the words of the dear old fairy tales, "And so they were married, and all lived happily till they died."

Afterword

Isabelle Holland

I first read *An Old-Fashioned Girl* when I was about thirteen, having already read the *Little Women* series and *Eight Cousins* and *Rose in Bloom*.

To an American child living in England, Louisa May Alcott was a revelation. My mother, feeling that I was seriously lacking in American background, literature, and lore, had her own copy of *Little Women,* given her on her twelfth birthday in 1890, repaired, reglued, and rebound, using the same covers as before, and gave it to me the Christmas I was nine. It was the most important and influential present I had ever received. I read nothing else for two years, horrifying my parents, who felt it was time I was on to something else. But with *Little Women* I had learned the joy of entering another world, and I found it magic.

When I got home from school each day, and as soon as I could reasonably claim I had done my homework (and sometimes not so reasonably), I opened up *Little Women*—it didn't matter where. I knew whole pages by heart. When I read one line of its dialogue I could quote the next twenty.

More than any other book, Louisa Alcott's book about a family of girls living in Concord made me into a reader. And once introduced to one of her books, I read all the others I could lay my hands on.

I have been told that today's child might find Ms. Alcott's "moralizing" and her enthusiasm for certain causes and scorn of certain customs "old-fashioned." Yet, appearing with a panel of twelve-year-olds only recently, I was impressed by the fact that two of the girls put *Little Women* among their top three favorites.

An Old-Fashioned Girl was the last of the Alcott books to come my way. Polly Milton does not have Jo March's rebelliousness. There is more of Meg in her than Jo. But there is so much reality in Polly and Fanny and Tom and Mr. Sydney and Maud that the author's periodic fulminations against fashionableness, whether in clothes or talk or *ennui* or affected manners, are a relatively small price to pay. And I have a fairly strong belief that they bother today's adults more than they do today's children.

Children, the wisest of beings in this, go for the story, for the people in it, and what happens to them. An occasional preachiness does not stand in the way of their pleasure as it does for an adult, far more aware of fashions in writing and therefore more disturbed by them than those who are coming fresh to the characters and all the fascinating events in their lives. And there is so much to laugh over as well as cry about: Who could forget Maud and her "fwactiousness" and Fanny's airs and graces as she tries, along with her equally snobbish friends, to appear blasé and bored?

Tom, Fanny's irrepressible brother (a little like Laurie, perhaps?) erupts throughout the pages. And whatever her views on what was seemly and desirable, it is obvious that Ms. Alcott, along with her feminism, has a great weakness for rambunctious, noisy, and generally prankish young men. She values the kind heart rather than the urbane manner and believes completely in the old Latin dictum *mens sana in corpore sano.*

The more than a century that young people have read and loved Ms. Alcott's books is statement enough. Many if not most of Ms. Alcott's values are still held in high regard: Her Polly Milton is honest rather than fake, she believes in giving along with receiving, she has no use at all for affectations or megrims, she believes in friendship, has a strong sense of the ridiculous, and prefers the simple over the fussy.

That could be said of wise young people in all the generations since Ms. Alcott blessed us with her books.